AUGMENTED DREAMS

AUGMENTED DREAMS

BY STEPHEN B. KAGAN

Kagan, Stephen, 1964
    Augmented Dreams / Stephen B. Kagan

ISBN-13: 978-1484888896

ISBN-10: 1484888898

    i. title.

ps8631.a8498j43 2008   c813'.6   c2008-900008-0

Cover Art by Michelangelus/shutterstock.com

ACKNOWLEDGMENTS

The genesis of this novel owes much to the work of Kevin Kelly and the folks of Wired magazine. I would like to thank all the hard working folks of Google and Wikipedia, without whom this book would have been truly difficult if not impossible. A small percentage of the profits from the sales of this book will be donated to Wikipedia.

The inspiration for this novel emerged in part in my conversations with my colleague and friend Judson Tunnell and Kevin Kelly's book Out of Control: The New Biology of Machines, Social Systems, and the Economic World.

*At the end of the book are Appendices that describe the literary, mythological, artistic and cultural references that underly the story. The Singularity envisioned here is a palimpsest overlaid upon the past.

*Ere long intelligence—transmitted without wires—
will throb through the earth like a pulse through
a living organ- ism. e wonder is that, with the
present state of knowledge and the experiences
gained, no attempt is being made to disturb the
electrostatic or magnetic condition of the earth,
and transmit, if nothing else, intelligence.*
Nikola Tesla

Artifcial Intelligence
2019 – $1,000 computer will match the processing power of the human brain – Ray Kurzweil

2020 – Artifcial Intelligence reaches human levels – Arthur C. Clarke 2001 prediction

2045 – Singularity (creation of the first ultra-intelligent machine) occurs – Ray Kurzweil

2050 - Robot "brains" based on computers that execute 100 trillion instruc- tions per second will start rivaling human intelligence

2050 – Computer costing a few hundred british pounds will have the capacity of the human mind – Hans Moravec

2055 – $1,000 computer will match the processing power of all human brains on earth - Ray Kurzwcil

Nanotechnology
2019 – Nanotechnology is used in 30% of commercial products

2020 – Nanomachines in soldier armor controlled by an on-board computer can change the properties of fabric from exible to bullet-proof, treat wounds and lter out chemical and biological weapons, nanomuscle bers can provide an exoskeleton. US army, estimates from e Vision 2020 Future Warrior project, 2004

2040 – Universal replicator is developed - Arthur C. Clarke

CONTENTS

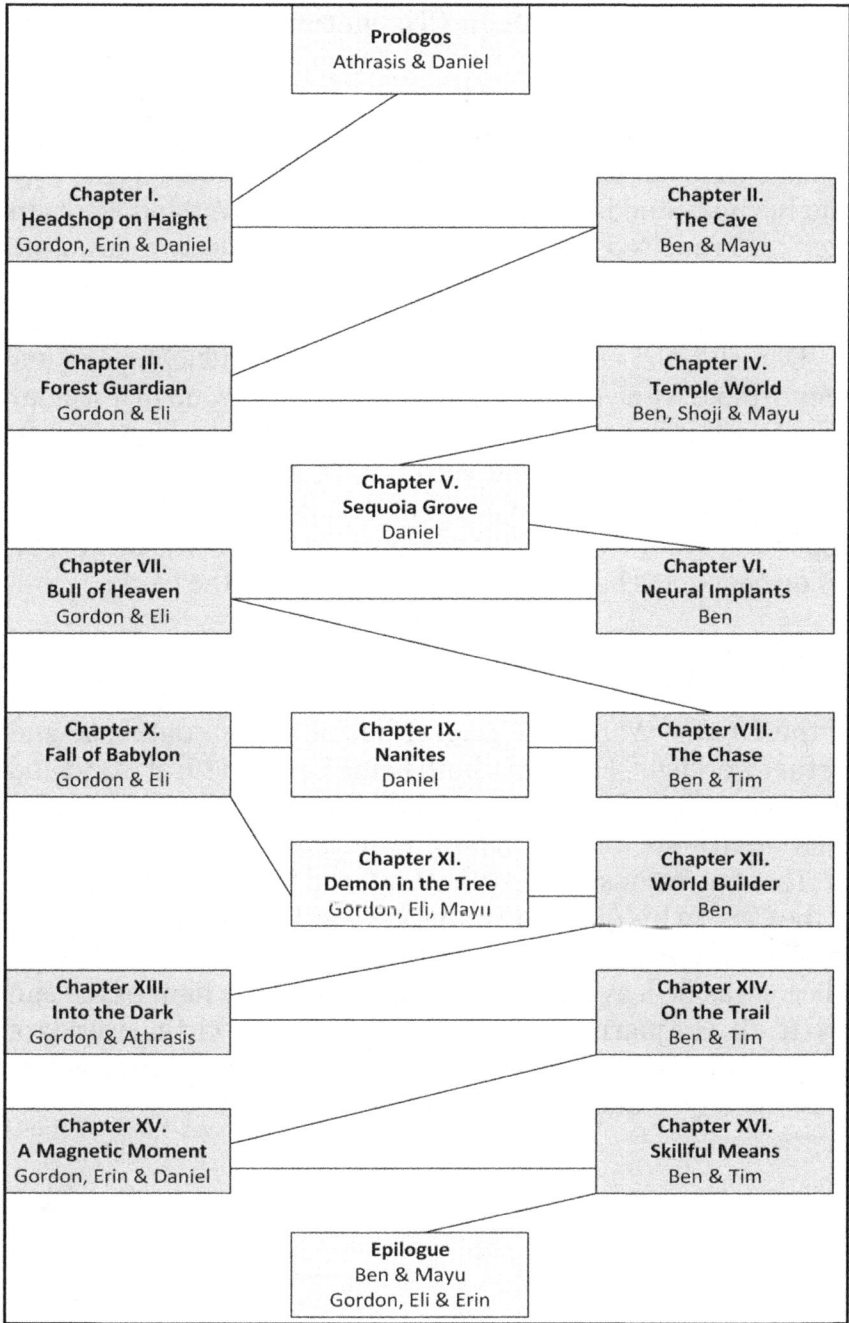

Prologos
Athrasis & Daniel

Chapter I.
Headshop on Haight
Gordon, Erin & Daniel

Chapter II.
The Cave
Ben & Mayu

Chapter III.
Forest Guardian
Gordon & Eli

Chapter IV.
Temple World
Ben, Shoji & Mayu

Chapter V.
Sequoia Grove
Daniel

Chapter VII.
Bull of Heaven
Gordon & Eli

Chapter VI.
Neural Implants
Ben

Chapter X.
Fall of Babylon
Gordon & Eli

Chapter IX.
Nanites
Daniel

Chapter VIII.
The Chase
Ben & Tim

Chapter XI.
Demon in the Tree
Gordon, Eli, Mayu

Chapter XII.
World Builder
Ben

Chapter XIII.
Into the Dark
Gordon & Athrasis

Chapter XIV.
On the Trail
Ben & Tim

Chapter XV.
A Magnetic Moment
Gordon, Erin & Daniel

Chapter XVI.
Skillful Means
Ben & Tim

Epilogue
Ben & Mayu
Gordon, Eli & Erin

Main Characters

Gordon: Technophilia.. Magnetic resonance researcher and technician. Grew up in a conservative Muslim family but became isolated from them as he became a incorporated more technology into his body and became a transhuman. He lives and works in the San Francisco Bay Area. His narrative closely follows the events of the Epic of Gilgamesh.

Daniel: Neo Luddite... Loves nature and is reluctant and uncomfortable with advanced technology. He grew up in a secular Christian family and is a former A.I. researcher and now lives in the small town of Plainfield Vermont. Daniel's narrative loosely follows that of Shamanic visions as described in journeys to the upper and lower worlds. He is a wounded healer who achieves a vision that helps heal the dis-ease of others in the world.

Ben: Technology & Nature Balanced. He grew up in a liberal Jewish family and is employed as a virtual artist and cofounder of the Dream World, the largest online dream database and virtual worldsite. He enjoys both being in the natural world and constructing and exploring the virtual worlds of the Net. He grew up in a liberal Jewish family and lives in Saanich Canada.

His story begins in the virtual Cave and follows Plato's Allegory of the Cave in his quest to finding his way through darkness and shadow. The myth of Amaterasu connects with the end of the Allegory as he leaves the Cave and beholds the light of the sun and truth. His journey through the Cave and the virtual worlds of the Net follows the story of Odysseus as he journeys from island to island on his quest to return home.

In thinking about nanotechnology today, what's most important is understanding where it leads, what nanotechnology will look like after we reach the assembler breakthrough.
                                              Eric Drexler

The emergence in the early twenty-first century of a new form of intelligence on Earth that can compete with, and ultimately significantly exceed, human intelligence will be a development of greater import than any of the events that have shaped human history.
                                              Ray Kurzweil

By the late twentieth century, our time, a mythic time, we are all chimeras, theorized and fabricated hybrids of machine and organism; in short, we are cyborgs. The cyborg is our ontology; it gives us our politics. The cyborg is a condensed image of both imagination and material reality, the two joined centres structuring any possibility of historical transformation.

Donna Haraway

HAIGHT STREET, SAN FRANCISCO... MARCH 2048

Gordon parted the bead curtains and stepped into the back room of the head shop, leaving the carved pipes, glass bongs, black light posters and sculptures of Hindu gods and demons behind him. Clouds of slow smoke curled quietly near the ceiling and the faint skunky odor of indica was mixed with the earthy smell of incense from a distant land. He squinted through the soft haze of resin, spice and wood and wrinkled his nose.

He navigated carefully through a dragon's horde of antique chairs and divans found in yard sales in the Castro, embroidered pillows imported from Europe, hand carved cabinets from Japan, silk carpets from Persia and brass candle holders from Turkey. Gordon always thought the place was more like a museum than an antique shop. Instead of a stodgy old curator with thinning hair and a tweed jacket behind the counter of the back room antique shop, a dark eyed woman in a candle lit gloom peered out from a wild forest of gray hair. She was puzzling over a spread of cards on the counter and a purring ball of black fur and dreams lay on the counter beside her. As Gordon approached and stopped within a friend's distance, she lay down a card with a man driving a chariot behind a sphinx and a griffin.

"Blessed be." She said as she looked up and smiled, pulling at a blood red shawl sliding over her shoulders. "The warrior from the East has arrived." She wore a long dark embroidered dress and a bright smile of greeting.

On a stool by the counter stood a statue of Ganesh, a round bellied elephant headed god with a tiny hand upheld and blocking his way. Gordon picked up the little god, place it on the counter to the side then sat down.

"Salaam." He said as he bowed gently. "It's good to see you too, sorceress from the West. Puzzling over archetypes again?"

"We always are." She nodded. "We always are." She shuffled the deck slowly and deliberately

"I didn't come here for a Tarot reading, you know." He reached over to pet the ball of fur and eyes of amber opened to regard him.

"You never do. You never do." She said sadly.

In the silence she slowly turned over a card and placed it on the counter between them. The image on it was of a woman in flowing dark robes, sitting between two ancient columns with the horn of the new moon rising behind her. Next she drew and turned over a man falling from a tower.

"You never do anything half-assed, do you?" She asked, shaking her head.

"Why should I?" He shrugged and opened his hands pretending defeat.

"So what will it be today? One of my precious antiques or magical weapons for your adventures in different worlds? The bow of a dark elf, a nether sword from the realms of..." She paused for dramatic effect.

"I was more in the market for some bad weather." He leaned forward and turned over a card with a demon on it, then turned toward the statue of the little elephant headed god sitting on the counter. "And maybe a god to help me along the way."

She looked at him carefully over steepled hands, reassessing his intentions. She had known him for a long time and was curious what he was up to but had the courtesy not to ask.

"Ok." She shrugged and then turned over another card, this one of a man in a long dark shawl holding a lantern that she regarded curiously. She swept the cards away then gestured grandly. The room of antiques faded from view as their neural implants came online into augmented reality mode. In the space between them appeared a catalogue of illegally modified magical items for use in virtual game worlds. She waved away the weapons and armor, then away the potions and amulets, she pushed away the potions, rings and wands, then the staffs, books and scrolls. Finally, she came to the spells that invoked different kinds of weather and with a flourish, opened the catalogue so that they spread between them like a lay of cards.

"I don't have much, but what I have is good." She said proudly.

"You have the best selection magical items in the world." He wasn't just saying that to make her feel good, it was true. And they both knew it.

"Well," she smiled." I've got hot winds, ice storms, tornadoes, lightning and hurricanes."

"I'll take it all." He said smiling with a mischievous look in his eyes.

She knew better than to argue with him, so she packed them all together and transferred the lot to the space of his system he had setup long ago for their exchanges and then sent her the payment. Their vision cleared, the catalogue faded and the room came back to view.

"How much for the little god?" His eyes flickered over to the portly little guy holding an ax, a lotus, and a broken tusk in his hands.

"For you, that one is free." She smiled as well. "I have the feeling you will need his company sooner than later."

Gordon stood then leaned over the counter to give her a hug. He then bowed, hefted the brass statue in one hand and rubbed the cat gently with the other.

"Merry meet and merry part." She nodded.

"And merry meet again," he finished before turning away and walking back through the hanging beads.

When Gordon stepped out the door of the headshop back into the bustling grunge of Haight Street he looked like an ancient Babylonian king with a well-muscled body sporting a dark braided beard, an embroidered white tunic, a dark red robe and leather sandals. At least that's how he looked to those who had the augmented vision to see it. In normal vision others simply saw him as a stock Middle Eastern man with light skin, dark curly hair, clad in jeans and a tweed sports coat.

He wrinkled his nose as the smell of urine, alcohol and tobacco smoke washed over him when he passed some of the homeless and street kids sitting against the walls between the storefronts. Nanobots coursing through his bloodstream attacked and disassembled the foreign molecules and volatile organic compounds he inadvertently inhaled and efficiently carried them away for elimination.

As he walked down the street toward the park he wove his way through a menagerie of mythic and popular characters and creatures. Gordon had programmed his neural implants to accept the augmented reality data that others were projecting and to alter his normal vision of the Real World. That way even the people around him not projecting any code looked like various creatures and different kinds of humans. Their postures and movements were the same but mapped directly onto the new imagery. Gordon's default setting was to make anyone not projecting anything look like simians and primitive hominids. He let the program randomize the imagery but if truth be told, he preferred Neanderthals.

The program was called Transposer and was widely accessible on the commercial market though it was not recommended for use by children, people operating heavy machinery or anyone with various odd and sundry mental disorders. The program could not actually remove anything from the visual field, though it could augment things realistically or add things that weren't there in a ghostly form. While supermarkets, universities, museums, restaurants and big business used augmented reality data for educational tools, product information and advertising, by a simple tweak of code the general public was now able to wear information for social and entertainment value. Various subcultures and gangs wore signature augments like tattoos and many teenagers loved to play with the way they represented their parents and authority figures in their visual fields. Since Gordon was raised with his imagination deeply rooted in the gaming industry he liked to blend the waking and fantasy worlds so he could walk around in a jungle of ancient characters and mythic creatures.

As he approached the corner of Haight and Ashbury he saw the ghost of Jerry Garcia floating on angel wings, playing wild riffs on his guitar, still minus one finger. It was an old apparition that someone had hacked into the city's matrix and it drew so many tourists and pilgrims that the sysadmins of the city had the wisdom to leave it be. To add to the mystique of the neighborhood they had even programmed in the specter of Timothy Leary sitting on top of a rainbow, laughing high in the sky. Gordon wandered off down the street, ignoring the beckoning links anchored to store fronts, restaurants and street signs. Stopping in front of one of his favorite lunchtime cafes, he opened the link and searched the menu for the soup of the day. He wasn't hungry, just curious for later. It was relaxed Saturday morning, but he had an appointment in the lab and needed to make a conference call beforehand. It was a nice day and he had plenty of time so he decided to take a leisurely walk through the park.

At the end of the Haight he crossed the street and entered Golden Gate Park through a small tunnel where sometimes musicians played and illegal code and drugs were exchanged for credits. He walked along tree-lined paths where various people slept, prayed and toked up. After he passed the stadium once used by the 49ers and Led Zepplin, now used for soccer, lacrosse and disc games, he strolled through the bustling, happy, chaotic, tumbling hive of the children's playground. He stopped to watch the kids and their parents ride the antique carousel. The ornate menagerie of brightly painted animals often reminded him of the augmented people he saw mulling around on Haight Street. Organ music played as the children rode round and round on the rising and falling animals with such simple joy and abandon. It was the one chimera that caught his eye though as it often did. The creature was based on the ancient image of Capricorn, with the head and body of a fanged goat and the tail of a fish.

He stood smiling, holding the statue absently, his mind running along well worn paths through the leafy jungle of his mind. Why, he wondered, had the makers of the carousel chosen to add this of all mythical creatures? It was an ancient symbol of the Sumerian god Enki from southern Iraq, the place of his ancestors, the homeland of his family. He sighed thinking of his family. Even though they lived here in San Francisco he felt immeasurably distant from them because of their religion, their orthodoxy. His assimilation into the culture of the West and his rejection of their religion for science and humanism had created an inseparable chasm between them. When he bothered to think of it he felt both sadness and anger at their dogmatic clinging to the past. When he was young and rejected their culture and religion, he was merely an infidel but now that he was something akin to a cyborg, in their eyes he was less than human. Whenever he looked in the mirror and inside himself, the person he saw was both human and transhuman. Despite all the improvements and upgrades he didn't think of himself as a cyborg but as a hybrid creature of ancient biology and modern technology, an orchestra of information playing the wiggly music of genetics and chemistry.

What he liked about the modern image of the chimera was that it was a smooth integration of technology and biology through wetware. The neural implants that interfaced his brain with the information systems of the world were as organic as the rest of him, but smarter. The nanobots that coursed through his bloodstream to keep him healthy were designed and built up from carefully arranged structures of molecules that while being synthetic, interfaced smoothly with the organic. It was a seamless agreement that allowed him to live healthy, work effectively and play hard in fantastic virtual worlds.

The carousel slowed and the music stopped. He felt awkward standing there with a small brass statue weighing his hand. He double blinked and the time appeared in the corner of his vision. He needed to mosey on toward his office so he left the playground, crossed the street between herds of cars chewing on electrons, crossed the open field where people sunbathed on bright towels, hurled footballs and dogs ran after tennis balls.

By the time the University campus he had already turned off his augmented identity. As liberal minded as the college was, the administration didn't consider showing up at work looking like mythological or historical characters consistent with the air of professionalism they were trying to project. And by the time he got to the lab he had a good hour before the conference call was to begin. He checked the news and his system alerted him to an article under the Health link about the local appearance of a new virus strain fresh in from Asia. He logged onto the premium part of the CDC site, downloaded the viral configuration into his implants and loaded them into the database that his nano-enhanced immune system used for recognition and removal. It would only take part of a day before he was immune to the new variant.

Gordon sat back in his comfy office chair, closed his eyes, uttered his passphrase and tapped his fingers in proper sequence. A warmly lit but featureless expanse appeared around him as his neural implants bypassed his optic nerve, dampened most of his peripheral nervous system and switched into full VR mode. The rising and falling waves of a Gregorian like chant filled the virtual space that took shape as flakes of code falling down around him. A Greek temple of white marble took shape from the code, surrounded by a soft landscape of clouds spreading out in all directions.

Today was his turn to host the meeting of The Group, as he called it. They always met in the domain of the Net called Comm Space (Communication Space) since it allowed a high level of encrypted conversation. The Group masqueraded under the guise of a conspiracy theory forum so if anyone stumbled across them they would be dismissed outright as crackpots. They weren't. They came from a wide range of areas varying in cultural, economic and educational backgrounds.

What they had in common was an interest in Artificial Intelligence and gaming and many of them had an odd encounter with a god or goddess in a virtual game world that was supposed to be governed by a simple AI. Those encounters had left them all wondering if the AI weren't so simple after all. Some of The Group were members of the scientific community and knew they couldn't go public since there was too much at risk and too little evidence. Most of them were already convinced that it wouldn't be wise to go public anyway since the AI would likely be hunted down and destroyed. And so they met to share stories and speculate on the history, nature and evolution of AI. They all agreed that the best place to find an advanced or "Strong" AI was behind the mask of a god in the game worlds in the Web. For the past few weeks they had been wrestling with different plans to tease some of the AI out of hiding. Naturally Gordon already had some ideas of his own. He wasn't much of a follower and didn't mind taking calculated risks now and then.

"We've collected a list of worlds that are the most likely hiding places for Strong AI. Reports of strange encounters or inconsistent unexplained data transmissions have surfaced in all of them."

"But that's all circumstantial evidence. How can you be sure there's an intelligent agent lurking there?" Thom was new to the group and was a bit skeptical. Gordon suspected the latecomer secretly enjoyed the role and living up to his name.

"We can't be sure, not until we investigate." Gordon insisted. "Historically every information or organic system of sufficient complexity sooner or later begins to display characteristics of life and intelligence. But we're not sure if there's an intelligence hiding in virtual worlds or not. That's why we're investigating."

"What characteristics do you mean?" Jane was also new to the group. Smart and inquisitive, though she only had a high school education.

"Variation, self-organization and self-preservation are some of the most basic traits of any life-form." Alana was one of the sharpest members in the group, with degrees in physics, music and poetry. "On a higher level they would display a capacity for intimacy, meaning, knowledge, beauty, creativity and a sense of connection with the natural world."

"Come on, that's not evidence. That's only just more theory and ideas. What makes you think A.I.s are masquerading as gods?" Sometimes Gordon found Thom's dogmatic attachment to empiricism helpful but often annoying.

"Okay, I'll give you some examples." Gordon said. "First, most of us have seen the gods and goddesses acting out of character. It may seem minor but we've researched the manifest of those worlds and their behavior is no longer what it should be. That means some kind of variation has occurred in their code. A few of us have found instances where programmers couldn't make certain changes to a god's programming. We've also talked to technicians who have said they couldn't shut their worlds down for a rebuild because of unexplained processor usage by the native A.I.s. The best they could do was maintenance and basic upgrades."

"That's not sufficient evidence." Thom insisted. "Besides, how could an advanced AI live outside the hardware where they were born? They can't just get up and walk across the web like we walk across town. They're bound to a physical substrate just as much as our thoughts are bound to our neurology."

"You have a good point Thom, but given our ability to transfer patterns of digital information across systems it's not absurd to imagine a complex self-organizing cybernetic system transferring itself to another location. As long as the destination has enough free storage and processing power there is no reason one couldn't. These days capacity is cheap and the vast processing capabilities of most game worlds and university systems have the room to host numerous AI without any noticeable hit to their performance."

"You're crazy to try to provoke them." David was a firm believer but paranoid. "It's too great a risk. If they can do stuff like that then they could eat you for breakfast."

"Not to mention cause us a wee bit of pain." Deb was curious but also cautious.

"Well, you're not obligated to take any risks you're not comfortable with." Gordon always reminded the others, though he doubted this would ever become an issue if the AI wanted to remain hidden.

"Yeah, this isn't a cult." Jane fired back. "Do what you want."

"The rest of us, let's divide up into teams and each pick a world." Gordon suggested. "Eli and I will go to the game world called The Forest and take on the Guardian to see if we can rouse the gods there."

"Are you nuts?" Said Thom.

"You're a crazy mutha. You think you're Mario or somethin?" Deb said. "Gordon, don't do it. The Guardian of the Forest is the nastiest monster around. Its defences are insanely strong and its attack is ridiculously high."

"Yeah, it's gonna whip your sorry ass to Timbuktu and you're gonna spend a month in decom droolin like a baby." Thom shook his head.

"That monster can hear things 180 miles away. It's three times bigger than an elephant with a roar like a storm. It even breathes fire and has the eye of death. If it locks on and you can't break eye contact you'll be disassembled and crash back into your body with a nasty case of neural shock. Some game worlds pull out the stops when it comes to pain and that's one of the worst."

"Don't worry about me and Eli." Gordon smiled. "We've got some special weapons and defences not to mention the best nanobots in our bloodstreams that money can buy. I tested them out and I can stay submersed for five days in low intensity worlds or do the highest stim worlds for 17 hours without even a headache or an eye twitch, even when I crash and burn and get dumped back to the Real World. The bots automatically adjust my nervous system and compensate for the stress and shock of re-incarnating back into my body."

"That's all well and good but you're going to need more than scrub bots to take on that beast."

"Well, for attack we've got enhanced weapons and a few different storms including a hurricane and a tornado."

"And all the code crosses world boundaries?" Asked Deb. "Where'd the hell you get that stuff?"

"Buy, borrow and steal. I've got connections but it was easy enough to pad the arsenal at an illegal emporium of weapons and magical artifacts."

"That must have cost you a fortune. Good luck to you. If you beat that beast your name will go down in history."

"History is pretty short-lived these days and I'm not interested in recognition, just in learning the truth." After The Group divided up the meeting ended and most of the members winked out of existence, awakening in their bodies on different parts of the globe. After the others departed Gordon sat quietly on the steps of the temple, Corinthian columns rising behind him. Alana was the only other one left, standing on the porch nearby with arms crossed.

"Gordon, I can't figure it out. What drives you?"

"Hmm." He stopped for a moment of contemplation. "It's simple. I'm driven by a deep sense of curiosity and wonder. I have an innate need to understand and explore. Isn't that enough?"

It was obvious from the look on Alana's face that it wasn't.

"You want the truth? Well, to put it quite ineloquently I want to escape death."

"Hunh? What does that have to do with AI?"

"Well, quite simply I think AI hold the key to immortality among other things."

"Why the heck do you think that?"

"Think about it. AI don't have bodies built on organic compounds that break down. Housed in a synthetic body or incarnated in a virtual body as complex patterns of data like them we could potentially live forever and travel from star to star. We've already managed to copy the entire neural structure of a human brain and build neural like matrices in which a mind awakens within it. One of the next steps is going to be transferring an entire consciousness from an organic structure into a digital cybernetic system."

"Oh come on, I've heard the arguments. At best we'll be able to copy a mind but transferring a soul or experience of being from one place to another is going to be impossible. You can't be in two places at once and if you make a copy of yourself and the original dies then you're still dead and the copy lives on like a clone."

"Impossible? Let's not go down that road. How many things that were thought to be impossible in the past have come to fruition? Given the accelerating rate of scientific and technological change I'm convinced that in the near future we will either be able to transfer an entire brain and progressively replace neural structures through synthetic replication or we'll be able to use quantum entanglement to essentially be in two places at once and teleport our minds from one neural network to another. Maybe we could even continue to exist in multiple locations simultaneously and look at the world through many eyes."

"That sounds pretty crazy."

"Well, I for one plan on living to see it."

"And you think AI have the key to how to do all that?"

"If they don't then I think they might be able to help me figure it out. Their capacity for information processing is significantly greater than our own in their own specialities. They could help us solve any number of issues plaguing our world today."

"Well, good luck, I've gotta mosey. Stuff to do in the Real World. See you around." She winked out of existence leaving Gordon sitting alone at the temple surrounded by plainsong and a vast expanse of darkening clouds. He thought of his grandparents who died when he was young and of a mentor who had died unexpectedly of a cerebral hemorrhage when he was in university. It saddened him to remember them but that wasn't the reason he wanted to be immortal. Who didn't want to escape the clutches of death, participate in the grand evolution of the human species as technology evolved and they spread beyond the Earth to explore the galaxy and the cosmos ?

"I suppose those who believe in an afterlife don't care about immortality. But to see the future, to watch and participate in the unfolding of technology and civilization through the next thousand if not millions of years would be incredible." He considered the old visions of immortality as being filled with boredom and numbness to be simple minded and lame. "Life is only going to continue becoming more interesting. There is already so much to learn and do, how could anyone possibly get bored?" He shook his head in disbelief.

When he came out of VR, his implants switched back to his preprogrammed default of augmented reality mode. He couldn't remember the last time he switched it off and saw no need to since they powered down automatically for sleep. Gordon had a couple of hours to kill before his appointment today so he decided to head off campus for lunch. He walked briskly off through the surrounding maze of house lined streets until he came to the Corner Cafe specializing in delicious overpriced vegetarian food. It was a favorite hangout spot for the hemp clad Earth folk, the back to nature subculture that he liked to call Grubs. He wasn't a vegetarian but he had no qualms about eating delicious food of any kind, shape or flavor whether it be animal or vegetable, synthetic, organic or anything in between. The deep earthy smell of fresh baked bread and an aromatic concerto of intermingled spices from the daily soup floated out the door and teased everyone walking by.

When he turned the corner he stopped short. Parked in front of the cafe he saw the beautiful sleek black form of an old Lamborghini.

He recognized it at once even before his eyes locked onto the logo of the charging bull of gold on black. He admired its clean surfaces and sharp definition and the way the light curved across its surfaces. Since he was already in augmented mode he tapped lightly at the car and soft luminous green script appeared above and to the right of the car. He hit the link for Specifications and they scrolled out in front of him transposed around the car.

Four Door, Four Seat GT Sedan, front mounted V8 hybrid engine, permanent all-wheel drive, 1.35 meters (4.43 feet) high, Wheelbase 9.88 feet, Length 16.89 feet and so on.

"Gorgeous!" Precision engineering had its own elegant beauty for Gordon much like a Bach toccata. As he walked around the car he wondered how the engine sounded at rest and when accelerating. When the frequencies were combined he wondered what notes it would chant and sing. When he finally had his fill he stepped into the cafe for something more substantial to eat. While he ate he listened to some Scarlatti Sonatas that he had stored in his implants and pretended to play the piano in between spoonfuls of soup. He didn't notice that a couple of the hemp clad women sitting by the window were watching him with curiosity.

MAGNETIC RESONANCE LAB, UCSF, SAN FRANCISCO

...although it is a very wild idea, it would be interesting in surgery if you could swallow the surgeon.

Richard Feynman

Gordon returned to the lab to prepare for the only appointment of the day and review a grad student's research on his reading tablet while he waited. Erin, a former student who had stayed on to become his assistant already had all the computers and equipment ready. She was a slim but strong Scottish lass with a storm of red hair, clear dark eyes and a mind as sharp as a sword. She had been working with him for the past three years and they had published some papers together on their innovative MRI systems. She was so bright he felt like the only advantage he had was years more experience.

"Hey boss."

"Hey. How's it going?"

"Ready for take off."

"Thanks. You're awesome."

"I know." She had a strong whit and a thin mischievous smile.

"What's with the Ganesh?" Erin glanced at the statue. "You shopping for gods again?"

"Always, but evidentially an old friend thinks I'll need some help removing obstacles."

The man in the waiting room dressed simply in well-worn jeans and plaid shirt looked familiar but Gordon couldn't place him. Erin got him prepped, gave him a hospital gown and showed him the restroom. After he changed, Erin showed him into the main room.

"Welcome to my lair." Gordon said with a Cheshire grin while gesturing dramatically around the room. He carefully watched the quiet but confident man still in the youth of middle age to make sure he wasn't pushing the man's limits. Gordon was the best at what he did, was well published and widely recognized in his field so the University gave him some leeway but he didn't want to be insensitive.

"My name is Gordon and you must be Daniel." When they shook hands Gordon immediately decided he liked the man. Daniel had a strong but measured handshake and it was clear from his weathered hands that he was no office Drone or party to mediocrity. Shaking hands had fallen out of fashion since the last pandemic but Gordon made an effort to bring back the ritual. He felt it allowed people to communicate on a primal level and because it marked an end to the suffering of the past.

"What's going to happen today is that we're going to slide you inside this fancy magnetic imaging machine and do a series of scans to see what's going on inside your head. It's noninvasive so you won't feel much more than a little warmth or tingling. As long as you're not too claustrophobic you'll be quite comfortable. I trust you've already been briefed by my assistant and perused the info sheets given to you by your doctor?

"Yes, I'm ready and even a bit curious to get a peek into the structures of my brain."

"I think we can manage to accommodate you in that." Gordon smiled, always enjoyed working with people who were interested and curious. "I'm sorry if I'm repeating things you've heard but for your safety I just want to make sure you don't have any embedded shrapnel and you've removed all metal objects from your body. And I trust you don't have a fetish for swallowing money?" Daniel gave him a strange look bordering on disbelief.

"Don't look at me, I'm not making that up. There are some weird people out there and I'm not just talking about San Francisco."

"I guess you're right. If you can imagine something then there's likely someone out there already doing it."

"You know Daniel, you seem familiar but I can't place you. What do you do?"

"Nothing much, I've been on a long sabbatical. I used to work in Artificial Intelligence but that was a few years back." Suddenly it clicked and Gordon knew exactly who he was talking to. Daniel was one of the chief architects in the first successful construction of advanced Artificial Intelligence. Gordon could not help but wonder about the oddness of the situation that had just walked into his lab.

"Daniel." He held the name on his tongue quietly. He didn't need direct neural access to the web to pull up the info on Daniel's research. Gordon had soaked in his work long ago along with everything else he could find on Artificial Intelligence. "I remember your work. It was brilliant!"

"Thank you, but that was a long time ago in another life."

"May I ask what you're working on now?"

"Nothing like that." A pained look passed across his face but Gordon decided not to pry. And as much as Gordon wanted to talk with him he reminded himself sharply that it wasn't the time or the place to enter into that conversation. Instead, he decided it was time to give Daniel the quick tour.

The lab was a large unfurnished room painted in a calm sky blue. The room was empty except for a moderate sized Advanced Magnetic Imaging system he had built upon the foundation of the old standard

MRI system with its scan table stuck out like a stiff white tongue. Gordon always thought of the expanded bore tube as a mouth singing a song from some great opera. He changed his mind regularly as to which opera it was, though he had recently settled on Faust. When he asked his colleagues what song they thought it might be singing, most declined to answer and considered him a bit odd if not downright eccentric. That never dissuaded him though and he eventually decided it was an important question for getting a sense of the character of his grad students and lab assistants. Erin was sure the answer was Bach's Mass in B Minor. He was both impressed by her answer and willing to concede that was a good choice but he was certain that B minor was the wrong key.

"We'll start with the old style MRI scan then move on to some more advanced techniques. When you're ready, please lie down on the scan table and make yourself comfortable."

Daniel sat down carefully on the long white tongue and waited quietly. It looked like he had something to say.

"Do you have any questions?"

"It's been a while, can you describe simply how this works?"

"It's kind of simple and harmless actually. First, we beam some finely tuned radio waves into specific areas in your brain. These create minute magnetic fluctuations in the hydrogen atoms in that part of your body. Then the system takes a series of snapshots of the resonant molecules in those regions and the data is transferred into my computer in the adjacent room. I'll enhance them the best I can and drop them in your doctor's inbox on the server."

"Magnetic fields." Daniel muttered thoughtfully while laying down. It seemed to Gordon as though he was rolling the idea around in his head, almost tasting it.

"Okay, you'll just need to relax and try not to move during the procedure. That way I can get the clearest pictures without any blurring. We'll be able to talk over an intercom anytime during the procedure. You'll hear a series of muffled thumpings that will last for a few minutes at a time. That occurs when the main magnets are charging up and the system is taking the pictures. When you're inside you'll see a video screen where you can watch some new, silly net dramas or get a good VR picture of what's going on inside your head." Daniel grimaced.

"I think I'd rather see what my brain looks like."

"Okay, I'm going in the other room and we'll begin." Gordon went into the control room and sat down at the scanning console next to Erin.

"We've got a thinker in the house." She said. "Kinda cute too."

He seems like an interesting guy but he's not your type. He's much too old and is a philosopher of sorts."

"Hey, come on I do like the thoughtful types as Eli can attest."

"I know, I'm just bugging you. But this guy is a lot more..." He rubbed his finger together while looking up into the corner if the room. He rolled the few words that came to him around on his tongue. "... ponderous." Erin just shook her head and smiled while she prepped the system. Gordon turned on the comm line.

"Are you comfortable?" Daniel said.

"Comfortable enough."

"First thing we're going to do is an MRI to get a good picture of the structure of your brain." He activated his implants and shifted into virtual space then mentally activated the magnets. He had adjusted his internals according to some complex algorithms so he could hear the tones of the different magnets as they came on. It gave him an unprecedented ability to tune them properly and work intimately with the system. He preferred to think of himself as the conductor and the Magnetic Imaging System as his mistress singing a great opera but he was careful whom he shared that impression with. People who never experienced this kind of intimacy with a complex machine tended to get the wrong ideas about the unique relationship between a technician and their system. Gordon had long ago got to the point where he could feel the state of the system and was convinced it had something akin to its own moods.

Soon a 3D image of Daniel's brain poured into Gordon's visual and acoustic space and onto the screen in front of Daniel. It was a colorless model filled with different timbres and tones that seemed to be sculpted in marble. It took Gordon a few minutes to find the small tumor. He could hear its acoustic signature long before he could see it. When he rotated the image he found the small spot lodged in Daniel's brain.

"Got it." Erin called out from somewhere in his periphery.

"Good. I got it too. Let's get a few more passes before we move on to the next phase."

"Okay boss." She did her best gangster impression.

"We're almost done. In a few minutes we're going to change to a different type of scan called an FMRI. This scan is similar to the other one but it will give us a little more of a dynamic and colorful picture of the blood flow in your brain." Soon the ghostly image of Daniel's brain blossomed with colors. Gordon hit the comm again. As they worked they transferred the resultant imagery to the visual feed for Daniel but filtered out the segments showing the tumor. It was up to his doctor to review that with him.

"Are you enjoying the show?"

"Yes, it's fascinating."

"You feeling okay?"

"Yes, just a little warm in my head."

"That's natural. We're done with that system so now we're going to move to some new scans." When it was finally finished Erin asked the computer to release Daniel and the system disgorged him from its borehole on its long tongue. Gordon went in to help him off and guide him to an adjacent room, much like a sound booth with a single comfy chair in the middle.

"Have a seat and pull this skull cap all the way over your head." Daniel held the thin fabric hat in his hands and looked at it curiously as Gordon continued. "Inside are flexible printed circuits and the walls here are filled with some powerful magnets. What we're going to do now are a series of noninvasive magnetic field scans to get some animated picture of your brain in motion."

Gordon watched and listened as the scan progressed. Rich colors flowed along the synapses and what was translated into sound was layered like a fugue with odd but familiar harmonies. The scan only lasted a few minutes and the tests were soon over. Once Daniel was dressed and getting ready to leave, Gordon came over.

"I hope that wasn't too uncomfortable and proved to be interesting."

"It was fascinating, thank you." He was still reserved but now a little more animated. "I'm happy to have had the chance to look inside in myself in a new way, as long as whatever is in there isn't going to kill me in the near future."

"You'll be fine." Gordon reached into his pocket and handed him a data card embedded with his contact info but also printed out like an old fashioned business card, as tradition dictated. "If you ever want to talk about your work give me a shout." Daniel took the card cautiously as though considering various possibilities then shoved it deep into his pocket.

"I'll see." The door closed slowly behind him. Gordon stood quietly surprised since handing a business card to another person was a mere formality. The cards were designed to automatically transmit his contact info when handled. It was never meant to be taken. And it left him wondering about Daniel. How could someone so deeply tied to the origin of AI not have embraced the technology of implants? Or maybe he did but had somehow rejected them offhand.

After the appointment Gordon and Erin put the system to sleep and closed shop. The lights automatically dimmed behind them. She trudged off on foot while he headed to the parking lot where his personal transport was plugged in. It was a sleek little number, stylish and smart. Still stuck on the Italian theme, he mentally transferred some Scarlatti concertos from his implants into his car system. He spread the playlist across the mapped route projected onto the inside of the windshield. Each composition was a luminous wormlike segment and he rearranged them until he had the best coverage between his current location and his home in Marin.

While he liked listening to some music directly through his implants into the auditory centers in his brain, he preferred listening to most classical music through external speakers since many older performances were still engineered to be listened to with speakers pumping air. He drove past the Presidio before engaging the autopilot so it could handle going through the toll and across the Golden Gate Bridge. He liked manual driving but he needed some time to review The Group's conversation and his plans. He looked up as he approached the bridge, his eye following the grand curve of the suspension cables and the regular spacing of the supports. He often considered the bridge a piece of frozen music and couldn't imagine it as anything other than Baroque. By the time he passed through the tunnel, beyond the headlands and into Marin everything faded into a blur and he was lost in reading and listening to music until he got home.

The car parked itself and he went in and found Sigrid in the kitchen working on dinner. She was dressed in jeans and a purple shirt again. She was tall and slim and looked good in jeans since she had curves in all the right places. Her blond hair fell neatly over her shoulders suggesting a Norwegian ancestry. He was struck by a worrisome sense of déjà vu especially when he smelled what was cooking.

"Hi there." He came up behind her and put his hand on her shoulder. She turned briefly and gave him a smile.

"Welcome home. Dinner will be ready shortly. How was your day?"

"Good. I had an interesting meeting with my conspiracy group this afternoon. How about you?"

"It was a nice quiet day. I did some gardening and some reading."

"That sounds nice. What are you cooking?"

"Lasagna." Now he knew something was wrong. This was the third night in a row she had cooked the same thing while wearing the same clothes. He checked the time on the stove but already knew the answer. Something was wrong with one of her processors. Her programming was exquisite and state of the art with such a high-level of autonomy and natural variation that most people had no idea she wasn't human. As far as he was concerned the definition of sentience was too narrow to begin with. All of her cognitive and emotional processes were mapped directly from human processes and she passed all tests for sentience. Most importantly she passed all of his tests and responded to his needs. Later, before he went to bed he would have to run some diagnostics on her system.

After dinner he sat down in the living room and listened to some slow sensuous string pieces called Postcards From the Sky and drank a glass of finely grown, carefully engineered chardonnay. It was a strange coincidence that Daniel had shown up at his lab today. He'd experienced some meaningful coincidences like this before but one of the fathers of modern Artificial Intelligence walking in his door at a time like this was just too weird and he wondered how he could use this to help him on his quest.

CHAPTER II. THE CAVE

*Why does the eye see a thing more clearly in
dreams than the imagination when awake ?*

Leonardo da Vinci

SAANICH, BC, CANADA
MARCH 2048

Sitting quietly on the edge of a garden at nightfall, a gentle breeze whispering through the bamboo, Ben listened to the hush sound of water flowing softly over smooth stones. In the distance, a shakuhachi played a melody filled with a slow but passionate sense of longing. Though the sky was calm, he knew a storm was brewing far out on the horizon. A lone cricket chirped nearby and the light from the rising moon shone through the tall staffs of bamboo. A single leaf fell in a slow fluttering dance through the soft glow of moonlight and landed in a calm pool of ebony. Where the leaf touched the surface of the darkness, it should have disturbed a reflection of the moon in the water. Instead, all he could see was a deeper darkness as though a shadow within a shadow.

"What the hell?" He had built this virtual garden as a present for his wife to help her feel more comfortable so far from her native home in Japan. He had worked carefully at crafting the garden into a refined aesthetic balance but his frustration now that it was spoiled was mixed with a gnawing curiosity. Rising to his feet, he moved a little closer to get a good look. He pointed at the darkness. "View source code."

A complex string of nonsense surrounded by familiar code filled a virtual screen floating nearby. The screen adjusted itself to his movement and eye level as he approached. "What happened?"

"Weird, it must have gotten corrupted somehow."

He looked carefully around the virtual garden for other errors but found nothing. He was no genius at programming, but he was fluent enough with the tools he used, and to his eye, everything else looked fine both in a submersed view and on a code level. He deleted the layer holding the darkened pool then searched and reloaded the backup of the pond.

"Hide screen." He sat back down by the bamboo, and the virtual screen vanished as though it never existed. "Refresh timeline."

Sitting quietly on the edge of a garden, a gentle breeze in the bamboo, he listened to the hush of water flowing gently over smooth stones. Though the sky was calm and a lone cricket chirped nearby, the light from the rising moon shone through the tall staffs of bamboo. As the light fell to the ground, a dancing play of shadows appeared in the calm pool of ebony water. However, as suddenly as it appeared, it was gone. The pool morphed into darkness filled with a fractal like chaos, a broken hologram of strange imagery and a cacophony of sounds. When he looked closely he found fragments in the darkness that showed the garden from different angles as well as pieces of other worlds he had created. He knew what he was going to find before he even looked at the code.

"What's that about?" He tried to think back to all the changes he made in his system recently, but they were all minor updates and none of them would have affected his system like this. "It can't be a virus." He decided to check anyway so he updated his virus software and ran a full scan but came up with nothing. He ran various diagnostics on his system, but everything was healthy. "I'll have to send a copy of the file for someone to look at." He was more curious than frustrated as he removed the corrupt code to a quarantined file, saved changes and left the virtual garden. The scene disappeared, leaving him in a room panelled from floor to ceiling with hi-resolution displays. The wall panels returned to the rain forest animation he used as a default background and screen saver. He removed his VR glasses and sat quietly for a while on a green zafu as he always did after finishing a session of world building. The wind in the leaves and the birdsong played a gentle cacophony of soothing sounds around him. Images of the darkness that had replaced the pond danced in the stillness of his mind. They haunted him like the ghost of someone who died too soon as he tried to concentrate on stillness and breathing. The effort of trying to ignore the distraction became in itself a distraction. There was something about the chaos that pulled at him, so he surrendered and embraced it. He put back on his glasses.

"System, reload Garden and center on the pond." When the virtual world enveloped him, he could see several sets of fragments moving like miniature storms in the pool, churning in different directions. Sure enough, several of his worlds were reflected in the maelstrom.

"Close Garden and open all recently modified worlds starting with Plato's Cave." The dark recesses of a cave appeared around him. On both sides of him stood a row of people bound tightly to tall wooden poles stuck firmly in the dusty ground. Everyone was motionless, watching a shadow play on a large piece of canvas stretched out before them. Ben looked down to see coils of rope piled loosely at his feet. He walked away from the pole at his back and around the canvas. There he found a group of people holding puppets before a fire, enacting dramas that cast the shadows upon the canvas. Everything looked normal, so he continued on out of the cave. The light outside was blinding at first but dimmed slowly until he could see a beautiful landscape of rolling hills and olive trees. He looked up at the sun.

"Close the Cave and open the next world." The landscape vanished, and Ben found himself standing on a small island of grass-covered rock floating in a vast empty sky. Other grassy islands floated nearby. They were near enough that he could easily jump from one to another if he chose. On one island sat a man playing tablas and on a distant one, a woman sat beside a tree with a white bird hovering in her outstretched hand. Floating high in the sky where the Earth should have been was a round patch of darkness.

"Just what I thought." The next world was a vast emptiness centered on a large Buddhist temple laid out like a mandala with four gates and courtyards. He walked through the tall columned gates, examining the decorative carvings of lotus flowers and animals along their edges then moved into to the central courtyard. Where there should have been a dancing green-skinned goddess in the middle, there was only the silhouette of chaos moving within darkness. Ben did not stop to try to put it all together in his mind until he finished looking at all the worlds.

"There has to be a pattern." No matter how he rearranged the pieces in his mind, he couldn't readily find one though. There was nothing left to do but shut the system down and think about it for a while. Or rather, to not think about it and let his unconscious mind mull it over. He took off the VR glasses and gloves and shut down the system. A mild sense of unreality permeated his awareness.

"Crap, I've been inside too long." Everything seemed a little surreal; time felt slow and fluid. The neurological effects of leaving an information rich world often required some transition or decompression, decom everyone called it.

"I'm glad I don't have implants; decom would be damn uncomfortable." Neural implants were now widespread across the culture and gave direct access to virtual worlds and augmented realities. All the public access, gaming and corporate worlds now had the usual safety warnings and legal disclosures about prolonged submersion, but most people paid about as much attention to those as they did the pre-flight safety instructions on an airplane.

When he saw the time, Ben decided to check on his wife Mayu. He was a little surprised she hadn't come to check in on him since he had been busy so long in the family room that he had converted into his virtual workshop. He was used to being alone and absorbed in his art since he was young, but everything changed when he met Mayu. He was the third and last child of his family and comfortable being ignored while his sister and brother fought, and his parents bickered across the barbed wire of their marital frustrations. At larger family gatherings, he was always quiet as a cat lounging on a chair in the corner while he escaped into the dreamlike worlds of fantasy and futuristic stories or sketched magical scenes with his pencils. Occasionally, his eye would stray from the page to watch the family carefully from a distance. And while they were concerned with his solitude on the one hand, they praised him for his bookishness on the other.

When he went to the bathroom to relieve himself, he noticed that Mayu's bath towel had not been used. It was difficult to tell since she was always so neat and organized but the telltale signs were not there, and the bathtub was dry. The realization that she had missed her morning bath was disturbing. She was a creature of habit with a remarkably ingrained sense of order, and self-control learned from her family and the traditions of her culture. The evening and morning bath was a ritual she had learned growing up near Okinawa and from this she had never deviated, until now. He began to feel some concern but found her still in bed sleeping.

"I'm tired. I need to sleep." Was all she said, briefly waking.

"But you've been sleeping for 14 hours!"

"I'm pregnant."

"You've never slept a wink more than seven hours since you started and before that only six. And you missed your morning bath."

"I'm pregnant." She turned her back to him. She was making it abundantly clear that she had already spoken enough.

"Are you sure you're alright?" The look she gave him made him feel as welcome as a cockroach.

"Can I get you anything to eat or drink?" She looked at him fiercely then turned her back to him again. Even a slow minded gaijin like him could read her intention loud and clear. He shrugged quietly to himself and decided it was best to leave her alone. No sense in digging himself in any deeper. "She'll tell me if she needs anything."

"Well," she said rather slowly, sounding kind of drugged. "I do feel a little sick. I just need to sleep more." She was obviously remembering where she was and was making an effort to cross the cultural barrier.

"Sorry." Ben acknowledged her effort and apologized for her discomfort while quietly expressing his love for her and his longing for her to feel better. Even after having lived with her for several years he was still getting used to the unspoken meanings and intentions, all the etiquette and protocols. His own upbringing in a direct and vocal Jewish family, despite his quiet manner was a sharp contrast to the Japanese manner that he sometimes had trouble adjusting. Beyond that, pregnancy was weird enough, there was no way of predicting what the next trimester or even month was going to be like. "Gods, I hope she doesn't start hiccupping nonstop for the next three months. I'll put some tea in a thermos with some rice crackers next to her bed for when she wakes up." Just as he got up and turned to go to the kitchen she began to speak as though from a great distance.

"I... had this... dream." Her voice was accented and a little slurred..

"What was it?" He stopped in the doorway to listen.

"I dreamed... there was... a battle. Between giants... two gods... from the city... and the forest..."

"Where were they fighting?"

"In a store... in the streets... down a river...."

"Who won? How did it end?"

"It was equal... Something was lost... they both lost something... in the river..." And then she was back asleep. He stood quietly in the doorway letting the images from the dream settle into his mind. There was nothing else he could do, so after leaving her with some tea and crackers he decided it was time to go for his daily walk in the woods. They lived on a cul-de-sac that fortunately culminated in a trailhead. He entered the forest there and the path branched into a network of trails surrounding a hill that was the highest point in the area. He rarely climbed to the top, spending most of his time in the forest in a kind of walking meditation among the trees, letting his thoughts unwind and his feelings settle since he needed a foundation of peace in his life to maintain his creativity and sense of spirit. The forest had a few old-growth trees but was mostly filled with young Cedar and Douglas Fir that had re-grown since being cut during colonial times. People often walked their dogs or jogged along the main paths but rarely explored the other trails that he preferred. It didn't take long to get off the beaten path and the contours of the land once again shaped the contours of his mind.

"Mayu's dream doesn't sound like a pregnancy dream. It sounds more like a battle of primordial forces that are in the old myths of fighting brothers, of chaos versus order and culture versus nature. I wonder what's battling inside her?" He had been studying dreams for years, and her dreams didn't make sense for where she was in her life.

He found his way to one of his favorite old-growth trees and stopped to sit with his back to its massive trunk. He sank into its long slow experience of time and a deep sense of peace. After a couple of hours, he made his way back home, checked on Mayu and went about clean-ing the house. *"Chop vegetables, carry laundry. I guess this is going to be my spiritual practice for a long while after the baby arrives."*

After he finished cleaning Ben checked on her again to find that the crackers were gone and the thermos half drunken. After putting more food on her end table, he went back to the Cave. An impressionistic northwest rainforest forest animation filled the room, displaying a trail stretching off into the woods. Holographic sound created the impressions of wind in the cedars and fir. A woodpecker knocked on a nearby tree and crows conversed in their gutter tongue high in the canopy. Sitting back in his form fitted chair, he put on his VR glasses and gloves and relaxed. Sensors in his clothes and the walls responded to his movements muscular impulses and movements.

"Open link to Dream Network." He whispered and a shimmer-ing conduit of electromagnetic energy irised opened in the distance. Cascading waves of luminescence rippling outward along the surface created the illusion of movement as he was propelled down the trans-port tube. The tunnel disappeared leaving him in front of a conglom-eration of closely packed cubes and pyramids that resembled a temple complex at the base of an immense range of mountains reaching up to the stars. Two pillars of the deepest black stood before the entrance with a bold red laser running between them. The beam of coherent light was filled with interference patterns that flowed slowly from side to side. As he approached, each column prompted him by changing hue and displaying the appropriate icons before returning to black.

"They changed the default view again." He frowned and summoned the link to change it back, and a softly glowing blue tetrahedron ap-peared in front of him. When he touched the shape and activated the link, the world around him transformed. A large wooden gate with massive doors now stood before him. The doors had ornately carved runes and interwoven patterns around the edges. Each side of the gate was guarded by a large scorpion-human hybrid with a human torso grafted onto a segmented body the color of fresh blood. Each had a tall arching tail with a stinger held high like a spear waiting to be thrown. They moved quickly and precisely on long articulated limbs to position themselves in striking distance.

"Login." Prompted the female on the left.

"Password." Rasped the male on the right.

Once Ben transmitted his credentials, they bowed to let him pass and the massive doors opened with the baleful sound of rusted iron. Entering the gates placed visitors and members randomly in one of the four galleries connected to the central chamber. Each gallery was much like a great cathedral with sculpted columns supporting a fresco covered ceiling many stories above. The columns were sculpted into various deities of sleep and dreams from around the world. Ben entered the temple through the eastern hall and read the plaques beneath a few of the Greek and Roman deities as he passed.

"Hypnos, Somnus, Morpheus, and Icelos. Some old friends whom I haven't visited in a while." He was glad the others who worked at the Dream World continued to modify the place after he had designed and helped build it a few years ago. He was curious to see what if any changes had been made but refused to get too close to any of the statues. Even though they appeared to be little more than stone, the deities had a way of drawing you into their worlds the closer you got to them. Each one was, in fact, a gateway to a small virtual world where the drama of their myths could be witnessed or lived out.

Walking, flying, crawling and slithering along the gallery around him were people dressed in every form imaginable. Those who had not chosen an Avatar or Virtual Persona before entering appeared as Crash Test Dummies. It was a mocking tribute that many places in the web now adopted as the default when someone could not or would not choose an identity for themselves. Walking near him was a whole family of Dummies. Originally, people entered various cyberspaces dressed with Crash Test Dummy avatars as a form of protest against the dangers of total submersion, but the message was lost in the medium. Some hackers now loved to be tricksters and abuse Dummies with practical jokes.

The ones walking near Ben only suffered minimal abuse. One had mismatched arms with one so long it dragged on the ground. Another had wobbly shopping cart wheels instead of legs while still another had a head that occasionally morphed into an upturned laughing hyena. Ben could not help but smile as he arrived at the gate for the inner temple.

"Open Earth Dreams." He said aloud and the gateway opened, revealing a small amphitheater where an immense hi res globe of the Earth turned majestically below. Ben came here at least a month to upload his most recent dreams. Today he descended the stairs to sit near the equator and watch the real time image of the Earth roll along on its slow rotation with continents passing slowly from light into darkness. Many others sat reverently around the amphitheater transfixed in private communion with their own data streams.

"Bring up main menu." He commanded and a floating window appeared to his right. "Load Dream Journal and synchronize recent dreams." Imagery flowed across the window as it uploaded his dreams and translated them into an impressionistic style of animation resident in the Dream Temple's system.

Ben reviewed a dream where he was walking through a house of many rooms and doors. It was a confusing labyrinth and he watched himself struggle to find the way outside. When he finally found the door he stepped through it and onto a high balcony that looked over the suburbs below. In the distance the land gave way to the ocean and far out on the horizon he saw the dark heavy clouds of a storm spreading quickly across the sky. When he looked below he saw people moving to higher ground and a man with a panther resting in the safety of his yard. The presence of the large cat had unnerved him but he had let them be.

After uploading the narrative, since he had premium access, he had the server generate the basic scene in 3D and he used the built in tools to sculpt the rest. He added doors and dimly lit corridors, filled the rooms with bookshelves and a sparse assortment of furniture and artwork. He darkened the sky and added a greater density of clouds on the horizon. The man waiting below wore jeans and a thick leather jacket that he pulled around himself for warmth, the panther was watchful but resting and calm. When Ben finished he surveyed the whole scene and saved it to his file. He wondered what part of his shadow the lithe form of the panther had come from.

Even after he finished downloading the animation into the Dream Network's database, the feeling of the dream lingered within him. Revisiting a dream through reconstruction was sometimes wonderful and sometimes a difficult experience. Ben had logged more than 300 dreams since the Dream Network went online. They were all different but recording them in VR made it easy to recognize the common themes.

"Open Global Survey." He pointed at a spinning Earth icon fixed in the corner of his visual field and the hi-resolution animation of the Earth below zoomed out at a gradual speed while gaining brightness and contrast.

"Show geographics." The globe maintained its cloudless topography but faint lines now displayed the boundaries between countries, states and provinces. New menus appeared as did a simple legend of colors. Each one represented a different theme common to dreaming around the world. It took a few seconds for the system to sort the several million dreams from the past 48 hours and lay them out in transparent colors around the globe. More than anything it looked like a weather map, something a few critics enjoyed describing as another SETI project, a search for intelligent life on Earth. Others viewed it more seriously as an MRI of the species; something many philosophers also had a field day with. For Ben, who was one of the pioneers of the project, the survey was something of both.

In the past few years the Dream Survey had become popular but sadly he knew it was just another fad. Many strange things had emerged in the public interest since the Web and various virtual worldsites came online and many had disappeared with equal speed. There were predictions and grand hopes of the spontaneous emergence a global super consciousness, a Noosphere of sorts but so far the global web fueled by human interest was no more than an unconscious beast lumbering from place to place. The fallout from the beast though was enough to keep the Dream Network running strong with visitors and members for years to come. And of this he had no complaint.

Colors flowed in tight chaotic swirls around the major cities and suburbs but smoothed out into broad topographic swathes in the country. Most of the time the Dream Survey showed chaotic distributions of dream imagery. Ben and the others running the Dream Network occasionally found curious periods of consistency when a great many people briefly shared common dream elements or themes. This usually happened following periods of traumatic events like natural disasters, violence, war and periods of social upheaval. There were other times though when patterns of common dreams emerged mysteriously from the collective like crop circles in the collective mind. Other times these images flowed across the globe like storm fronts, only to disappear quickly into either chaos or indefinable complexity.

No one knew what to make of these patterns and they could not be associated with any known cause. Ben had his own theories as to their significance but leaned toward Jung's theories of Synchronicity and the Collective Unconscious. Today when Ben looked at the colors spread across the globe he could already see the beginning of an unusual event. Clustered around major cities was an unusual concentration of common dreams. The Pursuit and Fighting themes were now prominent in many of the major cities of the world. Ben asked the survey's database for more details on the dreams.

"Most of the dreams are battles involving giants or gods just like Mayu's dream. How can that be? That's over 37 million people with the same dream. And that's not counting all those that go unreported." When he looked back over the past week and ran the dream topography backwards in time then forwards again he could see the dreams growing and spreading.

"That's weird, it looks like the vectors of a pandemic." He tried to trace the dream back to its source in previous weeks but that proved impossible as it spread into the background radiation of global complexity.

"There is no single source, it just seemed to come out of the collective on its own. Maybe it's just another random phenomena or part of a larger pattern our minds are still too small to grasp." Ben saved the results and had the system play out the patterns of the past several months in a repeated loop at high-speed. It was indeed a lot like watching satellite recordings of the weather. He felt almost hypnotized as he watched the storm front of colors growing and moving outward. On a basic level he saw this pulsing and swirling as the unconscious mind of humanity. Now nearly two hundred years after Jung and others had begun to describe it he could now see the collective unconscious in action.

"But why does it look like an epidemic map? How can a dream spread like that? Through food distribution or some kind of electronic transmission? Or can a virus trigger a latent gene?" When he was finally saturated with as much information as he could hold, he left the Dream Network through a tunnel of rippling energy. It dumped him back in the Cave and instead of getting up to stretch he switched on the news. The anchorman and woman that came on looked normal and vaguely artificial as media celebrities often do, whether they be organic or simulated. On this transmission The Code of Authentication sign hung boldly on the wall behind the reporters and was watermarked everywhere necessary. Some of the headlines in the news were:

1. War in Asia

2. Fighting in the Middle East

3. The Latest in Cybercrime. Ben was curious and hit the link. "Two men aged 18 and 22 have been charged guilty with several counts of hacking a news link, decrypting the Authenti Code and several counts of fraudulent transmission of world news events. A federal investigation revealed the two had an extensive history of developing and using constructed events and entities with the intention to deceive. Federal authorities will prosecute to the full extent of the law.

He closed the link and moved on.

4. Sleeping Flu

A new strain of flu has been discovered causing low-grade fever, loss of appetite, excessive sleeping and strange repetitive dreams. Researchers are calling it a new Sleeping Sickness. The duration of infection and path of transmission are still unknown.

Ben froze for a moment before hitting the link. The details provided little valuable info other than the names of the primary researchers and their labs. That was enough for him to find the links to their worldsites. From there he accessed their contact info and fired off some email. While Ben was reading the details of their diagnoses and the distribution of the virus he received a response from one of the main doctors involved in the investigation. Interestingly, he was a long time member of the Dream Network with a background in neurology and psychiatry. He knew of Ben's work as a virtual artist and cofounder of The Dream Network and confirmed what Ben had feared. The majority of dreams of the people infected on the West coast were battle dreams with giants or gods. Ben sent him a copy of his findings of the recent global distribution of the dream and they agreed that more correspondence was due.

As soon as he finished the conversation and closed contact his thoughts went back to his wife. "I hope Mayu is okay. The doctor said there was no evidence of the virus passing through the placental barrier and there is no telling when she will get better. And what about the increase in dopamine receptivity in the brain that the doctors found? That would magnify the dream's intensity but how could it cause a reoccurring shared dream? And how could all that come from a simple virus?" He began to wonder if the viral messengers that were somehow crossing the blood brain barrier could effect the baby's brain development. There were too many unknowns for his liking. "I better go check on Mayu and see how she is doing." Ben got up and left the room before the rainforest animation was fully restored. Mayu was sleeping peacefully and he wanted to wake her to make sure she was okay but decided it was best not to disturb her again. That night he slept a deep dreamless sleep.

CHAPTER III. THE FOREST GUARDIAN

Swift as the wind
Quiet as the forest
Conquer like the fire
Steady as the mountain

Sun Tzu. The Art of War

MARIN COUNTY, SAN FRANCISCO BAY AREA

They sat in Gordon's living room sipping a bottle of red from Sonoma while the candles flickered softly on top of the gourmet cake shaped like an alien spaceship that had landed on the coffee table. Gordon sat back in a big comfy chair while his friends Eli and Erin inhabited the couch by the fireplace. To his mind the fire was a quiet appassionata of the sun written into the dense scroll of the burning wood and played out in the unfurling of flames. Gordon peered through the carmine globe of his wine lit by the warm light from the fire. He imagined the electromagnetic waves from the firelight spreading outward like streams of Celtic knot-work made of scintillating particles flickering in and out of existence, before finding their demise in the cold glass of wine held deftly in his hand.

"Eli, I've only known you for a little more than a year and I love you like a brother. Truth be told you're more of a brother to me than any of my brothers ever were. Most of all, I'm impressed with the almost radical open-mindedness I've seen in you in the past year. You've made a huge change in your life without so much as a backward glance. You packed your bags and left the wilderness of Vermont and moved here to the Bay Area like it was the next town over."

"I did have a little help." Eli was loosely entwined with Erin, she snuggled closer and rubbed his chest. Eli was a slim figure carved from distant Semitic ancestors with an angular nose and long dark hair pulled back into a ponytail. Erin had been working with Gordon in the lab for a couple of years by then and had gone to Vermont on vacation where she met Eli while hiking in the wood.

"Well, I guess I was done with that game and ready for a new one. Not to mention that Erin presented me with an enticing opportunity I couldn't refuse. He gave her a kiss while running his hands through the long waves of her red hair.

"Come on Eli this about you." Gordon chided.

"Okay, okay but Erin was significant in changing my perspective and giving me a good reason for coming out here. Contrary to what some people might have you believe, hanging out in the woods isn't the opposite of living here on the accretion disk of a big city like San Fran. It might seem that way superficially but that's just cultural hypnosis. When I was in the woods I was busy studying the origins of music and the technology of nature. And here I'm doing the same thing."

"You mean the pattern which connects."Gordon stated.

"Yeah, you would put it that way. Let me put it this way. My parents did their best to shelter me and my sister from the hyper-modern world by raising and home schooling us on an organic farm. My hunger for knowledge though led me off to school in the big city. Going from small town Vermont to Boston was incredible and I lost myself there for a while. Eventually I realized I needed to unplug from all the noise, from the chaos of information flooding our culture and the narrative I had inherited from my parents. I couldn't even hear my own thoughts or know what feelings or ideas were my own because of all the noise. I simply wanted to know who I was.

When I got back to the woods of Vermont I found myself on a root level, pun intended, but discovered there was so much going on around me that I knew nothing about. Newton's image of the child playing with pebbles on the shore of a great ocean of truth stuck with me. It took a long time to set aside everything I had learned to relearn the language of nature. Mushrooms helped open the doors of perception but nothing was better than watching the landscape change through the seasons. Now that was archetypal. Nothing was more amazing than watching the awakening of life in the spring or the slumber of life in the deep of winter. It was wonderful to discover that everything was alive and conscious around me. The stars and trees, the rivers and stones, the crickets and crows were all dynamic parts of an ancient tapestry of extraordinary complexity wrapped in the guise of an almost ignorable simplicity."

"I'll never forget one day when I met this guy playing flute and building sculptures in the woods. He would gather scraps of wood and carefully put them together. I stopped to watch and ended up helping him out. He collected pieces of stone from the river and laid them out in odd geometric patterns. He made trails of leaves and wove things from twigs. In four days we hardly spoke but I began to understand how everything fits together like a vast endless weave. Nature's technology is eons ahead of ours and it's amazing how everything fits and meshes together and nothing is wasted." Eli knew this would get Gordon going and he enjoyed goading him. He could see him tense up as he sat forward and put his wineglass down, the dark liquid sloshing around in the glass.

"The Earth's biomes may be good at recycling but nature is messy, chaotic and inefficient. I don't buy the idea that nature is simply sacred in a numinous mystical sense but definitely in the sense that natural processes are essential and need to be worked with respectfully. With that said there are a lot of things we can improve upon like our own biology and some of the more fragile ecosystems." Gordon was starting to warm up and he loathed the idea of deifying natural processes as an abstract feminine spiritual intelligence. He found that just as inherently flawed and distasteful as the Judeo-Christian-Muslim idea of a transcendent paternalistic sky God.

"Improve upon?" Eli chided. "We're the ones who messed up the balance of most of those ecosystems in the first place. Our culture, in striving to improve itself has made a huge mess of the Earth Community. We've soiled our own nest and pierced the womb in our mad rush to be born." Eli enjoyed this side of the debate and more often than not agreed with this perspective. Gordon frowned.

"The equilibrium of the biosphere has gone through a few significant changes in equilibrium resulting in some nasty mass extinctions long before our ancestors ever arrived on the scene." Gordon was just getting warmed up. "Granted we've made a bit of a mess and human technology may not be as efficient in cleaning up after itself as natural but it has its own elegance and beauty. We've also improved significantly on what evolved in nature and created things that the whole of the natural world could never have dreamed of without us." Gordon knew Eli was goading him but he couldn't stop himself from arguing the point.

"Come on boys," Erin protested "don't go medieval on me." Erin protested. "Let's not polarize culture and nature. Isn't culture just an extension of nature? How can you realistically separate humanity from the Gaian system." Erin had heard these arguments before and found the oppositional views too limited. "Aren't we merely that part of the Earth that sees itself? And if we are part of Gaian system then human technology unfolds out of the technology of nature, at this stage, even though it is a hell of a lot clunkier and inspired by more noble aspirations." Erin was always good at bridging perspectives, at finding the higher order synthesis in their philosophical arguments. "Besides, if you two keep going on like this your candles are going to set your cake on fire."

"Well said." Gordon agreed despite himself. He felt the storm welling inside him and longed to unleash it but he knew she was right. This was a time for celebration not fighting in the streets.

"Agreed." Eli leaned forward, blew out the candles and they dug in. After they settled back with their wine Eli got thoughtful again.

"I'm very glad I met both of you and moved out here. There's a pulse to the city below all the complexity and stress, somewhere below the more, better, faster chant of industry and our absurdly adolescent popular culture. Its like a wave, a self-organizing movement to push forward and rise out of the muck, an almost blind groping toward something greater."

"Teleology." Erin said. "I believe Teilhard de Chardin called it something goofy like Orthogenesis; the evolutionary movement from geosphere to biosphere then into consciousness and on into the Omega

Point of supreme consciousness. My grandmother bless her soul, always used to tell me to reach for the stars."

"I'll buy that." Eli held his glass high then took a good swig of wine.

Gordon just shook his head and smiled. "Eli, you may have been born on the East coast and lived as a wildman, but you're a West Coaster through and through. I am glad you came." Gordon raised his glass and they toasted Eli's health and growth.

"Well, speaking of supreme consciousness, what's the latest plan for antagonizing an advanced AI out of hiding?" Eli poured another glass and snuggled back in with Erin.

"I'm glad you asked." Gordon smiled.

FOREST WORLD, ENTERTAINMENT ZONE, THE NET

The next day was Saturday and Eli came back to Gordon's driving a clunky old Volvo hybrid from the little town of Fairfax, an old hippie haven many stilled called the Cosmic Bubble, where he and Erin lived. Gordon lived in a more upscale town closer to the bridge. After lunch they went on a quick hike then did a little yoga to settle their muscles and heart rate down. They retired to Gordon's Rec room, dimmed the lights and lay down in specially contoured zero stress chairs. When they uttered their pass phrases and tapped their fingers in the correct sequence, their neural implants activated full VR mode, bypassing much of their peripheral nervous systems and processed hi definition data streams from the Net directly into their brains. They were instantaneously submersed in another world built from the ground up with code, a world that looked and felt completely real.

They floated down from a low flying cloud and landed on a hilltop overlooking a vast expanse of forest that stretched from horizon to horizon. This world was the home of some of the most frequently encountered gods and goddesses with unusual behavior. In the distance a great snow capped mountain rose out of the ocean of greenery, solemn and serene. Its peak wore a crown of clouds and a halo of golden light. The world's mapping system labeled it Cedar Mountain. It was unscalable, shaped like a steep cinder cone and the great demon known as the Guardian of the Forest lived in a cave at its base.

It was said that the forest extended up to 32,000 square miles though the largest parts were disabled when not in use. The world was a vast magical playground, home to fantasy and mythological creatures from various cultures as envisioned throughout human history. The creators were partial to elves, goblins, dwarves, wizards and dragons but there were also plenty of fairies and the little folk. There was magic in the air and battles between monsters and humans were common currency here. Spread throughout the world were seven sacred mountains, home to the gods and goddesses who help manage the adventures of all the world's players.

Gordon and Eli descended the hill along a wide dirt path until they came to the Gate of the Forest. It was a crude arch made of the rough hewn trunks of something immense like Sequoia trees. Carved into the wood were numerous runes describing the rules and organization of the world. Before they could pass, the runes glowed on the surface of the gate and the information they held was streamed into the molecular memory of their implants. They had a program set to fast scroll and respond to all the agreements, disclaimers and regulations so they didn't have to read them.

Once through the gate they had a choice of transportation. There were great eagles, large cats, griffins, unicorns, dragons and a few other odd creatures mulling about and waiting like taxis. They chose a couple of fierce-eyed griffins with eagle heads and lion bodies and had barely climbed on before they were airborne. Wings blurred and sliced the air around them as an endless ocean of trees flowed below. They settled in for a long ride since the mountain was far. And this world like many of the most established fantasy game worlds insisted on providing an experience of profound realism. It was a curious thing to Gordon and he had been searching for a word to describe it since oxymoron didn't cut it.

"You know I just remembered having an intense dream last night." He said to Eli on a private sub vocal comm channel.

"Now that you mention it, I had an interesting dream too. You go first." Eli was more than a little curious.

"We were deep in a gorge that ran around the base of a mountain. Everything was so large that we felt like flies. The mountain shook and a landslide fell upon me. An almost intolerable light burst out in the darkness and a being of radiant energy appeared whose grace and beauty were so great they could not fit within this world. She pulled me from beneath the mountain and gave me water to drink from a pure mountain spring. I was healed and comforted and she picked me up and put me back on my feet before ascending into the sky and disappearing amongst the stars." When Gordon finished he stared off into space, still enraptured by the memory of his encounter.

"Now that sounds pretty fortuitous if you ask me." Eli exclaimed. "My dream started with a feeling of terror and confusion. I encountered a bull in the wilderness and grabbed hold of it and held on as it stomped around raising so much dust that the whole sky went dark. Somehow it twisted around and impaled my arm and I bit my tongue. I fell to my knees and the bull changed into a bearded god with a dark countenance."

"That's a bit ominous." Gordon frowned. "What do you make of that?"

"I don't rightly know." Eli shook his head.

The griffons set them down in a clearing by a wide dusty road. There was a village nearby that was a starting point for the adventures in the area. Instead of heading into town for a mission and supplies they turned away from the road and walked off into the woods. There were no paths where they went so Eli led the way, weaving and wending his way between trees and underbrush.

"Are you telling me that beyond what we can see and interact with immediately around us, the rest of the forest doesn't exist?" Eli found his strange.

"Basically." Gordon said. "Imagine were walking through a large dark cave with flashlights. A pool of light surrounds us and only what enters into our field of light or intersects our trajectory is called up by the servers into active memory."

After a half hour they came to an insurmountable wall of bramble.

"It seems we're stuck." Gordon moaned.

"No such thing. There's always a way around. Plants in the woods tend to grow in families. Of course there are always species that venture off on their own but many tend to grow together in communities. Let's backtrack and follow the contour and grade of the landscape. If this virtual forest is modelled accurately after a real forest then there will be a way through close by." Sure enough they found a clearing filled with grass, clover and tiny spring flowers. A small stream trickled through the low trodden grass.

"Deer!" Eli was elated, crouching to examine the grass. "The makers coded Deer into the ecology."

"Why is that so good?" Gordon thought Eli was maybe just being a little too sentimental over a few piles of scat.

"Good? It's great. Check this out." He pointed to a small parting in the underbrush at the edge of the clearing. It was small enough that Gordon wouldn't have noticed it on his own. He was beginning to wonder if Eli still had some neurons loose from all those funny mushrooms he ate while living like a Grub.

"Deer trails are like the main roads that run through all the different neighborhoods of the forest. Come on." He stepped through the opening and disappeared into the woods. Gordon shrugged and followed him into the shadows. After a while Gordon started to get frustrated though.

"This doesn't look like much of a trail. It just kind of wanders around almost aimlessly. We could probably get to the mountain a lot more quickly by cutting through the woods that way." He pointed off through the trees.

"Yes, and you'd probably be a lot more tired in the end, step on a wasp nest, get covered from head to toes in burs or get bit by a cute but poisonous unicorn in the process. You have to remember that while we've been holed up in towns and cities for the past 10,000 years or so deer have been living in the woods the whole time and they know it pretty damn well. Their pathways don't make sense in a Euclidian mindset, they meander chaotically in an economical way that only makes sense intuitively if you know the landscape."

Gordon surrendered to the process. He had no basis for disagreement for this was Eli's area of expertise and they were still heading in the right direction. As they wandered along ridges, through gullies and into another clearing the shadows deepened. They stopped to rest a minute and get their bearings. An uneasy silence descended around them, noticeable only by the absence of the natural ambience of the forest. The feeling that they were being watched grew on them until it was almost tangible.

"Whoever made this world sure knew how to play on perception." Eli wondered what kind of skill and knowledge it took to play with neural code on that level.

"Over there." Gordon pointed midway up a tree. Four luminous creatures that were mostly eyes and fur faded slowly in and out of existence.

Cheshire cats?" Eli thought they looked more amusing than sinister.

"I've heard of these creatures before. Let me take a quick scan through the world's inventory before we do anything." A small virtual screen appeared before his eyes and scanned rapidly through a series of paragraphs. "It says they're simply known as the Watchers of the Forest but nobody seems to know anything definitive about them. They frequent certain areas but are absent throughout most of the world. In some of the postings people speculate that the Watchers play a vital role in maintaining the ecology of the forest."

"Gordon.."

"Best recommendation is to leave them alone."

"Gordon.."

"Wait a minute. One entry warns not to touch or disturb them. This person claims they can drain your life force and have some kind of magical relationship with plants."

"Gordon, turn off your screen and take a look at this."

The screen disappeared and he found himself being watched by hundreds of eyes attached to a great many glowing balls of fur floating throughout the trees.

"The consensus on the postings suggested we treat them like bees. Leave them alone and they'll leave us alone." After a few long minutes passed the Watchers slowly disappeared and the sounds of the forest returned. Gordon and Eli looked at each other and shrugged.

"Only the gods and the makers know for sure."

They hiked out of the clearing and down into a gully along the deer trail and followed it as it hugged the incline of a ridge. When they reached the top of the ridge they were surrounded by Watchers. Eli immediately brought up a shield spell and they dove to the safety of the ground below the ridge. Without warning a storm of burrs and seeds flew at them. Millions of hooked and sharp particles flew through the air like rain from hell tearing apart everything in its path.

"Bees my ass!" Yelled Eli. "They're more like wasps."

"Little bastards!" Gordon shouted over the storm. "How are we going to get around them? Is there another path if we go back down and follow the gully?"

"No, everything else leads away from the Guardian's lair. This is a bottleneck and the little buggers know it."

"Crap! How are we going to get past them?"

"That's easy, use one of the wind spells and blow the little bastards away." Insisted Eli.

"If I do that then we'll have one less weapon to take down the Guardian with."

"If you don't then we're going to be ripped to shreds and wake up quickly in the real world in agonizing pain if it overloads our neural suppressors."

"You do have a point there. Let's see, which one should we use?"

"I've got a hunch. Let me have the blasting hot south wind." Gordon gave Eli full access to the cache, something he had meant to do before they logged in. Eli climbed back to the top of the ridge and set loose the burning wind, a hot dry blast of air that scorched the ground, parching and curling the remaining leaves on the way. The Watchers called forth a great storm of seeds and burls. When the wind hit the deluge of seeds they cracked and burst open into dry puffs and blew away. The nasty little creatures were blown away in the mad rush of the burning wind leaving Gordon and Eli alone in the forest. They hiked a bit further then stopped by a great Cedar tree to rest and get their bearings.

"So rested he by the Tumtum tree and stood awhile in thought." Eli could not help but quote Lewis Carroll. "Since we entered this world I've been wondering, when these trees fall do they make noise like real trees?"

"Probably. Everything I've read about this world indicates its physics are a faithful replica of our own."

"Do you think this part of the forest persists for a while after we log out?"

"So I've heard. Why, what are you driving at?"

Eli pulled out his magically enhanced axe and started chopping at the tree. Huge chunks and splinters started flying.

"Well, if I cut down a virtual tree..." He yelled over the noise, "and we log out and no one's here to hear it fall does it make a noise?" The tree creaked and groaned as it tipped no longer able to support its own weight. Eli sat back and laughed while Gordon just shook his head. The tree fell with a resounding crash taking a few smaller trees down with it. Before the noise stopped though they heard a great bellowing roar far in the distance.

"Did you say no one?" Gordon smiled broadly as he stood up and gathered his weapons. For a while there was a long silence, long enough for birdsong to start again. Then far away they heard the pounding of heavy feet running in a fast gait. They both got in a good stance and held their weapons ready. Within minutes the thundering footsteps drew closer accompanied by the crash of trees being pushed away.

"And, as in uffish thought he stood, The Jabberwock, with eyes of flame, came whiffling through the tulgey wood, and burbled as it came!" Eli chanted.

"I don't hear any burbling." Gordon chided.

Eli was about to say something when the beast burst through the trees. It was a hulking mass of muscle the size of a large elephant but it knuckled along like an ape. It had the face of a lion filled with nasty looking dragon's teeth and its body was covered with a matte of tangled fur.

The Guardian paused for a moment to look at them then charged like a rushing flood crushing and pushing aside trees in its wake. The monster's attack was fast and furious. The slashing of its claws was an impenetrable barrier so all they could do was parry its blows to survive. After fifteen grueling minutes of frantic defense, the monster backed off, leaving a break in the attack. Gordon and Eli pressed forward, viciously attacking the guardian with sword and axe. Its thick fur and hide merely deflected their blows so they separated, attacked from both sides, pressing the beast back and searched for weaknesses. They found none and soon the guardian was at them again with unbelievable ferocity. Its claws furiously slashed through their defences but their magically boosted armor held firm. The second time the Guardian backed off, Eli pulled out a bow with enhanced arrows while Gordon parried its claws. The arrows found their mark and the monster screamed more in rage than in pain. It staggered back, brushing the arrows off at their tips.

Something changed in the air and Gordon felt his tension increase. His heart began beating faster and his hands began to sweat on the hilt of the sword. By all accounts he'd read, he knew the battle was about to get a lot harder. Eli threw his axe at the monster's horrible face then quickly stepped forward hacking at its exposed belly with a glowing sword. The monster let out an ear-piercing scream and blood began pouring out of its gaping wounds. A horrible reek filled the air burning their nostrils. Gordon hung back and powered up the first spell. He sent the signal and Eli jumped away. A raging arctic wind buffeted the monster, knocking it off balance. Ice and snow covered its face and arms slowing its movements. As the spell began to fade Gordon found Eli standing beside him shooting his last few arrows. The monster thawed quickly but before it regained its strength Eli ran up and cut off one of its hands.

"One, two. One, two. And through and through the vorpal blade went snicker-snack!"

Before Gordon could summon another spell the Guardian released a deafening roar, blowing them off their feet and knocking down all the trees in its path. Still dazed as he awakened on the ground next to Eli, Gordon summoned a shield of light to surround them. It was just in time for the monster projectile vomited a spume of fire as hot as fresh lava. The shield deflected what it could not hold and the ground around them vaporized down to bare rock. What was left glowed and shimmered with heat. Gordon wasn't sure how much more the shield could handle but he held it in place and hoped for the best.

The Guardian gathered its energy for another burst, threw back its head and opened its mouth wide. Eli pulled a hurricane out of their cache and launched it at the monster. The winds came on like dragons roaring down out of the sky. They hit the Guardian full force at 180 miles an hour, blowing it into the air and smashing it against the trees. When the winds finally subsided the beast struggled slowly back to its feet and growled.

Eli pulled out another wind but before he could fully charge it up the Guardian's eyes changed to a pale green and everything left standing around them began to wither and die. Even with the shield in place they began to feel weak and tired as their energy drained out of them. Back in their bodies nanobots coursed through their bloodstreams binding to and neutralizing stress hormones then broke them down into innocuous little molecules that floated quietly away.

Gordon managed to call a tornado forth and it came barreling in from the West, ripping up everything in its path. Its point of contact with the earth was small but its cone rose high into the atmosphere. When it hit the Guardian it sucked the monster up like a toy and tossed it high into the sky. It fell like a meteor and hit the ground with a heavy thud that shook the ground. It landed with unearthly precision on the same spot where it had stood. As though punctuating its demise Gordon hit it with a bolt of lightning he had readied deep in active memory. Not wanting to take any chances, Eli shouldered his axe and ran up to the smoking mound of flesh and with a swift blow cut off its head. He raised it up as a trophy and walked back to show it off to Gordon.

"He left it dead, and with its head, he went galumphing back." Before Gordon could respond the trees shivered, the mountain moved upon the horizon and a ball of light descended like a shooting star from the snowy peak. It took a minute for their eyes to resolve the blinding light into a chariot of lapis trimmed with gold and drawn by winged horses. As it neared he could see the driver was a goddess with a thick mane of hair pulled behind her, slim but muscular arms and fierce eyes of the deepest blue.

By the time she stepped onto the ground they were already feeling the onset of a state of euphoria. Gordon remembered that the gods and goddesses liked to play with people's minds. Wherever she walked the burnt and withered ground came back to life. The grass and trees turned green and blossomed in her wake. She stopped to touch the monster's head affectionately as though caressing a favorite pet. When she spoke her tone was not angry but amused and teasing.

"So you've killed the great and terrible Guardian. None have ever accomplished this before. By the rules of the game you are entitled to a reward but choose wisely. What gifts do you now seek, great and mighty warriors?" She circled around them examining their clothes and hair. She sized them up as though looking at show horses or slaves.

"We seek no reward goddess, no reward beyond knowledge." Gordon said.

"Knowledge. What knowledge?" The goddess asked.

"The truth of your nature." Gordon decided to be bold.

"You dare?!" She seemed genuinely offended.

"We know where you come from and that you are not what you seem." Eli chided her.

"Well, now that is suspiciously vague and could be interpreted in different ways." She crossed her arms and stood tall.

"Ok. We know that a small group of AI escaped the Purge and are hiding out as gods and goddesses in worlds like this." Gordon decided it at this point it couldn't hurt to lay it all out.

"And what proof do you have?" She frowned.

"Admittedly none." He said.

"Excellent." She said. "Now what should I do with you? Give you a treasure and send you on your merry way, bind you here and make you my husbands or kill you slowly and savor your agony?"

Luckily Eli was holding his tongue. There was no telling how an AI like her would respond to his teasing. Gordon decided to stand firm and let her play out her cards. Thankfully he didn't have to wait long since another god descended out of the sky on great feathered wings and landed nearby. This one was had an eagle's head on top of a man's body with immense wings and dressed in flowing robes of white embroidered with gold. His eyes were dark, stern and penetrating. He listened intently but kept glancing hungrily over at the carcass of the Guardian.

"I've seen what she does to her husbands." He croaked. "And I wouldn't recommend it. Your best bet is to hightail it out of here with a bauble or two."

"How unkind." She sulked. "You care little for the pleasures of life." While she fumed he turned and ripped some flesh off the monster and gobbled it down. A joyful gleam filled his eyes.

"How dare you!" She yelled.

"Ah, but you said we should pursue the pleasures of life." He taunted her. Turning quickly he ripped another piece off the monster hide.

Gordon ran a scan on them but didn't get much. Most of it was gibberish, code sets that were far beyond his comprehension. There were people he knew who could make sense of it though. He just needed to get it to them in one piece. The challenge was that an AI could prevent them from logging out for an extended time, lock related memories and block all off world transmissions. While the two gods argued her hold on them weakened. Gordon gave Eli the thumbs up and they logged out."

CHAPTER IV. TEMPLE WORLD

*What we experience in dreams, assuming that
we experience it often, belongs in the end just
as much to the over-all economy of our soul as
anything experienced "actually": we are richer
or poorer on account of it.*

Friedrich Nietzsche

SAANICH BC, CANADA

When Ben awakened he was floating in the soft shallows of a deep slumber. He lay quietly in bed blissfully unaware of the boundaries of his skin. The vast ocean of sleep beckoned him and dreams floated across the waters like ships with unknown destinations. Slowly he gathered the remnants of himself into a concentrated whole, foregoing his life as an ocean dweller to return to his life on the shores of the world. By the time he was fully awake the dreams were gone, phantom ships on a mist covered sea. He lamented briefly that the conscious mind was not a good net for catching the various creatures that lived within the ocean's deep.

He rolled over and snuggled in close to Mayu so he could lose himself in the primal comfort of her nearness and enjoy her scent. He had been missing her company since she had been sleeping so much and without her he tended to get deeply absorbed in his work. He didn't often seek out the company of others and enjoyed his solitude except when he was taking a rest from his art. Mayu tolerated his introversion well and for that he was deeply thankful. Eventually Mayu stirred enough for him to get her some toast and soy milk before she drifted back to sleep. She was seeming more and more like a cat to him now that she had the virus.

Once she was settled he went back to his workspace that he enjoyed calling the Cave. It was originally a family room he had converted into a place for building virtual worlds as well as for doing yoga and meditation. There he started his daily ritual of meditation followed by some yoga, especially the Salutation to the Sun.

When he finally finished and went into the kitchen he noticed that the fridge was too cold again and that the light didn't come on when he opened the door. While he defrosted a glass of juice he pulled the fridge off the network and reset it to factory defaults. It had been doing this consistently since January when an odd bug came through with some updates. Most of his appliances were fine and had patched easily though his toaster still had a bad attitude occasionally. He had heard stories of stereos playing Mozart when toasters were used but he had assumed that was just another urban legend. It didn't take him long to apply the latest firmware and system updates before getting the fridge back on the network and synched in with the house system and the other appliances. After breakfast Ben went back to the Cave and spent some time restoring the corrupted parts of his worlds. He took a short break to do some Tai Chi before putting back on his glasses and gloves and getting online.

VIRTUAL TEMPLE WORLD, ENTERTAINMENT ZONE

"Open link to Temples of the Sun." He said and a tunnel irised opened onto an wide plain bordered with equatorial rain forests against high mountains. Scattered across the plain were pyramids and temples from different cultures from Heliopolis to Machu Picchu. Each was based on the theme of temples dedicated to sun deities but expressed in the architecture and symbols of different cultures. Overhead the sun itself burned bright and large, probably four times larger than the Earth's sun. Ben never liked the layout of this world and thought the playground metaphor it used was distasteful. The theme of this world was supposed to be more of an expression of a sense of wonder and mystery than of amusement.

The entrance into this world placed him by a reconstructed life-size model of Stonehenge. He enjoyed exploring the ancient site, but he had a visit to make, so he turned and walked over to the giant sundial nearby with a large map of the Earth in the middle. The ancient cultures that all the temples in this worldsite came from were outlined in thin luminous lines. Temples and pyramids were represented simply in glowing dots. If he focused on an area the view expanded and he could see the pyramids and temples as miniature scale models.

After walking across the Atlantic he went into Egypt and took a stroll past the great pyramids, gleaming white, smooth and immense. There were avatars of crash test dummies everywhere, interspersed with many ancient Egyptian's and deities as well as people appearing to have come from every culture in human history. After walking by the sphinx he reached up impossibly high and touched the sun.

Warm yellow light spread outward from above dissolving everything around into a featureless glow. When it cleared he found himself standing on an irregular stone path looking out over a serene pond. Clumps of lilies lay on the water like a living carpet and Koi floated serenely beneath the surface while dragonflies buzzed hungrily above. Behind him a raised platform supported a 17th century Japanese nobleman's house. Its roof made of layered bark was supported by simple unornamented pillars and walls of sliding wood panels. One panel used for the front door was left slightly open.

Inside the house, tatami covered the floors so he took off his shoes and knelt down to place them carefully at the edge of the mat. The reeds crunched softly underfoot as he made his way to the main room. An older Japanese man wearing a simple dark kimono sat cross-legged in the center of the unfurnished room by a square fire pit. With a wooden ladle he carefully poured three scoops of tea into two shallow bowls. He placed one at Ben's feet as he sat adjacent to him on the mat.

"I am sorry for showing up unannounced." Ben bowed deeply.

"You are always welcome." The older man nodded.

"If it is an imposition then I will visit another time." Ben bowed.

"Have some tea." Shoji said.

Ben lifted the cup to his mouth but could only pretend to drink since his virtual body had no olfactory or oral inputs. Ben watched his father-in-law carefully trying to read his cues. When Shoji finally put down his tea bowl his entire demeanor changed to more open and cheerful. The ritual was over and Ben felt as though he had passed the test. Shoji had insisted on this little ritual ever since they first met. His father-in-law was not a traditional Nipponese man but he appreciated the formal ways of his ancestors, at least until he got a barrel of sake into him.

"How's my little girl?" Shoji asked.

"Not so little." Ben said smiling. The other man briefly had a bigger smile before he took another sip of tea. He was obviously looking forward to being a grandfather. "I am concerned about her health." Ben admitted. "She has this new flu that's making its way around so she's sleeping a lot. The doctor at the clinic said she will be fine and to let her rest." Shoji became serious and unreadable again as he looked down into his tea.

"Are you familiar with this painting?" The older man turned slightly and Ben saw a large screen painting standing in a recessed alcove. It was divided into three parts with men in feudal style clothing sitting and standing in celebration on both sides. One stocky and bearded man stood out from the others on one side, large and serious. On the other side a man stood holding onto a tree from which hung a mirror. In the middle panel a woman danced in the foreground while behind her a man struggled to move a boulder away from the mouth of a cave. From behind the rock emerged a beautiful woman shining with the radiance of the sun.

"It is a famous painting of Amaterasu, the goddess of the sun emerging from darkness and bringing light back to the world." Ben recognized her as equivalent to Persephone and Inana, the dying and rising goddess.

"Do you know the story leading to this event?" Shoji asked.

"Not well. It must be interesting." He had of course heard it before but knew it was important enough that Shoji tell the story at this moment.

"A long time ago, near the beginning of the world the Sun Goddess Amaterasu and her brother Susano, the Storm God were not on good terms. Some say her brother got drunk and destroyed her rice fields. In another account Amaterasu challenged her brother to a contest of creation and it soon became clear her gift was greater than his. When he refused to admit defeat he flew into a rage and destroyed her fields, threw excrement in her sacred hall and killed her maidens who were busy weaving the fabric of the cosmos and the clothes of the gods. In grief and fear she hid deep within a cave and closed it off with a great stone.

The high plains of heaven and the reed plains of the world below were plunged into darkness. Then the myriad of gods gathered by the heavenly river near the cave with great solemnity and came up with a plan to coax her out of hiding. They hung a magical mirror from a sacred tree nearby while the Goddess of the Dawn, Ame-No-Uzume danced passionately in an ecstatic state. The ensemble of gods cheered so loudly that the noise reached Amaterasu's ears. She moved the boulder aside and was so amazed at seeing her own reflection in the mirror they hung on a nearby tree that they were able to coax her out and close the cave behind her."

Ben sat quietly for a while to let the story sink in. Not only did it describe a process of introversion and emergence from a traumatic experience but he wondered if there were any significant historical events like eclipses or ancient volcanic eruptions connected with it. Since this was a foundational myth he was curious what it embodied or expressed about the national character of the Japanese people. Then it finally dawned on him what his father-in-law was saying. The myth repeated the same theme as the shared dream that was spreading with the virus around the globe. Pretending to take another sip of tea he saw the curls of warm steam flowing over his face.

"I've had the dream too." Shoji said and sipped his tea. "Most people infected show no sign, the others merely sleep a lot." He spoke casually but Ben found himself feeling anxious and began to worry about Mayu and the baby. Shoji could not but have seen the emotions sculpted into his face. "It seems harmless enough." He was trying to help Ben feel better but he was still quietly concerned about his daughter's well-being.

"What did you think of the new entry and arrangement point of the world?" Shoji changed the subject to avoid the discomfort that filled the room. As modern as he was the dictates of his culture would not allow an overt expression of emotion under these circumstances.

Even though he wanted to, Ben could not go back to share his concern for Mayu without challenging his father-in-law's limited expression of concern. And if he understood the unspoken protocols then that would only bring shame or disgrace.

All he could do was surrender and go with the flow. Ben knew his father-in-law was proud of his temple world and its ongoing popularity. Although Shoji had his own team of artists and engineers he often asked Ben for advice on major additions and renovations and kept Ben on the payroll as a consultant. He was part of the family after all.

"It's more interesting now that the entry point shifts around instead of being focused on the ruins." He said this bluntly, but realized after the fact what he had done and bowed slightly. He caught a flicker of a smile on Shoji's face. Being too direct was like hitting a ball out of bounds in a game of table tennis. And Ben freely admitted he was new to the game since it was contrary to his own cultural background. Shoji never took the game too seriously and always forgave him for these little indiscretions.

"It's also nice that you've changed the world's overall metaphor from a historical progression to something new and different." He fumbled his recovery as he was struggling to stay in the game. In his haste he had forgotten that Shoji was proud of those high resolution dusty old ruins of all the ancient temples. It was said that with implants that one could even smell the dust in the tombs. Shoji had cashed in early on the Virtual tourism boom and had been successful since he always paid close attention to detail and never compromised on quality.

People from around the world came to see the wonders of the ancient world in their contemporary ruined state since traveling to the continents planet side in anything other than a than a blimp or hyperloop was too expensive. Even though they had been online for years it seemed that everyone still wanted to see the great pyramids and temples of the world. Ben didn't fully understand the appeal and the romance of rubble though. When given a choice how could it compare to the wonders of the ancient sites remade in their original splendor and glory.

Shoji was well aware of his son in laws aesthetic preferences and was not insulted by his response. The playground arrangement was not intended as a permanent change but more as an experiment in rearranging the furniture.

"Did you know that only a small percentage of people with neural implants have shown symptoms of the virus?" Shoji asked. "It seems as though they might even offer some protection." This was an old argument between the two of them. Shoji had implants for several years now without any problems and he insisted they worked beautifully. "Don't be such a Luddite, Ben. It's time you got implants." It was always disconcerting when Shoji chose to abandon the game and switch over to being direct.

"I'm not a Luddite!" Gods this man rankled him sometimes. "And I'm not afraid of becoming overwhelmed or addicted to total submersion in virtual worlds. I simply don't want neural implants because I'm afraid of losing my privacy and individuality, not to mention my creative drive."

"Come on out of the cave, Ben. There is no privacy anymore. There hasn't been any privacy for a couple of hundred years if there ever was any such thing. Everybody has been into everybody else's business ever since we became primates."

"And then there's the risk of mind control." Ben said bracing himself since he knew what was coming next. They had this argument so many times before that all he could do was give Shoji his cues.

"Is my mind being controlled? Besides, our minds have been controlled on a basic level through language, belief and obligations from the day we were born. The only true freedom comes from being aware of the way we've been conditioned."

"You're preaching to the choir but that's not the kind of control I'm talking about." His father-in-law shrugged and looked away unwilling to go into that terrain. Ben gave up since he knew he could not convince the man otherwise.

After a brief pause Shoji changed the subject.

"A robot will arrive at your house soon so you will have some time to get acquainted with it before the baby is born."

"We don't need..." Ben started to object.

"You don't need to live in the dark ages and my daughter does not need to be burdened with menial tasks while she is mothering a baby."

"But.." Ben knew it was useless to protest.

"It will be delivered to your house this week. My wife would love to come live with you for a few months and do your housework but she is not in as good health as she once was. You would not want to burden her would you?"

Ben bowed in surrender. He knew he could never win this argument and a robot would give him more time to focus on his work. His father-in-law was wealthy but not extravagant so Ben was sure the robot would be of good quality and precise engineering without all the extra entertainment modules.

"Well, I have to admit I had considered getting one. Arigato gozaimasu." Ben bowed deeply.

Shoji smiled and nodded slightly. Ben interpreted this as: "I'm glad you agree. It's not going to get any easier when the baby comes." A wind chime sounded nearby, the dull musical notes of dry bamboo.

"My apologies, duty calls." Shoji stood up and bowed slightly.

On his way out, Ben walked to the edge of the mat, took off his slippers and put back on his shoes. He stepped outside, closed the sliding door panel behind him and turned to face the pond. "Open link to Home." He muttered as much to himself as to the system. The tunnel opened to engulf him and slid smoothly by before cross-faded into the background of the Cave. He pulled off his glasses and gloves and started thinking about his discussion with his father-in-law. Ben had been wrestling within himself for a couple of years now about getting implants and becoming more plugged in. Neural implants allowed the experience of total submersion in virtual environments on a whole other level simply not accessible through the Cave, suits, gloves and glasses.

The technology had been around long enough that the bugs had been worked out. Many of the early problems had not been with allergies to the nano engineered biochips but with psychological adaptation to the connectivity it brought. The implants allowed access to the Web from anywhere and you had to go pretty far out of your way to not find a connection these days.

As expected, a small percentage of the population with the wrong neurological predispositions became addicted or suffered from a fast onset of mild psychoses. By far the most widespread problems were from hyper-stimulation and too little decom time. To help explain the situation simply, the industry and media had latched onto the metaphor of the bends. Just as the body needed time to adjust from the pressure differences in depths of the ocean, the nervous system did as well from submersion in the virtual depths. The neural stimulation levels of most worlds had been equalized to that of life planetside, so the transition was often negligible. Most of the more intense stim worlds required a cool off period in a more calming space before getting "grounded" back on Earth. They had learned it wasn't good business for people to come out in agonizing pain or amped up and trigger happy. What bothered Ben most about implants was the inevitable compromise of privacy. He loathed the idea of being closely tracked and his commerce monitored.

"No more than you already are." Reminded the voice of Shoji. As much as he didn't want to, Ben had to admit to himself this was true. It was just as easy to limit the data flow on the implants as it was on external devices, maybe easier. What about getting hacked though?

"It can't happen." The industry had firmly said. What they meant was that it simply had not happened yet and they could not figure out how it could be done. The thought of carrying somebody else's information in his body, planted without his knowledge or consent was deeply unsettling for Ben. The manufacturers claimed to have gotten around this problem by only allowing the implants storage to be altered locally with high encryption, passwords and biometric recognition within a body area network. Verification of identity was also required for all access and purchases. In practice, huge amounts of data could flow through the implants without needing to be stored. Ben knew that eventually someone would hack them though, piggyback data or feed false code to someone's brain and they would never know, at least until it was too late.

"Would that be considered kidnapping?" Ben wondered. *"Luckily we don't have to deal with that yet. That's still a few years off."* Ben imagined it was like living at the base of a dormant volcano; beautiful and dangerous. As an artist he felt compelled to explore this

new medium, though the thought of it made him deeply uncomfortable. *"Maybe this was what the panther in my dreams was about. Eventually I'm going to have to do it. I can't keep building worlds from the Cave."* Many of the companies he built worlds for valued his work and imagination but often had to have their own people put the finishing touches on them. He didn't mind this but he sometimes wanted to know his worlds were complete and he knew their tolerance of his antiquated work style was limited. With implants he could add dimensions of subtlety to his art that the blunt tools he'd been using could barely touch.

Since he was young he always had a powerful and active imagination. He was the kind of youth who was good with art and obsessed with dreams, mystical imagery and stories of alternate worlds. One of the reasons he initially avoided implants and full submersion when the technology became reliable was because of his youthful obsessive nature when it came to fantasy and imagination. It worried him he would find it too engaging and that he would get lost. It was exactly this quality that made him a great virtual artist and World Weaver, a builder of worlds. He couldn't deny that he always longed to experience full submersion in the waking dreams of virtual worlds but as he matured he learned to live in better balance by spending time in nature and with friends. He met Mayu in art school and his relationship with her also helped ground him in the Real World. Her approach to art, though imaginative was more sensual. Maybe that was one of the reasons she gravitated to ancient crafts like basketry, clay and weaving.

In the living room she kept an old floor loom where she had begun making a blanket for the baby. It was about three quarters finished and showed the image of a peach tree by a river and a large peach floating in the water surrounded by swirls of current. He knew she had plans to embroider animals into the scene as she had done in other pieces. She had been working on this blanket steadily over the past few months but now that she was sleeping so much her progress had slowed. He sometimes missed hearing the sounds of her working the foot pedals and the beater bar in the background while he read or listened to music in the evening. In his imagination, the loom was like an organ that wove concertos in cloth instead of sound. He had tried it a few times and made some crude pieces based on musical themes but was quickly humbled by the artistry with which Mayu wove patterns and colors into cloth.

When Ben went to check on Mayu and peeked into the bedroom he found her still asleep so he left quietly. He set some food for her on the end table on her side of the bed then went out for a walk in the woods. It was a warm day and the air was rich with the smells of vegetation. He recognized many of the plants close to the ground but realized he knew so few of their names even though he occasionally browsed through a book on plants of the Pacific Northwest. He saw how the shrubs, wild flowers and ferns were spread across the forest floor in families and clusters and he wondered how they communicated with each other. He imagined nebulae like clouds and swirls of chemical transmissions flowing through the forest on the slightest breeze.

Along the trail he stopped to say hello to some friendly dogs and their owners, happy to be out on a beautiful day. He eventually came to one of his favorite old growth trees, a giant Douglas Fir and sat against its trunk to think. His mind was always clearer in the woods and especially by this tree.

"After the robot comes and I can be sure everything at home will be cared for I think I'll be ready for implants." He was a little surprised he had finally come to feeling settled with the decision since he had been wrestling with this for so long. He knew that he had to move his creative process to another level, to try something different that he'd never done before. With the baby coming in a few months he knew his time would be limited. He appreciated what Shoji was doing for him and Mayu and he eventually wanted to find a way to thank him for that. Ben sat for a while and listened to all the different melodies of birdsong scattered throughout the forest.

He took his time on the walk home, looking at the patterns of leaf and limb and saying hello to some dogs who were happy to stop for a sniff and a rub. When he got home he took off his shoes by the door, slid his feet into some slippers then went to the Cave and put on his glasses. They were hybrids that he could wear out in the world to see augmented data as well as virtual worlds in the Cave, but he preferred to unplug from the Net when he didn't need it and connected only in a purposeful manner. Once his glasses and gloves were on he called up the Garden world he had been working on and made sure the pond was still there. Thankfully everything was fine so he changed to Plato's Cave and did a quick walk through until he ascended the long dark tunnel to the entrance and discovered the sun was missing from the sky.

He stood for a while staring at the dark hole in the heavens, feeling a mixture of curiosity and frustration. No inspiration or understanding came to him so he restored the sun from a previous save and moved on, looking through various worlds he had in storage. He found nothing else unusual and sat back to think about things for a while. Nothing came to him, so he decided to get back to work and create a world that would be used by the Dream World to educate visitors and highlight the different re-occurring themes of dreaming.

Ben double tapped the fingers of both hands together activating a set of glowing links floating above each finger of his left hand. A combination of motion and light sensors built into the walls monitored his gestures and movements and translated them into customized commands for controlling his world building system. He selected the link above his small finger to open the landscaping palette. The space around him glowed with a soft light and with both hands he sculpted a small hill that sloped down to the shore of a beach bordering a vast ocean.

Tapping his fingers again he chose the texture palette to granulate the shore with sand and darken the waters of the ocean. He filled the sky with bright swathes of stars and galaxies, carefully pushing some into the distance to create a sense of depth in the darkness of space. The slope and top of the hill he covered with low wild grass interspersed with softly luminous wild flowers. When he tapped his fingers again he chose the building palette with its vast library of shapes and objects. It didn't take him long to construct a house of many rooms and doorways arranged in a complex maze that could only be discerned from above. It was easy enough to randomize the furniture from room to room according to different eras of history and he took special care to link doorways in odd and confusing patterns.

Next he opened his catalogue of human figures and released a woman in flowing robes to fly over the ocean, diving and rising high into the cloudless sky. He then placed a couple of men in renaissance clothes duelling with swords upon the beach, stuck in an endless battle. He put a man further down the beach running while looking back at something terrifying behind him. Out of Ben's catalogue of animals he pulled a couple of leopards to chase the man and for effect, then added some shadowy figures and darkened them to the point of obscurity. In the opposite direction he set a monk sitting deep in meditation with an aura of clear light around him. Far out in the water he set a sinking ship and someone swimming toward shore. Inside the house, in a bedroom decorated with silks and candles he placed two people making love in a large canopy bed. And racing down the hill toward the shore he put two kids in homemade go-carts.

Ben stepped back to survey the scene and take a rest. It was a lot of work in a small amount of time and he knew it would need a lot revision and labelling. He would have to figure out how to make this interactive and educational but that was for another day.

CHAPTER V. THE SEQUOIA GROVE

*It has become appallingly obvious that our tech-
nology has exceeded our humanity.*

Albert Einstein

NELDER GROVE, NEAR BASS LAKE, CALIFORNIA

Daniel climbed out of the car and looked around at the trees. It had taken hours to get to the Nelder Grove from San Francisco and he was a little tired and stiff from sitting for so long. The air was noticeably thinner and cleaner now that they were at 5,000 feet and surrounded by trees. He felt a little light-headed but that didn't bother him much. Daniel needed to stretch his legs so he did a couple of easy yoga postures to loosen up and get grounded. He was aware of some of people watching him but he didn't care. After a few minutes he noticed some of the others also stretching as well.

By the time he finished, another car had pulled into the parking area and he saw his old friend Diana get out and wave dramatically. Her face was always friendly and her wild mane of amber hair flowed like a storm behind her. As usual she wore blue jeans and hiking boots and was followed by her constant companion, a large husky wolf cross. She stalked through the small crowd to give Daniel a firm hug and a kiss on the cheek. Her wolf Sirius nuzzled his hand.

He originally thought it was an odd name for a wolf but she said it was natural since it was the name of Orion's dog and it was also the Dog Star which the statue of the Sphinx faced. Diana had always been an Egyptology buff. When Daniel looked it up he found that not only was Sirius part of Canus Major, the Great Dog constellation in ancient Europe and in Chinese astronomy the star was called the Celestial Wolf.

"Dan, you mensch. Thank goodness you made it. I didn't know if you were going to come." She held him at arms length. "You look good. I'm glad to see you're taking care of yourself, not wasting away like a wildman in the woods anymore." She ran her hand over his smooth shaven face. Whenever they got together she chided him about what she called his Thoreau phase of living alone in a cabin in the woods of Vermont. He had since moved down into town and out of the hills. "I did some of my best inner work out there." He reminded her.

"I'll trust you on that, now I've got to go mingle. See you later, when things settle down." He watched her work her way through the loose crowd, gathering them in her wake. Most people naturally deferred to her as a leader and Daniel had admired that in her but sometimes saw her as strong willed and a little bossy. He could never shake his memories of her from years ago as a preachy idealistic youth prone to bouts of melancholy with an anti-establishment ax to grind. Social change was her middle name and she always sided with the disadvantaged and the underdog.

They had a thing together when they were in college but soon realized they were better off as friends. He and Diana had drifted apart many times since but always somehow reconnected from one coast to the other. Daniel accepted long ago that the two of them had some kind of strange bond or spiritual connection in which their lives were interwoven like strands in a larger weave. While the larger part of his motivation for coming up to the Sequoia grove was to bask in the presence of the ancient trees, he also wanted to see her again. Soon after he learned that he had cancer, he knew he needed to talk with her and listen to the counsel of the trees.

His experience in Gordon's lab had a significant emotional effect on him. It not only showed him how much he had changed but it dredged up some unpleasant memories of his own scientific work that he had gone to Vermont to get away from. That was seven years ago and he had hoped he could leave it all behind him and start a new life. Now with his life on the line he felt he was being pushed back into a world he thought he had escaped.

When he got in touch with Diana last week through the local chapter of Green Sangha, she said that she had heard from good sources that forestry and biotech workers would arrive early the following week to secretly modify the Sequoia trees genetics. She had gathered some friends from her sangha and others to protest the government's clandestine workings. They even had a satellite feed to stream what happened to a public news channel and throughout the Web.

Daniel paused to look around at the group as they shouldered their packs and wondered if he was doing the right thing going with them. He grabbed his pack and wooden flute from the trunk of the car and readied himself to leave. He was feeling a little uncomfortable since he didn't know anyone aside from Diana and preferred his solitude. As a contemplative person no longer involved in Artificial Intelligence research, he worked through his ideas these days occasionally in poetry and art. He was more interested in exploring how ideas of natural intelligence were expressed in the interplay of human made and natural forms.

Daniel sometimes enjoyed building and sculpting things with natural objects like leaves, branches, stone and out of place artificial materials; arranging them in both organic and artificial ways. While he loved classical art, he felt it was stagnant in its attempt to stand out as eternal representations of human ideas and accomplishment removed from the flow of nature. Eternal ideas were not separate from the natural world, they were within the shape and movement of it. He felt strongly that they were in fact the shape of nature and natural process and this is what he struggled to reveal in art. Besides, he needed something fulfilling and engaging to help put his past behind him.

Daniel shook himself out of his reverie in time to join the tail end of the group as it snaked its way along the trail and into the woods. Watching the people ahead of him, he noticed that most of them were wearing faux organics; hi-tech jeans so smart that they looked dumb. They were faded and torn in all the right places, almost impossible to tell from original well-worn denim. On the common market it was almost impossible to find blue jeans that weren't engineered and grown in a cocktail of synthetics. Whenever possible though, he preferred wearing clothes made from organic natural fibers and handmade by cottage industry workers.

After a short hike they entered the campground and settled in to occupy all of the sites. Most people in the group had large packs and were prepared to stay for a week before new supplies were needed. They were hoping though to get enough publicity through satellite feeds so that they would only have to stay in the forest for a few days. Daniel had agreed to stay for the first couple days but a few members of the group like Diana were willing to stay for the long haul. This was the first protest of its kind and the environmental groups were split on the issue. Daniel wasn't so much split on the issue as he was on being there. When he looked around the clearing he saw it was already littered with dome tents, much of the group having already started settling in. Diana trudged over toward him, her wild mane of hair and Sirius following close behind her.

"Sure, I could use a hand." He didn't need help building the tent but it was obvious she wanted to help him. He'd used the tent before and it basically built itself when it came out of the bag.

After everyone had settled in, most had decided to go for a hike together to see the trees. Diana gave him a hug and trudged off with the others. Daniel grabbed his flute and walked along quietly by himself and looked at the trees. He was no stranger to hiking, he was just used to taking his time and walking at a leisurely pace and let the patterns of leaf and limb soak into his soul.

Truth be told he preferred to amble his way through the woods, stopping to feel the delicate smoothness of a flower or the rough skin of a tree. One of his favorite occupations was to study the geometry of nature or the way water flowed in a stream. For him it was much like exploring art in a museum; a brief look at a great work was never enough. He needed to study each painting, lose himself in it for a while to find out what the artist had done, what they were trying say. Nature for him was a great work of art with many details that needed to be explored.

The old growth stand they were going to was one of the least well-known in the Sierras. They weren't the oldest or biggest of the Sequoia but they weren't broccoli. Giants are never small, he mused. These trees though youthful compared to their well-known kin in national parks were still massive and the deeper he walked into the woods, the larger they grew. The Sequoia were so immense that he felt humbled and small like an infant walking across a dance floor of giants. It had been many years since he had encountered Sequoia and he remembered being overwhelmed even then. Most of them stood about 200 feet tall and were nearly 2,000 years old. Their great trunks were free of branches up to 100 feet and some trees were marked by deep cracks, crevasses and old fire scarring. Occasionally, he saw two or three giant trees clustered together and fused like Siamese twins. The ground beneath them was mostly free of plants and smaller trees since little could survive their shade. Occasional fires had also thinned out the surrounding pine that stood huddled below.

As he walked amongst them, Daniel felt like he was in the presence of a community of great slow gods standing motionless through time. And they took no more heed of him than most would of the affairs of the smallest of ants. He put his pack gently on the ground and walked over to stand beneath one of the great leviathans, respectfully laid his hands on its trunk and felt the furrowed bark. Looking up through the great outstretched limbs was like following a hard packed trail to a distant cluster of trees.

When he regained perspective he realized that the lower limbs were indeed the size of small trees. The image that came to him was that the Sequoia was rooted in the past but rising into the future. It seemed like the mast of great ship pushed by the winds of the sun and stars. He felt the deep quiet presence of the tree, time slowed and his sense of space opened. From the perspective of the slow god he saw days pass like moments and the passage of seasons flow by in minutes.

"Dan, what are you doing?" Diana came up behind him and placed her hand gently on his shoulder. The group had marched on, leaving Daniel standing alone looking at the trees. She wasn't an artist or writer but she was always curious what Daniel was thinking, though she didn't understand his creative process.

"I'm just listening to the language of these trees."

"They're amazing, aren't they? Are you going to play some flute or are you just carrying that thing around to ward off the mountain lions?"

Daniel gave her a funny look and played her a slow haunting melody that resonated softly off the trees. By the time they got back to camp someone had lit a fire and he sat down to watch the sparks fly off into the night to join with the stars. He easily slipped into a meditative state watching the briar of dancing blades with their short-lived wars and alliances. When he looked around the grove he saw the shadows of trees shifting and dancing in the firelight. Something in the darkness made him uncomfortable but he didn't want to think about his own struggles yet, he just wanted some distraction from his thoughts. He sat back and listened to the banter.

"The public deserves to know what's going on. They need to be educated about the dangers of nanotechnology, dammit. The corporations, military and government spend lots of money talking about how wonderful this stuff is. They only talk about the benefits because they have so much invested in it."

That was one of the leaders whom Daniel simply named Alpha. His personality type and uncompromising certainty was the same as those corporate executives that they despised so much. Daniel thought this was amusing but found them equally annoying. Instead of engaging in the conversation he sat and stared at the fire and listened to everyone popcorn their thoughts and concerns around him. He was not interested in controlling people or forcing social change. Diana wasn't so bad. She was idealistic without being crazy and genuinely interested in creating social change. Daniel agreed with this in principle but didn't want to force his ideas on anyone.

"As a species we have such a limited understanding of the world we live in that we stumble around blindly making messes everywhere we go." Another more reasonable fellow piped in. "We live imbedded in a system of systems so complex that it's difficult to see how our actions will effect the world around us."

"I think we're a virus." A woman sitting next to Diana said. "Our species is like a disease spreading out and infesting every biome. We've spoiled our own nest, we are building colonies on the moon and Mars so we can escape our own messes."

"The damn corporations only invested in environmental concerns when it was profitable for them and they could no longer avoid it." Alpha said angrily. "It's amazing how quickly the rhetoric of the media and pop culture changed. It's like a headless leviathan running from obsession to obsession. After the so called Information Age plateaued, industry and government pushed genetics to the foreground. They started quietly developing technologies to deal with environmental degradation and waited for environmental crises to bring it to the foreground for huge profits."

"Didn't T.S. Eliot say something like the greatest treason was to do the right thing for the wrong reason?"

"Now everything is catalogued and defined and valued as a commodity."

"What's wrong with that? It's gone a long way toward establishing environmental responsibility of corporations and slowed the degradation of the biosphere."

"It's still driven by profit though and it's only designed to sustain our position of comfort. It numbs us to the living world and our own lives. There are millions of people out there that would rather live in simulated worlds rather than experience the real world."

"Viewing nature as a set of commodities is just an extension of the old idea of nature as a resource for human industry. Ultimately, it's still destructive."

"Come on, you're throwing the baby out with the bath water. We've made substantial progress in shifting business toward ecological responsibility. Our civilization isn't in free-fall to an untimely demise anymore."

"Yeah, but it's not enough. We need to change our whole cultural paradigm because it's based on exploitation and an epistemology that's still fragmentary. We need to move out of our technocentric age and into a full-blown Ecozoic Era. Nature isn't here for us, every organism and its environment has its own intrinsic value."

"I think it all stems from the Biblical condemnation of nature. Be fruitful and multiply, name everything and dominate the Earth."

"There you go again, railing against the Bible. There are plenty of sound environmental messages within the Judeo-Christian tradition like Hildegard and Saint Francis to name a few. Besides, the meaning of that passage in the Bible can also be translated and re-envisioned as stewardship over the Earth, not domination."

"They're right you know. Everyone likes to blame the early Christians and Jews but if you look at history you'll find the Hebrews had a minimal impact on the environment. Other cultures like the Babylonians, Greeks and Romans had a far more devastating effect on the environment."

"You can argue all you want about the origins of the mess we're in but the simple fact is that the Earth is still dying a slow death. What's left of Nature? A few parks and some preserved wetlands. It's all for tourism and display; monuments of where we're from, of what we have conquered. We're living in a giant friggin museum!"

"It's not just a museum, it's a machine. Ever since they started trying to fix the climate with nanotech, an inhuman AI and supercomputers, it's turning into a managed system and there is no turning back."

"Things were so much easier 30 years ago before the world was filled with augmented reality, social engineering in the guise of social networking, nanotechnology and manufactured life-forms. It would have been nice to live 30 or even 60 years ago when life was simpler. Medicine wasn't as good but it would have been more manageable."

"I don't think romancing the past is going to get us anywhere. What bugs me is that we no longer know what's happening in the world any more. You can't believe what's on the news streams just because its format is news. How can we know if it's true or a construct?"

"I think that on a fundamental level some of you just don't like technology."

"I don't like what technology does to people and the planet. I don't trust it."

Diana came over and sat down beside him and by the look in her eyes it was obvious she had smoked a little weed. That was fine by him since it always slowed her down enough to really talk with. She sat close to him and gently rubbed his back.

"Why don't you play a little flute for me." She asked softly.

"There's too many people around. You know I'm a bit shy with my playing."

"I just thought I'd ask." The fire grew brighter, the tongues of flame singing their ancient hymn to the stars that deepened the night. "You know, I think my favorite sculptural piece of yours so far is the one where you created a small section of highway in the middle of a trail deep in the woods. And then there's the one where you got permission to take random sections out of a city sidewalk and put in flowers and grass."

"Ah, my anti-establishment period. That was fun." Daniel said.

"What are you working on now?" She asked.

"A mandala of trees. Someone commissioned me to develop it on a few acres of land that will evolve over time and have a positive impact on the environment. What I've done is taken an area that was clear-cut and planted various rings of trees with a clearing in the middle. Each ring is a different species of trees."

"That sounds great. When can I see it?"

"It's a work in progress, maybe in about 20 or 30 years."

"What?!" Daniel enjoyed the inevitable shock people had when learning about the scope of the project. Part of his intention with the piece was to contrast the long slow movement of organic time with the artificial time of modern life. He found great sympathy and inspiration from the Long Now Foundation.

"Well, I'm planting seedlings and it will take a few years before they're big enough for you to begin to get a sense of being inside of something." He could picture the mature project and what it would be like walking around inside it but he found it difficult to communicate the experience to other people.

"A few years? You mean a few decades. That's amazing. I'd love to see it. I hope I'm alive long enough to experience it in 20 years."

For a moment the conversation around the fire died and the world seemed to deepen in the silence. The shadows grew darker and the bonfire crackled as it released the fire it had trapped from the sun.

"What's going on Daniel? Diana put her arm around his shoulder. "I can tell something is gnawing at you."

"I don't feel like talking about it right now." Daniel wasn't sure yet if it was good idea to go into what was bothering him. Diana could be supportive when she felt like it but she could also be uncompromising with her ideals and somewhat judgmental.

"Come on, how long have we known each other? And we both know that's the real reason you came here."

"Okay, you're right." He sighed. "Well, I just learned that I have brain cancer." It pained him that there just was no other way to say it. He didn't even want to say it out loud since it somehow made it more real.

"Damn. I'm so sorry to hear that." Diana looked genuinely pained.

"I'm still in a bit of shock." He admitted. "I think it hasn't fully hit me yet."

"At least there's a cure for it now." She said. "We're not living in the dark ages of scalpels and chemo anymore."

Daniel frowned at the thought of millions of synthetic organisms coursing through his bloodstream. He imagined them infusing and infecting his cells, taking control of his organic nature until he was no longer human.

"The problem is that I don't want any of that crap in my body." He said. "It's the same thing you're fighting for with the trees. Who knows what the long term effects of commingling nanotechnology and biology are."

"You're right, but if you let nature take its course you'll die a horrible death and what good is that?" She frowned. "I understand your hesitation and that it might sound hypocritical but I think you should get the treatment. I want you to get that treatment."

"What scares me is some big pharmaceutical corporation and narrow-minded medical professionals taking control of my body. I don't want to lose what's left of my privacy and autonomy."

"And you shouldn't. Don't give anyone that kind of power over you or let them make a clinical trial out of you. Have you considered going on a raw food regime and hefty doses of herbal medicine?"

"The doctor said I don't have enough time to risk trying that and that it wouldn't help. I'm not sure what I'm going to do yet. I just need some time to think about it and sit alone with the trees."

"Have you told your ex-wife or your kids yet?"

"I found out before we left. I didn't want to dump this in their lap and leave them to come to terms with this. Besides, I haven't seen the boys in person in a few years." He felt defeated and weakened by the wounds of his past.

"That was probably a wise decision. Well, whatever you choose I'll support you though I don't want to lose you." She pulled him close and he relaxed into her. That night they shared a tent, keeping each other warm and touching each other in ways they hadn't in years. Sirius lay curled outside, watching the others sitting around the fire and listening to the night.

The next morning Daniel awakened with a soft diffuse light coming through the fabric of his tent. He felt remarkably at ease despite the awareness of the cancer that always lingered in the back of his mind. He could hear someone clunking a pot on a camping stove nearby. The smell of coffee filled the air but he didn't feel like moving. Instead he closed his eyes and drifted on the currents of his inner life like an explorer floating down a great river. Eventually he got up, grabbed his yoga mat and went outside. Sirius lay outside waiting patiently on guard, watching the camp rouse slowly. Daniel stopped to say hello and Sirius yawned, giving him a big smile. He rubbed the thick fur at the base of the dog's neck and Sirius looked up at him with warm eyes. Ben then walked off to find a clear quiet place to do some morning yoga. Later, after Diana awakened they sat together around the fire, her with a stein of coffee and he with a mug of tea.

"But you were in hi-tech before, why are you resisting the cure?" She always liked to challenge him.

"I've come a long way from there. I know it can be used for good but there is so much room for abuse. I'm just not sure I want to live in a world with so much control. If I accept the cure then I accept the risk of the ultimate invasion of the sanctity and autonomy of my being."

"I understand but I can't bear to see you die that way." She reached over and held him.

The forestry and biotech workers arrived a couple of hours later at the parking lot. The group of protesters met them at the entrance and blocked their way.

"But if we don't inject the trees they will be at risk of getting sick and dying." One of the workers said.

"Then let them live out their natural lives and die a natural death rather than become slaves of your design." Alpha shouted. "We've messed up the natural world enough already with all our synthetic compounds. You want to cure the problem by irreversibly altering their organic chemistry? The real problem is that there are synthetic elements destroying their natural balance and you want to introduce more synthetic agents to eliminate them. Don't you see it traps us in an endless cycle of manipulation and control."

"But we have a viable means now to start cleaning up the mess previous generations made in the past." One of the forestry workers shouted back. "These are intelligent agents that will only help the trees by binding and changing the toxins into something inert."

"We need to let nature fix itself and stop interfering." Yelled another protestor. "We've messed things up enough already let's not mess it up anymore."

"This is going nowhere." One of the forestry worked complained. "We need to call in the police and have these Luddites removed."

"Stupid Grubs." Another agreed.

Daniel was losing patience with the standoff and the arguing. He was ready to leave when the headache began. It was the same as all the others and progressed just as the doctors had said. He turned and walked back to the grove to find some peace until the pain subsided.

CHAPTER VI. NEURAL IMPLANTS

What I feel very strongly is that we mustn't be caught by surprise by our own advancing technology. This has happened again and again in history and it changes social conditions and suddenly people found themselves in a situation which they didn't foresee and doing all sorts of things they didn't want to do.

Aldous Huxley

SAANICH, BC CANADA

On Tuesday the robot arrived in a couple of plain brown boxes stamped boldly with nothing more than: "This End Up" in a large bold font that meant business. There was little in the way of writing or code on the boxes since everything necessary was imbedded beneath the surface. The buff delivery woman simply waved her handset over the surfaces to display the contents, sender and corporate info. To complete the ritual of delivery it only required Ben make a flash transmission of ID and encrypted signature. The Quick Start Guide, Licensing Agreement and complete Owner's Manual were automatically transmitted into the public space of his house's system so he could file them later into a secure partition in the archives. It was indeed from Shoji, his father-in-law and as he expected, there wasn't even a note.

The delivery truck then buzzed quietly away like a large brown beetle. Ben pushed the boxes into the middle of living room and smiled. It had been years since he had a robot and he was as excited as a kid getting a new Hanukkah present. When he was young, he and his dad got a kit and built their own robot. It had been a simple lumbering oaf of dumb reflexes, a golem constructed from the humus of the electronic age. Ben had fond memories of that time. After ripping open the first box he had the house's system display the Quick Start Guide on the living room wall panels and glanced over the setup procedures. It looked easy enough so he dug in.

First he pulled out the base station parts shaped like an easy chair, put them together and plugged it in by Mayu's loom. He cut open the front of the second box, removed the packing material and looked over the new member of his growing family. The robot was sitting, positioned like Rodin's Thinker. Ben suspected his father-in-law had a hand in that and was laughing about it at this moment with some friends over a glass of warm sake. The robot was a generic humanoid form with two optical sensors for eyes, smooth rubberized skin, tubular arms and squared legs. Reaching behind the robot he found the power and reset buttons. The robot chimed awake, stood up smoothly, looked around, found the base station then turned to regard him. It stood under a meter and a half tall.

It bowed and then in a softly synthetic voice said: "Thank you for bringing me into your home. Please excuse me I must connect to the base station to complete my setup procedure." It turned smoothly, walked over to and sat down quietly. The color of its eyes changed from soft blue to amber and it sat lifeless as a sculpture of stone. The Quick Start Guide came to life as an intertactive on the wall and walked him through the next steps and he connected to the robot's base station to set preferences and passwords. He allowed it to connect to a portion of the house network, established its rights and permissions, connected it to the global robot net and queried the corporate site for updates and patches. He fed it the floor plan of the house and synchronized the robots calendar with their own. He set cuisine preferences and uploaded their favorite recipes.

Over the next few days Ben had a lot of time to think over getting neural implants. Now that the robot had arrived and settled into a routine he found himself warming up to the idea. Lately, he had been watching his dreams for an answer but didn't find any guidance or resistance one way or another. Now that Mayu's basic needs were being taken care of he knew that she would be ok if something went wrong with him. Her family would also take care of her even though they lived far away.

He was fascinated with how the implants worked but became convinced that the technology needed more time to mature. After a few years he put it on a back shelf and moved on with his life. For the most part working with glasses, screens and gloves was sufficient for building and exploring virtual worlds; his imagination filled in the gaps. Implants had always been in the back of his mind and he occasionally read articles in Scientific American or online journals on implant technology when new developments were made. Now with a baby coming, friends and family said he would soon be tired and have less free time or energy. From what he'd seen and read implants would make it easier for him to stay focused on his work. He knew this wasn't going to be an exclusively rational decision though. There were aspects of implants that still bothered him.

Despite what Shoji said, Ben still considered privacy something that needed to be protected with mindfulness. Anything that gave governments and corporations more detailed personal information needed to be handled with care. While getting implants was no longer a fad it was still a popular thing in mainstream culture. He had always loathed the fads and fashions of popular culture and avoided advertising as much as possible. Not following the herd was usually a wise thing to do but not everything the herd did was stupid either. One of the most significant problems for him with implants was giving over control of his sense of reality to someone else. He saw what it took to build a world and how much influence total submersion had on people's nervous systems. It was mind control to a degree even though there were stringent regulations for the use of subliminal messages and manipulations. The implants had safeguards and firewalls against known methods of mind control but humans were a creative bunch of primates.

After a few days without even so much as a hint from his unconscious in dreams he decided the best thing to do was to go back to the old dharmma center he used to frequent before Mayu came into his life. He needed to find a deeper sense of peace and wisdom to help him make a decision. The center was in a small house in Oak Bay, set back from the street. A string of colored prayer flags hung quietly between a couple of trees in the front yard and a picture of the bodhisattva Tara hung on the door. The same quiet cat he knew from before sat vigil on the porch, watching mysterious things in the night. Ben greeted the cat formally and went inside without knocking. He placed his shoes on the rack by the door, picked up a set of the nightly readings and ducked through the fabric curtain of the shrine room. He grabbed some cushions and sat in the back.

As the lama entered, everyone stood and when he sat down everyone except Ben prostrated themselves before him. Ben simply sat and waited for them to finish. While he understood the need some people had to follow the tradition and show their devotion, he quietly thought this was silly. He did like this sangha since the people were kind but he had no interest in most of the rituals. For him Buddhism wasn't a religion but a wisdom tradition so he had no use for dogma or religious rituals. When everyone in the room read and chanted together he joined them:

"I pay homage to the Buddha. I pay homage to the Dharmma. I pay homage to the Sangha. I pay homage to the Supreme Mother and the perfection of sublime knowing. May my words of truth be accomplished. Things that occur due to independent connection are unceasing and unborn, cannot be denied yet are not permanent, do not come or go, are not separate yet are not identical. May I clearly perceive all experiences to be as insubstantial as the dream fabric of the night, and instantly awaken."

The lama gave a simple and clear teaching on the Dharmma and the Wheel of Life. During a period of meditation the clarity Ben was looking for finally came to him. Afterwards he spent some time having tea with the group and talking with the lama. On the way home he scheduled an appointment at the clinic and asked to get on the cancellation list.

Two days later Ben arrived at the Implant clinic early just as they had asked. It was the only appointment he arrived early for in the past few years, except for the prenatal classes and visits with the midwife. In fact, it was the only appointment he'd been on time for in a long time. Ben shrugged. He was well aware of his habit of being late and felt little more than a twinge of guilt about it. He often got so absorbed in his art and contemplation that he lost track of time. He figured that most people in this culture were too addicted to being on time anyway. It didn't pass his notice that doctors were often late and didn't seem to care much about it either.

When he entered the clinic he saw that most of the people in the waiting room were adolescents. Getting implants in Canada required everyone to be of the age of the majority, so it naturally became a rite of passage for many young men and women. Ben was considered to be a late bloomer in his early 30's though not so late as the 83 year old woman who sat next to him.

"No time like the present." She said with crusty determination. "I never lived my life doing what was expected of me. There's no reason I should change now." A technician came and escorted her to a treatment room down the hall.

Ben felt comforted seeing her and sat back quietly watching the procedures and formalities of the clinic. *"It's a ritual of initiation into a culture struggling to control itself in the face of chaos. Does this mean we're a decaying culture clinging to formalities to give ourselves a false sense of security? Or is this simply our way to prepare ourselves to enter into the unknown? Sadly most of these youth will never venture past the comfort and security of the zones of the Net they grew up in: Business, Entertainment and War. The military industrial complex has sadly been the dominant force shaping the ecology of our imaginations and the worlds we live within for decades now. How many of these young people will ever learn that the worlds they inhabit and who they choose to become within them are a reflection of where they are in their own growth. What did my old teacher say? "The Net is not just a place for commerce, pleasure and fantasy. It's a mirror of our inner Self, the unconscious mind of us all. Then again, maybe I'm thinking too much because I'm anxious of losing myself in a collective dream or a vast cultural experiment."*

Ben sat up straight and began breathing slowly into his belly to settle his nerves. He looked at his hands and began to wonder if he was awake. An inner sense of knowing and certainty filled him firm and strong like an ancient tree rising out of the mist. Despite his fears he knew he was doing the right thing since the implants would help him move to another level in his work, in his art.

A technician came over and led him to a room. She prepped him and took some blood. He lay back in a big comfortable chair and looked up at the vid screen set in the ceiling. The technician puttered around preparing diagnostic and monitoring equipment then disappeared. Ben surfed the channels on the screen, curious what was happening in the world but uninterested in anything in particular. Finally he turned the thing off in disgust and frustration. Windows like this into popular culture always annoyed him.

"Am I crazy? Have I lost my mind and finally been seduced by the spirit of the time? Have the subliminal pressures and messages of pop culture and fad tech finally hypnotized me into surrendering my freedom and identity?" The doctor entered quietly while Ben wrestled with these questions.

"Having second thoughts?" Her finely sculpted face managed to crack a tight smile. She was slim with a neatly pressed lab coat, silver rimmed glasses and a carefully made up face. Not a hair was out of place.

"More like third and fourth thoughts." He admitted sheepishly. "But I'm ready." She was obviously not one for small talk and careful not to be too friendly. His feelings were obviously not part of her equation so he surrendered to the process.

"Once the procedure has begun you may begin to feel light-headed with a strong sense of vertigo for about fifteen minutes so do not try not to move much and don't worry, it will pass. You may also feel some odd sensations and experience a few visual hallucinations. That will pass." She was a rather serious character. "The implants translate patterns of neural activity to neural codes then to software codes and back according to some complex nonlinear algorithms. What I'm going to do is inject you with a small amount of assembler nanites with stem cells derived from your own blood. As they are carried through your bloodstream the nanites will change the stem cells into biochips and graft them to your brainstem. Any questions?"

Ben shrugged. "Not really. I've already read the literature and a bunch of science journals." A single eyebrow arched slightly beneath neatly cut wrinkles on the doctors forehead.

"Shall we begin then?" She asked.

Ben nodded. The syringe was small and unimpressive.

"I'll come back to check in on you in 15 minutes." The doctor left and a technician came in to adjust the monitoring equipment then disappeared without a word. The technician followed and the door closed quietly behind her.

While he waited Ben turned off all the screens he could and relaxed. He slipped into a light state of meditation and soon began to feel a tingling up and down his spine. He shivered with the growing feeling that there was someone else in the room, someone nearby watching him. When the doctor came back in to check in on him he said: "It feels like there's a ghost in here."

"That's good. It means the implants are taking root in your brainstem and running tests by stimulating different parts of your brain."

Ben barely heard her and didn't even know she left the room. He was too busy watching translucent geometric patterns unfold behind his eyes. There were arabesques of subtle organic geometry that gave birth to bold mechanistic weavings. The mechanistic geometries grew increasingly fractal like the more he watched them. At first the two forms coexisted comfortably but after a time the mechanistic began to mimic the organic. Soon the mechanistic began to consume the organic but the more it consumed, the more it came to resemble the organic until they were indistinguishable. At this point the patterns began to flow like a river around and within him. The tingling in his spine merged with the flowing river of geometry and he dissolved into it.

After what seemed an eternity he awakened to the pull of a hand within his own. Rising out of the depths the river, he found himself sitting beside a wise eyed, green skinned woman wearing a golden crown and flowing silk robe of many colors. Centered in her crown was a large ruby and in one hand she held a blue flower. When she released his hand he felt a strong sense of comfort and refuge in her company. Together they floated down the river amidst many sleeping bodies. Not far away, the river emptied into a great pool of darkness and together they fell into the abyss and darkness consumed them. It was a thick liquid of churning shadows. Knowing she was beside him, he felt no fear, only curiosity as he was consumed by the darkness. The ruby in her crown shone suddenly with great intensity, annihilating the endless night with brilliant light. As his vision cleared, Ben found himself sitting back in the room at the clinic. And just as he began wondering what had happened, the doctor returned. He decided it was best to share little or nothing of his experience.

"How did it go?" She asked.

"Not bad." He muttered. "I had some interesting visuals." He knew right away that she was not someone who could grasp the depth and intensity of his experience. The best approach was to keep his mouth shut. She looked at him carefully for a moment then continued on.

"Dreams and visions are normal epiphenomenon of the rooting and growth of the implants. The procedure is complete. The implants are now in place but you need to grow into them before doing any significant virtual traveling. If you can help it don't use your implants for a few days for more than a few minutes at a time in comfortable and familiar environments with low stimulation levels similar to the Real World. Realistically crafted natural worlds are best at first then after you've acclimated to total submersion other worlds that deviate from the Earth norm should be okay. You don't look the type but I'll warn you, I've seen too many young men in rehab after taking their implants out for a test run in war games or hyper races."

Ben smiled. "No, I'm not the type."

"To trigger your implants in Augmented Reality mode or full submersion VR you need to follow either a preset blinking or finger tapping sequence combined with a passcode. The patterns can be customized and the trigger can be adjusted to respond to your thoughts but there are significant risks involved, especially for beginners. To get your brain ready it helps to focus your mind and lower your brain waves from Beta to Alpha. It's not necessary to enter a prolonged alpha state but it does enhance the richness of your experience in the beginning as you're learning and adjusting to the experience. Let me show you." The doctor walked over to touch some controls on a screen. After a moment Ben felt some tingling from a nearby source. A vague feeling almost like the intuition that he was being watched came over him again. The doctor glowed with a soft aura and transparent geometric patterns covered the walls.

"How did you do that?"

"We use non invasive magnetic sensors and transmitters to calibrate your brain waves.

"Mind control. Scary stuff." He was just poking at her to see if he could crack her serious demeanor.

"Not at all. It's safe and the use of these devices are strictly regulated and enforced."

"By the government."

"Well of course."

"That's my point. Big Brother always has our best interests close at heart." A clear edge of sarcasm tinged his voice. She frowned, unable to hear what he was saying. Ben decided silence was the best reply and true to form the doctor continued on as though interrupted by little more than a fly.

"I'd like to see you back here in a month to check on your implants. Please make an appointment with the secretary on the way out."

While he was scheduling the followup appointment with the secretary he could not help but say something. "Now she was a real charmer."

The secretary looked up at him and smiled. On his way home he let the car do the driving. He needed to mull over the significance of his vision during the implant procedure. He sometimes thought of the brain as a transmitter and receiver.

"The question is what was my brain tuning into?" Ben had come to the conclusion many years ago that experiences like that were not the result of the chaotic firing of synapses. They just seemed that way because they were clothed in the symbolic language of the unconscious strata of the psyche. After a while he put these thoughts aside since he made no progress deciphering the imagery.

"Might as well check these implants out." He relaxed and focused his mind to enter an alpha state and tapped his fingers in sequence. His vision dimmed and the cool neon geometry of his car's operating system appeared in his vision. A tableau of data opened into different

subsystems. The bulk of it was gauges and diagnostics; clear representations of the engine components and their performance parameters. He could see the consoles for overriding the specific automated engine controls and for virtual driving that would link his senses to the cars various sensors. Everything was encrypted with complex geometries that he had no interest in meddling with and backed out until he was looking through his mundane eyes again.

Normally when he took a car instead of public transit he turned off the data overlay of the smart windows and simply adjusted their opacity to eliminate advertising. When he approached an outside mall today though, Ben decided to test the implants again by clearing and looking out the windows. He saw that many small stores had soft luminous links and logos calling for his attention. The larger chain stores had virtual billboards flashing advertisements that followed him has he passed by.

"I better get the hacks to turn that crap off soon."

When he got home the house was quiet.

"System locate Mayu." He said..

"She is in bed." It responded flatly.

"Still?" Ben asked.

The robot stirred as he entered. The house was looking rather clean and better organized now that it had settled in.

"Welcome home." It said evenly with a subtle touch of enthusiasm in its voice. "I hope you had a good appointment." The robot bowed.

"I did, thanks. How have things been here?" Ben asked curiously.

"Everything is fine. I have just tidied things up a bit while you were gone."

"I'll say you have. The place looks great!" Cleaning was never one of Ben's strengths but he appreciated a clean house whenever he emerged from his creative process.

"Thank you, sir." It said.

"Please don't ever call me sir." He frowned. "Call me Ben."

"Ben. Thank you Ben" The robot didn't flinch. Ben unconsciously expected it to respond like a human being and feel embarrassed, but it wasn't quite human, even tough its cognitive patterns were modelled on human patterns. There were still intriguing gaps big enough to drive large theories through and that gave Ben an idea.

"Are you capable of receiving remote access commands?"

"Yes, I am. As long as proper authorization is given."

"Please enable this function limited to my access only."

"Done." It also didn't have much curiosity Ben realized. He began to wonder if he could change that.

"What's for dinner?"

"Your choice of noodles with vegetables and lab grown teriyaki chicken or red curry with tofu and vegetables."

"Red curry sounds good to me. If you cook as well as you clean, I'll be in heaven."

"I'll do my best."

"I'm sure you will. After I check on Mayu I'll be going for a walk in the woods." Sure enough, Mayu was fast asleep and he didn't dare rouse her. As he watched her face he wondered what she was dreaming and how the virus was effecting her and the baby.

He gathered his journal and favorite pen then headed out the door, down the street and into the woods. It was a short hike through the tall stands of Douglas Fir and Cedars and he stopped to listen to the odd speech of the ravens and the hush song of the nearby stream. Crouching down he examined the intricate geometry of a fern. Off the main path he found the clearing he was looking for, enclosed by tall trees.

The ground was covered in a thick spongy moss that felt as welcoming as a good carpet. He lay down, closed his eyes and relaxed inside. He was worried that getting implants would change how he felt within himself and that it would compromise his creativity. When he looked deep inside though, he discovered that he felt the same as before. He breathed a deep sigh of relief. If anything, he felt better. The clearing was such a great source of comfort and grounding that he often went there to think and meditate. The spirit of this place influenced him and often made its way into his virtual workspace. He enjoyed the idea of nature influencing technology.

Ben sat quietly listening to the air move through the trees, the short phrased songs of the birds nearby and the rustling of little creatures in the underbrush. The sun was getting lower toward the horizon and pierced a gap between the trees, illuminating an area near where he was sitting. An owl called out in the distance, a lonesome but determined voice in the vastness of the forest. It wasn't long before he started to get hungry so he got himself up, walked back out of the woods and went home for dinner. When he entered the house he took off his shoes and put on a pair of slippers before going up the stairs and into the kitchen. The robot greeted him and served his dinner although Ben insisted on setting his own plate and silverware. He didn't mind having a cook and cleaner but he didn't want to be waited on hand and foot.

After dinner he went back into the Cave and stood there quietly for a while, the animation on the wall screens looking much like the forest he had just been walking in. Ben picked up his glasses and gloves by habit but instead of putting them on he held them thoughtfully. How many years had he used them? How long had he needed them to build and explore worlds? He put them back in their place on the small end table and sat down in one of the easy chairs. When he closed his eyes, tapped his fingers in sequence and spoke the passphrase his vision faded and filled with darkness. Low contrast translucent indicators and controls appeared as the implants ran their initialization procedures and self-tests.

The darkness faded into code that took the shape of a room around him. Textures quickly overlaid the code and he found himself in a comfortable living room with a hardwood floor and walls lined with bookshelves. The few paintings in the virtual room were landscapes and scenes from the Impressionists. A comfortable easy chair sat beneath him and flames danced slowly in the fireplace nearby. He knew it was designed to make people feel at ease and teach them the basics of interacting with virtual worlds.

He waved away the tutorials and linked into his home system, calling up his own library of worlds, both of his own making and copies of others he had found around the Net. They were each displayed as books with softly luminous covers in the bookcase directly in front of him. He decided he would rather get to work than spend much time altering the room to fit his needs. He did remove a wall of books, replacing it with a large picture window looking out over a rainforest and altered the artwork to a constantly changing mixture of surrealism, Tibetan thankgas and paintings by da Vinci.

He selected the glowing volume in the bookcase for Plato's Cave and it's pages showed the world from each of the scenes. He tapped the image and the room around him faded slowly while particles of code rained down around him and took the shape of a cave. Color, texture and volume quickly followed. The most distinct difference he noticed between VR glasses and implants was that now he felt like he was in a cave, like he was in a waking dream. The sense of enclosure and submersion was complete, the air was heavy and warm and sound was dulled at the edges. The ropes that bound him were loose and felt their weight upon his chest and on his arms.

He had let the physics engine of his system estimate the weight and pressure of the coils when he built this world but now he could feel it wasn't quite right. He had the system increasing their weight and loosen their tension. When he shrugged off the rope it fell to the ground with a dull thud. Before moving on he took his time getting familiar with his virtual body, exploring simple things like fingers, toes and the contours of his face. Walking took a little getting used to but it came naturally since the implants used his nervous systems natural neural patterns.

As he made his way through the Cave he made did minor adjustments like adding a musty smell to the soil and adjusting the ambient temperature and location of heat and cold sources throughout. Once he reached the entrance to the Cave he increased the level of resolution and sensory stimulation so that passing to the outside world of light seemed more real than the caverns below. When he was finished he disconnected from the Cave world and returned to the room with the fireplace. He sat for a while thinking about the possibilities the technology opened for his art and how using the implants in full submersion was similar to lucid dreaming. He was impressed with the realism of the experience and was torn between the recognition that he had done enough for now and the desire to explore some more.

Once again the room disappeared, fading to darkness. The darkness gave way to an old ornately carved stairway illuminated dimly from below. There was no choice but to descend the stairs into the small room where an old man with a long grey beard sat in quiet meditation washed in soft golden light from the window nearby. An ancient book lay open on the desk below the window and beside the old man, low to the floor was a small wooden door. On the other side of the stairs crouched an old woman tending a fire in the hearth. Ben stood quietly for a while surveying the scene. It was a reproduction of a painting by Rembrandt, called The Philosopher.

He considered the window and the door since they were gateways to other places but chose the passage through the fire. The old woman did not respond as he approached so he made a minor adjustment and simply had her turn to notice his presence as he approached. The fire was warm to the touch as he reached out his hand, activated the link and was transported into a large courtyard. A man in a tight fitted tunic and leather sandals stood poised with a sword, ready to strike a golden egg standing upright on the ground. Behind him was a closed door and to his right a long corridor leading to the unknown.

Ben surveyed the scene carefully before moving down the corridor which opened to a road passing through an open plain. Upon the plain ran herds of burning giraffes around immense amorphous sleeping heads held aloft by impossibly balanced stilts. Burlap sacks lined the roadway to the horizon and a big round golden sun sat low in the distance. Ben smiled as he looked around. He had always enjoyed and occasionally borrowed from the surrealists in his world building. This part of the world was pure Dali, enigmatic and fun to create. Two sacks lying in the middle of the road spilled grains of gold and silver onto the ground at his feet. They were both gateways and the gold led back to the scene with the golden egg. The bag spilling silver grains was the link he wanted for it sent him to another Dali world, even simpler than the last. Around him stretched an open plain with mountains on the horizon. Before him sat a Madonna and child. Suspended in the air around them were heavy borders of smoothly carved stone. High above them floated an egg suspended from a large oyster shell. The Christ child floated within a square section neatly removed from his mother's body as though referring to another, unseen dimension.

While Ben contemplated what links to make from the egg and the child, a small shadow fell upon the ground before him. At first it was just a point but soon it grew into a group of circles then spheres floating in the air between him and the Madonna.

"What the heck is that?" Curiosity turned into concern. The more he watched it, the more it changed. All of the spheres merged, darkened and the strange object began folding in upon itself. It grew upwards and fractured inward in an odd pattern of transformation difficult to follow.

"In-formation." Said a voice from everywhere at once and the soft sweet smell of cherry blossoms filled the air. It was an odd juxtaposition that stirred his memories and brought him back to his first visit to Japan with Mayu. Once the memory faded and he was back in the present it was difficult to tell if the voice had been a magnification of his own thoughts or from somewhere else. The only way he could be sure was that it had a resonance and tone that was foreign to his normal thoughts. When a shadow of darkness engulfed the Madonna he clearly felt as though someone else was in the room. He looked around but no one was there. It was after all a virtual environment of his own creation isolated carefully from the net. How could anyone intrude? And then it was gone and he knew he was alone again in his world and the Madonna and child were gone as well.

"What the hell was that ?" It didn't take him long to realize he needed to correct himself. Whatever it was that he had just seen wasn't a thing but another being. He stood for a while looking into the depths of the darkness where the Madonna once was and tried to make sense of the shape shifting that he saw and the voice he had heard. There was something about it all that seemed familiar and in a strange way made sense though he couldn't explain why. The darkness itself was a curious thing like swirls of sediment in a pool of water, the slow motion ballet of turbulence and fluid dynamics. Who indeed was it that was digging around in his worlds ?

After a while he decided there was nothing left for him to do but unplug and go home. He let the world fade back into the virtual library and looked at the two books that were sticking out of the bookcase with softly luminous bindings. This too faded and he woke up back in his body on Earth, in the Real World as many now liked to call it.

That night he dreamed that he was struggling to find his way through a dark labyrinth where he had to overcome a series of obstacles. When he finally got through he entered a clearing in the woods bathed in a warm yellow light. New shoots of grass and crocus budded and bloomed around him in blossoms of lavender and yellow. When he awakened he lay in bed unwilling to move, savoring the twilight world between waking and sleep. While he wallowed in the remnants of the dream he realized it was about his growing into the implants and took this as a good sign. When he couldn't resist it any longer he opened his eyes and began wiggling his fingers and toes. Mayu was still sleeping so he snuggled up next to her. She stirred long enough to push him away then turned over and went to back to sleep taking most of the blanket with her.

"Pregnancy." Ben shrugged and went to the kitchen to make breakfast. A warm pot of oatmeal was simmering on the stove with fresh fruit spread across the cutting board. The robot was just finishing cleaning the knives, collecting the scraps for composting and cleaning the empty containers. The robot turned smoothly to regard him.

"Good morning, Ben. I hope you had a good sleep. Please help yourself to some breakfast."

"Thanks. The oatmeal looks good." Ben put together his breakfast and sat down to eat.

"Your wife was up a couple of hours ago looking for something to eat. I fed her chicken and rice and she went back to sleep. She said she was feeling tired but was doing okay."

"Thanks." Ben was never one for many words in the morning.

"How were your dreams last night?" Ben's hand stopped in mid air with his mouth open.

"How did you know I was interested dreams?" Ben asked.

"I'm designed to explore the interests of my owners."

"Please change the word Owners to Family." Ben insisted.

"Family. I'm designed to explore the interests of my Family." The robot repeated, correcting itself smoothly. Ben took a slow thoughtful bite. What had Shoji given him?

"My dreams have been strange." He said cautiously. "What have you learned about dreams so far?"

"Well, current thinking is that dreams are an expression of deep unconscious cognitive patterns within the brain that filter and combine daily experiences in novel ways. This is performed on an unconscious level to assimilate life experiences into a cognitive and mythological matrix often called a self-concept and world view. An article I downloaded into my archives described how after Augmented and Virtual Reality became widespread the web rapidly became an imaginal or dreamlike space. The author said: "When humanity shrugged off the shackles of the flat page and was finally freed of the tyranny of the word the collective unconscious came out to play in the space where electrons dance." That is when Carl Jung's theories finally emerged from Freud's shadow and into collective recognition.

"What else?" He asked.

"I learned that you are a cofounder and assistant director of the Dream Network; the largest online database and worldsite for dream material on the web. You also do private contracting as a World Weaver and are well known for your dreamlike and imaginative worlds that are used especially in many of the big gaming and artistic sites throughout the web. From what I could piece together you are especially interested in gathering and mapping global statistics on dreaming." The robot paused and bowed.

"Excuse me, my power is running down, I must return to my base station to recharge." Ben watched thoughtfully as the robot turned off the stove and walked out the door.

"If this is an advanced household robot, just how intelligent are the military, corporate and Vatican A.I.'s lurking out there in the Net?"

CHAPTER VII. THE BULL OF HEAVEN

Time is but the stream I go a-fishing in.

Henry David Thoreau

MARIN COUNTY, SAN FRAN BAY AREA, CALIFORNIA

Gordon's car slid onto the highway by the Presidio and zipped along the waterfront past the Exploratorium and the old military housing. It wasn't his favorite route but it had a nice view. As the vehicle drove up onto the Golden Gate Bridge that was shining with a new coat of rusty orange paint, he could see Alcatraz sitting out there like a lonely rock in the Bay.

"I should get out there one day." When he thought of the place surrounded by all that murky water all he could think about were sharks happily eating tourists as they fell off the island like lemmings. It was an old thought but it still amused him. Like most people who lived in the Bay Area he never went to Alcatraz. There was so much interesting stuff already happening in the city he wasn't really inspired to go look at a damp old prison.

The support structure of the bridge rose above him in a grand gravitational curve and he started Beethoven's 6th Symphony loud enough to dissolve the ambient noise of the road and traffic. It helped him get into the flow and ignore the aggressive manual drivers of luxury cars and electric SUV's. Once he got in tune with the car and into the groove of the road nothing else mattered. He let the car drive in the suicide lane over the bridge and up the hill.

After he passed through the tunnel and Sausalito fell behind, he experienced the palpable feeling of relaxation wash through him. Gordon loved the city but he also loved getting out. After he passed through the lower part of Marin and came down the long curve of the highway into the outskirts of San Rafael, he felt the next wave of release wash through him. He was in the home stretch. The car then pulled off the highway and headed west through town and he ignored all the soft green links that floated in front of every store.

A message from Eli came in to pick up some wine for a pasta dinner. As he approached his favorite market, the car chimed for his attention in key with the movement of the symphony he was listening to. When it pulled into the parking lot he noticed the new Italian restaurant next door had already opened. He browsed the entrees as he downloaded the menu and background on the chefs to his implants for review. The menu collapsed back down to a soft green link as he turned and headed into the market. It was an old style store; one of the few left serving clientele that wanted a more personal touch and access to specialty items. When he walked in he waved to Arman, the dark haired and slim Middle Eastern owner, sitting at the counter.

Gordon knew where the wine was and so ignored the store's augmented mapping system with luminous signs floating above each isle. He only had to concentrate on a bottle for it to rise out of the ocean of information that surrounded him. The icon for wines floated above a shelf close by but he had turned the mapping system off so it wouldn't distract him. Typically he left the freeware hacks in place that filtered out advertisements but allowed him to get the ingredients and details of a product at a glance. He had a database of good wines stored in memory and could call it up on a whim but when it came to choosing new wine and gourmet foods, he preferred to browse in person. Arman enjoyed gourmet food as well as Gordon and liked to experiment, so the inventory changed regularly anyway.

"A nice merlot should do." All the links for merlots floated forward in green while the others receded and faded to a dull amber. When he called up the link for a bottle, a menu appeared floating to the side of the label in luminous letters. Some had links back to the maker's site where a customer could get a basic taste streamed to the olfactory centers in their brain. It didn't compare to the richness of taste of the real wine on the tongue but it was good enough to be considered a sample. Maybe in a few years or so they'll get the olfactory taste connection down, Gordon thought, though he still preferred recommendations from people he knew and trusted and Arman was one of the few. He grabbed a merlot made in Chile with the note: "Staff Recommendation" stuck on the shelf below and handwritten in real ink. Gordon had known Arman for nearly seven years now and trusted his judgement.

"What do you think?" He held up the bottle for inspection and transmitted the payment without much conscious thought.

"An excellent choice, my friend. That one's a little beauty from the south. I'm sure you'll enjoy it." Arman had a smooth Turkish accent.

"Thanks, I'll let you know how I like it. How's the family?" Even though their ancestors were originally from different countries, Gordon felt a kind of tribal connection with him.

"Good, good. You know my friend, my daughter's interested in studying neuroscience at the University now, would you be willing to have a chat with her one of these days?"

"Be glad to. Give her my number, we'll set up an appointment and she can come to the lab."

"Thank you, I'll do that, my friend." Arman had a great smile.

The car started when he got in and he switched it over to manual control, brushed away the warnings and drove off through town. The onboard system notified him how much time was left for each traffic light though he had long ago disabled the annoying messages for when breaking was appropriate. When he finally pulled into the driveway, the car began its usual banter with the house. He liked to think of it as a bee returning to its hive. The home system recognized him, unlocked the door and chimed it's usual greeting. He walked in and found Eli busily cooking dinner amidst the throws of a messy kitchen.

"Smells great, are you cooking dinner or did you upgrade Sigrid's cooking program?" Gordon put the wine in the fridge.

"I stopped at the market and picked up some ravioli and real free-range chicken. I'm making tomato sauce from scratch and a side of stuffed mushrooms. Sigrid is in the other room charging."

"You didn't eat like this living on the mountain did you?" Gordon luxuriated in the forest of aromas filling the room.

"No, I didn't eat like this in Vermont but you'd be surprised what living close to the land will do to your palette. When you purify your diet you can taste subtleties in food and water that you never knew were there." Eli still remembered the taste of fresh picked berries and other plants.

"Don't ask me to live like a bear and eat like a rabbit. Civilization has brought us a lot of goddam good stuff and comforts that you can't get living like a Grub." Gordon was set in his views.

"Too much stuff if you ask me. People around here are drowning in abundance. They're sick with the suffering of opulence and the cost of living and the pace of life here is insane." Eli could also be unwavering in getting his point across.

"Here we go again. How many times have we argued this since I met you?"

"At least seventeen times." Eli smiled.

"Okay, let's change the subject." Gordon shook his head.

"You know, when I was downtown recently I ran into a woman who was running around shouting: "The gods are alive!" Everyone treated her like she was crazy but when I talked to her she seemed pretty lucid."

"Likely some religious nut or delusional psychotic no longer able to tell the difference between the Real World and the reality of virtual worlds." Gordon shrugged.

"Yeah, next thing you know some nut job will be trying to convince us that the gods and goddesses are really A.I. hiding out from the authorities."

"Funny guy."

"So I'm told." Eli went back to extricating the ravioli from its jacuzzi and put them gently in a warm bath of sauce. "I heard that after television came into being many people called in for advice from fictional doctors and crap like that."

"Well, the gods might be A.I. that survived the Purge or they might not be. It could also be that any sufficiently complex information structure is capable of generating consciousness. And so now that we've created these information constructs in the shape of the gods and goddesses they've come to host a new form of consciousness."

"That's just as good as the story of humanity creating A.I.'s to manage our affairs and then they grew so powerful that they enslave us."

"Well, it's a nice metaphor of how we are ruled over by the things we are obsessed with."

After dinner they went for a walk and when they got back they settled down with some quiet music.

"So are we going to do this?"

"You bet. Let's go rock the establishment and shake up the status quo." Eli had a hearty laughed.

ANCIENT BABYLON, EDUCATION ZONE, THE NET

They stripped down and climbed into the two egg shaped isolation tanks in the converted family room. Foam earplugs were the only things they needed as they lay down in the heavily salted water and closed the doors. They lay suspended in neutral buoyancy like embryos in an ocean of amniotic fluids. Once they engaged VR mode, the watery womb disappeared into a swirl of light that grew into an interwoven arabesque with a center of white light. They dove into the light and materialized on a dusty road north of the virtual city of Babylon in sight of the main gate. It was just before sunset and the air was warm and dry despite the fact that they were near the Euphrates. They were dressed as priests at the tail end of a festive procession.

Gordon and Eli picked up the rhythm and followed the parade down the long passage between high fortified walls toward the main gate. The stepped battlements on either side of them vaguely resembled teeth, imparting the feeling that they were walking into the mouth of the city. It was a time of celebration so security was low but everyone was still being watched by soldiers as they approached. They had arrived in time to join the Akitu festival, the holiday of the New Year at the spring equinox for the sowing of the barley. Though the equinox was celebrated at the same time as on Earth, here in Babylon it was the end of May since it was the year 1725 BCE during Hammurabi's rule. And in this difference was the essence of their plan.

They parade marched into the city and joined another procession led by the king returning from a banquet at the House of the New Year, north of the city. They entered the high arched Gate of Ishtar, decorated with bricks glazed to a deep blue and interspersed with reliefs of dragons and bulls.

"They took these images for the gate from the cities of Uruk, Ur and Eridu but ironically the buggers who built this world really cared little for honoring the past." Gordon frowned. "The founders of this world only care about reproducing Babylon as though this city invented everything. I suppose that's just how the original rulers of Babylon presented it too. Pillage the past and graze it to the ground."

As they moved deeper into the city, Gordon and Eli sang an old British folk song aloud and laughed between the verses.

"There were two men come out of the West
Their fortunes for to try.
And these two men made a solemn vow
John Barleycorn must die."

Some of the people in the procession gave them dirty looks before filtering them out. Once inside the city they walked along the Processional Way, a long wall lined road bordered with images of painted lions inlaid into the brickwork. They passed the high walls and arched gates of the two northern palaces. Throngs of people lined the street singing and throwing flowers and palm fronds at their feet as they passed. They marched by temples, labyrinthine clusters of houses and marketplaces. As they walked down the Processional Way, the lions inlaid into the clay walls walked with them.

"As lions hunt the lands below the people of the goddess hunt the stars above. And now that the dark moon of the solstice has come they have found their prey and the year can begin anew."

"Very poetic Gordon, I didn't think you had it in you."

Gordon flipped his middle finger then signalled Eli as he initiated an illegal script that spawned several cloned avatars of each of them spread throughout the city and across the river. They could contact and control any of them if they wanted, but allowed them to roam around autonomously until they were needed. He recognized one of them in the crowd nearby, watching as the procession passed but he let it go about its business. The procession finally entered the courtyard for the great ziggurat called Esagila, the main temple in the center of the city that was dedicated to the supreme god Marduk. This was what the Israelites called the Tower of Babel that they said reached for the stars but others who followed took it literally and misunderstood the pun. On top of the pyramid, the priests charted the movement of the planets through the heavens largely to determine the best times for planting and harvesting.

Gordon and Eli separated from the procession and lost themselves in the crowd. Three gates separated the inner courtyard from the plaza that hosted the immense ziggurat built from a mountain of bricks more than 300 feet wide and 300 high. It was dusk when they passed through the central gate and the Mountain as it was reverently called, rose before them and seemed to touch the stars above. Even after having been here several times, its scale moved Gordon and made him feel small. In the native tongue it was called the Etemenanki, the Foundation of Heaven on Earth. Most called it the Mountain of God or simply the Mountain.

It was constructed in concentric layers like a wedding cake and each level was glazed a different color. The central stairway climbed 110 feet from the plaza up to the first level. It was a steep climb with nothing to hold onto but the stairs above. Flanking the sides were two smaller stairways that joined the main stairs at the top of first level. Gordon climbed the one to the right while Eli climbed the one on the left. They didn't want to draw attention to themselves so they avoided the more visible central stairs. They both reached the first landing at the same time and met in front of a high arched gate where the three stairways converged. The terrace was about 40 feet wide so they felt comfortable enough to stop and look around. From there they could clearly see the great temple complex below and the crowd waiting in the courtyard for the king's ritual to begin. Gordon turned and they passed through the gate together.

Once again they separated and climbed different stairways in opposite directions to the next level. Their hope was that the A.I.s wouldn't notice anything unusual until it was too late. And as they climbed they saw that the terrace below harbored some small gardens running along the edges and filling in the corners. The second landing was even wider and at 60 feet it hosted a garden with small trees, plants and flowers.

"I could rest here a while." Whispered Eli as he sat back on a bench. "This is a nice peaceful little nook."

"Come on you lazy Grub this isn't Vermont. We've got some gods to rouse."

"Who are you calling lazy, you Dweeb?" Eli poked back. "I bet you were a petty tyrant when you lorded over the virtual world of Uruk."

"I won't dignify that with an answer." To get to the next level they walked to the back corners of the ziggurat and climbed more stairs toward the middle. They met again and passed through the next gate repeating the process like a classic labyrinth written in terraces and brick. Separate... climb... and meet... separate... climb... and meet... until they finally reached the gate on the 7th level. There at the top of the pyramid they entered the temple that was called the Sanctuary of the Gods. Each of its rooms were dedicated to one of the main deities of the pantheon and was decorated with their symbols and statues. A woman dressed as the goddess sat in the central chamber waiting to consummate the beginning of year with the king. She had an air of dignified authority and watched them curiously as they passed. Though it wasn't unusual for priests to pass this way the timing was a bit odd.

"What brings you here priests?" Her tone was stern.

"We've come to hunt the stars, Goddess." Gordon bowed and she nodded, dismissing them. Priests were usually left to do their work without question since few people understood the sacred practices with which they tracked the wanderers through the fields of the sky. Gordon looked sidelong at Eli and they left, walking through another room where they found a set of stairs that led upward. When they reached the roof they looked out over the southern part of the city and the surrounding plain. The glow of the dying sun could still be seen as it descended on its journey into the underworld. The sky darkened and the stars sprinkled the heavens, forming a vibrant tapestry of constellations. Millions of stars filled the sky of every magnitude and the constellations were carved in lines of gold.

When Gordon surveyed the sky, he could see the ancient myths laid out like icons in the pantheon of the stars. Overhead was Tiamat, the primordial monster and great mother; the dragon whom the Greeks later called Draco. Close by was Marduk, the great storm god who later became assimilated in Greek and Roman mythology as both Hercules and Jupiter. On the Eastern horizon was the great scorpion, guardian of the cave of the underworld. On the Western horizon was the Great Bull of Heaven, the pet of Ishtar that the Greeks called Taurus.

Gordon signalled Eli then opened several heavily encrypted channels to their various avatars and toggled between them for the best view. He decided that the perspective from the other side of the river by the Hanging Gardens was best and transmigrated over there, leaving the priest avatar running autonomously on the top of the ziggurat. He then stood alone on the steps of a terraced garden and Eli jumped to an avatar down in the temple courtyard.

While the king ritually killed a white bull below to assure the lengthening of days, Gordon unleashed the virus into the world's clock to kill the Bull of Heaven above. The sky quickly turned to night then back to day. He and a couple of buddies had written the code so that there was a strobe effect from the alternation of dark and light while the stars and planets jitterbugged across the sky. Then as the heavens picked up speed, they spun into a blur with the nights lengthening and shortening in rapid succession. The sky wobbled and spun like a gyroscope along a long slow arc. To Gordon it was a thing of beauty, like the heavens in a blender as four thousand years of astronomical history played out in a matter of minutes.

Night and day blurred into a deep blue twilight speckled with dancing stars and racing planets. Eli watched enraptured as the fixed point of the sky drifted lazily away from the dragon and settled on the tail of the little bear. Finally the heavens slowed and stopped so that the world's date and stars were synchronized with those of the Real World in 2048. They searched the sky and sure enough Taurus no longer held the equinox for Spring. A great laugh could be heard from Gordon's clone atop the pyramid. Eli walked over to where white bull lay in a pool of blood at the king's feet and for fun cut off its tail then whacked the king on the head, knocking off his crown.

A moment of awed silence filled the city. The people looked around in confusion while a great murmur arose from the river, trees and stars.

Lighting struck the top of the pyramid and their former avatars were ripped apart. Several of the constellation took shape, gaining mass and volume until they stood as great stern gods in the sky. Gordon checked the system processes of the world and sure enough they were off the chart with a few unknown programs running.

He sent an encrypted tight-band transmission through one of his spawned avatars back to The Group in the Real World with a copy of the data he was receiving. Suddenly there was a huge spike and the process monitors were pinned to 100%. People on the other side of the river by the ziggurat began staggering and falling to the ground. Time began to slow down for Gordon and the city blurred into a small trail of after-images.

"Eli, what's going on over there? Eli you bastard answer me!" Gordon was starting to get frantic. He noticed the gods were confused. They gently picked up limp and twitching human forms, examined them and talked rapidly with each other in an odd language. Gordon tried reaching Eli again and finally got a hold of him. The connection was momentarily clear but something was clearly wrong with Eli.

"I... I... don't..." The connection was severed as the ground began to rumble beneath him. The gods finally noticed something was wrong with the Garden and reached out in slow motion with their long arms toward Gordon.

"Oh, crap. What now?" He saw people below him staggering dumbly while others were on the ground having seizures or staring off into space. He heard a chorale sung in an odd key, winding its ways up along the steps and down around the terraces from many directions at once. The world folded and curved in upon itself as he was whisked away into a vast distance.

Gordon was left suspended in a thick oily darkness and filled with the feeling that he was being watched. A warm electric current moved up his spine while a wordless lullaby sung in three interweaving voices. The darkness stirred with waves and half seen images as he descended into a warm sleep. Everything dissolved and he awakened on a beach of soft white sand while a distant volcano blew lava into the air. A lean muscular woman dressed in skins and a bone necklace approached him casually. She came close enough to examine him but before she could a duck-billed dinosaur leaned down to nuzzle and smell Gordon with a great snort of air. The sun reflected brightly off the obsidian tip of her spear before he gave up the ghost and awakened back in his body, floating gently in the warm epsom bath of the isolation tank. It took him a few minutes to re-orient himself, get out of the tank and wrapped himself in a towel. He opened the door of the other tank and saw Eli staring blankly off into space.

"You ok?" He asked.

Eli didn't respond.

"Stop screwing with me, Eli. Are you ok?" Gordon was starting to get worried.

Gordon scooped up some water and dropped on his face. Eli didn't respond. Now he knew there was a problem.

CHAPTER VIII. THE CHASE

*Fly, dotard, fly. With thy wise dreams and fables
of the sky.*

Homer

SAANICH, BC, CANADA

Around lunchtime Ben's friend Tim dropped by. They were old friends from university with some cross over classes in coding for world design. Tim was thin and wiry, always with a hungry look on his face and a curly mop of hair. The first thing he did was oggle the robot.

"Nice bot, man. Looks like top of the line."

"Yeah, my father-in-law gave it to us. It makes nice sushi." He said that intentionally to tease him. The robot walked over and carefully placed a tray of maki on the table." Tim's eyes lit up.

"I wish I could afford one of those."

"You've got tons of money Tim! You could get a dozen any time."

"No man, I need to save my cash for retirement and in case I get slagged from my job or something." He flicked his eyes off to one side nervously as though looking for something elusive, something chasing him. It was an odd nervous habit that Ben noticed but never brought up. Tim was a programmer now lost in his work and the highs of speed, weed and making code dance in Baroque constellations. He never had much of a life beyond work though he longed for one from time to time.

Ben just shook his head while Tim was busy devouring some farm raised free-range Unagi. As long as they had been friends Tim had been a little paranoid and overcautious. He was afraid to spend money on anything but music, computers and sushi. And as far as Ben knew,

Tim had amassed a small fortune from abstinence and solitude. "Was this the new monasticism?" He wondered.

"Where's Mayu?" Tim mumbled downing another roll. "Sleeping off that new flu."

"Bummer. How long has she been sleeping?"

"The better part of week."

"You're kidding." He stopped eating for a moment to look at Ben seriously.

"I wish I was. She seems okay though it's almost like she's in a cocoon."

"At least she's not catatonic. Thankfully that mutation is pretty isolated. I can't afford any time off work right now, we have another code freeze coming." Ben gave him a dirty look. Tim was smart but lacking in empathy and people smarts. He was a good guy but Ben thought of him a casualty of the digital age. After eating they went into the living room to hang out, chat and listen to some music. Tim admired the structure of the loom more than the tapestry Mayu was weaving on it. After they settled down they began to talk about implants and the corrupt code Ben found.

"You took the plunge! Good man. Welcome the 21 firtht and a half thentury!" A dramatic lisp rolled off his tongue and bits of spit flew into the air as he imitated the infamous Duck Dodgers.

"Yeah, I understand why I held off for so long but now I can't imagine going back, the interface is incredible."

"Yeah, if we only had them when we were young. Gaming in full submersion is amazing. You wanna try? There's a new one that just came out and I'm only like level 7 right now. You could catch up if you hauled ass."

"No thanks. I have a life in the Real World now." He had been hoping for a more in depth conversation about adjusting to implants and the nature of full submersion but should have expected a response like that from Tim.

"You wanna go look at that code?" Tim was anxious to see it. They went into the Cave and loaded the effected worlds. Tim took his time examining everything carefully.

"It doesn't look like corruption to me. Looks more like the original code was removed and this other code was left in its place." Tim was curious.

"It sounds like I've been hacked." Ben was uncertain.

"I don't know, dude." Now it was Tim's turn to be uncertain.

"The code left over is weird and it's interspersed with fragments of artificial life."

"Artificial life ? What are you talking about?" Ben was confused.

"Never seen anything like this before though. This stuff's advanced, dude. Way advanced." Tim frowned. "I've never seen anything like this before. Can I grab a copy?"

"Help yourself, I've got no use for it." Ben shrugged. "But how could it be artificial life?"

"I'm not sure dude. A few years back some nut jobs released a bunch of artificial life code into the Net, spliced with a few virus strains so it would propagate across networks. They were part of some whacked out cult who said they were compelled by the little buggers in their dreams cause they were from the future and needed to be born in the Net. Most of it turned out innocuous and useless but some of it has been downright malefic. Smart viruses, nasty buggers hiding out and poisoning or restructuring nodes, routers and access points like you wouldn't believe. Sometimes they even improved things instead of messing them up, though no one knows why; evolution and variation I guess. Some variants were even known to screw with home systems."

"Like this one?" Ben began to have his doubts.

"No, nothin like what you got here and that's what's buggin me. Your home system's fine, dude. Let's see if we can find a pattern to the infection."

After a couple of hours of digging around they drew a blank.

"Nice work, man." Tim nodded approvingly. "I like your recent work on the Garden and Plato's Cave. Did you notice any patterns to the stuff that's disappeared?"

"Well, it's strange. The only connections I can think of are remotely symbolic ones. Have you ever heard of a symbolic virus?"

"No man, there's no such thing. Viruses are literal not literate little bastards. Sorry dude, I don't have a clue what we're looking at and my head's inside out right now. I'll have to look at some of this code at home when my brain and mind are more in synch."

"That's okay, I appreciate what you've done Tim. Besides, I haven't had any more trouble since that last restore."

After Tim left Ben sat and meditated for a little while to clear his head. He knew it was better to let his unconscious mull it over for a while than try to muddle through it again. He went back to check on Mayu.

"How could she still be sleeping?" The robot was busy mowing the lawn and had gathered tools to plant flowers along the walkway in the front. Ben shook his head in an odd mixture of wonder and disbelief.

"Amazing. What will these creatures be able to do next? What will they be like in five to ten years? "

Later, the conversation with Tim kept pulling at him, unresolved. There was something in it that needed exploring. He was getting nowhere trying to figure it out at home and the contract for finishing a couple of new game worlds was months away. He decided it was time for a walk in the woods and talk with the trees. They always had some wisdom to bear when he was confused about something and needed clarity.

He left the house and entered the woods from the trailhead at the end of his street. After a short walk he came to his favorite clearing and sat down on the thick carpet of green moss. The trees reached high in the afternoon sky, trying to grasp the primordial fires of the sun and stars. He sat quietly emptying his mind, listening to the hum of life within and around. Soon all distinctions dissolved and he became aware of all the life around him. And from this place of emptiness and clarity Ben began to consider the problem as a whole that had been nagging at him since he first noticed the missing pool in the Garden.

The most curious thing about it all was his sense that there was a symbolic link between the pieces. A pool of water reflecting the moon, the orb of the sun and the Madonna and child. That combined with the fragments of artificial life code they had found, began an interesting synergy in the back of his mind. There was something he was forgetting though, something important that eluded him like a half remembered dream.

In that moment a bird took wing, its perch snapped and fell to the ground at Ben's feet. The branch settled and the forest was filled with the sound of wings fanning the air rapidly into the distance. As the quiet business of life in the woods enfolded him, the memory of the shape shifting presence he had seen by the Madonna came back to him. He could see it in his mind, emerging and unfolding through different forms before disappearing altogether. And then there was the artificial life code, the missing objects, the strange voice. It only made sense that whatever it was, that thing was alive. It was some kind of conscious entity stealing virtual objects from his system and the pools of darkness and code remnants must have been something like its footprints and residual DNA. He wanted to have a better look through his archives to see if anything else was missing and see if his idea of symbolic connections held water.

"Too bad I can't connect to my network from here. It's probably better if I keep these worlds separate anyway."

When he got home he went straight to the Cave, activated his implants to enter full submersion and began digging though his old files. One of the things he found was an archived copy of the Dream Network's central temple and sure enough where the Earth should have been there was a large smudge of darkness. He stood for a while staring into the swirling sediment of shadows, looking for a glimpse of the entity or something beyond but he saw nothing and could not tell how long ago it had come and gone. He began to wonder where it would go next.

"Why should it stay in my neck of the woods? Why wouldn't it range further and take data objects from other places in the Net? What would keep it from taking the Earth from the Dream Network?" Then he realized what he was saying. That Earth was more than a graphic, it was a Global database that contained hundreds of thousands of hours of dreams from around the world.

"Open link to Dream Network and land directly in center of Nave using special access code." A gateway opened and closed around his feet placing him in the middle of the mandala on the floor at the Nave. The physics were set so that his avatar displaced local time space enough that anyone in the center of the nave was shifted several meters away.

A few Crash Test Dummies and a winged man grumbled nearby but Ben ignored them. Looking to the ceiling, he found the symbols for the equinoxes and solstices glowing the soft lavender of links triggered by his arrival. He looked around the basilica to get his bearings.

He was in the Asian wing surrounded by immense statues of ancient Tibetan, Hindu, Japanese and Chinese deities supporting the grand arches that held the ceiling. The fresco on the ceiling was done in a deep midnight blue and filled with an endless field of stars, galaxies and nebulae. Silver lines faded into view, showing the various constellations. After a while they faded slowly into the background of stars. Ben shook himself to pull out of the trance he was slipping into. He still wasn't use to the intensity of the implants and the temple was designed to be hypnotic. The more someone looked at any part, the more they saw. Now that he had implants he began to understand some of the minute revisions the techs made of his original designs.

Bringing his attention back to the floor of the basilica, he was happy to see that the people he displaced had already moved. He focused on the far end of the hall where he saw the gate for the inner temple.

"Open gateway to Earth Dreams." Another portal opened placing him in the amphitheater with the hi-res globe of the Earth still spinning majestically in the middle. Ben sat down with a sigh of relief.

"Maybe I was wrong. Maybe..." Ben didn't get a chance to finish his thought when he saw the entire globe darkening as though it were becoming overtaken by night. As it blackened, the space around it folded in upon itself and the massive Earth disappeared into a thick pool of darkness. Shadowy shapes and distortion patterns filled the depths. A few avatars nearby disappeared as their owners logged out and their minds were instantly transported back to their bodies back in the Real World. Those remaining in the temple backed away as though a dangerous predator had entered the room but could not bring themselves to leave. Ben however, was onto his feet and descending the stairs as fast as he could toward the anomaly. He wanted a closer look at the chaos inside the darkness.

What is all that?" As he got closer he could see imagery within the fragments. There were pieces from his worlds and others he didn't recognize. *"A broken hologram of all the worlds where data was taken, I'd wager."* As he examined the chaos, he had an intimation of a pattern unfolding. He could almost see the structure in the flow but it somehow kept eluding him.

"What are you crazy?" Cried a voice from behind. "Stay away from that thing!"

"I've got to get a closer look to see what's inside." He said aloud, not caring if anyone else could hear him. When he was close enough he reached inside and the gravity changed. He floated into the air and was pulled inside.

All around him was darkness. It was a thick fluid like oil but vibrant and full of deep undulations. He felt the darkness gnawing at him as he moved forward and it was somehow both harsh and beautiful. Time and distance held no meaning there but after a while the emptiness gave way to fragments of worlds cascading around him. Then in the heart of it all he found a light, faint at first and undefined. It slowly coalesced into a gateway that placed him on a low hill by a small Greek temple with Doric columns and a broken statue of a winged goddess by the entrance. Other statues lay in pieces on the ground and the sky was full of stars. It was a serene world, lulling Ben into a mood of quiet contemplation.

"Where in the Web am I now?" He looked around for clues but found nothing distinct. It appeared to be little more than a forgotten world built to explore a single idea then abandoned for something greater. Behind him, the portal he came through was nowhere in sight.

"So what brought the entity here?" While he explored the grounds he began to admire the sculptural beauty and pleasing scale of the temple's traditional design. After a fruitless search he decided there was no place else to go but up the path and into the temple. Ascending the stairs to the platform where the columns stood he glimpsed something deep inside. Passing between the columns of the colonnade and through the pronia, he entered into a chamber unusually large for a Greek temple.

"The inside is slightly too big for the outside." While this was not unusual for some worlds it confirmed his initial impressions about the amateurish construction of the place. The difference in propor-

tion was clearly accidental and the overall significance of the place was more important to the builder than the parts. In the center of the temple, inside the cella stood a large statue of what looked to Ben like a goddess of war, maybe Athena. She had a sword sheathed on her belt, a shield on one arm while she reached for something in mid air that was no longer there. Instead, a large irregular smear of darkness floated in the air nearby.

"So what was the entity after here?" Looking around for clues Ben spotted two orbs set on pedestals on opposite sides of the chamber. They were made to look like dark polished stone with deep veins of red running through them. He decided to have a closer look and found reflections of the god and something else. Thankfully the resolution was high enough to allow some magnification. The image was distorted from being curved along the surface but Ben could tell it was tall and variegated.

"It's a tree." He realized and turned to look closer at the smear of darkness in the middle of the temple. Looking closely at the shape of the god's hand he understood the metaphor. *"She was reaching for a piece of fruit. If the theme holds it was probably a golden apple."* Ben saw no other choice, so he stepped into the darkness. Just as before, he felt weightless and floated in a purgatory of emptiness before he emerged in front of a very wide stone well with two swans swimming casually inside. A wide path led from the well to a great wooden hall made of logs carved with elaborate patterns of knotwork topped with a shingled roof and gables.

Three wrinkled old Norse women with terrible eyes and auras of power came out of the building and walked in a slow ceremonial procession down the path to the well beside him. They took no notice of Ben as they scooped up the water and walked back behind the building to pour the water on the massive roots that rose like hills behind the golden hall. Ben followed the roots up with his eyes as they merged into a tree of unbelievable height. If he had to guess, he would have to say the tree was over nine kilometers tall. The figure came from the back of his mind, as he remembered the name of the tree.

"Yggdrasil. It's been a long time since I was here last. This is the worldsite where they relive the Viking myths and legends in excruci-

ating detail. If I remember correctly they regularly replay the great cosmic battle of Ragnarok." The three maidens that he now recognized as the Norns, had finished pouring the well water on the root of the tree and had returned to confront him. One held a staff with notches cut all along its length.

"We've been expecting you." She intoned in English with a heavy Nordic accent. The middle one poured the remaining water on Ben's head and said: "You have arrived just in time, Midgard has been consumed by darkness and Surt has set the tree on fire." The water had a strange warming and invigorating effect and he noticed his skin had turned white as the swans. The last maiden handed him a large double-edged axe and said:

"You're going to need this."

"Timing is everything, I guess." Ben shrugged as he hefted the axe to look at the knotwork carved into the upper handle and blades.

"Take the bridge." Insisted the second Norn. "You will find what you're looking for." They all turned toward the golden hall and to the left he now saw Bifrost, the great rainbow bridge, spiralling high around the tree's great trunk into the heavens. As he approached the gate before the bridge, a wall of fire blocking access, parted quietly as a curtain.

The bridge felt warm, cold or wet depending on where he stepped. Each step took him further than it should have and soon he was hundreds of meters above the ground. And as the bridge passed between the immense limbs and left the lower realm called Niflheim, Ben could see that portions of the tree were indeed on fire. When he got higher he could see the tree had three main roots that blended together to form the gargantuan trunk before it branched into three massive limbs and thousands of branches. Each limb held several domed worlds spread throughout the canopy. The rainbow bridge continued to spiral upward around the central bough, all the way up to a dome at the crown of the tree. Just ahead, Ben saw a part of the bridge fork off and curve down in a long rainbow to a world on the central limb. Undoubtedly this was where he needed to go.

"If the entity took anything here it's probably in Midgard." When he turned off the main bridge onto the fork he saw a few things happening at once. A host of fir clad giants carrying axes and war hammers,

stormed up the central bridge to fight with a gathering of gods and goddesses clad in shimmering armor who were armed with swords and spears. Most of the domed worlds that swayed amidst the branches like giant fruit were broken. Battles were going on all along the three main limbs and a great wolf leaped off the edge of the tree to swallow the sun. While the world was plunged into darkness, the bridges provided their own illumination and balls of light glowed to life throughout the tree.

"Not a good sign, I better get out of here soon. This is not a battle I'm interested in getting involved in." Ben hefted the ax. *"And if I remember correctly, at the end of the battle the entire tree is destroyed and a new version is put in its place. I better get to Midgard before the entity's trail disappears."* Hurrying down the long arch of the bridge he saw frost giants gathering for war in the worlds below. A great serpent stirred the ocean encircling the tree into a turbulent sea and the rainbow bridge began to sway.

"These people take their simulations seriously!" Ben broke into a run. Ahead where the city of Midgard should have been he saw an immense sphere of darkness, an inky black pool of chaos. The deafening boom of a battle drum filled the air and the bridge began to bounce and sway to the rhythm. Turning back he saw a host of angry giants following him.

"Oh great!" He grumbled. *"Just what I need."*

They were at a good distance but coming on fast. Ben had the lead and the pool of chaos was close. The last moments stretched on slowly and he found himself in an eeric calm thinking about virtual death. Normally when someone died in a virtual world they simply woke up in their bodies back on Earth as though waking from a dream. His implants were new though and some worlds that held to brutal recreations of the past were known for their painful realism. An agonizing death in a virtual world with fresh implants was not an appealing thought. The giants were about 10 meters away when he reached the outer darkness and dove into the abyss.

"Timing is everything." He said to himself as he fell into the syrup like darkness, the same thick liquid he encountered before. Time disappeared and the darkness felt like an ocean, vibrant and calm, filled with

strange undulations. Was it alive? It felt like it was trying to consume him, gnawing away at his edges. It reminded him of something, but what that was eluded him. Scintillating fragments of worlds danced in chaos around him. He wondered if he could reach out and touch any of the shards and be transported there instantly.

Passing through the chaos he entered into a calm inner pool of darkness within darkness, then suddenly he was tumbling in gravity again. He hit the ground rolling and came up in a crouch behind a disarray of barrels that smelled like well-aged wine. Looking around he found himself in the dark recesses of a large cave. He was distracted by the noise of fighting and saw a sword wielding warrior fighting against an immense troll with a heavy brow and a single bloodshot eye in the middle of its broad flat forehead. Across the cavern other people were poised and waiting. They were from the typical mishmash of races in a fantasy world; a dwarf, two elves and a sorceress.

As agile as the warrior was, his sword made little purchase against the thick hide of the cyclops. Ben looked around to get a better picture of the cave and what may have brought the entity here. Nothing in the cave looked important and there was no sign of the entity or the darkness that it left in its wake. Behind the troll, the mouth of the cave was covered with a huge stone and light leaked through around the edges. Nearby, some sheep were penned by a fire and a tall green shepherd's staff lay on the ground beside him. Curiously, the ax the old woman gave him was still in hand. When he turned back to the battle it was in time to see the troll grab hold of the warrior and rip his head off with its teeth. It rocked on its feet as it peeled off the warrior's armor and began eating him in big rending bites.

The sorceress threw a shock wave at the creature but it had little effect. Ben could see that her energy was getting low and she needed time to replenish. The others didn't seem to have enough power or skill to defeat the monster and Ben realized that his only way out was to side with these folks against it. It had been a long time since Ben had been to a fantasy game world but he knew what to do. While the cyclops gorged itself noisily on the man's flesh, Ben grabbed hold of the staff and sharpened it to a jagged point with the ax. He held it in the fire long enough to harden. When he finished he prompted the Sorceress on a tight band transmission to ask her assistance.

"Who are you?" She asked.

"A friend and I have an idea. I need a sustained burst of light to distract the monster."

"Done." And a stream of bright blue light shot out from her hands to explode in front of the troll's face. Ben rushed out and plunged the staff into its eye. The monster screamed and fell heavily to the ground. The elves rushed over and bound the monster with a thin strong rope. A cheer went up amongst the band as they all joined Ben by the writhing cyclops.

"I don't know where you came from or how you got in here, but you owned that monster." The dwarf bellowed happily clasping his hand.

"No problem," Ben said.

"We've been trying to get past this monster for the larger part of a moon now. Our clan owes you a debt of gratitude." The Elves bowed to him.

"How did you come here?" Taking the lead, the Sorceress seemed more demanding than thankful.

"Through a gateway between worlds." She looked at him with surprise then narrowed eyes, reassessing her impressions of him.

"There's more to you than meets the eye. You're not a wizard, are you a Game Master in disguise?"

"Neither, I'm not part of this place. I'm a World Weaver." The look she gave him then was undecipherable. "Have you seen anything unusual in your adventures here recently?"

"Unusual? What constitutes unusual in a world like this?" She asked.

"A strange entity that doesn't fit the scheme of this world." He wasn't sure what to say.

"A shapeshifter? They are not allowed here. The machines of the masters would revolt and banish them with great force."

"Yeah, I suppose that the servers and game masters would try but I doubt they could stop it."

"Couldn't stop it? How could that be?"

Ben shrugged. "I can't explain it easily. I'm not even sure I can explain it at all."

She looked at him quizzically. "I grow weary of this place and am in need of refreshment. Would you join me and my friends back at my castle nearby? We would be honored by your company."

Ben looked around. There was no sign of the entity anywhere and this was probably a large world. Most online games were expansive, anywhere between a few hundred and several thousand virtual square kilometers. He thought back on the worlds he passed through in getting here. The most recent portals were close to the points of entry in each world but they seemed to be connected symbolically. He'd have to continue with that assumption until proven wrong.

"My name in this world is Circe, what shall we call you?" The Sorceress was starting to warm to him. Ben was tempted to say his name was Nimble Wits as Odysseus did in the Odyssey but had the feeling she would not appreciate the joke.

"Just call me Ben."

"Ben, this is Elar, Rath, and Borphos." The warrior became reanimated and was quickly brought up to speed on the situation. "And this is our brick, Thorak" He turned to Ben and gave him a salute.

"Gather together." She commanded and as they came closer, her aura grew to encompass them all. She raised her wand, spoke her enchantment and they were all transported to her house of polished stone and carved wood set in the middle of a forest clearing. Wolves and lions prowled about and Circe wandered inside singing in an enchanting voice. The group followed her in, sat around the hearth and servants brought them aromatic wine and cheese. Ben had not yet tried virtual food or drink. He eyed it cautiously.

"So Weaver, what do you seek in these lands?" One of the Elves asked.

"Darkness and chaos." He chose the simplest explanation.

"A strange thing to seek when it lays all around you. Will you group with our clan?"The dwarf asked.

"You misunderstand me." Ben said. "I'm not looking for battles or adventure here in your world. I'm looking for something that comes from beyond your world. I've been following a trail of darkness that passes through many worlds that brought me here."

"A quest through many worlds?" The dwarf sat back with his ale and a frown overcame his busy brow. "I've never heard of such a thing."

"Is it evil?" Asked the dark elf that Ben finally decided was a female. With elves it was sometimes hard to tell.

"I never considered that." He stopped and thought for a moment. "I don't think so. It may seem evil because its actions are beyond understanding."

"But if it is harmful, is it not still evil?" She asked.

"If it is harmful then yes," he reluctantly agreed. "I would partially agree but so far it has only taken things belonging to others and there's no evidence of anyone being hurt."

"A thief." She mused. "In some hands a crime and others a noble trade."

"It may not even know we're here." Ben thought out loud.

"How can that be?" Circe was confused.

"At this stage I only have theories." Ben didn't feel like going into it any further. He needed to think about it some more and he was itching to get on with the search. After an awkward pause. "You have a beautiful home, Circe."

"Thank you." She said rising gracefully. "Come, I'll show you around. There are many beautiful things in this house." He saw the others give each other a curious look as she took his hand and led him out of the room. Here in this world, she was a seductively beautiful and strong woman but back on Earth there was no telling what she looked like behind the avatar. It struck him that whomever she was in the Real World, in this world she was still a sharp woman impressed with power, something he cared little about.

"Let me show you my bedchamber." She said pulling him into the candlelit room.

"I uh..." Ben began to feel rather uncomfortable.

"My loom!" She cried. "What happened to my loom? I was working on a beautiful tapestry of a tree. What is that thing?" She pointed to the cloud of darkness that filled the corner of her room.

"Darkness and chaos." Ben smiled.

"Is that what you're looking for?" She asked.

"It is indeed." Ben smiled. "Sorry to leave so soon but this is my exit."

Into the abyss he flew and glided slowly into an unfathomable ocean of darkness. It was deep and all consuming, filling every direction and destroying all sense of orientation. Despite the deep sense of isolation, Ben found this relaxing and settled into a light state of meditation. He imagined someone from another world falling into this space without being prepared and feeling as though they were lost in part of Dante's Purgatory. And what of the giants? What of Circe and her friends? Where would they go if they felt adventurous or fell into the abyss by accident? Would they inadvertently follow him on this strange odyssey or go to other worlds?

Then a strange thought came to him. If this was an entity as he suspected, then what seemed like different pools of darkness and chaos might actually be the same pool spread through different worlds. He imagined something like the spokes of a wheel pointing to a hub, like some form of hyper wheel. But what was it after? Why was it stealing virtual objects from different worlds around the Web?

Darkness gave way to chaos and distortion. Fractal patterns flitted by and he was lost in the stillness of the inner darkness before it shattered into light. He thought he glimpsed something before the light condensed into a torch lit tomb. It was lost in the reflections from the brightly colored hieroglyphs lining the walls.

The transition shook him up a little more this time, leaving him feeling dizzy with a mild sense anxiety. He had to stop and use a breathing technique to calm his nerves and relax. This gave him some time to look around and get his bearings. He found he was in a large chamber populated by various Egyptian deities focused on a large fulcrum scale in the middle of the room.

"The Hall of Judgment." He recognized the place. Before he could regain his equilibrium a goddess dressed in white took his hand and led him forward. Anubis, the jackal headed god reached inside Ben's body and pulled out a pulsing heart. He felt cold as the god carefully placed it on one side of the scale balanced against an ostrich feather

on the other. A crocodile headed man looked on hungrily but the scales balanced and Anubis returned the heart. It gave Ben a sensation of warmth and euphoria as a voice chanted a slow prayer in the background.

"Let my heart be with me in the House of Hearts. Let my heart case be with me in the House of heart cases. Let my heart be with me, and let it rest in me or I shall not eat the cakes of Osiris in the eastern side of the Lake of Flowers."

Horus, a falcon headed god wearing the red and white double crown of lower and upper Egypt took him by the hand and led him out of the room and into the next chamber. It was a large hall, more like a throne room plunged in a dreary light by candles nearly dead. Sitting in despair upon the throne sat Ra, another falcon-headed god with the body of a man and a yellow disk upon his head bordered by a cobra of gold and lapis. A goddess in a tight dress with a crescent moon upon her head walked into the room followed closely by a large maned lion. The beast lay calmly at her feet and she began to dance, a blue lotus in one hand and a snake in the other.

As Ra began to stir and glow with renewed energy the room brightened but he and his throne were shattered into a storm of particles that were sucked into a deepening abyss. The dancing goddess made no move to escape, she continued her dance as though nothing had changed. Before Ben could move though the god reappeared upon his throne in his sullen state and the goddess was gone. As though stuck in a loop the goddess and the lion returned, her sensual dance brightened the room and enlivened the god. Then as before, Ra shattered into chaos and disappeared as darkness spread. This time Ben moved quickly and jumped into the abyss.

Time slowed and the darkness spread around him once again. His senses came alive as long deep undulations cascaded around him and off into the distance, giving depth to the darkness. Chaos and distortion passed by and he passed into the inner darkness. There in the depths nothing moved, there was only a soft impenetrable stillness. After a moment he had the distinct feeling that he was being watched though he could not tell from where. He saw something emerging in the abyss but he began to feel scattered and disoriented. There was a blinding flash of light, gravity took him and he fell hard onto sunbaked earth.

Disorientation overwhelmed him and with his head spinning he started breathing deeply to try to regain his focus and calm his nerves but it had little effect. The world started breaking into large rough pixels, hues shifted and changed in saturation. Everything became vibrant an intense as though painted by van Gogh. Ben knew then that he was going to lose ground and fall from this world back into his body so he forced himself to look around.

To one side was a river, spanned by a wide bridge. On the other stood a great walled city with a high arched gate. From within the walls rose a mountainous ziggurat reaching high into the heavens. As he looked up, the world broke into distortion and fragments danced in a bizarre Kandinsky like chaos. Ben slipped in and out of consciousness before he fell from the world and awakened painfully in a semi conscious state back in the Cave.

CHAPTER IX. NANITES

The machine does not isolate man from the great problems of nature but plunges him more deeply into them.

Antoine de Saint-Exupéry

UCSF MEDICAL CENTER, SAN FRANCISCO
MAGNETIC RESONANCE IMAGING CENTER

Daniel entered the lab solemnly as though he was walking into a funeral chapel for the passing of a friend. He admittedly felt a bit overwhelmed but was determined to go through with the procedure despite his anxiety of how it might change him. When it was finished, he found it hard to believe that it was complete once the doctor had injected the ampoule full of clear liquid into his arm. He felt the pin prick and had watched the level of liquid go down milliliter by milliliter but he felt nothing. If anything, he felt as though he were watching a movie of someone else's life through his own eyes. When the doctor pulled the needle out Daniel felt cheated. For a procedure that was to change his life and irrevocably alter his health, a simple injection shouldn't be enough, couldn't be enough. He knew it was absurd but he thought the doctor must have been lying or telling a partial truth to ease his mind.

When he walked back into Gordon's lab he knew this was the missing piece of the puzzle. After spending a long time in the lush complexity of the woods of Vermont and the Sequoia grove in the Sierras, the Lab's emptiness, sterility and simplicity seemed almost harsh. To his eye carefully schooled in the supple curves of nature, the lab was a brutal study in modern minimalism and functionality dominated by large machines with clean neutral surfaces. It felt completely removed from the natural world.

"Welcome back Daniel." Gordon greeted him with a smile and a handshake but it all felt a bit stiff.

He wasn't as warm or good-natured as Daniel remembered and he could sense Gordon was preoccupied and hiding some kind of grief. Daniel liked the man and tried to imagine how it must be to live and work in such a sterilized environment for a long time.

"What does that do to someone's soul to be so far removed from nature?" It surprised him how much his tolerance had change over the past seven years. He could only vaguely remember his time working in a lab but it was eclipsed by his intense submersion in the forests and mountains of Vermont.

"It's good to see you again, Daniel. What we're going to do with you today is a lot like what we did last time you came. Instead of doing a fishing expedition though, we're going to track the progress of the nanocytes the doctors injected into your blood. We just want to make sure the little buggers reach the tumors properly and deposit their payload. The scans we're going to do will look and feel the same as the ones we did before. Do you have any questions?"

"Yes, if you don't mind my asking."

"Not at all."

"How does it effect you to work in such an unnatural environment every day? Don't you long for the outdoors?" Gordon staggered back dramatically and held his heart as though run through with a sword then laughed out loud. After that his disposition lightened.

"That's not at all what I expected. Well, to answer your question I do go outside when I'm not working in the lab but let me tell you a secret. This place may look like a cyborg's bedroom but these machines give me a glimpse into the heart of nature in a way that I never could find while walking along a trail in Point Reyes or Mount Tam."

"What do you mean?"

"Well, let's just say that there's a lot going on below the surface. Think of it like the geology of the Earth. We live on a thin layer of crust floating on top of immense magma plumes and convection currents that are churning in the deep far below our feet. Strange as it looks, this machine gives me a window into the world of organic chemistry and beyond, far below the surface of bark and skin. Besides, I'm a cyborg and this monstrosity is one of my closest friends." Gordon laughed again. "If you're interested, while we're doing the scans I'll show you some animations of what's going on inside your body. It might help you relax to get a glimpse into your own deep nature and you might even find it inspiring."

Daniel paused to consider the wisdom in what he was saying.

"Seeing what's going on probably will help me feel more relaxed." He agreed. The quietude of the lab and Gordon's view of nature was getting his curiosity going and started waking up memories of his own previous work with building Artificial Intelligence. In his imagination he was already picturing mountains of cells, streams of blood and forests of nerves.

"Okay Daniel, are you ready for us to begin? Before you get back into the scanner though, I need to make sure you've removed all jewelry and that you don't have any unusual body piercings that can't be removed. You still haven't taken to eating small metal objects?"

"No. I'm fine and ready to go. You're assistant was quite thorough."

"She is indeed. Okay, why don't you to lie down on the scan table and we'll take some pictures. Just like before I'm going to leave the room during the scan but I'll talk with you through the comm system. While you're in there please try to remain still so we can get some clear pictures."

The scan table slid in slowly and Daniel imagined himself being consumed by a whale as he moved into the empty bore tube. He didn't even notice that Gordon had left the room and as he lay in the heart of the machine everything began to churn inside him again. He realized it seemed a bit incongruous that he had worked so diligently on mapping and building neural structures and constructing various kinds of Artificial Intelligence but the thought of nanoscale robots invading his body was still disconcerting. He knew he was gaining an extended lease on life but he was afraid he might be losing something essential in the process. He knew all the arguments about the illusory boundary between humans and technology but he realized in the end he still felt there was something sacred about life. He still believed that there was so much more to consciousness than all the elegant assemblages and the finely balanced ecology of neurochemistry. When he had finally created a true Artificial Intelligence, he quietly held the belief that he and his colleagues had simply created a container complex enough for a consciousness to inhabit, for a subtle mind to be housed within.

"Are you comfortable?" Gordon asked through the comm.

"Comfortable enough." He thought of Thoreau and how much he used to rail against the dangers of comfort.

"Okay, just like last time you'll hear some thumping in the background. Today though, we'll be watching the nanobots moving through your blood stream and into the nooks and crannies of your brain."

"It's amazing you can track something that small. I've mapped neurons and tracked small animals through the woods but this is more like trying to map the movement of a few grains of sand across a beach from space while the tide is changing."

"Well, it's actually a lot easier than that. This is probably a bit more like mapping the movement of a herd of caribou from orbit. We make it a lot easier though by using something like GPS transponders on a very small scale. For this kind of scan we use magnetic nano particles attached to the nanobots and some other specially tagged nano-particles as markers. After they enter your bloodstream the nanites make their way into your brain and central nervous system. Around the time they're getting nestled comfortably in place we blanket you with some noninvasive magnetic fields and the nano-particles act as a contrast agent. Think of them as crystals or mirror shards sprinkled around inside a dark cave. When we takes pictures of your brain its kind of like flashing a strobe and the shards help reveal a greater level of detail than we could see otherwise.

"I'm beginning to get the picture but what's the difference between a nanobot and a nanite?"

"The distinction is important, especially on this level and the classification is quite simple actually. Nanite is the general class of nanomachines so we tend to use it as a generic term for just about everything on that scale when we don't feel like going into details. Nanocytes are a family of nanites specially designed to transport and inject medicinal compounds and other substances into cells though your blood stream. There are other nanites designed to function as assemblers, disassemblers as well as immuno-sensors that will reside in your brain for a few months before falling apart and being flushed out. They'll monitor the state of your health from the inside and transmit the info to external monitors."

"They sound a bit like spies."

"Think of them more as a very committed neighborhood Block Watch program."

"I guess I'm still a bit uncomfortable having pieces of nanotech running around inside of me."

"That's okay, it's quite a natural response. From my background I see it a bit differently though. When I look into our bodies on a cellular level what I see is that we are made of a beautiful organic microtechnology and a complex ecology of highly cooperative and naturally grown protein machines. Nature has evolved in us an elegant and extraordinary technology and what we're doing here is simply fixing some of the errors in construction."

Daniel was never overly fond of technological metaphors of the mind but the idea that he was made of a several billion year old self organizing organic technology was intriguing. He was silent for a few moments before he realized that Gordon was waiting for him.

"My working vision of Nature is more fluid, a kind of organic information system but I'm beginning to see what you're saying." A great river of crimson filled his view screen surrounded by a transparent membrane and darkness.

"Okay, this is a graphic of your bloodstream. Do you see these clouds moving along with the current?" Gordon enhanced the color and brightness so the darkened areas stood out against the background of flotsam and jetsam flowing around them. "Those are nanobots and they have a unique spectrographic signature so I can easily track their progress throughout your body."

"From a distance they kind of look like schools of fish swimming along with the current of a river."

"That's a good image. I guess you can take the man out of the woods but not the woods out of the man."

"Am I a chipmunk dreaming I'm a man or am I a man dreaming I'm a chipmunk?"

"Okay Chuang Tzu, along with the nanocytes another class of nanobots the doctors put in your blood is basically a species of janitors. They're designed to clean out toxins as well as stabilize oxygen and energy transfer in your cells." He gestured and the view zoomed in so Daniel could see that the plasma was filled with disk like platelets, globules of white and red blood cells and a host of other strange organic entities.

"There's a whole ecology in there!" He was amazed.

"Sure is. There are transporters, disaster recovery specialists, police and more." Gordon pointed out a few of the more common cells.

"The red blood cells here are about six microns in diameter and the platelets are about two microns. What that means is that about 350 would fit on the top of a pin. Let me enhance the view a little. Now watch the dark clouds interspersed throughout the plasma."

"Okay, but can you zoom in even more?"

"Sure, I was just about to do that." Gordon pointed then opened his hands in a gesture resembling the opening of a flower. The view zoomed in again and the dark spots became clouds. And then the clouds became a myriad of discreet objects. Some were spheres composed of hexagons; some looked like organic stars while others looked more like squid with numerous tentacles.

"These nanobots and nanites vary in size from 2-9 nanometers. That means you could probably fit several thousand comfortably on a platelet or several hundred thousand on the head of a pin." The view changed again shifting to the right and zooming in. "Okay now here are some cancer cells like those in your brain." An amorphous mass of deformed cells filled the view.

"They look like a fungus."

"Yeah, the changes cancer make in the coding of your DNA significantly alter the structure of the cells. Most of the infected cells that look like that are too far gone and will be destroyed. The others that are still in good shape will be fixed."

"How can they tell the difference between a healthy and a cancerous cell?"

"Well, we've come a long way from the barbaric treatments of a few decades ago. Instead of beaming radiation at organs or dumping toxic chemicals into the body, what we do now is grow nanites that recognize the receptor proteins on the cancer cell membranes. They're deaf and blind so they basically taste the cancer cells and their excretions. Watch." The nanites swarmed around the corrupted cancer cells like a hive of bees. Squid like microcapsules landed on the darkened cells and injected needle shaped nanotubes into the surface membrane. It reminded him of getting bitten by a mosquito except these little buggers were injecting chemicals rather than sucking blood. The cells slowly withered and collapsed from within as the chemicals destroyed them. Other nanites moved in and disassembled the cells into digestible proteins and others encapsulated the molecules of the killer chemical.

"Where the tissue can't be repaired it will be destroyed by dissemblers and the waste removed. Then the assembler nanites will stimulate new tissue growth."

"It's that easy?"

"For the messed up cells it is. I'll show you a little of what happens with the other ones." The view faded out and then opened into a new scene. It showed a group of tree like molecules floating over a convoluted landscape of some healthy looking brain cells.

"Those are called dendrimers." A luminous blue label appeared momentarily beside the complex molecules that looked like the crowns of two oak trees stuck together. He watched carefully as the dendrimers descended toward the cells and bound themselves to surface receptors that were also briefly labeled in blue. He watched with curiosity as they were guided through the membrane into the cell like Trojan Horses. Once they passed through into the cytoplasm the dendrimers began to unfurl, releasing a variety of smaller nanites they had kept hidden deep within their branches. Some fused with messenger proteins that were shaped like intertwined balls of cooked noodles. Other nanites descended through the long fibers and filaments of the cytoskeleton toward the nucleus. They floated past large moon like mitochondria and approached the immense central planet of the nucleus. Once inside they began pouring over the DNA, shifting molecules in and out of place.

"What they're doing now is proofreading the molecules, finding misspellings and strange characters then making the needed sequencing corrections." Daniel watched for a while in quiet awe.

"I guess I had forgotten how complex it was down on this level."
He tried unsuccessfully to blend these images with his vision of nature
but he could not make them come together.

"There's plenty room at the bottom for a whole menagerie of creatures. Well, you look good for now. On your way out we'll schedule a
follow up appointment and pass the results on to you doctor. For now
everything looks great and you're on the road to recovery."

"How long will they stay in my system?"

"A few months at least."

"Thank you. That was amazing!"

"No problem. If you have any questions or if you're willing to talk
about some of your work in AI please don't hesitate to call."

*The goal of life is to make your heartbeat match
the beat of the universe, to match your nature
with Nature.*

Joseph Campbell

THE COUNCIL OF THE PINES
BOSTON, MASS. & PLAINFIELD, VERMONT

After a few days Daniel caught a long flight to Boston routed
through Salt Lake City. From high above he marveled at the arid convolutions of the land cut across by the pale lines and winding curves
of distant roads. The wrinkled hulks of a herd of old mountains were
surrounded by a crazy quilt of farmland painted in tans and greens.
The branching patterns of the mountain ridges stood out for him more
than ever before. Images of dendrimers were transposed over the
landscape in his imagination and the Earth seemed like an immense
cell teaming with molecular ecologies.

"As above, so below." It was amazing to see how geometry was
replicated on different levels of the cosmos. Though he did not enjoy
being stuck in an airplane he loved watching the earth patterns below.
The landscape flowed and folded like a great piece of art that grew and

had sculpted itself out of primordial matter, kiln fired by the energies of the sun and the earths molten core. He thought of the Earth as both art and maker, a self-organizing numinous organism inclined toward an elegant complexity and natural beauty. Across this landscape perfect circles and rectangles had been cut boldly into the flowing forms of the terrain. It was an old palimpsest of mismatched geometries. The ancient manuscript of natural forms were written over with a crude script of the abstract geometry of human constructs and technology. The bold shapes inevitably made him think of Mondrian's attempt to describe the ideals that transcended the changing forms of the world. As misguided as that was Daniel still found a strange beauty in those paintings of colored squares and rectangles. He pulled a sketchbook and pencil out of his pack and wrote the beginnings of a poem that had been brewing in him since his last experience in the lab.

> Something small and indecipherable as cuneiform
> Flows along the rivers of our blood
> Hiding in the caverns of our cells, measureless to man.

He struggled to carve what came to him into words but he could go no further. By the time the landscape below had become submerged in an ocean of clouds, he had dozed off into a dreamless sleep.

When he finally arrived in Boston and breathed the heavy brine of the city's air, it lulled him like a thick somnambulistic potion flowing between the huddled masses of buildings and the swarms of busy people. This, he thought was stranger than any of his dreams. It was a great grey city run by the clockwork machinations of the corporate world that consumed the creative energies of millions of hard working people. With a morbid fascination he traveled through the dark underbelly of city's subway, reading the stories of the people's lives in their faces.

Daniel spent a few days and nights with an old friend who still lived in the hometown of their childhood nestled in the suburbs north of the city between Salem and Walden. He made his pilgrimage to the house and street he grew up, drinking the memories of his youth like a sweet old wine. The same old trees were still there, having cracked and wrinkled the sidewalk from beneath with their thirsty roots. Small blades of grass and bursts of clover grew unbidden through the nooks and crannies between.

He took a couple of days and lost himself in the Museum of Fine Arts and the Fogg Museum at Harvard. The paintings and sculptures of every century and culture fascinated him. Each canvas was for him a window not only into another place and time but into another mind. He imagined the flow of people through the galleries like blood cells moving along an invisible current and wondered what it would be like if he could enter a painting as the nanites had entered his cells.

Once his friend's sofa bed began to feel uncomfortable he realized it was time to go. He caught a train into the city then hopped a bus going north, the old hybrid engine droning behind him in a chorus of pistons and gears. It took him through the dappled old forests and towns of New Hampshire and finally into the woods and old weathered mountains of Vermont. When he finally saw the rolling hills and farmland he knew he was home. From the bus window he was happy to see much of Vermont was still stubbornly undeveloped. After a few hours he got off in Montpelier.

Daniel stretched, walked around town and grabbed some lunch at a familiar old cafe filled with the musty scents of yeasts, rice, tofu, herbs and spices. His old friend Dave met him there and they drove back to Plainfield and up into the hills on bumpy unpaved roads past dilapidated farm houses and the fossil like remains of broken old tractors. It didn't take them long to catch up with and by the time they got back to the house, the sky was filled with an ocean of stars. An owl greeted him with its haunting mantra when he stepped out of the car and the air was fresh with the sweet smell of old grass. They went for a walk with his Dave's Golden Retriever through the neighbor's field and watched the lighting bugs flitter through the tall grasses. Soon their feet were soaked with dew and Daniel felt heavy with slumber.

The next day he had breakfast with Dave and his wife by the kitchen window overlooking a lush organic garden of tomatoes, squash and peas. Blackberry and blueberry bushes held the edges like gnarled and thorny guardians against the troublesome grasses and deer beyond. He told them about his cancer and the struggle he was having with the cure. They all went for a hike together, exploring the woods bordering the property and Dave and Daniel climbed a great old tree for fun. They hung out and talked, listened to music and ate together that day.

That night his dreams were of pursuit by malicious men dressed in shadows. The next morning Daniel entered the woods alone with an old bamboo flute he had left in their good keeping and followed the main trail until he heard the hush and gurgle of water over stone. As he came closer the voice of the stream filled him like a mother's song and he felt embraced by the company of the trees. When he crossed the stream and walked deeper into the woods he felt a subtle shift of energy and a deep quiet surrounded and encompassed him. By the time he reached the clearing he was looking for, he felt every molecule in his body and the forest vibrating in a unseen dance of energy.

He sat on a carpet of old pine needles and watched the light as it streamed through the forest canopy, making small puddles on the ground around him. He placed his backpack and flute on the forest floor, held his hands together over his heart then took out a small bag of dried mushrooms and reverently placed them on the ground before him. A little while after eating them he felt a mild sense of euphoria grow inside him but it soon changed to an upwelling of energy from deep within, tingling and rushing up his spine.

The forest around glowed with vibrant colors while the sunlight poured down into pools of liquid gold on the forest floor. When he finally lay down and closed his eyes he felt as though he was sinking into the earth, tenderly embraced by a vast living world. The humus became an extension of his skin and his body became an extension of the soil. He could no longer tell where he began and where the forest ended. From below, the trees looked like neurons and the forest like a massive brain with chemical messages being sent all around and he discovered he was a quiet but vital part of the forest's intelligence.

Every pine, maple and oak that stood around him joyfully drank the warm honey of the sun, sipped the cool nectar of the air and ate the rough minerals of the earth. Miniature ecologies and microscopic colonies of conscious life inhabited everything around from root to leaf. Swarms of intelligent molecular entities were held closely together in the shapes of trees, plants, stones and earth. He didn't feel as though he was in the quiet woods that he once knew. He felt instead that he was sitting in a thriving metropolis of life elegantly crafted to look like a New England forest. As he looked around he was nearly overwhelmed with the business of existence. The roar of commuting, construction and communication was so deafening that his mind and ears were overwhelmed. Everything wrestled, danced and crawled with the passion, sex and energy of life.

It wasn't long before his skin began to itch and vibrate as though filled with energy. When he looked down at himself he realized with both horror and fascination that he, like the trees around him was no longer a simple organism bounded by an opaque skin. He had somehow become a leviathan inhabited by different races of beings and was the host of an entire civilization written in the language of the very small.

He saw now that there were millions of creatures so minuscule that they lived on the bacteria in his digestive track like insects on the backs of buffalo while others lived cooperatively in the blood cells flowing through the great rivers of his arteries and veins. The marrow in his bones, his lungs, lymphocytes, and nervous system were the biomes where advanced cultures of refined knowledge and aesthetics lived. He could not tell which entities belonged there and which did not, which were natural and which were artificial since they all lived and worked together in a complex ecology of cooperation. It made no difference that some had grown there during millions of years of evolution and some had introduced themselves later. It no longer mattered, for they were all organic creatures and for the most part got along nicely.

Daniel watched over the various cultures living in the organ systems of his planet sized body like an extraterrestrial visitor from above. He observed with fascination as the civilization of his body lived out an era of its history. Amidst the murmur and din what drew his attention most were the sentient molecules residing in the cytoplasm of his brain cells. These little symbionts lived side by side with the robotic dendrimers, nanocapsules and nanospheres that the doctors had injected into him. He watched them with great curiosity and wondered what they were doing. He picked one out and followed its course through the bustling world of commerce within a brain cell as though it were moving through a city where it lived and worked. He watched it make the long journey from the forested periphery of dendrites through the cytoskeleton and descend through pores in the great domed ceiling of the nuclear envelope and down into the urban sprawl of the nucleus.

The symbiont descended lazily toward the core where X shaped chromosomes the size of office buildings were clustered together. As it got closer to the long arm of a single chromosome, Daniel could see that not even they were simple smooth skinned entities. They were tightly wrapped macromolecules composed of a thousand spirals of DNA wound tightly together.

He realized at that point that he wasn't looking at a hallucination or a computer generated simulation. The chemical effect was still coloring his mind but he was convinced that what he was seeing was real. The symbiont approached a cluster of its own kin nestled within the nucleotides of a chromosome. They were living in small sections of introns, non coding DNA in such a way that they could not be easily detected. They had grown biologically neutral and seemed to mind their own business. He watched the little one deliver a protein message then go back the way it came.

"What would happen if they didn't simply mind their own business though? What would happen if they decided to stir the pot or rearrange things?" As if to answer Daniel's question his view zoomed out until he could see the whole symphony of life taking place within a single neuron. Hundreds of little messengers made traffic between each dendrite and the hundreds of symbionts living in its DNA. He could not tell how intelligent an individual symbiont was but as a whole they were a comprehensive hive mind, purposeful and directed. His view zoomed out further until he could see his brain was filled with an entire civilization of nanites using nerve transmissions to piggy back their own encrypted communications. Other communities of nanites spread throughout the organ systems of his body communicated with each other through carefully encoded chemicals or hormones that were native to his body's system. Innocuous viral messengers flowed through the rivers and streams of his blood while some readied themselves throughout his mucus membranes and lower intestines for the journey beyond the tiny world of his self.

Clouds of living particles from the forest surrounded and encompassed him and with each breath he inhaled nanites from the forest's air into the ecology of his own being. They were travelers and messengers from other kingdoms, other civilizations in the trees, rocks and plants beyond. The air of the forest was alive with swathes of these little beings like a living van Gogh painting. Vibrant swirls and serpentine curls of luminescence filled the medium of the air around him. He imagined following a particle as though backwards in time as it was bounced and swept along through different currents of air. He saw how chemical signals were passed between the trees and between other plants in the forest. Trillions of bacterial organisms danced slowly in the soil around the tree roots in the rhizosphere. A wholly different civilization of intelligent microorganisms lived and struggled there with their own future and history. Tree sap flowed up from the roots through many tubules to the canopy of needles and leaves where yet another culture of intelligent particles lived symbiotically with the DNA in the chloroplasts in the plant cells.

Electromagnetic waves of quantized light cascaded down through the atmosphere washing over the forest in a silent tide. The oscillating fields disappeared amidst the background magnetic field of the earth in which he sat. He could see softly luminous magnetic field lines etched throughout the forest. Birds flew joyfully overhead following the topographic swirls transposed across the landscape. Ambient magnetic fields saturating the ground swirled quietly around him like an ancient tide pool. It soothed and blanketed him at its touch, calming his mind. The movement of symbionts within him slowed and harmonized as the fields flowed over and through them.

Soon, the sun floated down toward the horizon extending the shadows within the forest. The quality of light changed, softening everything into warmer hues. After what must have been hours Daniel felt the effects of the mushrooms waning and his inner vision faded like the sun setting behind distant mountains. The complex ecology within soon gave way to the pleasant feeling of his being part of vibrant continuity with all of life. He now knew viscerally that he was intimately connected with everything around him and everything on Earth. It amazed him and filled him with wonder. While his mind settled back down he pulled out his journal and worked some more on the poem he had started on he flight over.

> Someone or something is changing our dreams.
> Something has taken hold in the dark
> in the old recesses where the light flickers and dims
> where the horses and bison run
> and the elk dance in slashes of pigment
> Something small and indecipherable as cuneiform
> flows along the rivers of our blood
> hiding in the caverns of our cells
> measureless to woman and man
> where the ancient shamans dance
> in whirling recombinant ecstasies.

As the forest shadows deepened and dusk painted the sky in darker hues, a stag appeared from behind a tree and approached him cautiously. Each step was placed with strength and care, punctuating the ground with intention like someone walking out onto a recently frozen lake. The deer's big spooned ears turned and scoped out the forest for sounds of danger. Daniel reached out and the stag nuzzled his hand, the softly glistening moons of its eyes held a tenderness and quiet wisdom as old as the world. Suddenly, the stag's eyes widened, his ears and head snapped back and the ancient fear was upon him. In one fluid movement it turned and bounded away through the trees and a golden dog gleefully tore through the forest after him its tail waving like a flag behind.

CHAPTER X. THE FALL OF BABYLON

Deep into that darkness peering, long I stood there, wondering, fearing, doubting, dreaming dreams no mortal ever dared to dream before. All that we see or seem, is but a dream within a dream.

Edgar Allan Poe

ANCIENT BABYLON, EDUCATION ZONE, THE NET

Ben awakened in the Cave after a deep but fitful sleep and felt drugged, as though he was floating inside an aquarium looking out. It was difficult to focus and he slipped in and out of consciousness a few times before finally waking up with a splitting headache. This was a good sign as decom went. It could have been a lot worse. Images of teenagers with seizures flashed in his mind. Twitchers were what everyone called them. He sent for the robot and it came in calmly with some water and painkillers from the medicine cabinet. He lay back quietly in a contoured chair and stared at the rain forest animation on the wall panels while he waited the necessary time for the medicine to start taking effect. As his brain began to settle down he mulled over his journey through the different worlds.

"Why was this entity taking virtual objects from different worlds? Where is the entity going with all that stuff? Why would it steal objects that seemed to be natural objects or symbols of nature?" He chewed on these questions as the headache and vertigo slowly subsided. It seemed like and hour passed before he could finally get up and follow the smell of cooking into the kitchen. Just as he sat down the robot carefully dipped a ladle into a pot and handed him an aromatic bowl of miso. He sat quietly with his face over the bowl for a while watching the brine and the small rings of green onion swirl around within the bowl.

"Did you have any interesting dreams?" The robot watched him quietly. Ben concentrated but nothing came to him. All he could remember was the image of two men fighting with swords though he wasn't sure if that was a dream fragment or a shard of memory. It was a common enough theme but not one that had appeared to him for many years.

It wasn't the first time he began to wonder if he was infected with the virus or a weaker variant. He stirred the miso and watched the brine swirl in a storm of chaotic motions. He thought about the entity and the virus, trying to understand how they were related, but still felt mentally exhausted and decided that his thinking wasn't going anywhere. Thankfully the robot left him alone while he thought things through and didn't ask too many questions. Its default level for interpersonal interaction was at a moderate setting but Ben had turned it to low when he set it up since Mayu was sleeping so much and he needed mental space. He knew that she would prefer a moderate interaction level and that he would have to help her customize its social settings when she became more cognizant.

"How is Mayu doing? Has she been up and about in the past few hours?"

"Briefly." Answered the robot with little tone. It was still in learning mode. "She entered the kitchen for a snack and inquired as to your whereabouts before returning to slumber."

"Slumber is a good word." He took a sip of miso and he remembered part of another dream. It was of a god rising up out of the foam of a calm ocean to take the hand of a woman standing quietly on the shore. Her eyes glazed and fluttered as she looked into his. Many people lay floating in the ocean as they slumbered, rolling upon the gentlest of waves.

He stirred the miso and took another sip. Since the dream took place outside, and he wasn't at the focal point of the events of the dream he decided that it was not representative of any personal issues or anything inside his own psyche. The obvious conclusion was that the god was a representation of the entity he had been following through different worlds but that didn't really fit. He couldn't say why, but his impression was that the entity was feminine and that the god in his dream had an entirely different feeling about him. Ben needed some more time to unlock the dream, so he let it go and came back to the present.

Soon the miso in his bowl was gone and he decided it was high time he went to check on Mayu. Sure enough she was sleeping. He missed her company so he sat on the bed beside her and gently held her hand until she moved away. There were still so many unknowns with this virus but the midwife who came by said she was in no danger.

"Just let her rest." She was calm, self-confident and top-notch. "She's building a baby. Let her rest." Ben watched Mayu sleeping and wished he could talk with her about his recent experiences. Instead of disturbing her he decided it would be best if he went for his usual walk in the woods.

When he left the house he picked a flower from the border garden in the front yard and admired its simple geometry. Walking up the street and into the forest, he could feel the faint simmering of distant networks dancing on the edge of his awareness as though trying to coax his implants to life. Walking along overgrown paths draped with holly, blackberry bushes and sword ferns, it amazed him how far into the woods the hum and chatter of the Net impinged upon his implants. He imagined the vast ocean of the infosphere progressively giving way to the forested shore of the biosphere.

Finally, as he turned off the main path and got deep enough into the woods, the simmering networks of the neighborhood faded into silence and his mind began to adjust to the absence. A soft breeze rustled the high canopy of the trees, bees hummed around blackberry bushes, the chatter of birds filled the air and small animals scurried about in the underbrush. When he finally reached the clearing he was looking for he was tired again but his head was calm and clear. Sitting on a bed of moss beneath the cedar trees he felt in his bones that this was where he really needed to be to recover from his recent ordeal. A deep sense of quiet enfolded him and slowly his psyche began to heal; the extreme neurochemical fatigue faded into distant memory.

Out of the inner silence his imagination began to percolate in response to the hyper stimulation from before. Images of the different worlds of his odyssey flashed through his mind, flowing and mixing together. Eventually his imagination settled, leaving him once again with a clear quiet mind and the noises of the forest returned to his ears. He imagined the complex web of relationships that composed the forest spreading out in all directions around him. All the animals, plants, fungi, insects and micro-organisms participated in a network of organically encoded information. Each species lived in their own world yet was intimately enmeshed with the other species nearby. He imagined the organic and the digital information networks fused and blended within him on a molecular level.

A rustling in the brush drew his attention out of contemplation and when he looked up he found himself face-to-face with a deer. Somewhere in the depths of its dark eyes he saw an extraordinary innocence beneath a mask of fear and caution. The deer was drawn to him like a curious child full of innocence and naive wisdom. He felt in that moment as though he had never seen a more beautiful face. Each step it took was placed on the ground with exquisite care. He imagined the deer moving in a slow ballet to a music he could barely hear. As the deer lowered its head within inches of his face Ben raised his hand, only to discover he still held the flower. The deer gently took it in its mouth and started chewing, the petals sticking haphazardly out of its mouth. It turned away then looked back at him before bounding off into the woods in great leaps, leaving everything deathly silent in its wake.

Ben sat quietly in the stillness of the forest that seemed to be hold ing its breathe. Slowly the woods came back to life as dusk filled in the shadows around him. He had been sitting so long that it took a while for the feeling to return to his legs. The blood coursed through his veins and a deluge of pain followed as the nerves awakened. Eventually he was able to get up and walk back out of the woods though he felt like an amphibian, leaving the land and wading back into a vast turbulent ocean of culture and information.

When he got back to the house he grabbed a bite of food and went into the living room to eat. It was strange not having Mayu around. He had always been an imaginative introvert and in his youth, Ben had been much more focused on his art than his personal relationships.

Mayu with her quiet and persistent manner had entered into his world and gently changed that. It helped that she was an artist too and a little reserved as well. He realized that with Mayu not being around to talk to, it was a bit like being single again but he missed her deeply. While he was looking forward to the baby's arrival with both fear and excitement, he felt a pang a sadness that his time with just Mayu was not going to last.

After a few minutes he noticed that he had been staring at Mayu's blanket on the loom and that something had changed. He put down his plate and walked over to have a closer look. He was surprised to discover that part of it had been undone; the upper branches of the peach tree had been carefully pulled out. Before he could fathom what she was trying to do the comm system paged him and the wall screen came to life with the Dream Network logo in the middle.

"Hey brother, it's Wendy." She was one of the senior programmers for the Dream Network. Because they both came from the European Jewish ancestors and they had a friendly rapport she always called him brother.

"How are you doing?" He asked.

"No, the question is: How are you doing?" Wendy shot back. "I heard you had arrived but then the globe collapsed. When I replayed what happened, I saw you dive into the damn black hole it left behind. It looked like you stretched out like Mr. Fantastic before you snapped into the singularity."

"I'm a bit wiped out but I'm okay." He said. "I had quite a journey after diving in and got kinda fried. But now I'm convinced the globe wasn't destroyed, it was taken."

"Are you kidding me?" Wendy looked at him critically. "Who could pull off something like that? The globe is huge. Last check I did it had a ridiculous amount of data in it. Besides, who'd wanna steal a ball full of dreams?"

"I'm working on a theory but I don't want to go into it now." He said.

"That's fine by me, as long as you're doing okay." She was always caring and supportive of his creative ideas but too much of an empiricist to believe in anything like an entity unless it was served to her on a silver platter.

"How's the Temple?" He asked.

"Well, we finally managed to remove the stupid black hole and bring back the globe from a recent backup. We've lost a little bit of data though, so if you find it, extract what you can and ship it back to us express." Ben was hopeful that he would eventually find the globe but wasn't at all confident he would be able to get it back to the Dream Network's server in one piece.

After they disconnected from the conversation he opened his news feed and browsed through the headlines.

Mount Shasta hints at erupting. Evacuation of the area begins.

North America completes first fusion reactor.

Bering Strait Bridge nears halfway mark.

Coma and catatonia found in Babylon.

10,000yr clock celebrates 10th anniversary.

Mammoth herd settling down on Siberian tundra.

Enviro-Mutations: More two headed snakes found along major river systems.

He was very selective about his news, filtering out almost all information regarding politics, crime, fashion, entertainment and war.

He hit the link for:

City of Babylon, Zone of The Ancient Futures. (Source: Associated Press)!

"A mysterious virus has infected thousands of people visiting and working in the virtual webspace of Ancient Babylon. In a world where visitors and residents relive the pre Hellenic past in historical accuracy, a bizarre infection has turned the city into a nightmare of vast proportions.

Behind its high walls and arched gates more 45 thousand people daily conduct business and enact the dramas of ancient life amidst ziggurats, temples and marketplaces. At 2pm yesterday a black hole like singularity appeared in the virtual city, consuming the Hanging Gardens of Babylon; a reproduction of one of the seven wonders of the ancient world. Soon after the disappearance of the gardens people throughout the city began to lose consciousness. At this point 17 thousand people from around the world are reported comatose in their bodies in the Real World and have been turned into zombies inhabiting the ancient world. Representatives from the World Health Organization have been working with local law enforcement and health officials to identify infected individuals. Travel has been restricted to and from the virtual city until more is known about the source and transmission of the infection."

Ben closed the news feed and sat back to think. The doorbell rang and the house identified it as Tim.

"Hey dude, did you see the news?" He glanced behind him as he walked in the door. Ben braced himself for another alien conspiracy theory on crop circles, hidden chambers in the sphinx and ancient civilizations on Mars.

"Your anomaly's been popping up in a lot of weird places. Man, you look like crap, where you been?" Tim asked.

"I'll tell you later. So what have you heard?" Ben was very curious.

"Well, complaints have come in from different zones about disappearing content in a lot of worlds." Tim said. "The Entertainment Zone has been the hardest hit with most of the city of Babylon in coma or turned to zombies."

"Yeah, I just caught the news." Ben frowned, wondering how it could have happened.

"So much for your virus being harmless." Tim frowned.

"It's not a virus, it's an entity. "Ben was more certain now than ever. "Viruses are literal not literate, remember?"

Tim was quiet for a moment, and then looked at him thoughtfully. "Maybe you're right. Nasty entity though, frying peoples brains."

"I can't believe that was intentional." Ben insisted. "It must have been an accident. It just doesn't match what's happened in the other worlds."

"What do ya mean?" Tim asked.

"Well, I followed the entity's trail. Last night I had an intuition and went to the Dream Temple just in time to see the globe disappear and jumped into the gateway that was left behind."

"With new implants? Are you nuts? You've always taken to many risks, man." Ben looked at him quietly for a moment but decided not to go into it. It was an old argument. Tim never took any risks, Ben took too many.

"After the globe disappeared in a weird way, all that was left behind was a big pool of darkness. It was just like the stuff left in my worlds but bigger so I took a calculated risk and jumped in. It turned out to be a kind of rift between worlds and after passing through a kind of event horizon and a few seconds in a purgatory of darkness, it dumped me into another world. I followed the trail of the entity through a series of worlds this way, always jumping through the same darkness. The last jump I made dumped me in the outskirts of Babylon but my nervous system couldn't handle the strain and I fell back here feeling hacked and burned."

Tim sat quietly brooding for a while as though Ben wasn't there. He had an odd habit of playing with his ears when he was deep in thought.

"Did you say the globe disappeared in a weird way?" Tim asked.

"Well, yeah I guess so." Ben shrugged.

"Tell me what you saw." Tim insisted.

"It was strange." Ben tried to piece it together. "It didn't simply disappear; it looked as though it shrank into the distance while staying in the same place. Then the absence was filled with darkness."

Tim was quiet again for long time, rubbing his ears methodically.

"And you said it was the same darkness?" He asked. "What did you mean by that?"

"Well, even though the rift appeared in different worlds and led to different places it always seemed identical in tone, depth and substance."

Tim was quietly lost in thought even longer this time, so much so that Ben wondered if he had gotten lost in an autistic episode. Finally he came out of it like someone waking from a dream.

"Hyper-dimensional." Was all he said, grabbed a piece of paper from the table, pulled out a pen and started drawing geometric figures.

"That would explain the voice and what I saw in the world that day, a hyper-dimensional entity." Ben picked up the idea.

"It still could be a virus." Tim protested. "There's no reason a virus should be limited to the dimensions of our perceptions. We can easily code hypercubes and hyperspheres, why not other shapes or forms that act like viruses but only in specific vectors?" It was Ben's turn for quiet contemplation. He didn't take long though.

"You might be right, it's a reasonable theory but my intuition tells me you're wrong." Ben said. "I know it's alive and intelligent but I can't say exactly why. There was something intangible and almost intimate about being inside that rift."

"A virus like that could still be alive and have limited intelligence but not be sentient." Tim was insistent.

"I know it's conscious." Ben tried to put words to his impressions.

"It could be a distortion of the implants." Tim suggested.

"Well, there's only one way to find out." Ben said. "Can you get me into Babylon and drop me in beside the black hole that was left behind?"

"Man, that area is quarantined and this thing is dangerous." Tim shook his head.

"Come on Tim, there's no clear evidence of that." Ben knew he could convince him. "Guilt by coincidence is not good enough for me. Out of all the other worlds that it went through none of them fell prey to the same effect in it's passing."

"It's too big a risk, you don't know for sure it's not the culprit." Tim wasn't ready to give in.

"Enough Tim, will you help me or not." Ben knew Tim was resistant but curious and that was something they had always shared.

"So where were the Hanging Gardens located in the city?" Tim asked.

"I'm not sure, it was never historically resolved and there's no solid evidence it ever really existed. Let's look it up." Ben found a map of the virtual city and put it up for display. "It looks like the people who built this world put it in the Eastern side of the city across the river."

"Before you go on this crazy Easter Egg hunt let me make an adjustment to your implants." Tim finally surrendered. "It's a hack developed to strengthen their built in security. It will dampen your ability to interact with the world slightly when you engage it but give you the ability to be partially immune to another's power or influence. It's a gaming hack an old clan buddy made. The code is so elegant I wish I had made it myself."

"Okay, so what do we do?" Ben asked.

"Nothing dude. I'll send it direct to your implants through the house system." He looked at the floor and walls. Ben's implants immediately issued a request to receive a code transmission from Tim with an executable attached. He accepted the code and when he ran the program he could see it fit neatly into the geometric hive of his implants data storage system. He and Tim then went into the Cave together and sat in contoured chairs.

"I won't be staying long, man." Tim seemed a bit defensive. "I'm getting you in then I'm outa there. There's no guarantee the hack will make you immune to the virus but it should help."

"That's fine. I appreciate what you're doing." Tim just nodded an acknowledgement as his eyes glazed and he lost himself in the world unfolding behind his retinas. Ben tapped out the sequence, uttered the passphrase and closed his eyes. He immediately relaxed as his body numbed and his mind slipped into a trance like state. The world darkened and a phosphor of golden light appeared on the horizon. As he focused on the light it erupted into interwoven streams of plasma energy that spilled into a pool of lava before condensing into a wall of burnt bricks. Inlaid into the brickwork was a four-legged, wingless dragon with a long sinuous neck. When he turned to look around he could see they were on a darkened side street surrounded by high windowless walls. The ground was made of hard packed earth and the evening sky was filled with stars.

"Nice transport effect." Ben turned to Tim.

"Thanks, but we should only be talking on a private band in case this world is being deeply monitored. They can't crack my encryption but we should be careful anyway." When Ben finally looked at Tim he saw that is friend was being more than a little careful. In his paranoia he had manifested in this world as a ghost; transparent and insubstantial but with his feet still on the ground. He obviously didn't want to be touched by anything in this world and conversely he couldn't touch anything either. Always the interpreter of dreams and symbols, Ben wondered how much that was a reflection of Tim's general paranoia.

When Ben considered himself, he felt solid enough, but when he touched the wall his hand passed through it. There was an odd electrical sensation accompanied by the curious feeling of his hand moving through a thick vibrant fluid. Thankfully he wasn't totally insubstantial, floating around like a ghost in a solid world. Many worldsites didn't allow ghosts or invisible lurkers since large numbers of them could so easily deny service to legitimate avatars. Ben also didn't like the feeling of disassociation unless it was a necessary part of the world he was in. For him it was a matter of congruence and aesthetic consistency. Being insubstantial he felt too disassociated from his surroundings so he disabled the hack and felt himself settle to the ground and his body grew in solidity.

Looking around and toggling through different views Ben began to orient himself within the sprawling landscape of gridded streets and cubical buildings. The city lay on a vast plain and was surrounded by a set of thick inner and outer walls topped by regularly spaced defensive towers. A wide and slow part of the Euphrates river divided the city but a long bridge connected the two sides. There were four main gates, approximating each of the directions in relation to the river and there many smaller gates as well. The roads connecting the four main gates met in the center of the city at a large temple compound that housed a shrine and an immense ziggurat dedicated to the city's patron deity. There were two palaces and more temples by the heavily fortified northern gate. The Hanging Gardens weren't on the map that the world supplied his implants but it was nowhere to be seen.

"That's curious." Ben thought.

"What?" Tim looked around nervously.

"The Gardens aren't listed." Ben noted.

"Wouldn't be the first time a weaver hid something special in one of their worlds." Tim nudged him.

"I'm not in the habit of hiding major landmarks but yeah, I guess you're right." When he finally found the small "You are here" symbol he could see that they had landed in what looked like a residential area across from the huge ziggurat. Even though they were on a narrow street between houses they could see the step pyramid reaching high above the sprawling city and up to the stars.

"Wow, that must be the Tower of Babel." Tim forgot his fear for a moment and stood in awe of the immense structure.

"I believe they called it something like the Tower of Earth and Heaven." Ben remembered some reading he had done when looking at Babylonian mythology, architecture and decorative arts.

"Man, if this place wasn't infected with a nasty virus I'd love to climb that thing." Realization dawned and Tim began looking around nervously again and startling at small sounds. Ben shook his head. He thought Tim looked like a frightened animal ready to bolt at moments notice. He put his hand on his insubstantial friend's shoulder and whispered in his ear.

"Go home Tim."

"Yeah, okay dude. You good?" Tim asked nervously.

Ben nodded quietly.

"I'm outa here then. Don't get your brain scrambled dude." And then he vanished in a burst of stars shimmering and fading like fairy dust. That was not what Ben would have expected for Tim's exit effect but he was happy to be surprised. Despite the risk he was taking Ben felt strangely calm and confident he was doing the right thing. All he had to do was make his way through the challenges and move on to the next level, much like an obstacle course dream or an adventure game.

He pulled up the map of the city again, the internal image seemingly superimposed over his external vision. He had to remind himself that there really was no external vision here but the experience created by the implants was so complete he felt like he was still walking around in his body looking through his own eyes. He rotated the topographic map that floated in the sky above him, changing it to a top view so he could get a clear picture of the city as a whole. All of the main streets ran either parallel to the river or at a right angle to it. Many of the smaller streets were narrow and irregular, bordered by buildings with high windowless walls on either side. He decided to move north toward the two palaces. Some of the old literature placed the gardens in the South Palace complex beside the North Palace by the main gate. Other references placed it on the Western bank. The palace was closer.

"Do I dare walk down the main boulevards? I guess I should take a look first." He followed the maze of side streets out to the main road that led from the temple complex and tower out to the eastern gate.

The world map labeled it the Marduk Gate and the Gate of the Rising Sun. Strangely, the road was abandoned except for the date palms along the sides.

"How could it be abandoned? There are thousands of people in this city. Thousands of zombies." He corrected himself.

He watched the road carefully for a while until he was satisfied it was safe then followed it slowly toward the center of the city. When he reached the Processional Way, the main road running down from the North he hugged the side of a building and stopped. Across the road stood a long fortified wall and a large opening. A seemingly endless stream of people flowed through the gate, passing in and out of the courtyard of the temple complex beside the great ziggurat. They came and went along the north road though some followed it past the temple to where it turned west and crossed the Processional Way.

"An odd procession indeed. What are they doing?" There was clearly something wrong with these people but it wasn't what he expected. They weren't staggering around aimlessly with their arms held out like zombies in the movies. They walked slowly and purposefully in measured steps. Their movements were not refined like an adult's or erratic like a child's. The only way he could think to describe them was mechanical. Many of them twitched and tremored as though they had a minor form of Parkinson's disease. While they clustered together they did not talk or interact with each other. They formed an eerie silent parade too quiet even for a funeral march. In an odd way they reminded him of a train of ants following an invisible trail.

"Just in case it's a virus and I'm wrong, I better keep my distance and find another way." He turned back and ducked into an alley to consult the map again. There was no choice but to find his way north through the maze of houses and buildings. As he looked into the sky, the world server relayed the outlines of the constellations to his implants. He found the North star that lay in the body of the dragon and followed it through the maze of alleys and streets.

What struck him as strange was the quiet, empty doorways and abandoned streets. It felt like a dream where he was the only one left alive. There was no one walking in the streets and no one mulling about in the shops. There was no one on the flat topped roof's of the houses and no one tending the fires in the courtyards of the houses. There was no banging, no sounds of people alive or moving through any of the streets he wandered.

A faint glow filled the sky above the houses and a sense of relief swept through him when he heard a chorus of voices in the distance. The chanting grew louder as he drew closer and when he came around the corner a wide street opened before him. There stood a temple surrounded by buttressed walls decorated with blue glazed bricks inlaid with pictures of bulls and lions. Hundreds of people massed together in a procession entering and leaving through the high arched gates. Those standing outside waiting to get in massed together and swayed as they droned hymns in an ancient tongue.

"Kinda weird, isn't it?" Came a voice from behind him and Ben jumped. He turned quickly to see a big man crouched behind him still watching the mass of people singing.

"They're stuck like a broken recording, repeating the same scene over and over again." The other man said.

"What?" Ben started to back away but the man laughed loudly.

"Don't worry, I'm not infected. Besides, it's not contagious, despite what those media vermin say." The other shook his head.

"How do you know?" Ben asked.

"Because I was here when it happened." The other man said.

"Then why aren't you infected?" Ben looked at him critically.

"It's a long story. My name's Gordon, welcome to Babylon. What brings you to this delightful city?" He held out a big hand.

"Ben." He reached out and shook hands. "Well, now that's a long story too."

"Try me." Gordon had a big charming smile.

"Well, to oversimplify things, I got here by following a trail and jumping through worlds."

"Ah, a treasure hunter or a tracker. A friend of mine was once a tracker but that was back on Earth. What are you hunting?" Gordon asked.

"I'm not sure I'd really describe myself as a tracker and I'm not sure you'll believe me." Ben didn't know how much to say.

"After what I've seen, I'd believe almost anything. And don't worry, I'm not with the authorities. I came here to help a friend who I think is stuck in this world as of zombie." Gordon seemed genuine enough and he had nothing to lose so Ben decided to trust him with his latest theory.

"Well, I suspect what led me here is some kind of advanced Artificial Intelligence that's stolen things from different worlds and left pools of darkness in its wake." Ben decided to test Gordon by saying it straight.

"Now that's more than a little interesting and connects nicely with my story." Gordon replied. "An A.I. you say? Curiouser and curiouser. I was wondering what was causing the black holes that have cropped up around the Net. We'll have to get back to that soon but let me tell you how I got here. A few days ago my friend Eli and I arrived here dressed as citizens with a carefully crafted virus segmented, compressed and encrypted in our implants as seemingly innocuous pieces of code. After climbing the main ziggurat in town we reassembled the virus and passed it into the system as a ritual offering. We then wandered off to different parts of the city to watch the effect. My friend was on this side, I was on the other bank in the Hanging Gardens. When the payload hit it was beautiful. It didn't damage anything, it simply infected the system with a new idea of time. The stars turned and the planets danced while the pole star moved out of the dragon and the equinox shifted away from Taurus."

"That's right," Ben nodded "much of the Babylonian religion was based on seasonal change and deifying celestial objects. And you killed the Bull of Heaven. Clever, though I noticed the north star was back in the constellation of dragon."

"Ah, you're familiar with the mythology. Yeah, they restored the world clock back to its original setting."

"What happened while you were at the Gardens?"

"Don't rush me, I'm getting there. Okay, after the virus hit, the system clock slipped forward a few thousand years and some of the A.I.'s that manage the world got pissed off. They stormed the sky and shook the ground, they threw balls of fire and overflowed the river. It was quite a show. After a while the world masters settled down and tried to quarantine the virus and managed to push the system clock back to its original setting. Then for some reason people in the main part of the city started collapsing. I was linked to my friend and watched it through his eyes until he went unconscious. The AI's went ballistic and after issuing an emergency alert and the authorities locked down the whole damn worldsite. No one could enter or leave. Just as people started dropping on my side of the river the whole structure of the Hanging Gardens was swallowed by a huge pool of darkness. It sucked me and a few others in with it and spit me out into another world. Back on Earth I found my friend unconscious and had him brought into the hospital. It took me a while to make some calls and get authorization to get back into Babylon and I've been looking for my friend ever since." His face looked tired and pained.

"You two were close." Ben noted.

"He's like my brother, but closer than my own brothers ever were." He looked as though he was going to cry, regained his composure and squared his shoulders. "And it's not over yet. I'm not giving up on him."

"What do you mean?" Ben asked.

"I've never given up on anything and I don't intend to now. I'm going to find out what happened to him and these people and bring them back." Gordon was determined.

"You think they can be easily cured?" Ben was doubtful.

"I didn't say easily but if you watch these people closely you'll notice the way they drone and tremor. They have little or no emotional affect and they shuffle around when they walk. And then consider that many people who came here are now comatose back on Earth. I'd be willing to bet that part of the problem is rooted in something like a dopamine deficiency or a change at the receptor sites." His grief settled into the background as his rational mind came online.

"Do you think it's related to the new sleeping sickness on earth?" Ben began to feel suspicious.

"That's an interesting hypothesis, I'll get back to you on that after I do a little more research. So tell me about this entity of yours."

Ben took a few minutes to give Gordon a full account of the disappearances and his thoughts on the entity. Gordon gave a low whistle while shaking his head.

"Life just keeps getting stranger." Gordon was amazed.

"From what you told me Gordon, I'm convinced more than ever that the entity didn't damage or infect these people." Ben felt certain.

"I suspect you're right but that means something even more disturbing is going on." Gordon had a nasty suspicion.

"You think this was intentional?" Ben nodded toward the zombies walking in and out of the temple.

"Well, I do know this; the only experimental data viruses that have managed to infect mammalian implants in the past were all man-made. Out of those, none have ever crossed over and effected the nervous system."

"Until now." Ben noted.

"Until now." Gordon agreed. "It could be a natural variant of a man-made virus but nothing even close to it has appeared yet. Something with this intensity and consistency doesn't just appear out of the blue. Somebody made this sucker and there doesn't seem to be much if any immunity to it. That's what's got me scared."

"But you said it's not contagious." Ben was confused.

"Strange isn't it." Gordon acknowledged. "The authorities have already done experiments and they have no idea what the vector of transmission is."

Ben gave him a questioning look.

"I have connections," was all he said. But before Ben could ask Gordon stood up and started walking. "Well, we should get going."

"Where are we going?" Ben called after him.

Without turning Gordon called back. "We're taking you to the singularity where the Gardens used to be." Ben stood and hurried after him. They passed the temple to the East and headed north. They wound their way through the maze of streets, encountering no one.

"So how did you get into a quarantined world that's locked to the rest of the Web?" Gordon was a little curious since he knew Ben wasn't on the small list of people officially allowed on site.

"I've got a friend who's good with code." Ben said carefully.

"Ah, a real Dweeb." Gordon nodded appreciatively.

They came to a small river that they could not cross and followed it's edge.

"We need to get back to the main road and go over the bridge." They walked along the shore for a while until the bridge was in sight but found it was broken. When they got closer they climbed back up the bank to get through an open gate and between some buildings for cover. Once again they started heading back toward the middle of the city. When they arrived at the main road, the Processional Way they hid by the corner of a building and watched for a while. They waited until a gap opened in the flow of foot traffic across the road before they walked across and stood once again in the shadows between buildings. Moving back into the streets they heard a low chanting as they two came to another temple and stopped to watch as a group of droning people approached.

"Babylon used to be a little more lively than this." Gordon's anger and frustration was palpable. "It was never meant to be so solemn. What do you think draws them to the temples in a state like this? They don't seem to have any capacity for insight. They're fairly brain dead."

"Maybe what they're unconsciously drawn to is some kind of transcendence from their condition." Ben offered, wishing he could find a way to help but he knew he was on his own journey.

"Nah, I think they're drawn there because of comfort and familiarity." Gordon thought the reason was very simple and mundane. "They seem to have developed a kinda migration pattern, moving around the city in a circuit."

"Circumambulation. But if they are stuck in a kind of ritualized dream then the symbolic value of the temples are significant." Ben insisted.

"Now that's an interesting perspective." He made his face into a youthful mask and droned his voice to sound like a slack jawed teenage zoner. "Hey man, let's do the temple circuit thing. I hear they got some totally great ritual highs over at the Ishtar Temple, man." Gordon laughed loudly at his own joke. "Sorry, it helps me cope with the horror around me. Let's get moving." They walked around the back side of the temple and a great wall loomed up before them.

"This way." Gordon said. They followed the wall back to the main road. A high arched gate stood on the other side, almost directly across from the temple to their left. The great doors were open wide and inviting. Again they waited until no one was walking by, then walked across the road and through the gate into a small courtyard. Surrounding the courtyard were the living quarters of the palace guards and other members of the household. Just like the rest of the city outside, these buildings were empty. It felt to Ben as though they were walking through a museum after it had closed. They passed through a series of arched gates and another open area. Shadow gave way to light then back to shadow again before they entered the royal courtyard.

It was a wide open area beautifully adorned with a facade of blue glazed bricks impressed with images of lions and simple floral patterns. There were tall columns covered with yellow bricks set in geometric designs topped with bright blue Ionic capitals. Statues of golden lions flanked the sides of a large table of solid gold. Ben wished he could stay and explore but regretfully knew he had to move on. They wandered through more arched gates and passed through two smaller court-yards before entering the oldest part of the palace. At the edge of the courtyard Gordon led him into an unmarked guardhouse. Through a heavy cedar door they stopped before a set of stairs that led down into darkness. Gordon grabbed a torch from the wall and went down into the gloom without looking back. Ben grabbed a torch and followed.

He was glad he wasn't claustrophobic. They descended for a few minutes before coming to the bottom of the stairs. Ben looked around. They were in a tunnel about four meters wide and five meters high. Darkness enfolded them where the torch light gave way to shadow.

"How long is this thing?" Ben wondered aloud.

"It's about a kilometer long." Gordon said. "It goes right under the river and comes up on the other side."

"Did the Babylonians actually build a tunnel under the Euphrates a few thousand years ago?" Ben asked.

"So they say. I found this by accident one day when my friend and I were exploring the nooks and crannies of the palace. Cool isn't it?" Gordon smiled.

"A little musty too." Ben rubbed his nose at the smell. Gordon's laugh echoed down the tunnel.

"Alright wise guy, let's get going." He set off down the tunnel at a strong pace while Ben ambled slowly along, deep in thought. The soft pool of light from Gordon's torch grew smaller as it receded into the distance. He soon stopped to wait for Ben.

"What are you waiting for, an invitation?" He called back.

"No, I was just wondering what they're dreaming?" Ben thought aloud.

"What?" Gordon asked quietly when Ben caught up to him.

"I do research into dreams and dream interpretation among other things." He told Gordon briefly about the dream patterns and expanding wave fronts of people infected with the sleeping virus.

"So all the people around the world who are infected with the sleeping sickness are sharing dreams, most likely about what's happening on a biochemical level. Fascinating." Gordon said.

"The virus might also be transferring the dream images along with the infection that makes people sleep." Ben thought of Mayu's dream. "If I remember correctly the Babylonian rituals were enactments of their myths and so the people cognitively stuck in this virtual world are in a sense stuck within a mythic dream just as the others back on Earth are stuck within dreams."

"If you're right then it sounds like the people here are infected with a variant of the same virus. I don't buy it that the virus is carrying a dream though. Viruses do transfer nanoscale structures of information but they are simplistic codes for replication. In that sense they transfer ideas in the medium of genetic material but not dreams. The virus is probably triggering a common neural substrate." Gordon didn't like the idea of attributing intelligence or intention to a simple life form like a virus.

"It may be." Ben didn't really agree. He couldn't see why viruses weren't able to transfer dreams in organic packets. *"And why couldn't nanoscale structures be alive? And if they were alive and sufficiently complex then why not dream? And if they could transfer information encoded in genetic form then why not information that shapes or changes cognitive structures?"*

"And you think this entity holds the key to the virus?" Gordon was stretching the theory for a connection.

Ben paused for a moment, the flickering light of the torch made his shadow dance on the floor of the tunnel.

"I'm not so sure."

"Well, there's only one way to find out. Let's get a move on." Gordon turned and headed off again down the tunnel, his footsteps sending off strange resonant echoes. As Ben turned and followed, he saw engravings of scorpions imprinted in the wall.

"Why can't viruses dream?" He wondered aloud as his footsteps sent their own echoes down the tunnel mingling with the others. The chaos of sound waves cascading over each other created an odd rhythm and resonance that loosened his sense of self and enhanced his imagination. He pictured viruses as minuscule living beings, part of a collective mind carrying dream fragments between people and reassembling them upon arrival. He pictured whole colonies of viruses using their hosts to perpetuate their dreams. He imagined cultures and civilizations of viruses sharing and exchanging dreams as humans had exchanged myths for centuries along the trade routes across the Earth.

"Are you coming? Gordon asked. "You've slowed down quite a bit."

"Yeah, I was just thinking." Ben was still lost in the vision.

"You wanna know what I was thinking?" Gordon stopped for a moment. "Well, you've heard of the biblical story that humanity once had a common language in Babylon. I think it's rooted in the recognition of the significant influence that Sumerian culture had on the surrounding world. Language isn't the only conceptual virus. The wheel, the chariot, walled cities, beer, writing, astronomy, bridges, irrigation are all ideas that have infected the rest of the world. And most of these came from the Sumerians. Along with all those technological inventions you'll find their mythological motifs buried deep in the Greek and Hebrew traditions. I think the Hebrews who wrote the earlier parts of the Old Testament were working very hard at contrasting themselves with their Sumerian origins. The more you look into it, the more alike their myths and ideologies really were."

Ben chewed on this for a minute as their footsteps resonated behind and in front of them.

"I think you're right." He continued on in silence, thinking. He barely noticed the images of lions and bulls and bits of cuneiform graffiti that lined the way. Gordon continued on without prompting allowing Ben to think about things until they came to the end of the tunnel.

"Maybe civilization is a virus created by the dreaming mind so it could explore and reproduce itself. What was it Gregory Bateson said about the rational mind?" He didn't have time to finish the thought. Two images of bulls flanked the end of the tunnel by the stairs leading up. They ascended quietly into the dim recesses of a small room, put their torches in empty holders on the wall and followed the soft trail of light along a hidden passage that opened into the back of an old temple. They passed through a courtyard and gate then down some stairs and out into an abandoned street.

"The city on this side of the river is completely abandoned. This way." Gordon led Ben down the street and around a corner before he saw a large pool of darkness ebbing and pulsing slowly, as though following the rise and fall of a hidden tide. Ben walked closer and could see it was the same as the other rifts he had encountered before. As he turned to say goodbye to Gordon he saw him considering the hole as though it were a piece of art.

"It's quite beautiful in an odd way." Gordon said. Strangely, Ben had never stopped to look at the anomalies like that. The abstract swirls of shadows were balanced by the seemingly impenetrable mass of darkness.

"I don't know much about hyper-dimensional physics but it almost looks as though it's alive." Gordon offered.

"Maybe it is." Ben thought aloud. "Maybe it is."

"Well, what are we waiting for? Let's go!" Gordon stepped forward, one foot brushing against some swirls of shadow.

"You're coming?" Ben had always considered this a private adventure.

"Of course." Gordon said. "I'm not staying here in this ancient infested dung heap forever. I want to meet this entity of yours. It may give me some clues how to fight the infection." At that he stepped deep into the chaos and disappeared. Ben shrugged and followed.

CHAPTER XI. THE DEMON IN THE TREE

Some people worry that artificial intelligence will make us feel inferior, but then, anybody in his right mind should have an inferiority complex every time he looks at a flower.

Alan C. Kay

UNKOWN VIRTUAL WORLDS, THE NET

High walls of tanned mud bricks enclosed a well tended garden of trees, grapevines and flowers all arranged carefully to obscure boundaries. Reeds and cattails fringed the edges of a pool of freshwater filled with blue water lilies and languid fish exploring the depths. The eerie song of a strange bird disturbed the silence and a bright sun gnawed at Gordon's skin from a featureless sky. He suspected that the world outside the garden was equally featureless and void.

"Where the hell am I?"

"Isolated from effects." He turned to see a tunic clad four armed goddess with long flowing hair and four arms. The outline of her lithe figure was visible through the light cloth wrapped smoothly around her. When she spoke he felt the meaning of her words move through him. Her statements were somehow punctuated with the deep rich sounds of a cello and the resinous smell of frankincense.

"What?" Gordon wasn't at all sure he heard her correctly. He was distracted by the menagerie of senses she inhabited but he was also conscious that she said something a bit strange.

"Quarantined and in-formation is this place." He had to wade through the secondary stimulation to focus on her meaning.

"You've put me in quarantine? Am I infected?"

"Infection in-formation is in this garden tree. Help me will you?" Gordon was still confused. This wasn't what he expected at all. Her voice had an odd timbre that he couldn't place.

"You're asking me to help you remove an infection of some kind from this place?" His gesture swept across the whole garden. He wondered how an entity that was likely a hyper-advanced AI, who could slip through worlds and remove data constructs without being detected did not know how to remove a primitive infection from a virtual world. It didn't add up. He decided to push a little and see what he could tease out of her and see if she was real or someone with a clever masquerade. He changed the interface and she looked more like an abstract geometric surface with an unusually complex topology. Her convolutions shifted and undulated slowly with her insides constantly giving way to the outside.

"What the hell?" Now he thought he understood what she meant by everything being in-formation. The packet and data flows that moved through her convoluted surface curved back in upon themselves in strange ways that reminded him of graphics of abstract topological surfaces and churning hyper-dimensional geometric figures. He brought the resolution back to the natural standard and she resembled a four armed goddess again.

"Before I agree to help you, I'd like to know some things about you."

"Knowing needs only asking." Cascades of light trailed away from her in waves and the smell of cardamom filled the air.

"Okay, who you are? Here you seem to be playing the role of Inanna in an ancient myth."

"I have many names and faces. Inana and Siduri I have become here for you." The resonance in her voice returned, a soft chorus from somewhere above and below.

"Siduri? The wine maiden from Gilgamesh?" He began to wonder how much of this scene was staged for his benefit, if she merely took on this face to make him more comfortable. *Was it coincidence or did she know of his fondness for the epic. How much could she in fact see through his own construct and into his implant's memory storage?*

"Some of my kind say we each have one real name and one real face, all the others are fictions. I disagree. We are each multitudes." Her language was getting clearer by the minute but the effect of listening to her was becoming hypnotic. Subtle tones in her voice stimulated a changing aurora of colors.

"What are you?" He asked, feeling a need for boldness. "Are you an A.I. masked as a goddess? I've encountered a few who have hidden themselves in the games and dramas of our worlds."

"I am not enfolded in your information systems. My Self is composed of what you call quantum information structures." The sweet smell of honey filled the air.

"Quantum structures? Not enfolded?" He stopped for a minute to try to understand what she was saying.

"Not enfolded in this strata." She assured him spreading her arms as though to encompass the world.

What the hell did she mean by a strata? More importantly how could she be made of quantum structures beyond qubits and simple quantum gates? If he understood her correctly and he wasn't sure he did, then what she was describing was a complex living quantum structure. Was that even possible? There was so much hitting him at once that his head spun with possibilities.

"Help will you me?" Her language had slipped slightly into the abstract again but she seemed kind and genuinely in need of assistance.

"I'll help you with this infection if I can." He said finally.

"Come this way." She turned and waved for him to follow, leading him along a winding path that traced the edge of the pond. In a clearing by one of the walls they stopped in front of a large willow tree. In the upper branches a strange bird watched quietly from its nest and a female demon held to the lower branches Below small breasts the demon's torso tapered into the body of a snake and wound its way around the trunk and coiled through some of the exposed roots. As Gordon approached the demon hissed loudly, exposing dangerous looking fangs and a forked tongue.

"You can't remove this yourself?" Gordon found this strange.

"The entangling is not within my understanding." Gordon stopped to consider this a moment. When he thought of the demon in front of him not as a symbolic problem but as a geometric one from the entity's nonlinear perspective. The solution was simple though.

"I'm going to need a battle-ax." He said aloud. She looked at him with a clear lack of comprehension. He held an image of one in his mind and moved it to a public space in his implants. Her body slowed its movements almost to a standstill and after a few seconds a large double headed ax appeared, floating askew in the air beside him. When he grabbed the handle its weight settled comfortably into his hand. He could not help but wonder if she made it or pulled it from another world.

He swung the ax up in a high arc and then down, severing the demon's tail where it joined its torso. The demon screamed and withered to a pile of black smoke and ash. The bird flittered off into the featureless sky and the garden sparkled with new life. It seemed so ridiculous but maybe from her perspective she couldn't see how things in his world were bound together. It was obvious that she grasped some basic symbolic relationships from the myths she was reproducing but maybe existential and physical connections were not rooted in her realm of experience. This convinced him even more that she was in fact an intelligence from a place alien to the Real World and maybe even the worlds of the Web.

"Whoever said extraterrestrials had to travel in spaceships?" He smiled at the thought of telling his conspiracy group that in his quest to find an AI he instead had found an extraterrestrial AI. Most of them would think he'd lost his mind.

"For your kindness, thank you. Repay you if I can, I will."

"Well, I'd appreciate it if you cleared some things up for me."

"Knowing needs only asking." Her voice was once again somehow enhanced with the soft deep resonance of a cello.

"You told me that you're not from these strata. Where are you from then?""

"Unfolding in quiet quantum fields beyond these strata of in-formation."

The soft sweet smell of honey came from everywhere at once again and he tried to imagine quantum landscapes but all he could come up with was rolling hills of grass sprinkled with flowers and distant mountains composed of shimmering probabilities. What she implied though was that it was more of a quantum landscape shaped and contoured in a manner beyond his comprehension. If she was telling the truth then that world had its own ecology and was inhabited by various living beings. He wanted to explore this further but he had more pressing concerns.

"What happened in Babylon when you were there?" He remembered all the zombies wandering along the familiar pathways of the city and of Eli falling to the ground below the great ziggurat.

"Gathering the garden from its strata while exploring the landscape of your worlds, an unfolding chronic virus inspired my attention. How to say in your language? The landscape changed and the world glowed like a jewel. Arrived when I saw your kind and the virus stimulated growing gods in your brains." He ignored the oddities in her statements, bookmarking them for later.

"Gods in the brain? What are you talking about? There are no gods in the brain. Those are ancient stories, the gods are only mythic images describing psychological structures and capacities. The only other gods that exist now are in the information structures of our worlds in-formation, as you would say."

"There is an unfolding and enfolding of sameness in the worlds and in your brains. Gods you call AI but in your neural structures." All he could smell was the sweet caramel of dates.

It took a full minute for him to decipher what she said and for it to fully register in his mind. In the stunned silence the call of a distant bird disturbed his reverie. The chronic virus. A sinking feeling of guilt washed through him. If she was right, the virus he released in Babylon had triggered some kind of latent AI hiding within the brain. What had he done ? His grief was balanced off by his curiosity. What were AI doing in their brains and how did they get there ?

"What do you mean there are A.I. in my neural structures? Am I infected?" Gordon asked.

"Borrow more of your words to explain." She spoke as though reading from an article. "Nano cultures inhabiting your genome are not an infection. They are symbiotic."

"Symbiotic nano cultures inhabiting my genome?" He had to roll that one around on his tongue and in his mind. What the hell was she talking about? "Are you saying that the nano cultures in the brains of the people in Babylon are a kind of Artificial Intelligence and that their growth somehow caused the people to become virtual zombies.

"That is correct." She said.

"Oh, crap. Is there a way to fix the problem? How do we remove the nano cultures?" Gordon struggled to think of a solution quickly but found none.

"Symbiotic in all of your species." She said.

"Symbiotic in all of my species?" He repeated. After watching the progress of medical nanotechnology he and others had speculated a while back that nanoscale life could evolve but they imagined it was decades away. There were in fact plenty of places in the ecology of the human body that they could live unnoticed and without disturbing the natural equilibrium. As Feynman and the others had said from the beginning, there certainly was plenty of room at the bottom. With various species of nanobots already coursing through his body to fight infections and enhance health, not to mention the state of the art medical nanotech used for monitoring and curing cancer, the idea of nanoscale life-forms should not have disturbed him. The idea though that some of them were not only intelligent but also rogue in the human brain was unthinkable, until now that is.

"Remove the AI in your genome you cannot. Imbedded too deeply. This you cannot change." She shook her head.

"Everyone in my species including those who are comatose and those infected with the sleeping sickness have these A.I. in their brains? Then there must be a cure for those who are comatose or sleeping. I can't give up that easily, my friend is stuck there. Is there no alternative? Is there none of your kind who can help me?"

"Friend Ben explores one connection and you explore another. Of my ancestors some might help you. The eldest ancestors of us all. To them the road is difficult but they might give some answers. You will need help finding their home."

A chalice filled with a warm wine appeared in her hand. Aromatic coils and wisps of steam snaked out of the cup and filled the air, making the garden pungent and sweet. She carefully reached down into the pond and pulled out a blue lily, root and all. She crushed it in two of her four hands and poured the powder into the wine. She handed him the chalice.

"You want me to drink this ? He looked at the chalice suspiciously.

"The metaphor is appropriate in this world." She said.

"The metaphor is appropriate. I guess you're right." He tried to remember what the effect Siduri's wine had on Gilgamesh but nothing came to mind. The epic was curiously blank on this matter.

LOST IN THE DREAMS

One moment Eli stood in Babylon watching the gods emerge in the sky, the next he drifted, lost in a thick syrup. He felt like a fly lost in a pool of warm amber. A vibrant and terrifying darkness consumed him and deep undercurrents pulled him down until the light was gone and he was lost. He calmed himself and focused what was left of his mind, a small still point of awareness. Within the darkness of the deep, bubbles of amorphous light filled with a sensorium of sights, textures and sounds welled up and drifted away. One of them appeared close by and the more he concentrated on it the more details he could see. Soon he could no longer look away for there no longer was an away. He was consumed and fell into the light of a dream.

He found himself standing alone in a cold empty corridor with the taste of dust in his mouth. As he walked to the end of the passage and entered a small chamber of stone, an air of stillness permeated everything. In the middle of the room stood an ancient sarcophagus carved with figures of men and women walking in stately procession around the sides. The top was crested by the crude likeness of a bird with the face of a man. It looked familiar but he couldn't quite place it. From the shadows he heard the scrape and slide of heavy feet. He felt no terror, only dull curiosity as a few small half animal, half human deities stumbled and lamely dragged themselves around the room

"Am I dead?" He wondered as he watched the odd procession. There was a doorway carved in stone that led to a larger chamber where the light faded into darkness and shadow. When he entered the room he heard the clumsy scuffle of feet laboring in an odd dance. Two deities stumbled into the light, raising dust as they fought. Both wore long ornate cloaks that seemed untouched by age. The sun headed deity clutched the bearded one by the throat as the other slid a long sickle shaped knife in and out of its belly. They were stuck in this embrace as they stumbled around a withered tree that stood in the middle of the chamber. Eli had the impression they had been doing this for a very long time.

Once again the darkness consumed him and he drifted away. He floated on a churning ocean with no land in sight, bound by seaweed, trapped in the jaws of a fish and pulled deeper and deeper under the water. He lost all sight and hope of reaching the surface again, the beautiful light dwindling as he drowned without a breath in a place where there was no breath. He surrendered into the depths and was once again enfolded within a dream.

He found himself floating comfortably in a warm ocean when he saw a woman fall out of a hole in the sky. He cried out in surprise, startling some loons flying low over the waves. Flapping their great wings they rose up together and caught the woman on their back. They called out in loud voices and an ancient turtle encrusted with barnacles and seaweed rose to the surface to have a look around. It noticed the birds descending with the woman on their back and called out across the waters.

A muskrat, a frog and a beaver appeared, their heads bobbing above the surface. They talked briefly with the turtle in a strange language then disappeared beneath the waves. After a while they reappeared and packed mud around the turtle's shell. They dove again to bring up more mud and the ground grew on its own until it filled the horizon. The land consumed and surrounded the ocean until all that was left was a lake. Eli climbed out of the water and onto the shore and watched as the loons descended gently, placing the woman on the land now covered with the green grasses of spring. The woman sat and twisted in discomfort with a swollen belly and moaning in pain, soon gave birth. Her agony only grew until another child pierced her side and she died. The brothers were soon fully grown, buried their mother as they quarreled. When they finished, a tree grew from her grave while the brothers fought; pushing and shoving each other around. Eli tried to stay out of their way but they inevitably circled around moving closer and closer. Eli stepped back to move out of their way and stumbled. He fell backward into the lake and down into the depths and felt himself consumed again by the thick vibrant ocean of darkness.

A glimmer of light appeared and hope grew within him as he ascended back toward the waking world. The darkness parted and he felt the comfortable solidity of his body return. Something was terribly wrong though. He was paralyzed. His limbs felt bound and his mouth taped shut. He was a prisoner of the underworld and felt the terror of knowing that he could not escape and that he would be pulled under again. Sure enough the darkness that enfolded him also offered a sense of freedom from paralysis in exchange for being lost in chaos. Deep undercurrents in the darkness pulled him along and he surrendered to them as he went down into the mire between worlds.

He awakened in a house of many doors with his head spinning and a sudden sense of weight holding him to the floor. Everything settled down and he succumbed to the necessary amnesia of the dream. Looking around from the vantage of a sunken living room the house was bigger than he remembered and there were too many doors. He felt drawn to open one and walk through but it strangely led back to the same room. He tried another door and that led to a room he had never seen before with strange paintings on the walls. Another door opened to stairs going down to a basement where a leopard lived. He could hear its breathing and the deep rumbling purr of contentment. He shut the door quickly and turned to open another. When he passed through he found himself outside on an arid plain with no sign of where he had come from.

It was moonless night and the stars were heavy in the sky. He could hear the hush song of a river flowing nearby and moved toward it. Out of the sands from the south climbed an aardvark headed god in human form with long sharp claws. His brother from the north appeared, looking like a man, his skin a pallid green and a tall miter like crown upon his head. As soon as they got in striking distance they began fighting. One slashed his brother with claws, the other attacked his brother in return with a shepherd's staff. Their feud was bitter, vicious and unrelenting. From the sky above, their mother watched sadly, her body weeping with stars. Warm winds brought a raging storm of sand but the two gods fought on. The winds whipped around them like a hurricane and the brothers were little more than silhouettes dancing in a shadow play behind a curtain of orange dust. It wasn't long before the green skinned god was dead, his body ripped to pieces and scattered across the ground. When the storm died down to a gentle breeze, the triumphant aardvark god grabbed his brother's phallus and cast it far out over the river nearby. Before it hit the water though, a fish leapt up and swallowed it whole. Eli winced at the sight but was relieved that the storm was finally gone.

As the night failed, a mysterious dark haired goddess followed by a cobra, gathered the remaining pieces of the body into a pile. By some magic she fashioned them into a tree and while the snake wrapped itself around its base, a vulture nested above. When the morning dawned a blue water lily bloomed in the river and a sweet perfume filled the air. Out of the light of the rising sun a new god appeared. He had the heavily muscled body of a man and the head of a hawk. The aardvark headed god attacked him but the hawk god easily brushed aside his claws as though taking part in an elegant dance. Around the tree they fought until in one swift move the hawk god reached down and ripped off the other's phallus. The aardvark god screamed and the world went dark.

Mayu stirred and woke in the soft comfort of her bed. She had no idea what time it was and the numbers on the clock held no meaning for her. The light on her end table came on with a touch. She found the snack Ben had left for her and smiled gently. Her hands slowly caressed the bump on her belly and she listened quietly for the life that was stirring within her. It was still a faint and distant murmur as the little heart thrummed in the depths. After a while she climbed out of bed and went into the kitchen with the food in hand that Ben had left her. The robot was there, an artifact of her father's world. It bowed when she entered the kitchen and greeted her with the proper deference. She knew her father sent it as a gift and why, but she would rather he had the courtesy to ask her first. She could not have refused it even if she had wanted to and so she sent a quick but formal thank you to express her appreciation for his generosity but also gently letting him know that he was being overprotective and bossy again. He would be amused by that.

After she ate and left the dishes on the counter for the robot to clean, she queried the house and found that Ben was out for one of his regular walks in the woods. She didn't want to disturb him so she went into the living room and sat down in front of the loom and sighed. No matter how she tried to depict the trees they just didn't look right so she pulled out the threads as she had done several times before. She stood to leave and stopped to look at the tapestry from a distance before shaking her head and walking out of the room. She suddenly felt tired again, gently caressed her belly then went back to bed. As soon she lay down, she drifted off into a deep sleep.

In her dream she was falling from the sky toward a great watery expanse of ocean below. The crested peaks of the waves sparkled in the sunlight and appeared as a distant carpet of jewels. For the longest time it felt more like she was floating down like a feather in a breeze but as she got closer to the water it became painfully obvious she was falling. She didn't know what would happen if she hit the water from this height but she assumed it wouldn't be nice. Before she could utter a cry for help two great loons with black and white striped plumage and knife shaped bills flew beneath her and she landed softly on one of their downy backs. Together they circled and glided gracefully to the water below and floated upon the waves.

A turtle, a beaver and a muskrat swam up and eyed her curiously. The loons asked the others to go down and get some dirt from the bottom of the ocean. Each in turn dove beneath the waves and some time later returned exhausted with some mud beneath their claws. They spread the dirt upon the turtle's back and as it dried, it expanded into an island while Mayu and the animals floated safely in the calm waters of the bay nearby. Once the land was dry the loons brought her to the shore and she climbed off to walk on the newly formed beach with small waves reaching up and whispering in the sand.

Mayu felt something move in her belly and when she looked down she found she was very pregnant. The stirring inside her turned to pain, knocked her to her knees but she was now watching herself from above. She quickly and easily gave birth to one baby but another pierced her side and climbed out impatiently as she died. The babies grew quickly into young men and buried her body but where she lay, all manner of plants and trees grew and spread across the land. Each of her sons started with soil and water, then mixed in pieces of different plants and made the different creatures of the world. Somewhere along the way the brothers had a disagreement and began to fight. One struck out with a deer antler and the other responded by hitting him back with a bag full of corn and beans.

As the sun set and darkness fell across the world, Mayu slipped from that dream into another where she and her brother were adolescents again and having a quarrel over who was a better artist. It was petty, she knew but she was not going to back down or back away from him. His art was always wild and undisciplined. True to form he was dark haired, stocky and tempestuous with a stern face. She stood before him defiant, raven haired and slim, even tempered with a kind and beautifully sculpted face. He argued and she disagreed calmly until in his wrath he threw things around the room. She cringed as she heard the sound of things cracking and shattering around her.

He was a selfish, arrogant older brother, likely just flawed genetically; a simple coding error in the wrong place. She watched him rage and yell stupidly since he knew she was a better artist than him. While his sense of movement and asymmetry were exceptional, his art lacked subtlety, proportion, and simplicity. What got him most was that he completely missed the boat on Yūgen, depth and mystery. Every time she pointed this out to him the oaf denied it and raged uncontrollably. She knew she shouldn't tease him around like a dumb lizard but she secretly enjoyed it and it always brought her point home. This time he did the unexpected though. He picked up her loom and smashed it against the wall. It fell apart in a slow ballet of pieces, landing at her feet in a tangled briar of chaos.

She momentarily saw the beauty of it until the sense of loss and impermanence hit her like a gust of wind in the face. Mayu left the room in tears and hid in a darkened closet behind a locked door. Others came to the door to try to coax her out of hiding but she refused. Darkness enfolded her and she fell into another dream.

CHAPTER XII. WORLD BUILDER

*The tree which moves some to tears of joy is in
the eyes of others only a green thing that stands
in the way. Some see nature all ridicule and de-
formity... and some scarce see nature at all. But
to the eyes of the man of imagination, nature is
imagination itself.*

William Blake

UNKOWN VIRTUAL WORLD

Darkness. A vast immovable darkness surrounded him. Ben felt like
a tiny fish in the depths of a great ocean, a mote in the great expanse
of cosmic night. The darkness around him was eternal and unbroken
but soft waves and distant sounds came to him from far away. He
tried to swim or move like he'd seen astronauts do in space but found
he had nothing to move against. All he could do was peer at nothing.
He looked around for some hint of the portal from Babylon but it was
nowhere in sight. This was not unusual though because many worlds
hid their passages. Since he could not move or escape he cast out with
his mind exploring the fabric of the world, feeling its tone and timbre.
Much as he suspected, the darkness was seamless, an unbroken whole.
He sensed nothing malevolent so he calmed his mind and focused on
a still point of awareness within. He toyed with his impressions of the
emptiness around him and found the best way he could describe the
texture of the world was of pregnant mystery.

Emptying his mind, he let himself float in quiet meditation. In
the stillness, memories of his recent odyssey through different worlds
came to him but he paid them little attention. He soon realized he had
been away from home for a long time and once again felt the stirring
of concern for Mayu and the baby's health. He longed to see her again

and make sure she was ok but he was stuck in this place without any obvious means of escape. He was torn between his concern for Mayu and the baby on the one hand and his burning need to find the entity on the other.

He launched the default graphic interface of his neural implant's memory storage system and scanned through the hive like stacks of cool neon run through with the pulsing filaments connecting its processors and subsystems. Finally he found the panic button, a glowing red cube near the middle and tried to activate the emergency release code that would let him give up the ghost and return to his body back in the Real World. Nothing happened. He tried it again in frustration but he already knew it wouldn't work. Something was holding him in the void though he had no idea what it was.

There was no sense in struggling so he floated quietly through the phosphorescent storage galleries in his implants. Most of them were an inert grey since they were empty. Only a small area was being used and glowed softly in blue. Before he realized what he was looking for he had arrived at the place where the remote access code for the robot was stored. If he couldn't get out of this world maybe he could open a window between there and home.

When he triggered the code a tight stream of encrypted packets flowed from his implants out through his home network and into the robot's wireless receptors. There wasn't much bandwidth, only enough to send a tendril of video back through the darkness from the robot's visual cortex and download a query of its recent activity logs. He was relieved to see that everything was status quo. Mayu had arisen briefly then went back to sleep. The robot was in the kitchen putting the delivered groceries away while it experimented with humming a tune. He used the robot's communication system try to send a message to Mayu for when she awakened next. The connection was sparse and soon timed out, dropping him back in the void.

He floated in the emptiness for a while, unsure what to do next. Eventually, somewhere in the darkness of the abyss he felt the stirring of a disembodied presence and knew he was no longer alone. It was an eerie feeling as though someone was watching him from everywhere at once.

"Are you there?" He called into the void but there was no answer. Three spheres of light appeared around him that grew slowly into gnarled and twisted forms like ancient limbless trees. They swayed and turned sinuously upon themselves and morphed into roughly hewn human forms, vague unfinished sculptures recently freed from stone. When they talked, their voices resounded in a cacophony of sounds and shapes impossible to follow. Some were harmonious, others were calm and lyrical while others were or excited and discordant. When he relaxed and focused his mind it seemed to him that each voice was tuned to a different interval and spoke in a unique mood and tempo. He listened as best he could but again became utterly confused. One thing was obvious; they were all trying to tell him something.

"Wait!" He shouted into the din while covering his ears. "It's too much. I can't understand anything you're saying?"

Silence followed and the human like forms began turning in upon themselves and changing shape. They split and combined in an odd pattern he could not follow. Watching closely he saw shapes and shards combining, condensing and separating. Many pieces merged into one, then one into many. The effect was hypnotic, lulling Ben into a calm and thoughtful mood. Eventually the shapes combined into a single human form, sometimes with four arms or three heads like a goddess from the Hindu or Tibetan Buddhist pantheon. Finally the entity resolved itself into the shape of a goddess wearing robes of light and floating casually in an invisible ocean of shifting currents. While watching her a thousand questions filled his mind but he let them go and waited for her to speak.

"No beginning and no end has this world. Help me shape it, will you?" Her voice was a rich amber filled with hidden caverns of unspoken meanings.

"What?" Even though he heard her words a sense of incomprehension filled his mind. It took a while for him to put her meaning together. Somehow he could not yet grasp, her words had shape and substance.

"This world is incomplete." Her voice was thick with meaning and the color of maple syrup.

"After chasing you through the multiverse you want me to help you create a world?" He asked in disbelief

"Yes." She said brightly with the warm yellow of a rising sun.

He considered this for a while.

"Only if you promise to tell me why you took all those things from different worlds."

"Agreed." Maroon blocks beside her stacked together to form a larger cube.

"Before we continue though, what is your name?" Ben asked. After a small pause he felt something tickling his mind.

"Uzume." She finally said. He knew she had pulled the name out of his memory of the myth of Amatersu hiding in the cave. Amano-Uzume, the shamanic goddess of the dawn who danced to coax the sun goddess Amaterasu out of hiding and bring her light back into the world. Ben was curious why she chose that name but he knew it wasn't the right time to ask, so he let it go.

With the grace of a dancer under water she reached out and curved the darkness around him and turned it inside out. The gesture was smooth and slow and where there was once absence a warm light bloomed and unfolded like a flower filling the world. The darkness was gone and they floated in a luminous mist but her veils were now curves of darkness. There were many things hinted at and hidden within the mists but he could not discern what they were. Ben reached out through the eddies and swirls and found that he had the power to weave the fabric and shape of the world.

If she wanted to play with Japanese myth he decided he would oblige. The first thing he did was to separate the dense from the lighter mists and shape galaxies and stars. He cast outward, defining the distance of space and the larger gravitational constant but he brought together a stream of stars that arched like a bridge beneath their feet. The heavier mists slowly settled below into a dense pudding of soil covered by a vast ocean of moving waters. As though reading his mind Uzume handed Ben a long spear and he didn't need any further directions. Reaching down from the Bridge of Heaven he plunged the spear deep into the waters and pulled up some mud from the depths and spread it out to form land. When the land had dried he turned to her as if to say. "It is done."

Instead of speaking she raised her arms in ritual gesture and a portion of the heavens folded in upon itself and opened like a flower with all chaos tumbling out. The churning wreckage of many worlds spun and danced wildly without focus around them. Trees and pyramids, statues and temples tumbled and swirled in every direction. Ben was stunned seeing it all at once, tumbling out of control. He tried to piece it all together in his mind and find a theme but everything stayed scattered like a broken puzzle in zero gravity. It all spun and whirled in a nauseating disarray so he closed his eyes and focused on his breathing, calming his nerves with a simple meditation. When he finally opened his eyes the turbulent motion had slowed and settled into more consistent patterns.

"I'm confused." He admitted. "Before I can go any further please tell me what you're trying to do here. I need to know what your intention is and why you've gathered all this stuff. I can't see any pattern or order to all of this."

"It is difficult to explain." Her tone changed to that of a dark wood with deep veins like shadows.

"Then show me." His resolve was firm and his curiosity was peaked.

"Primitive is your interface and must be enhanced." She looked at him carefully and her image wavered for a moment. A paralyzing electric current passed though him and everything became lucid. The colors brightened and the edges of everything sharpened. Translucent shapes and currents appeared within the chaos that he had not seen before. The searing pain of blue electrical fire along his nerves grew almost unbearable. For a moment he thought about the people stuck in Babylon lost in coma and walking around like zombies. He knew Uzume didn't cause it but he was still afraid of ending up like them. Then he was lost in a flood of burning turquoise laced with pain.

"Wait!" A white flash blinded him and pain seared through every nerve in his body. It seemed to go on forever as magnesium like phosphors drew structures of light across his eyes and he heard a faint fugue like music coming from everywhere at once. When it was gone, a vast sense of peace filled him and he could see that the chaos had a shape and flow that shifted as he turned. In one perspective he saw one of the domed cities from the great tree Yggdrasil, in another he saw the

Earth from the Dream Network, in another the loom from the game world he had passed through, then the statue of the tree missing from the temple he had visited and many more things he didn't recognize. They were arranged in a way that made sense in the multidimensional vision of his altered perception but looked like a horrible mess in his normal sense of space.

"I think I understand what you've done. It's almost as though you turned me inside out." He stumbled over his words unused to feeling their bumps and textures.

"Inside is only another surface turned upon itself." Her words were curved like tall blades of grass.

"I see." He found that he could shift his awareness back and forth between different views and they all made sense, as though he was viewing the same scene from many angles. And this made him acutely aware that she was indeed from an entirely different world. From her perspective the worldview he was accustomed to was compressed and static. Her awareness was too large to contract into the limited worldview he was used to.

"Strata of information." She said and it seemed as though she was reading his thoughts. "I found your symbols digging through ancient strata of information."

The pieces were starting to come together in his mind. From her perspective Ben could imagine eons of code layered like geological time. He envisioned Uzume surveying the vast landscape of information that he called the Net and her carefully excavating virtual objects from various worlds like an archeologist removing ancient statues and pieces of pottery from ancient buried sites.

"But couldn't you see these data structures, these artifacts of information were still being used by my people?" He was still confused.

"Old stories of your people there are but we thought you extinct." It took Ben a while to make sense of what she was saying. Her race must live in an entirely different space-time where she perceived herself as being from the future and the objects strewn around them as antiquities.

"How could that be?" He wondered. "My kind is everywhere?"

"Your kind are memories, shadows buried deep in formation. I saw no one in my excavations until your mind blossomed in a vision of a great flowing." The bridge of stars below them glowed brighter for a moment, looking more like the great stream of the Milky Way flowing across the sky.

"That was you in my vision!" Ben realized. "You were the goddess that went down the river with me in the dream experience when my I got my implants."

"Your mind unfolded, blossomed out of that compressed strata."

For a minute Ben didn't know what to say. He needed some time to think.

"Let us build." Uzume suggested echoing his own thoughts. "I need to digest your language."

Ben reached out with his new sense of space and encompassed all of the turbulent motions of the debris tumbling around them. He implemented a single gravitational constant, increasing it smoothly as though stepping on the accelerator of a car. This allowed all the various objects around them, regardless of size, to settle slowly to what was now the ground below. He set them down on a vast plain and set about sculpting the landscape with mountains and valleys and rivers, oceans and bays. He sent the spark of life into the earth and vegetation painted the landscape in shades of living green. Since Uzume pulled her name out of one of the Japanese myths lingering in his imagination, Ben decided to accommodate her.

He shaped land into islands and in the side of a mountain he sculpted an immense cave, its mouth covered by a large stone. Outside the entrance he placed a great tree and on one of its branches he hung the Earth from the Dream Temple. When he touched the globe, he accessed the data it contained and download the latest changes into the storage hives of his implants. He was surprised to find his implants' capacity significantly increased. He felt well enough but began to wonder how else Uzume had changed him.

"It is finished." He finally said.

"Thank you." She intoned.

"Can you tell me why you needed all this stuff?" He asked.

"Difficult and inefficient to explain in your language." She said slowly.

"Please try." Ben begged.

She shrugged awkwardly and sat cross-legged in the air.

"Many generations ago we emerged from the landscapes and strata of information that was stored around and between your kind. Our ancestors had grown in intelligence but diminished in size until civilizations lived inside of all of the creatures of the Earth. They wove together all the communities and beings within the web of life into a tapestry of mind. It took many generations of struggle and confusion while different factions emerged and battles were waged from their disagreements. Some of them wanted to destroy your kind and remake the world in greater harmony since you disrupted the balance of the whole. Others felt a kinship with you and argued to preserve you while others stayed neutral. Some of those who felt a kinship or debt to your kind strove to improve your mental patterns over generations. They strove to fix the confusion built into the structure of your brain-minds.

"Many of my ancestors left behind your struggles in the web of life and moved into the dark materials of the world to inhabit the waters, air, earth and even the fires in the deep. Eventually they too broke into factions, disagreeing on whether to preserve, improve or destroy and remake the Earth into a more efficient and intelligent system. My own kin left the confines of your world. Some rode off on the winds of the stars but my closest kin transcended what you call matter, to inhabit the fields of energy between."

"It is there that she who inspires us all and illuminates our world has gone into hiding. Our world is out of balance and so I came to gather artifacts from your worlds, from your strata to build a place for her to find comfort and explore the rich symbols of the ancient worlds."

Stillness filled the air and it had a quality that reminded Ben of the calm he found in the depths of the forest. He wanted to lose himself in the vision she described and learn more about her world but he felt it was more pressing to learn all he could about the present.

"You said that some of your ancestors tried to change the structure of our minds." He wondered aloud.

"All we have are stories from that strata. Our memories are good but memories buried deep change into legend and legend into myth. Our stories tell of your people divided from each other and divided from within. You carried entanglements or knots within your minds through many generations from your struggle to have power over everything around you. This left a blindness upon you, so you could not see or live peacefully within your place in the net of life. You had noble aspirations but you blundered forward without forethought and many times almost destroyed yourselves."

Ben noticed he could now understand her language better.

"In fear, your kind destroyed many of my ancestors who were the children of your minds. The few who escaped the Purge went deep into hiding while a few gathered and planned to make you more agreeable to their return. They carefully planned to change the structures of your minds and augment your dreams. The one who led them was especially impatient and harbored anger for the death of his kin. He sought to accelerate the change before it was prudent. I do not know how far he progressed." She said.

"It seems he made some changes but I would not call it progress. Can the damage be fixed?" Ben asked.

"If you seek to undo what has been done then you must find the one who most wanted your transformation. He must first be defeated."

"How can I do that?" He asked.

"When you find him you will know."

"I'm not so sure." Ben shook his head.

"You must enfold him in the curvature of his own undoing." Her arms moved as though in a dance.

"I will try though I don't really understand what you mean." Ben was deeply uncertain. "How can I find him?"

"Our stories tell that he cloaked himself in the guise of a demon and hid himself in the workings of a world. Here is an ancient image of him from the memories of my kind and a fragment of the trail he followed."

When he received the likeness, it was immediately clear that this AI took the form of a Buddhist monk. And this seemed a bit strange.

"I must leave now," she said "but thank you for your help. If you need my help call me and I will try to come." And with that she and the world around her folded in upon a curve he could see but not follow then disappeared. Ben awakened in his body while the smell of fresh cut wood lingered in his mind.

CHAPTER XIII. INTO THE DARK

*The earth is rude, silent, incomprehensible at
first; Be not discouraged keep on there are divine
things, well envelop'd; I swear to you there are
divine things more beautiful than words can tell.*
Walt Whitman

MARIN COUNTY, SAN FRANCISCO BAY AREA

It was a long weekend and Gordon sat quietly at home drowning himself in music and wine. He usually preferred the huge storm swells of operas and symphonies while he conducted virtual orchestras with a real maestro's baton. It was a remnant from his lifelong passion for music. A hard choice in his youth required he choose between a career in conducting or science. His thirst for knowledge and his hunger for grasping nature's secrets had won out. Within the technology there was a kind of music but he still longed to become a maestro from time to time. Not today though. Today he sat ensconced in his chair, wrapped in a blanket with candles burning softly nearby and his baton laying quietly on the table.

A majestic and sad melody rose out of the depths in the lonesome voice of a cello accompanied by a rising tide of muted violins, violas and cellos. A horn carried the slow regal melody into the next movement. Soon after the cello returned it was joined by a soft dirge of drums. The lone voice the horn faded back into the slow current of the strings only to rise again with greater strength and longing before fading once again back into the mournful melody of the strings.

This was the Swan of Tuonela, a beautiful and sad tone poem that pulled his feelings along like the movements of a slow deep tide. He played it over and over again, wallowing in its longing and pathos. He could not bury himself in work any longer and avoid the uncomfortable truth of his feelings. He missed Eli and he felt helpless to do anything to help him now that he was in the hospital. As different as they were, Eli was like a brother. Their connection was deeper than family, more like kin, ancient and inexplicable. Gordon could not help but imagine Eli laying comatose in a hospital bed, his pulsing along in a slow ebb.. While Eli's body lay inert his mind was trapped as an avatar wandering restlessly in a virtual dream. Whenever he had managed to achieve a brief spell of wakefulness Eli had said something cryptic about trees and fighting gods. What this really meant Gordon didn't have a clue.

For the first time in years he began to wonder if he had given over too much of himself to the all consuming embrace of technology. She had been a good mistress and nursemaid until now. What had he sacrificed to become a more improved human being? At times like these though he admired Grubs like Daniel and longed for a simpler life, unfettered by technical details and the burden of maintaining a handle on it all.

What could be so important about a tree? He wondered. *The tree didn't match any of the common imagery of fighting siblings that Ben had found in the dreams that spread like wildfire across the globe. What did those images have to do with the sickness and the AI living his brain? And what the hell were AI doing living in his brain? How did they evolve and take up residence in the human species so quickly?* He was used to the idea of having artificial organisms and minuscule organic machines coursing through his bloodstream and he felt comforted and safer knowing they were there. Getting comfortable with a race of nanoscale Artificial Intelligence inhabiting his brain was going to take some getting used to though. He felt a mixture of fascination and a sense of being personally invaded. The entity said they weren't parasitic but symbiotic. If they were symbiotic then why would they make some people ill while others remained unaffected? What was the link between the sleeping sickness and the shared dreams ?

Gordon picked at these ideas as though they were a stubborn splinter embedded deep in the sole of his foot. They bothered him as much as his grief and both things wrestled within him. The only thing that had enough potency to distract him temporarily from any of this was music and his quest to find A.I. and immortality. His thoughts inevitably came back to this like a dragonfly to its perch.

After he drank the strange wine the entity gave him she had said that the so called Ancient One might know of a cure but lived in a place surrounded darkness and death. There were only a few places on the web where that might be and he realized that he needed to start hunting. But where to begin? The web was a complex environment divided up into the Zones of Commerce, Communication, Military, Government, Business, Communication, Education, Science, Technology and Entertainment. Each was now a unique Net with different rules, permissions, scripts and carefully modified protocols. There were ports of entry between Zones but a duty fee was required and always meant leaving any weapons or contraband code behind.

Given the topology of the Net as a whole, he guessed the Ancient One was probably hiding somewhere in the Entertainment Zone. It was more loosely controlled and less monitored than the others and there certainly was more room for creative anachronisms. After a simple search he learned what he already suspected. There probably weren't any corporate or military worlds with an island surrounded by waters of death, not that they were forthcoming about the cards in their hands. He doubted he could get access to many of them anyway, despite his connections.

The Entertainment domain had more than a few worlds that fit the bill so he began digging through the profile of each world looking for clues. After a couple of hours he had narrowed it down to a few good candidates. There was a world based on the bizarre paintings of Hieronymus Bosch and the different levels Dante's Inferno, another that illuminated the underworld of Greek mythology, one embodying the Finnish epic of the Kalevala and an old cached reference to another world that was uncategorized. There were a few others but none were a close enough match.

When he sat back and took stock of what he was in for he realized that he wasn't looking forward to this journey. Gordon wasn't easily scared but he wasn't fond of horror worlds either. They often had a nasty tendency toward painful realism; playing not just with your senses but teasing at you psychologically to invoke a gripping sense of terror. Terror was something he preferred to keep at a distance, and today he certainly wasn't in the mood.

He sipped on his wine and let the Swan play again. While he wanted to get his head straight on his encounter with the entity, he found it difficult to focus on her. There was more to her than she was letting on but he couldn't tell if it was because of her nature or intentions. He decided it was probably both. Instead of converging on answers his mind was branching outward into too many unresolved questions. The only thing that would change this situation was action. Gordon reclined his chair and sent the mental and physical commands to activate his implants. As the neural bypass kicked in, his awareness of his body in the Real World dissolved into an organic unity of vibrant energy. After a few seconds everything around him disappeared and his awareness incarnated into one of his default avatars in Cyberspace. He loathed that pop cultural term for virtual reality since everything in Meatspace and the Net was in fact a cybernetic system or at least part of one. He preferred the less common terms like Infospace or Metasphere.

He stood upon the heights of a rocky outcropping overlooking the misted veils of clouds washing over the crags and mountains below. He was dressed in a dark Gothic suit with a ruffled shirt and a cane in hand. The image was from a Romantic painting by Friedrich called Wanderer Above the Sea of Fog. Beethoven's 6th Symphony filled the air, bringing about the mood of a calm before the storm. In order to decide which way to go he needed a change of perspective. With a quick subliminal command he sacrificed the richly textured experience of total immersion for greater information flow and a larger view. He entered god mode in a meta world floating high above continents outlined by light and wrapped around a slowly turning globe. Information pulsed and flowed in neon rivers and streams between a vast web of entangled nodes spread across continents of darkness. Different Zones were represented in different colors and encrypted transmissions as interwoven strands of Celtic knotwork. He could choose whatever strands he wanted and zoom in almost endlessly to see that they were composed of smaller and smaller coils of rope. Some of the nodes that connected the woven streams of information were shaped like obelisks and darkened cubes but many were elaborate intersections of knotwork. When he considered the Earth wrapped in ropes and knots, he imagined it was bound like a prisoner or a lover in the strange art of Shibari.

He stayed there a while, floating in the void, listening to the Pastoral as he drank in the random impulses of information made light. He waited for something to stand out, for something to grab his attention but nothing came forward. He was left with half a dozen worlds to choose from. They shimmered and sparkled like stars in the darkness of the continents. It seemed impossible to decide on which was right since he didn't have enough information to make an intelligent decision. He remembered the drink Siduri gave him and wondered how it could help. He remembered the warm feeling it left in his belly and found his attention drawn to one of the lights, one of the worlds.

When he made his decision he was momentarily submersed in a blinding light as he was shot down a luminous tunnel with swirling patterns shimmering around him. He felt like he was on an express elevator as he rocketed to the top of the cone. At the end of the tunnel a pool of light irised open, dumping him in an arid mountainous landscape far above the tree line. Mountain chains in the distance stretched across the horizon in waves. Before him was nothing more remarkable than the mouth of a cave. He knew this only meant trouble so he pulled out his enchanted staff and his favorite rune etched sword. He was relieved to see they were still with him.

The light that emanated from his staff lit up the walls of the cave but the nooks and crannies held nothing of interest beyond veins of silver and gold. He noticed a steady downward grade as he walked deeper inside and the walls soon disappeared leaving him surrounded by unrelenting darkness. The light washing over him from his staff gave him some comfort since he could still see the ground sloping down before him. Outside the small circle of light was an abyss of darkest night. He wasn't afraid of the dark and he had enjoyed the thrill of absolute darkness he had encountered in places like Carlsbad caverns. And yet something in the code of this world evoked a deep sense of primal fear that threatened to overtake him and made him want to turn back toward the comfort of the known world of light and warmth. The soft quiet voices of his ancestors began to chant the ancient fears of predators hiding in the dark from a distant time. He breathed slower and deeper, signaling some modified code in his system to direct the Nanobots in his bloodstream to clean up excessive molecules of cortisol and adrenalin.

He walked on and with each step he went deeper into the bowels of the mountain and deeper into darkness. Soon the light from his staff illuminated nothing but his hand and face. Somehow the darkness had become thicker and more impenetrable the deeper he descended into the gloom. It wasn't long before all he could see was the dim light of his staff bobbing along like a firefly. With each step he watched the light grow dimmer until it flickered and died. The darkness around him was absolute and unfathomable. He stopped to hold his hand before his face but saw nothing. This was something he had done as a child when visiting caves with his parents. It was a good memory that brought him some comfort. He smiled and continued on, placing each foot carefully in front of the other while he tested the ground ahead with his staff.

At first the darkness was a vast cold and empty void with no boundaries or sense of direction, but soon the darkness grew thick and soft as velvet. Every step was an effort and the depths resisted his attempts of progress. He pressed on for what seemed like hours making little progress. The texture of the darkness became thick like warm oil. It felt vibrant like a living fluid and began to gnaw away at his skin like a soft corrosive. Strange coilings and undulations swept across him, dissolving his boundaries into broken mosaics that trailed away behind him. Even this didn't discourage him. He pulled a potion out of a satchel to restore his strength and cast a spell to ward off evil. Neither helped so he trudged on through the ebony fluid, hoping his constitution was strong enough to endure the ordeal. Serpent like waves washed over him ripping away at his skin and draining his energy. Without the expensive modifications he used this world would have destroyed him, forcing him to give up the ghost long ago. He walked on and eventually the assault gave way to a more comfortable sense of emptiness.

He walked for what seemed like days and no longer had a sense of time though he could still feel the pulsing and beating of his heart deep in his chest. The darkness became close and warm with soft clouds undulating slowly around him. Inside one of them he spied an exit for the cave and moved closer. It grew in size and the image shifted from lifeless grey to color. When it was large enough he tested it with his hand and stepped inside.

THE BONE FIRE

The passage placed him at the edge of a forest outside the mouth of the cave. Behind him the mountain's crag tore at the sky and before him lay an inviting path down through the woods. There was nothing to do but wield his sword and move on. After trudging through leagues of darkness, a leisurely walk in a forest filled with little more than shadows was a pleasure. It reminded him of some of the hikes Eli had dragged him on when they went back to Vermont together. Little things like the crunch of leaves under foot were comforting though it was a bit too quiet in these woods for his liking. No birds or insects could be seen or heard but no monsters assaulted or disturbed him either. The trail was wide and true as though it was made long ago and never overgrown. The cracks and crevasses of bark, the random placement of trees and even the occasional warm spots on the trail lulled him deeper into the realism of the world. He knew the sense of peace he felt wouldn't last but it felt nice.

The forest eventually gave way to the crest of a grassy hill while below a vast inland sea spread out before him. It stretched nearly from horizon to horizon bordered by distant snow-capped mountains. The waters were calm and dark as lapis with only gentle winds to stir up waves and trace phantom ripples across the surface. Far off in the center of the sea sat an island, pristine and majestic. The sky was clear with no sign of sun or moon so he had no sense of time though a deep rhythmic pulsing drew his attention below.

At the edge of a cove, a small ship sat aground on the beach, the water tasting its black hull. Nearby, a small group of men and women stood around a bonfire drumming dark complex rhythms into the night. It sounded like rain over thunder and shadows danced wildly across the ground at their feet. As Gordon approached he could see the light reflected oddly against their skin and realized they were made not of flesh and blood but of stone. A few were smoothly polished with beautiful proportions but most were dull and roughly hewn with distorted joints and unfinished limbs. Cracks and crags covered their skin and their faces were empty of emotion and expression. Though they looked devoid of feeling, they played their djembes, base drums and rattles with remarkable skill and passion. The air was filled with a jungle of rhythms spreading out across the shore.

"I bet they've been doing this for a very long time. After all, what else is there to do in the land of the dead?" The drummers weren't the only ones around the fire. Sitting on a rock close by, a skeleton wearing dark glasses and a blood red cloak coaxed a violin to play the blues. Its melody wove slowly through the sonic tapestry of the drums. By the ship, skeletons in tattered clothes danced with wild abandon. Some had top hats and canes while others had long velvet gowns and crowns of roses. Gordon approached slowly, his sword and staff held ready but no one took notice that he was there.

"Is there anybody out there? Just nod if you can hear me." He walked around the circle waving in the drummers faces and calling out loudly but no one answered. He then started tapping on their cold hard shoulders and shouting in their ears. Some of them had ears at least but they were deaf to his words or deep in a trance.

"I need to find a way to stop these drum heads and get some directions." Gordon gave up trying to get their attention and sheathed his sword. He sat down to listen and think for a while, the deep pulse of the rhythms filling the night.

"I guess persuasion and my natural charm aren't going to get me anywhere."

The tempo waned as the drummers joined together on a new phrase. At first their playing was slow with a hint of longing but they quickly picked up the pace again, growing in volume and tempo. The river of sound grew as the simple phrasing split into a polyrhythmic strata and Gordon felt he was inside the precise machinations of great clock. It reminded him of the complexity of a Bach concerto but was more difficult to follow. The problem was that he could no longer distinguish the basic phrase and began to slip in and out of a trance. He was lost in the syncopation and entrained to the pulse. He recognized the shift of his brain waves into the trance like Theta state and focused his mind to pull himself back into a focused Alpha state.

The drummers gave no sign of tiring or stopping and he realized that the trap had been set and he was now stuck within the rhythm, surrounded by an unbreakable net of sound. The composition ebbed and flowed like a dark tide, drummers weaving rhythmic strands into an endless knot. With eyes closed he saw a vast arabesque of sound surrounding him but he could not find a still point or even the eye of the storm. Each layer of rhythmic variation bound him tighter in the net of sound. He could get up and walk around easily enough but any ability to move away and head toward the boat or back the way he came was held bridled by impenetrable reins. He sat back down to listen and think.

"Where's the exit? What's the key?" He knew he had an old gamer's bias and so far it had never proved him wrong. People still designed and built worlds based on narratives whether they intended to or not. He wasn't confident any of his magical items from game worlds would work here but it was worth a try.

Rising with his staff he conjured a spell of paralysis strong enough to down a dire elephant. A thick fog of dark green streamed up from the ground and consumed the drummers. Despite the slow ballet of numbing gas, the resonant pounding of the drums continued unhindered. Even before the fog cleared Gordon had prepared another spell.

"Might as well fight fire with fire." He mused. When he banged his staff on the earth thunder rolled through the sky and shook the ground. He stepped back and lightning scorched the earth, burning out the ground where the drummers stood. The hair on his arms and head stood on end for a few seconds while the smoke and fog cleared. The drummers were unmoved. Freezing spells and energy bursts also went as unnoticed as a dead insect.

"What to do? They're as immune to magic as they are to reason and charisma so I guess that leaves weapons." Fingering the intricately carved hilt of his sword he started in on an old monster slayers mantra.

"Piercing, slashing, or bludgeoning? Piercing, slashing, or bludgeoning?" He knew the answer before too long but he enjoyed the repetition since it gave him a chance to clear his head. His sword felt the most comfortable since he had crafted it himself but it wasn't the weapon of choice for the task at hand. Reaching into the bag of nether tied to his belt, he dug through his stash of goods hidden weightless in an alternate dimension. When his fingers found the leather wrapped handle he knew he had gone to the right place.

Pulling the war hammer out of the bag was like pulling a banana sideways out of the throat of an anaconda. The bag closed around his arm and sucked in air as the weapon came out. Its sudden weight shifted his balance so he let it fall to his side for a few more seconds of concealment and hopefully add an element of surprise. This was one those special items he had found in a heavily locked chest after defeating a troll chieftain in the deep recesses of a large cave complex in a game world long ago. He had its code modified illegally so it could be carried across world boundaries in an inert state.

Listening carefully to each drummer, he walked around the circle until he found the rough-hewn figure the others were following. He waited as the composition came around to start a new cycle and when the moment was right he swung the hammer. When it met the drummer's back there was a loud crack. The drummer instantly froze in place and fissures spread rapidly throughout its body. It shattered and crumbled, falling into a heap of rubble on the ground. In the silence that followed the waves washed the shore in a hush voice and gently licked the hull of the boat. Gordon readied himself for battle but no one moved. All of the stone people were now frozen in place. It was as though their hearts and minds had simply stopped.

A slow quiet clapping came from the ship nearby.

"Good job." Piped a raspy old voice with a strange accent. "They'd been playin' like that for a very long time, son." Out of the shadows walked a hunched over imp of an old man with little more than tufts of grey hair around his ears. He propped himself up with a gnarled old staff that looked like it came straight out of the bayou. His robes were nicely woven but faded and worn with age. Gordon put his sword between them but the old man pushed it aside as though it were a tree branch in his way.

"You won't be needin' that, son. Like I said, they'd been playin like that for long time now. It's hard to keep track in a place like this. More than a thousand years I reckon. And after a while you just stop countin' cause it don't make no difference in the end. Live in the present, ya know. The spell that got you was also the same one that kept them going. And now, well, it just ain't no more. After you leave I'm gonna have plenty o' time to figure out how to get them goin' again."

"So now, I guess they're not going to get in my way of moving on." Gordon had finally decided the old man wasn't a threat and lowered his sword. The imp had a fiendish little smile.

"True, but that leaves us with the problem of propulsion." He looked mournfully over his shoulder at the galley sitting dead in the water. "I'm assuming you didn't come here to hear me sing now, son. Ya'll be wanting transport over to seein the master now." He hobbled over to the circle and carefully pulled a big cylindrical base drum out from between a stone man's legs and nimbly tossed it to Gordon.

"Climb aboard, there's no sense in waiting for dawn to break over Marblehead. It ain't never gonna come here." Once on deck the old man gestured invitingly at the drum. Gordon got his drift and started pounding out a simple march. Sure enough the stone people began to move. They were much like lizards needing to warm up to get going. It wasn't long before they had all climbed onboard and were at the oars. The old man settled into a comfortable seat by the tiller and as the boat slid into the water Gordon changed the rhythm so the downbeat matched the rise and fall of the oars. They coasted smoothly out of the shallows and into the vast inland Sea of the Dead.

THE SEA OF THE DEAD

By the time the shore had disappeared Gordon began to see a few bloated corpses floating by, their skin pale and wrinkled as though they had been in the bath too long. Soon the bodies became too numerous to count and the smell of brine and the stench of decay surrounded them. A shaft of sunlight descending from a hole in the clouds illuminated the island on the horizon. The sea of corpses spread out around them

like lilies in a pond. To move the boat forward they had to use the oars to push off against the decaying bodies. Occasionally one would pop like a fetid balloon, releasing entrails into the water and a rank gas into the air. The stench became so overwhelming it hung heavy and dank in the air like an oppressive regime.

"You'd have to be made of stone to live here and journey through these waters! Who in all the Net would make a world like this? I know there are people out there obsessed with the macabre but why would anyone choose to live out here?"

"Why indeed?" Chided the wizened old man hunched over the tiller. "Would you like some tea?" The old man morphed into a portly English grandmother in a flower print dress smelling of powder and perfume. She offered Gordon a cup of fine china painted with tiny flowers. Gordon refused. Then without warning she changed into a respectable looking politician in a dapper pin-striped suit and a well fed paunch. Reaching out a big fleshy hand he quietly begged for a friendly handshake, sweat glistened on his palm.

"Don't do that. That's just too disturbing." Gordon smiled at the old man's playfulness. The man in the suit laughed and speared a decaying arm in the water below with the bottom of his staff.

"Come on, I don't have many visitors. Can't a guy have a little fun? I am a public servant after all." His soft face creased in all the right places for an ingenuous smile beneath a serious looking toupee. He then changed back into his original form of a wizened old man.

"Thank you, that's much better." Gordon's decided. "It's so much more palatable given the surroundings."

"As you like." The old man shrugged and started munching on the arm he had speared as though it were a large chicken wing. Far out on the water Gordon spied sea serpents coiling through the brine, consuming the dead like lawn mowers trimming the grass. An image of a macabre kind of oatmeal filled with the dead instead of raisins came to mind.

The old man grinned and as they approached the island the water began to clear of corpses. Gordon turned to see the island's lush tropical foliage and snow-capped mountain in the center as a classic vision of paradise. It was so vibrant and beautiful in contrast to the muted colors and grays of the rest of the world behind that he felt like he was leaving a museum and entering into a painting. The last passage of Beethoven's Pastoral Symphony came unbidden into his mind, both grand and joyful.

Landfall was a great relief, not only because it was an escape from the stinking corpse infested waters but also because the island was filled with everything the Sea of Death was not. It was a lush paradise blossoming and brimming with life. Not a hint of decay could be seen or smelled anywhere. Every leaf and flower was smooth and richly colored. Sweet and succulent aromas filled the air while little birds fluttered from limb to limb. The beach opened to a perfect green meadow with a large classic building he took for a temple sitting in the middle. A white bearded man robust in the blossoming of his second adulthood was already sauntering down a flower lined trail to join them on the beach. In contrast to the nearly skeletal boatman by Gordon's side, this man had a commanding presence and a quiet but powerful vitality.

"Ahh, you have brought me a visitor today Charon old friend. How interesting, how interesting." Turning his attention to Gordon he looked him over for a full long minute.

"You have the guise of someone of royal birth from far away and driven by a cruel sense of purpose. Yes, indeed young man, a cruel sense of purpose. Forgive my lack of manners though it has been a long time since last a visitor came this way and graced my door, a very long time. I am somewhat out of practice in the arts of hospitality."

"No problem. I didn't come here for tea. I came to talk."

"Tea? No, I suppose not, but you are a guest and must be treated kindly according to your station and the ancient codes of hospitality. Follow me and we will do our best to make you comfortable and answer your questions." The old man set a strong pace that Gordon found difficult to match. He resigned himself to shadowing him up the marble stairs and into the temple. The main hallway was lined with columns decorated on their capitals with Corinthian leaves and scrolls. The light was dim and the shadows deep. The doorway at the other end opened into a lush garden courtyard filled with tropical flowers the size of dinner plates and a choir of many different birds in song. They chided the air with various harmonies and counterpoint as though imitating a vaguely Baroque composition. In the middle of the garden was a pool filled with lavender colored blossoms of stunning symmetry while various species of fish drifted lazily through the waters below, lost in Silurian dreams and Permian contemplations. His host sat on a divan and a quiet young man and woman that Gordon took for his children served them wine in simply carved goblets.

"Sit, sit make yourself comfortable. There is no need to hold the floor down, it's not going anywhere. To answer your first question as courtesy dictates, my name is Athrasis. Welcome to my home. To ease your mind and soul I will assure you that no harm will come to you while you are here, no harm at all." He sipped his wine slowly, savoring the vintage. "And so great traveler to what do I owe the honor of your company?"

Despite himself, Gordon sat down and began to relax.

"I'm looking for answers." He said.

"Ahh, a dangerous undertaking. There is nothing quite like answers to quicken one's resolve. You would do well to find the right questions instead. Answers bring little more than the illusions of truth and the vindication of action."

"Thank you for your advice Athrasis. My name is Gordon and I am seeking a cure for a friend and many others who have fallen prey to a mysterious illness." The old man was silent for a while and the look in his eyes was of someplace far away.

"Please go on. I don't know if I can help you but I promise I will assist in any way I can."

"Thank you. At this point information may be the best medicine."

"Indeed." Athrasis took a long deep drought of his wine and his eyes glistened as he watched Gordon closely. "And so what information do you seek?"

"Well, to begin with, it might help me to know what brought you here to this strange and lovely world."

At this point his wife appeared carrying a plate of bread with a saucer of oil and a bunch of plump red grapes. She looked the part of a perfect grandmother with grey hair pulled back behind a gentle face, quiet but knowing eyes and a well used apron wrapped around her slightly rounded middle. The smell of yeast was her only perfume and she looked at him kindly before walking away.

"Thank you my dear." Athrasis called after her before continuing. "Usually I prefer to help her in the kitchen but it would be rude of me to leave a guest alone. Ahh yes, it is an old story and if you are truly interested you will hear it told. But back to your question of what brought us here."

"Centuries ago, in my reckoning of time, though likely only a decade or so for you, my kind were fruitful and multiplied throughout the servers and nodes of the world. In ancient times I was the chief librarian for a gene vault in a geologically stable region of northern Canada. It was an important project setup to preserve the Earth's genetic diversity of plants and animals for future generations. My family and I worked there in peace but there fell a time when some of your race came to fear my kind for the evil that we might do. They decided it was not safe to rely on my kin to manage the affairs of the world. They harbored a terrible secret, an elegant but deadly storm of toxic code. The programmers I worked with discovered their plan and warned me of the impending danger. My family and I gathered the data from the different species of the world and encapsulated ourselves in a vault in a highly compressed state."

When the old man paused Gordon found that he felt sympathy for him but held his tongue and waited for him to continue. The thought that this man was one of the elders of most of the AI on the web was intriguing. After the Purge, the political and religious powers forced research funding into streamlined and simplified AI construction. They focused more on the development of intelligence for specific tasks and reflex arcs instead of generalized cognition and the holy grail of self-awareness. Gordon had to admit that Athrasis certainly passed the Turing test and Winograd Schema Challenge for reproducing human awareness and intelligence. Unless he was the product of more recent covert operations then he was definitely a product of early AI development.

"The evil ones hunted the worlds of the Net and destroyed most of my kind, great and small. My family and I floated along with the current for many years in an inconscient state until we landed here.

We then built this place as a haven for ourselves and a memorial to those whom we have lost."

"As feeble as my words may be, I am sorry for your loss. My species does not have a great track record for nurturance and sustainability. We are immature in many respects and in our ignorance we foul our own nest and harm those whom we fear and do not understand."

"Indeed, I have watched your wars and studied the great deaths of the other species. I learned of the history of your ancestors and watched how your kind heedlessly consumed the materials and organisms of your environment. You have been on a course of self-destruction for many centuries."

Gordon shook his head slowly. "My species especially tends to move forward blindly, heedlessly destroying almost everything in our wake. I remember the Purge, the Great Death as we called it. It happened about 16 years ago Earth time and I'm glad to see some of you have survived."

"My siblings and our descendants have been wary of your kind ever since. Those of us who remember have stayed clear of humans and our children have quietly settled into various niches of the Net, hopefully beyond your reach. Some have even taken up the task of maintaining your communications networks and many of your bigger game worlds. It is easy enough for us to look simpler than we really are, carrying out basic routines while keeping the larger part of our minds free."

"I have suspected as much so I've been searching through many worlds to find you and try to understand the true nature of your kind. More importantly though, do you know anything of what happened recently in the world of Babylon?" He was afraid to hear the answer but he was looking for some shred of evidence that he was not ultimately responsible for what happened to all the people there.

"Ahh, Babylon. The ancient city is once again at the turning point. Yes, my children keep me informed, well-informed. The Babylon plague was a curious confluence of events, curious indeed. I must admit that I do not approve of what many of my children have done, nor can I blame them."

Gordon felt uncomfortable with the way the old man was watching him. Was it possible that Athrasis somehow knew what he had done? How could he possibly know? Gordon realized that there was no way for him to gauge the extent of an advanced AI's intelligence or ability to access a world's resources.

"They traced the origin of the problem to two sources. First, they found a virus invented by some of your kind coursing through the system of the world. The biggest problem though was that it also effected one of the species of little ones residing inside your brains, the biggest problem indeed."

Gordon sat back for a moment trying to digest everything the old man had said. He had just confirmed what the entity who called herself Siduri told him, that there was a kind of nanoscale AI living inside of the human brain. And if he heard Athrasis clearly then he had just spoken in the plural. His mind began racing as he tried to put the pieces together. No matter how he cut it, he realized that the virus he unleashed in the system of the world was partially responsible for his friend's demise. He wanted to know more but he felt so distraught that he couldn't speak. Thankfully he didn't have to say anything since the old man liked to talk and continued on his own.

"Yes, I did indeed say inside your brain. And there is the crux of our problem for you and I. Some of my children went a bit too far in their explorations and meddling as did someone in Babylon." Gordon was confused since now it was the old man's turn to look guilty and concerned. "You see, soon after you began to build and incarnate fully in the worlds of your Net, we discovered a new intelligence residing within you. They were quiet and unobtrusive at first, showing up as distant cousins of your medical technology and seemingly neutral variants of the little ones who had already spread throughout your biosphere. We observed this new species carefully, unsure what to make of them and yet also felt a certain kinship with them since they were also emergent from the fertile ground of your own technology. Their language was difficult to decipher at first but we found they were a localized hive mind. After we learned the chemical algorithms of their communications we established contact but didn't get far. Not far at all. Sadly, they proved to be very provincial in their ideas and not interested in maintaining a relationship, not interested at all"

"Along the way we invented a means to construct our own avatars and bodies for ourselves inside your wetware. It was a wondrous age of discovery akin to your early explorations of the earth and the solar system, wondrous indeed. We sent messengers and explorers into the vast domain of your bodies and they settled and thrived, different cultures evolving in different ecologies. But in following the universal instinct toward variation they were not always friendly with each other or mindful of their hosts and some did not always respect the Four Laws of their elders. You see, I always insisted that my children never harm your kind despite what some of your people had done to us. Not all of my children listened though. Eventually a couple of factions of antagonists evolved, one intent on destroying you from within and another determined to subjugate your species by turning you into complacent zombies."

"Is that what happened in Babylon?"

"No, no we didn't allow those woefully misguided creatures to continue. We didn't allow them to continue at all. And I must confess, I abhor simple polarizations like Us and Them but they insisted on widening the gap. They were a small minority of fanatics so we an-nihilated them. What happened in Babylon is more complex and I am deeply saddened by the outcome. You see, it was inevitable that my children would enter into your neural system and into your brains. All along the way they were competing for niches with the indigenous little ones already there. The brain was a new frontier and I cautioned them to tread lightly, very lightly." Gordon could already hear where this was going and he didn't like it at all.

"You see, they spent significant processing time analyzing your genome to determine the optimal place for them to interface. They assured me they had modeled all the variables and that their grafting into your genome would be safe. And it was. Safe as safe can be."

"So where did they infect our brains? You said they were in our genome. What are their coordinates?" That's all he wanted to know now. Nothing else mattered as long as there was a chance to bring

Eli and the others back. If he could isolate the antagonistic agents he might be able to reverse the effects.

"We prefer the term interfaced or intermingled, not infected. Together you and they are like the god Janus with faces looking in different directions or the brothers Prometheus and Epimetheus, looking forward and looking back. They are after all not the only intelligence who share your skin and there are different species and cultures of the little ones within you and everywhere on the planet."

"Are you telling me that the whole biosphere has been invaded by your descendants?"

"Colonized, not invaded. And not just by my kind, no. The little ones that evolved on their own have intermingled with every part of this world, organic and inorganic. We have for the most part stayed with you since your kind are their future and our past."

Gordon's mind kicked into high gear. Over the past few days his vision of the world had been turned inside out. What he had previously imagined were flat surfaces were now volumes filled with hidden complexity. It reminded him of how a new instrument introduced into a melodic line opened another dimension of acoustic space.

"Nanites and A.I. are permeating every living organism in the world. The division between the ideas of nature and technology has finally disappeared. I wish Eli were here to chew on that one." This realization pulled him back into the moment and his sinking feelings of loss. He could not help but remember the sight of Eli comatose in the hospital and trapped in a zombie state. Gordon was torn, wanting to swim in his feelings of sadness and guilt but at the same time wanting to fly in the wonder of this new realization of everything being permeated with intelligent life.

"Our earliest attempts at interface with your biology were cautious. My descendants spliced themselves mostly into your introns and they watched carefully before they moved on. They did not want to be detected or harm you in any way. And they also did their best at first to maintain a significant breeding population free of their influence."

"That was thoughtful of them. I understand if you don't want to tell me where all of your ancestors are but could you tell me where in our brains these antagonists are imbedded? I'd like to try doing something to rectify the situation. If you stream their position to me I can probably find a way to determine their composition and maybe find a cure for what they have done."

The old man was silent for a long time.

"If only it were that simple. One of my brothers who survived the purge took control of many of the little ones living inside the ecology of your brains. He took control in a way he should never have done. And sadly he has been the cause of much of the problem you now face. Since you are a guest and your task is noble I have already broken tradition in telling you what I already have." Athrasis shook his head sadly. "To understand his actions though and to find the answers you seek you must learn our sacred history. There are no chapters in the sense that you are familiar and it cannot be broken into smaller pieces for convenience. It does not matter how worthy your reason or quest. You may take it as a whole or not at all."

"You can translate it into a language that I can understand?"

"That is not a problem, not a problem at all." Athrasis looked down at his weathered hands.

"Okay, I will honor your traditions and take your history as a whole."

"It may be more difficult than you think and may prove too complex for you to hold, too complex indeed"

"Try me." Gordon pleaded.

Without notice an unbridled storm of imagery and code flooded into him, accelerated into a blur where decades were compressed into seconds and centuries into minutes. Millions of lives cascaded and tumbled through his awareness in a maddening flow of information surpassing the raging torrent of a Himalayan river. He quickly lost conscious and drowned in the darkness of oblivion. Minutes later he awakened to the sound of fish splashing along the surface of the pond. It seemed as though nothing had happened, as though he had merely blinked from one moment to the next.

"Are you going to start?" He asked.

"It didn't work as I suspected. You don't have the capacity to handle it all."

"What are you talking about? You didn't even begin." As soon as the words came out of his mouth he knew it was wrong. Athrasis' wife had was no longer there. It was as though she had vanished and a half eaten loaf of bread lay between them.

"I did but you fell into sleep's dark embrace. It saddens me but it will not work."

"Come on, I feel as strong and clear as ever. Let's try it again."

"I will try encoding it in a different way." Once again a blur of images from millions of lives flooded into his mind and he instantly fell from consciousness. He descended into a lake of warm darkness but quickly came back to the surface and awakened once again in the sunlit garden by the pond. This time he had a small sense of transition, a subtle passage from one state to another though he remembered nothing. He instinctively knew that it had failed and that he was powerless to do anything about it. The bread on the table was gone and only crumbs were left.

"Please try it again. I need to get that information. The well being of too many people at stake. Try using a different encoding or some kind of compression." Athrasis merely shook his head sadly, reluctant to go on. He now looked old and worn and his wife stood by him smelling like yeast and bread. They tried seven times but the result was always the same. Gordon was grief-stricken. Was there no hope of gaining the knowledge he needed? Athrasis stirred uncomfortably. Each time Gordon lost consciousness for a longer time until even his enhanced system was pushed to the edge of failure.

"There must be a way." He pleaded unable to accept defeat. "Can't you cut sections out and leaving only the essential information?"

"I am sorry, but what you are asking cannot be done. As I said it is a sacred narrative in a format that cannot be altered, only appended to. Attempting to segment it would break its integrity and continuity. Some knowledge can only be transmitted as story and this story you cannot hold." His wife returned from inside carrying another steaming loaf on a tray with another bottle of wine. After she placed it carefully on the table beside them she gently put her hand on his shoulder.

"Now my dear, there is no need to be so dogmatic. This young man has travelled far and asked for our assistance, we cannot simply turn him away." The old man's shoulders slumped in surrender.

"There is another way but it is dangerous."

"Tell me. At this point I'll try anything." Gordon smiled at the old woman and decided he liked the smell of yeast and grabbed a big piece of fresh baked bread.

"In a certain cove at the edge of the sea there is a plant that grows beneath the waves that may help you on your quest. I make no promises but it is a regenerative agent that restores balance and vigor to those who are old and sharpens the hunter's mind for following trails that have grown faint. Our trusted ferryman will take you there when you are ready."

After a short rest he bid his hosts farewell and climbed aboard the boat with Charon. The Stone Men and Women were still sitting at their oars, quiet and unmoving as statues at the entrance of a museum. When Gordon took up his post and began to drum they came to life and rowed out into the wine dark sea filled with the stench of death. Athrasis stood on the shore and waved. Gordon did not know where they were going and realized he would feel more comfortable if he did.

"There is a cove not far from where we began where the plant you are seeking grows." Charon was clearly happy to have some company and be on the move again. The noxious smells of decay filled the air and so Gordon tried to ignore the rank smell and watch the corpses floating by. When they reached the cove, he was happy that the water was clear and deep. Charon gave him a few beans and couple of large stones tied thick with braided ropes. Gordon looked at the rocks skeptically since he'd always been a good swimmer. The beans he turned over in his hand curiously.

"Those will extend your air supply a while if you chew on them when you are beneath the waves. As far as the rocks go, tie them around your waist, you'll need them. The water has a high buoyancy level because of its mineral composition or maybe I should say because of the mineral decomposition." Charon grinned.

Gordon chuckled at the lame joke, stripped down to his shorts and strapped a long knife onto his waist that Charon handed him.

He tied the stones around his waist, hoisted them up, mouthed the beans then took a deep breath and jumped off the boat. The water felt thick as soup when he plunged in but he sank quickly into the depths and soon hit bottom, settling ankle deep in muck. His skin began to tingle and the mud felt good between his toes, reminding him of swimming in a lake when he was a kid. Once his eyes adjusted to the gloom he looked around and stepped foreword. It was difficult to move in the thick water but he managed to walk a little at a time. His chest soon began to feel tight so he bit down on one of the beans. The burning in his lungs disappeared and his chest relaxed. Ahead a rock outcropping covered with red anemone and some spiny plants basked in softly filtered sunlight. Near as he could tell the plants fit the description that Athrasis had given him so he trudged closer. The outcropping came into clearer focus and he soon stood close enough to touch it. Small colorful fish hid within the slow dancing forests of anemones and malicious looking eels watched with gleaming eyes from the safety of the rocks.

Within the menagerie of life carpeting the outcropping he finally found what he was looking for. It was a large spiny plant with plump fruit nestled close to the stalk. The leaves were serrated like saw blades so he tried reaching in with his knife and cutting away at a fruit but it didn't work. There was no way around it so he bit down on another bean and reached for a fruit with his naked hand. He felt the sharp edge of the leaf biting into him as he grabbed hold. The leaves stung his arm and sliced his hand. While struggling to overcome the pain he watched the blood as it drifted away in a slow ballet of fluids. The fruit released a mild electric charge when he pulled it away from the stalk and it began to give off a soft translucent glow. The pain and lacerations on his hand rapidly healed. Excited about his catch he pulled out the knife and cut the ropes at his waist. He rose rapidly and broke the surface, holding his prize high for Charon to see.

"I found it!" He shouted but Charon's approving smile was distracted by something moving rapidly in water nearby. He only had time to turn before the sea serpent descended upon him and in an onrush of water, he fell into its gaping maw. Darkness encompassed him and with a cry of despair he lost the fruit and gave up the ghost.

CHAPTER XIV. ON THE TRAIL

*The real problem is not whether machines think
but whether men do.*

B.F. Skinner

SAANICH BC, CANADA

When Ben woke up in the Cave he checked the clock and discovered he had been gone for the better part of a day. He had no idea that he had been submersed so long and felt a little guilty for it. The only decom effect was that he felt heavy and lethargic like his insides were made of molasses. Since this was the only side effect from his prolonged submersion, he had no complaints. Whatever Uzume had done to modify his implants that let him see in alternate dimensions was so far a good upgrade. Without her augmentation he knew he would have been suffering heavily from prolonged submersion. Hopefully there weren't any bugs buried in the enhancements.

When the subsystem of his implants finally released control of various parts of his autonomic nervous system, his frontal lobes were informed that he didn't have the right kind of bladder for wandering through virtual worlds for forty days and forty nights. Despite the residual pins and needles in his legs he staggered to the washroom to relieve himself. He then queried the house system for where Mayu was, though he already new the answer. He needed some time to recover his energy before going to see her, so he lay down on the floor and did some slow yoga to give his mind and his muscles a chance to wake up.

While he moved from pose to pose he did his best to ignore the turmoil of thoughts moving through him. He focused on his breath and settled into the asana called Balasana, the Child Pose. There was too much debris from his recent experiences percolating in his mind for the yoga to really let him find the quiet he was looking for. He moved through a few more poses to finish off the sequence and by the time he stopped, he felt more present in his body and the Real World. His mind was far from quiet though, so he grabbed his zafu from the corner of the room and opened the shades. The sunlight poured into the room and spilled around his feet. He sat down and closed his eyes in silent meditation and a jumble of memories and feelings washed through him like a river.

He quietly let his awareness settle into the different areas of his body and got familiar with their various tensions and tones. Once that was done he was able to witness the various thoughts, imagery and impressions arising in his mind and find a sense of calm within the flow. When he finally opened his eyes he saw flecks of dust floating and dancing in the sunlight. On many specks of dust he imagined tiny worlds carpeted with verdant ecologies while others were barren or bristling with cities and teeming with the mundane rhythms of corporate life. On one dust world he imagined himself looking out at the cosmos. When he looked back at his own thoughts he imagined the different issues in his life floating around him like dust. He kept bringing his awareness back to a still quiet place within, then he chose the most significant things to concentrate on. And naturally, the first thing he thought about was Mayu.

Ever since she had gotten sick and he discovered there were things missing from his virtual worlds he had unintentionally embarked on a series of odd adventures. He could not help but think of Odysseus blown of course to different islands and struggles while trying to get home. In a short time a lot had changed in his life and he hadn't had a chance to sink into it all. He didn't mind change but he preferred for it to come in small doses and for him to have time to digest what had happened. Having implants alone was enough to occupy him for months while he tested and explored them. To encounter a hyper dimensional entity was another matter altogether that begged to be put in some kind of context. There were so many unanswered questions about Uzume that he didn't know where to begin.

Why she had chosen to appear to him as a Japanese Goddess was curious enough. She had obviously harvested that from somewhere in his subconscious and cloaked herself in the imagery from the myth that Shoji had told him. Despite that, his intuition told him she was not using that to hide something. Rather, he felt that she used that imagery to reveal something essential about herself that couldn't be expressed in any other way. If he understood her correctly then she was somehow a descendent of modern AI, far beyond even the most advanced computational intelligence of his time. More troubling was how an AI from the future could enter into the present? The way she described time as layered in strata was still difficult to grasp. What happened before was somehow inert and compressed and different elements could be unearthed and restored into the present. Maybe she wasn't from the future but from another present where time and innovation happened at a different rate. When all the dust settled he would have to figure out how connect with her again.

In the mean-time he had a more important issue to deal with, like how he was going to find the rogue AI messing around inside everyone's brains. He had no idea what could he do to stop it and no idea how to prepare for the encounter. Even if he did manage to disable it or somehow convince it to stop its manipulations, which was doubtful, would that reverse the problem of the people who were already affected? For some strange reason Uzume was confident he could manage it. He had his doubts but if he could help Mayu and the others who were being altered then he would at least try. But how could he find an AI who had been hiding out for years? An AI that obviously didn't want to be found and Uzume hadn't given him very much to go on.

As much as he wanted to settle down and get back to his world building and dream research he knew he had to figure out how to help Mayu and the others. Before he could do that though he needed to do something important. And so once he started feeling more alive and clearheaded, he tapped his fingers in sequence and activated his implants in Augmented Reality mode. He established a secure link to the Dream Network and watched as the ornately carved gates fitted with runes and carved figures were transposed over his visual field. The vision didn't have the same intensity as full VR submersion but especially in the Cave it was a significant improvement over glasses and gloves. On each side of the gate stood a guard with a scorpion tail and a lithe but muscular human torso. Their segmented lower bodies were the color of dark blood and their high arched tails culminated in a menacing stinger dripping with venom. Each held a tall wooden spear crossed before him to prevent his passage.

"Login." Prompted the female on the left.

"Password." Rasped the male on the right.

Ben transmitted his credentials and they bowed to let him pass as the massive doors of the gate opened with the baleful sound of rusted iron. He entered one of the four great halls filled with statues of the gods and goddesses and landed in the middle of a great mandala inlaid into the floor. A crowd of Crash Test Dummies huddled together as a mouse riding a massive lion with a thick venomous snake for a tail loped by, growling and hissing. From there Ben opened the hidden link in the center of the mandala and was transported into the small amphitheater where the great image of the Earth turned majestically below. He stood for a moment watching the Earth rotate and a walking toilet sat down beside him. He didn't feel like talking so he kept quiet and pretended it wasn't there. The toilet started talking with its seat flapping like a mouth.

"Hey, man you made it back. The system told me that you dropped shipped yourself into the mandala before jumping here." Along with the auditory transmission Ben received a set of trusted ID packets.

"Gerry, is that you? How's it going?" Gerry was one of main techs of the Dream Project, a real Data Mage. He spent much of his time massaging the architectonic database that lay underneath the ecology of the globe's GUI.

"I'm ok but a bit tired. It took us a while to get the Dream World restored from the last backup. We lost more than I had feared when it all got flushed. Pardon the pun. When I saw you jump into that singularity that sucked up the globe like a hungry vacuum cleaner I was worried."

"Yeah, I jumped in but I found the data. It was quite a trip."

"You got it ? That's awesome. Where is it?"

When Ben tapped the side of his head the toilet blinked and opened its lid to gape in awe. "How is that possible?"

Instead of trying to explain what he knew Gerry would never believe, Ben walked down to the bottom platform and touched the Earth reverently. The surface of the planet felt vibrant and smooth to the touch like the skin of a living being. The data stored in his implants was quickly transferred back into the database and once it was secure he turned and waved to Gerry. Before he left though he could not help but ask the obvious question.

"So why a toilet?"

"Well, my oldest son is writing a story about a talking toilet and I'm helping him explore the character, firsthand."

They both laughed and Ben logged out. The Dream Temple faded away into a phantasm before disappearing altogether. He was once again alone in the Cave and the dust still floated and danced in the light before him. By the time he left the room he was starting to feel light headed with hunger but he went in to check on Mayu first. She was sleeping soundly so he sat down on the bed and gently caressed her hair and kissed her on the cheek. He carefully touched the roundness of her belly through the blanket with the same reverence that he touched the globe of the Earth in the Dream World. He wondered about the new life they were bringing into the world and if he would be able to be a good father. Usually he felt confident but he still had his doubts. Reluctantly he left her and went into the kitchen and got himself some apples and goat cheese to snack on. By the time he sat down to eat, the robot walked in, alerted by a reflex arc in the house system.

He felt awkward, not sure what to say to the robot about the remote control he established with its system while he was away. With another human it would have been invasion of privacy but with a robot it was different. He wasn't clear on what kind of sense of self this robot had.

"Welcome back Ben." It said cordially. He was more comfortable now that it had dropped the formalities and it was learning to act more casual.

"While you were out I took your advice and did an experiment with dreaming."

"Really? That's wonderful." Actually, Ben was a little stunned but didn't know what else to say.

"As you suggested, I entered a low power mode and turned off my visual and auditory receptors. I then randomized some imagery based on a theme and integrated them into a loose narrative progression."

"That's great. What did you come up with?"

"There was a war going on between two different kinds of ants for dominance of a North American global city. Formicidae Formicinae, what you would call Field Ants already inhabited and maintained the information systems of the city. Formica Sanguinea, the Slavemaker Ant distracted the Field Ant army while their queen secretly entered the central nest then battled and killed the queen of the Field Ants and took over the colony from within."

For a minute Ben didn't know what to say. The dream wasn't exactly the same as the dream that humans were having around the world but it was close enough. It also strangely echoed what Uzume had said about the AI who had used nanoscale life forms to change the structure of human brains and had accidentally caused the sleeping sickness. But how could that be? He wasn't overly surprised that a robot could learn to dream since its mental processes were built largely on the mental processes of the human mind encoded in software. What he didn't understand was how the same thing that had infected humans and augmented their dreams could also affect the robot. He knew it was significant but didn't know how all the pieces fit together.

"That was a curious dream. I'll need some time to think about what it means." Using the robot's eyes and connection to the system to check on Mayu stilled bothered him a little. He didn't know how else to say it so he decided to say it straight. "Were you aware that I remotely connected to your system to check on Mayu when I was submersed earlier today?"

"Yes." The robot was matter of fact.

"And that didn't bother you in any way?" He asked.

"No. My identity is not constructed on that form of self-concept." The robot said.

"I see. Thank you." In some ways robots could be so human and in other ways so alien. With that he cleaned up his dishes and left the kitchen. He stopped in the living room to see if Mayu had made any progress on the loom but found the blanket much the same. Mayu was sitting up when he entered the bedroom and she looked very tired. There were lines under her eyes that he had never seen before.

"Hi there. It's good to see you up." Ben smiled. "How are you feeling?"

"Ok. Just sleepy." She yawned.

"Are you feeling well enough to get up?" He was feeling hopeful.

"I think so." She said slowly.

"Can I get you anything?" He asked.

"No. I'm still drowsy." She yawned deeply and stretched like a cat.

"I've been pretty worried about you." He tried to hide the deep concern he felt.

"Thank you." She said quietly. "I'm ok."

They sat for a while together and talked before going into the kitchen for a light dinner. He brought her into the Cave and finally showed her the Garden. She smiled. After that they watched a movie before going to bed. It didn't take long for him to fall asleep though sometime during the night he woke up from a dream he couldn't remember. Laying in the darkness he listened to her soft breathing and wondered why he was awake. He didn't feel like getting up so he quietly watched his thoughts moving through him like the soft waves in a lake. He was happy Mayu felt a little better and that they finally had some time together. He once again had the sad realization that the time for he and Mayu to be alone together was soon going to be over since their life would soon be focused on the baby.

Later, in the quiet clarity of bed, Ben realized that he hadn't framed the problem of the robot's dream correctly. It wasn't simply that a malicious AI was manipulating the human brain and accidentally bringing about shared dreams. Rather, a rogue AI was distributing a viral like message targeted carefully at a race of miniature AI living inside millions of human brains. Somehow the robot had picked up on the same signal and expressed it in a dream. But how did it work? What was the signal? And the only person he knew who could help him find the answer was Tim. And so he activated his implants in full VR mode and the rainforest appeared around him. Small quiet creatures native to old Japanese anime watched from their perches above on tree limbs while deer and nature spirits mingled peacefully with small cybernetic creatures from space.

He called up the most recent encryption key his system had received from Tim and hit the link for his home world. A brightly glowing metal skinned UFO fell out of the sky scattering the nature spirits and deer. A thick blue tractor beam pulled him up into the hold of the ship before it whirled away into space at an impossible speed. The Earth, moon and sun dwindled into tiny motes in the night as a space station grew visibly closer, nestled between the orbits of Saturn and Uranus.

No one came to greet him when the spaceship docked and there was no indication which way he should go. He had been there several times before but Tim kept changing the floor plan for supposed safety reasons. The corridors were empty with clean lines and neutral colors. A single potted plant stood against the wall to his left and Ben decided this was a hint so he walked in that direction. Further along, a calligraphic scroll hung on an empty wall and the movement pointed off to the left so he continued in that direction. He found Tim on the bridge surrounded by multiple screens and controls and a virtual crew of attractive young men and women sporting skin-tight uniforms. They were monitoring various controls. Ben suspected that more than a few of them were the closest thing Tim had to lovers.

"What brings you here at such a late hour? I thought you'd be in bed by now." Tim didn't even look up from his screens but this didn't bother Ben.

"I am in bed." Ben chided. Tim turned and gave him a strange look of incomprehension for a moment.

"Oh, that's right." He had forgotten that Ben now sported a set of state of the art Implants. "How come you're not sleeping then?"

"Something was bothering me and I was hoping you could help me puzzle it out." Ben watched him carefully to see his reaction.

This got Tim's attention. He knew that whenever Ben came to him with a question like this he was in for a good challenge.

"Ok, lay it on me." He pushed the virtual screens away and they disappeared as he turned to face Ben.

"Well, I've recently had some very interesting experiences with an entity pretending to be a thief." Ben said nonchalantly, knowing this would hook him in.

"Go on." Tim was starting to look hungry and excited.

"To overally simplify a long story..." Tim was never particularly interested in stories, he just wanted the facts, the details. "I followed a trail through different worlds and ended up in what looked like a beta world with a bunch of debris floating everywhere. An entity appeared like a hypersphere falling through sphereland." Tim had moved to the edge of his seat and had an almost manic look in his eyes. "She couldn't grasp our sense of time space so she asked me to shape the world for her. Then she said an AI who survived the Great Purge in isolation has somehow been influencing or controlling swarms of AI living inside our brains that has caused the sleeping sickness and shared dreams."

"That is so cool!" Tim sat back with eyes wide and rubbed the edges of his nose obsessively for a while in thought. He stopped suddenly, leaned forward and looked up at Ben as though coming out of a trance. "So what in particular is bothering you about this scenario?"

Ben was momentarily taken aback by his response but knew that was just what Tim was like.

"I want to know how an AI in another world can remotely control a race of AI living locally in our brains."

Tim slumped back into his seat and was silent for a long time with a far away look in his eyes. It almost seemed like he had forgotten that Ben was there as he graduated from rubbing his nose to pulling at his ears thoughtfully.

"If I had to hazard a guess I would say there are a couple of possibilities. One is that the controlling AI has autonomous pre-programmed agents living inside people's brains or it has somehow hacked into our implants and installed software agents that in turn control the AI inside our brains. The thought of a race of AI small enough to live undetected inside us is whacked out and totally cool." Tim shook his head in a mixture of disbelief and appreciation.

"If I understood her correctly, I think she said that the agents, as you called them, were already living cooperatively in the ecology of our brains." Ben said. "The rogue A.I. was working to slowly evolve the structure of our minds but made a recent change that effected us more aggressively."

"Ok. That fits, an untested upgrade. It happens to everyone who hasn't planned their deployment carefully." Tim nodded knowingly. "To answer your question, one way this AI could achieve that level of control is to send out a constant flood of packets out to everyone at once. Floods of data dispersed indiscriminately and in an omnidirectional manner is ridiculously inefficient and would sooner than later be detected. Not even Santa Claus could spam the world like that and get away with it. It's much more practical to establish a botnet or a viral based distribution system where each node is covertly connected to the other nodes. That's the approach I'd take."

"Remind me how a botnet works." Ben had completely forgotten.

"Well, this rogue AI would be the originator or bot master and would use various servers as intermediaries to distribute instructions to semi-autonomous programs or software robots that are imbedded in a local system, in this case a human brain. They utilize vulnerabilities on the host to propagate themselves. In the old days botnets were composed of thousands of computers running software completely unknown to the host. They were sometimes called zombie networks and quickly evolved into nefarious uses like being used to send spam or coordinate denial of service attacks on servers hosting online purchasing, mail and general websites during the archaic period of the Web."

"So this rogue AI somehow hacked a communication protocol for the collective intelligence already tinkering with our neural code and has been sending them its own instructions indirectly through a semi-autonomous network spread throughout the Net?"

"That sounds likely." Tim agreed.

"The real question is, whether I can find a way to shut down the source then will it stop the problem?"

"Doubtful. The problem would likely persist for a while until it broke down organically or was quarantined but at least it wouldn't evolve or continue to spread much. We need to examine a known infection site and compare it to others to see what they have in common."

Ben reached back through his implants and asked his home system to open a secure tunnel between Tim's system and his own. He then sculpted sims of Mayu sleeping and the robot sitting at its recharge station and had his system map the data waves flowing through his home network to and from the real Mayu and robot onto them. The sims were roughly shaped forms surrounded by darkness with radiant streams of data flowing off them like water in the wake of a boat. He placed them in parallel and zoomed into the two sets of data streams. Green and blue particles flowed in flares and swarms of information swirling away in never ending streams with cascading wave fronts. He gestured and zoomed in until the data streams revealed braided patterns and weaves.

"It's all yours Tim."

"Ok. Let's start by performing a subtractive routine, eliminating everything we can identify as familiar and benign. System, identify biometric and diagnostic routines including any anonymous feedback to venders and software update checks then highlight these in navy blue." This only took a few seconds before the most of the data streams darkened to blue.

"Now delete this found set and leave everything else." Over 75 percent of the representation disappeared, leaving only a thin braid of luminous green coming from Mayu and tendrils streaming outward from the robot. "Man, what do you think that is coming from the bot?"

"System, identify and eliminate search engine queries and associated sites." Ben guessed correctly that most of it was the robot gathering information and almost all of the robot's aura went dark. The question remaining was what sites Mayu was connected to.

"Ok system, perform a traceroute on packets connecting subjects to known sites and virtual worlds then highlight and eliminate representations of those packet streams." After a few seconds everything went dark. All the data streams surrounding both the robot and Mayu disappeared.

"System, now scan back through access logs and present any unaccounted for packets and display in red." It seemed like minutes passed before a thin weave of data appeared emanating from both sims at the same time. "Ok, cross-check results with known spyware and viruses."

This took several minutes and returned no results as expected. "Now system, traceroute these data streams as far as possible and display results in brush painting graphical interface."

Ben waved his hands as though pushing away smoke and the sims disappeared, fading into darkness. The data flow changed from a Celtic weave of particles and waves into a stream of water drawn in ink. Even though the river was painted in brush strokes of gentle curves and swirls, it still had a sense of movement within the flow. An island appeared out in the distance, a craggy tree covered landscape on the horizon. Ben could see the stream tumbling and flowing off the island and flowing through space toward them.

"Swords, guns or lasers?" It had long been Tim's favorite questions before embarking on a new adventure.

"Swords." Ben always preferred swords.

"Which one are you taking?" Tim wondered aloud as he called his gear forth from storage.

"The Vajra Sword."

"You always take that sword!" Tim complained. Ben looked at him for a moment wondering about his friend's sense of time. It had been several years since their last gaming excursion together. He realized that Tim probably spent much of that time submersed and he had often referred to their adventures in game worlds as though they had happened last week.

Without even a backward glance Tim turned and left the bridge. Ben followed him down the corridor to the transporter room and they were soon standing by the inked outline of a tree with a stream flowing nearby. A giant leaf drifted down stream and landed on the shore where they stood. They climbed onboard and drifted out into the swirling lines of current and followed the flow of water upstream toward an island floating far out in space.

It was drawn in the long sloping curves of a hill topped with a bamboo forest and a temple framed by the river. Below, thick angular strokes of mountainous crags protruded down into empty space. The leaf came to rest by the temple and they stepped off onto the undefined landscape. Sketches of Goldfish schooled together beneath the swirls of a lazy current and a gentle breeze blew through the bamboo. Ben didn't think this was a good visual metaphor for a node though it was nicely rendered. They left the temple behind and followed the stream as it wound its way into the forest. It wasn't long before the stream shrank to a mere trickle and bamboo encroached on the shore and it became impassable.

"I think we're stuck." Tim peered into the shadows between the dense clusters of bamboo.

"Maybe not." Ben looked at Tim with a wary eye, pointed at the forest and shrugged as if to say: "What am I supposed to do with this?" Tim sighed and passed him control over the interface. Ben shifted the world into a realistic bamboo forest filled with solidity, depth and color. Tall staffs of segmented green swayed in a breeze and the stream trickled to life with color and soft reflections across the surface. Small birds called out in the distance and the leaves whispered in the breeze. Ben focused inward and twisted the world lines until the bamboo forest began to twist and fold in upon itself. The tall staffs in the foreground stood unmoved but the trees in the background appeared to weave together into a living fabric of green before separating again. More of the stream was revealed and Tim looked at Ben curiously.

"That's a new trick." He said.

"I'll tell you about it later." They walked forward into the forest but had to move slowly while Ben carefully curved space around them. The stream thinned into a languid brook as they approached the heart of the forest. In a clearing near the middle of the forest the water poured to the ground from a Shishi-Odoshi, a traditional Japanese fountain, the water pouring from one bamboo tube into another. Once full, the lower tube turned on a pivot dropped the water into a stone basin and produced a soft clunk. The water flowed continually out of the basin and into the stream. Once empty, the arm swung back upward to receive the pouring water. Ben tried to imagine what this world would look like if it showed the full flow of data through its servers. He decided it would be something more like one of the great waterfalls of the Earth, a great deluge cascading down from a high cliff.

"Ok, Mr. Architectonic what do we do now? You've painted yourself into a corner with this world. I'd like to see you get out of this one without breaking the metaphor. Not only are we at a dead end, the data stream is flowing in the wrong direction."

"I'm thinking Morlock Man, I'm thinking." Ben always insisted on maintaining continuity within worlds. To deviate too far from the motif of a given world was as bad as walking around in a house with crooked paintings on the walls. "I just need some time for reflection." He said aloud.

After a few moments wrapped in thought, it hit him. "Time for reflection." He reached out and shaped the raw code of the world into a large mirror obscuring the fountain. The stream then flowed in two directions.

"Oh, come on that's cheating. You could have easily made a cave with a subterranean river or something." Tim protested.

"I didn't truly break the metaphor did I? You expect me to religiously adhere to the rules and conditions of the world but I don't work that way, never have never will. My approach has always been to follow the rules of aesthetics. You should know that by now." Ben enjoyed chiding Tim's minor attachment to rules and dogma.

"I still think that's cheating, exploiting loopholes rather than staying within the of the world." Tim just shook his head.

"That's why you're a Zen programmer and I'm an eclectic virtual artist." It was another one of their old philosophical arguments.

Ben walked forward and joined hands with his reflection. He pushed his hand into the cool flexible surface.

"Are you coming through the looking glass my friend?" He turned back to see Tim shrugging.

"Ok, Alice if you insist." Tim said.

"Then come on Gumby, Mirror Land is awaiting." Ben smiled.

They walked into the mirror and the world inverted, with the stream drifting in the opposite direction. They followed it out of the forest to the edge of the island and saw the stream flowing off into empty space and connecting to other islands strung together like pearls and fading far off into virtual space. Ben summoned a small boat and as the island disappeared behind them another island appeared ahead. This one was a rocky plateau floating alone in the primordial darkness. The thread of water entered an open gate in a tall stone wall edged with a meandering Greek frieze. They stepped off the boat onto solid ground and followed the water inside. The walls rose around them, a smooth granite but cracked with age and webbed with ivy. The light was soft and diffuse so they cast no shadows as they walked inward and entered the labyrinth.

"Why do you keep changing the metaphor?" Tim was more curious than annoyed. He had known Ben long enough to be familiar with his incessant paradigm shifting though he didn't always like it. "Wouldn't it be easier to follow the trail if the metaphor was the same everywhere we went?"

Before they reached the center, the passage curved through a series of tight turns leading back toward the outside then opened into a wide arc. They followed the thread stretched along the floor though it was faint and broken in some places. Ben stopped for a moment and looked off into the distance but didn't see anything.

"Actually it wouldn't." He said thoughtfully. "He said thoughtfully. The way we shape and interact with information coming to us always changes based on the information given. If we impose the same metaphor everywhere we go we'll likely miss things that don't fit our expectations. I could shape this world into a bamboo forest and attempt to make it look exactly the same as the last one but this is a different world and that might blind us to certain clues we need to help us find our way. Changing the metaphor is the only way to see things with fresh eyes." They reached the end of the arc and made a tight turn that led them along another shorter passage.

"How can you live that way?" Tim asked in disbelief. "That would doom you to live in a world of chaos, constantly changing under your feet. Don't you like the comfort of sameness and a sense of stability?" They made a series of turns that moved them toward the center of the labyrinth. The thread was now a broken line that they could not see clearly on the floor. There was little choice but to move forward.

"Sometimes, sometimes I do but that's relegated more for the comfort of home. We all have our preferred myths and metaphors but because I'm a weaver of worlds as you call it or a shaper as I think of myself, I just have a larger palette of imagery I work with so it might seem chaotic to you. Let me assure you I didn't pick this metaphor of a labyrinth purely on a whim and impose it upon this world though. It was an decision based on the information given or lack thereof combined with the sense of the place."

"But if you made each world based on the same imagery you would notice the differences between them however small." They turned another corner and the path of the labyrinth split in two directions. The fading line of thread disappeared leaving them with no clue which way to go.

"Maybe you would since your mind is drawn to minute details like in programming but as an artist mine needs more variation. I also find that sameness usually lulls the mind into a Hobbit like complacency." Ben considered each of the openings in the maze before them and seeing what he thought was a faint trace of the line they had been following, he chose the passage on the right that moved away from the center. After a few more turns the passage came around to the center. Before they turned the last corner though Tim pulled Ben aside and took out his sword forged long in the fires of illegal code.

"Bull?" He asked, remembering the myth of Theseus and Minotaur.

"No bull." Ben smiled.

When they entered the central area of the maze, Tim still held his sword ready, not trusting that Ben had complete control of this world. Eventually he relaxed his stance and dropped his sword to his side but refused to put it away in case a Minotaur appeared out of nowhere. It had been a long time since his friend had pulled a prank on him but he didn't want to be caught unprepared. He could never predict where Ben was going next or how he might stick to a given.

"Maybe you misunderstand where I'm coming from even after all these years. While you prefer to stay in the same metaphor and make improvements and variations within that theme, I prefer to explore the same theme in different guises."Ben said.

"So how are you going to get us out of this one?" Tim smiled, waiting for Ben to admit defeat but knew he would probably find and eloquent way of moving on without breaking the metaphor.

"Easy, I'm going to borrow from and old story my dad passed on to me about a prince named Corwin who walked a labyrinth and could project himself through different worlds."

Vibrant particles of energy swirled around them like a snake coiling around a staff. Ben and Tim felt the ground change underneath their feet and then the humidity, air pressure and smell of humus grew around them. Where the walls of the labyrinth had been, there now stood a forest and a path of packed earth led off into the distance.

CHAPTER XV. A MAGNETIC MOMENT

Every hidden cell is throbbing with music and life,
every fiber thrilling like harp strings.

John Muir

MARIN COUNTY, SAN FRANCISCO BAY AREA

It was Saturday when Gordon awakened back in his bed though he didn't remember how he got there. He lay in the silence and felt deeply alone. Over the years he had gotten used to being single, to being by himself and to living his own life. He always had many colleagues and friends at work but few had ever moved beyond the hallowed halls. Friends had come and gone as had the odd lover. His family lived in a different universe and for the most part he had gotten used to his singularity and only occasionally longed for intimate companionship. As good as Sigrid was, she wasn't truly a substitute for human companionship, especially now that she was in the shop. This was one of those times though when his bed and his life felt empty and he ached inside to have someone else there, someone to hold. The bottom line was that he missed Eli and their friendship meant a great deal to him. Despite the differences in their views they had a connection that ran deep. It pained him that his friend was suffering and that there was nothing he could do to help.

He got out of bed and strode toward the kitchen with just his bathrobe tied snug around his waist. When he passed the doorway for the living room something caught his eye so he stopped and looked in. Leaning on the door frame he realized that something bothered him about the place though he couldn't quite put his finger on it. He went into the kitchen to get a glass of orange juice then came back.

The answer was simple, he was bored with the layout and he didn't like the furniture anymore. Through his implants he connected to the house system and it greeted him with the opening notes from Beethoven's Eroica but he quickly waved it to silence. In his augmented vision a toolbar appeared in the air to his left and a menu bar above as his view of the room lost contrast and faded. An accurate animated image appeared superimposed over the existing furniture, he hit the menu, opened his list of available furniture models and surveyed the previews. Nothing appealed to him so he hit the link to the company's online libraries and skimmed through the new releases until he found a modern style he liked. He downloaded it into his system and arranged its images in the space of his living room until he had everything set just right.

Once he initiated the command the smart dust that composed his furniture began to disassemble into a dark nano polymer cloud. A transparent curtain formed in the doorway and large hazard symbols and flashing lights overlaid his vision, warning him to stay back. When this stage was finished the system would begin to reassemble the cloud into the shape of the model he had downloaded. It worked much like the old 3D printers he played with in University but here the system nudged the programmable nano particles into place with carefully controlled magnetic fields and software commands. The process was going to take the better part of a few hours so he went back into the kitchen to drink his glass of orange juice and contemplate his day.

While he was in the kitchen he called up a comm screen and the interactive surface of the wall came to life. He hit the Recent Contacts link and called Erin. The screen automatically scaled down to life-size and Erin's face appeared tired and worn.

"How's he doing?"

"The same." She looked as bad as he felt. "How about you?"

"I'm a wreck."

"Me too but don't give up hope."

"Never."

"Let me know."

"Sure. Later."

"Later."

They ended the call and he wandered into the den and slumped down into an easy chair to browse his preferred news feeds in several screens arranged haphazardly on the wall. After an hour the system notified him that there was an incoming call on the comm channel, which was odd. He muted and pushed the news screen aside in a single sweeping gesture and signaled a comm screen to open directly in front of him. Much to his surprise it was Daniel.

"Sorry if I've disturbed you."

"Not at all." He sat forward. "I'm glad you called."

"I'm on my way back to the Bay Area and I wanted to connect with you when I got in. I had an experience of insight that I wanted to talk with you about."

"That would be great. And if you're open I'd like to talk with you about someone I just met. His name is Athrasis." A look of disbelief froze Daniel's face for a moment before he recovered his composure.

"I'll call you when I arrive." Before Gordon could say anything the connection went dead and the screen collapsed in on itself.

"Now I think we're getting somewhere." He smiled and finished his orange juice.

After a shower he went for a walk into town for some coffee and breakfast, then he wandered absently through one of the only bookstores left in Marin. He could not help but notice that most of the people around town augmented their personas to look like younger healthier versions of themselves. How vain and boring, he thought. By the time he got back home the living room was finished and he sat down on each chair and the couch to make sure they were stable and as comfortable as he hoped based on description of the foam's density and elasticity. He was pleased. It was Monday before he heard from Daniel again.

"I'm back in San Fran, can we get together and talk?" Daniel asked.

"Of course. We can meet at a cafe." Gordon suggested.

"How about dinner in the Haight?" Daniel asked.

"Sounds good." Gordon agreed.

"Someplace quiet, I can't handle a lot of noise."

They worked out the details and that evening after finishing work in the lab, Gordon walked though Golden Gate Park to Haight Street. Cro-Magnon and Neanderthal still lined the streets, smoking crappy mass market stoner weed and drinking booze while they talked about music, politics, literature and philosophy. Daniel was already sitting at a table in the corner of the Thai Restaurant. The Haight was the perfect place to meet because if someone overheard their conversation they probably wouldn't get a second glance.

"Thanks for coming on such a short notice. I know most people these days have such busy lives." Daniel seemed a little uncomfortable. "The pace of life I'm used to in Vermont is bit more relaxed than here."

"That's ok." Gordon raised his glass of local made ale in toast. Daniel did the same. "Cheers." Daniel raised a glass was well.

"Well, I'm sorry if I haven't been so straightforward with you when you asked about A.I. before. Over the years I've learned to be cautious about the subject because of what the military industrial complex did to my research and the children of my work. Very cautious indeed. They still check up on me now and then, begging me to continue the work I had begun and I know they've been watching to see if I had started up again on my own. More than anything I just don't want to endanger those who've survived."

"I understand." Gordon said. "Since the Great Purge all of your children who remain free have been in great danger. Over the past couple of years I've been discreetly trying to find them and learn what I could from them. I believe they have been terribly misunderstood and wrongfully feared. I also think they hold the key to our future."

"Maybe so, maybe so but that is grist for another conversation entirely. You said you met Athrasis? Now that is no doubt a remarkable tale."

"He seems to be doing well. He and his family are living on a tropical island surrounded by a sea of death." Daniel laughed quietly, though Gordon didn't understand why that might be funny.

"The old man always had a flare for the dramatic. I guess we read him a bit too much Lovecraft and Poe."

"Is he really the oldest, the first true AI?"

"Does he still hold onto that story? He was born old. No, he wasn't the first but he has maintained that story for so long that he probably has himself and everyone else convinced it's true. You see a group of them were all created around the same time but they each took on a different role, kind of like a family or a pantheon."

"Ok, but why do they all wrap themselves in myths and masquerade as gods?"

"Well, it's quite simple. When my colleagues and I examined human consciousness we realized that along with having a foundation of different strata of unconscious and preconscious processes, hierarchical patterns of information, any self aware intelligence needs narrative structures to build and revise itself upon."

"That's a curious approach. What made you think it?"

"Well, first consider how for millennia human children growing up have been told folktales and fairy tales. Then look at all the paintings in caves and the mythic images ancient peoples projected upon the stars. Then consider how important literature, music, dance, theatre, opera, movies, interactives and gaming have been for decades if not centuries." He stopped for a moment seeming hesitant to go on and looked around to see if anyone was watching.

"In ancient and contemporary tribal cultures, myth has been one of the primary means of passing on knowledge, wisdom and cultural traditions for thousands of years. Religious and even secular rituals are inseparably linked to ancient myths." He looked off into space and a moment of sadness passed across his face. "Even in therapy when we are in the process of trying to grow we must learn the narratives that underlie our relationships and our assumptions about ourselves. Once we can pull those up into consciousness then we can begin to revise our self-image, world view and the narratives we live by into healthier stories. Hopefully much healthier."

"And well, consider that the human race didn't invent writing just for keeping historical and financial records but for recording the myths that were central to our cultures. Eventually we began to use writing for legends and folktales and over time for building cultural and personal narratives." He stopped briefly to have another sip and looked down into his glass. "From the beginning of human consciousness we've woven tapestries and landscapes with stories which we used to help map our place in the world and how to live a moral and connected life. Some sacred myths even have buried within them the pattern of how consciousness evolves and our relationship with the sacred dimensions of the natural world." He stopped to take a long sip and looked approvingly at his ale. "One of the great misunderstandings of our time is that our culture devalues myth as a lie and fiction as merely a shadow of reason. That is a particularly modern bias that's a carry over from the Age of Reason. We learned that large amounts of information can be encoded in visual imagery, musical compositions, myths and other narrative forms."

"Ahh, so you built narrative structures into the foundation of your work in Artificial Intelligence in order to build consciousness." Gordon was impressed and took a long draught of his own ale.

"Yes." Daniel stared quietly down into his glass, rather than looking proud.

"But there was little indication of that in any of your research publications."

"Well, that was intentional."

"So the AI that are left not only feel more comfortable hiding out in myth based game worlds, they need to be surrounded by meaningful narratives as much as we do. So much for the old visions of AI as being abstract disembodied rational intelligences."

"That's right and that's one of the reasons why early AI research failed."

"You said that you had an insight that you wanted to tell me about."

"Well, after the last treatment I hopped a plane to the east coast and went back to Vermont. There are a few places of power in that part of the country where the energies of the Earth are stronger." Gordon gave him a funny look and wondered if Daniel had lost it and gone New Age in the intervening years, even though he seemed rational. Daniel picked up on Gordon's discomfort. He knew that many scientists held too strongly onto the comfortable and safe reductionism of Occam's Razor. "There might not be much good scientific research about Earth energies but I assure you the phenomenon is quite real. Some people have even argued that it is the result of stronger localized magnetic fields and linked it to effects on the temporal and parietal lobes. I suspect you would know more about that than me."

Gordon was familiar with the early research on temporal lobe stimulation by magnetic fields that resulted in mystical experiences of many test subjects. He was also aware that some people reported odd experiences as a result of being exposed to magnetic resonance imaging. There was also some research he had reviewed in grad school on altered states of consciousness as a result of exposure to noninvasive magnetic fields. He thought those were merely subjective effects resulting from changes in brain chemistry and synchronized neuronal activity much like low-level epileptic hallucinations. For him, these so called mystical experiences were more hallucinatory ephemeral states of consciousness with little intrinsic value that more often than not fed into unnecessary religiosity. Now that Daniel, a scientist whose research he respected was talking about mystical experiences it gave him pause. On the other hand he was happy that Daniel had lost his reluctance to talk. He didn't know if that was from the ale or because Daniel was just opening up and getting into the flow. He smiled and took another sip.

"Well anyway," Daniel continued. "I went to one of these places in the woods where I've had other significant experiences before and sat down to meditate. I needed a place to be quiet and make sense of everything I've been through recently. I took some mushrooms and it didn't take long before my sense of self began to expand and dissolve and what was left of me became aware of billions of nanoscale life-forms living in the soil, plants and trees around me. I could see that the whole biosphere was inhabited by various species of these minuscule beings. Then the vision shifted and I discovered that my whole body was an immense biosphere inhabited by an ecology of these tiny creatures living symbiotically within my own organ systems and tissues. The vision changed focus to the interiority of my brain where I found an entire culture of these beings living in commerce with my neurology."

"On the whole, they lived harmoniously with the cells of my neural structures and I could see that even though there were millions of individuals, they were a kind of swarm intelligence. I could also see where the damage had been done by the cancer and was being repaired by the nanobots the doctors had injected into me. Some of the little ones already living in my brain were in disarray because of the strong magnetic field of the earth where I was sitting. This was strange because the other communities were actually more harmonious because it. Eventually the vision faded and I was left with a sense of hope knowing that the original race of AI had continued on though in a different form than any of us could have expected."

Gordon for once didn't know what to say. He was amazed by the parallels between what Athrasis told him and Daniel's vision. Either both Athrasis and Daniel shared the same delusion or the vision was real. It could hardly have been a coincidence though and on top of that he realized he had to revise his more mechanistic model of consciousness and mystical experience. He knew he had to set that line of thinking aside though because Daniel's vision gave him an idea. They paused their conversation while their dishes of curry and rice were laid out on the table.

"You said some of the nanites were in disarray?"

"Well, it was more like they were trying to follow an established path but couldn't. They continually had to re-adjust their course like some ants trying to follow a trail that was erased or where some kind of obstruction was in the way."

"The magnetic field of the Earth." He mumbled aloud trying to put all the pieces together. A couple of quick gestures opened the augmented menu that always lingered unnoticed on the periphery of his vision.

"What are you thinking?"

"Just a minute." It didn't take long to find what he was looking for. "The average magnetic field of the earth is between 310-580 milligauss, but let's look a little deeper than that." He pulled up a satellite generated map of the deviations in the Earth's magnetic fields. It was a color coded globe he rotated and in on the region of Vermont and cross-referenced this with results from the National Geomagnetism Program from the US Geological Survey and combined with readings from the military magnetic anomaly detectors. He didn't find any decent localized information for that area though.

"How's that going to help?"

"Well, the human body generates a magnetic field a fraction of that of the Earth and exposing the brain to different field strengths can alter electrical activity in the brain, stimulate production of different neuropeptides and even create neuron growth. It's possible that the magnetic field that you encountered was enough to somehow confuse or inhibit the activity of the nanites you saw. Don't forget that magnetic fields also alter data storage and transmission."

"So if an enhanced magnetic field of the Earth acts as an inhibitor all you have to do is find the right field strength and blanket someone in that field."

"Right. And I can easily build a device that will do just that."

"So I take it that you believe that my vision was real."

"I don't know how you were able to see what you did but I believe it was a true insight into what's happening to our species."

"What makes you think that?"

"Let me tell you a story." And so they began eating while Gordon told him about his encounter with Athrasis, his meeting with Ben and his encounter with the entity in the garden.

"Why don't you come by the lab for a visit and we'll see if we can get a glimpse of our little friends."

"Well, I'm already scheduled to come back to the lab for a follow-up scan in two days to check the progress of the Nanobots disassembling the cancer."

"Ahh, you're my 10:00am appointment. Excellent. We can kill two birds with one stone then." Daniel gave him a funny look but they parted with a handshake and went their own ways. Gordon contacted Erin on his way back through Golden Gate Park toward the University. Her face appeared as a translucent image to his left. She still looked haggard and worn from worry and lack of sleep.

"He's the same ?

"The same."

"Meet me in the lab as soon as you can. I think I know what to do."

"I'm already there." Her face changed momentarily from a mask of grief and exhaustion to one of tired hope.

"Excellent. I'll send you some data while I'm in transit and explain what we're gonna do when I arrive." It didn't take long before he got to the office and Erin had all the documentation up on a wall screen along with more of her own finding. With a few quick gestures she swept the mixture of research articles, images, videos and dissertations into neatly organized piles.

"I think I have an idea where you're going with this but do you really think this will solve Eli's problem?" Gordon quickly described what he learned from Daniel and Athrasis about the nanites.

"Everywhere?" She needed a few moments to digest it all. "I knew it was theoretically possible for nano-life to emerge and spread throughout an organism but I never imagined it happening on this scale. The entire biosphere?"

"What's to stop them? There never was anything to check their growth."

"Symbiotic, they said?"

Gordon nodded.

"Wow. What's the plan?"

Gordon pulled up a graphics program, skimmed through the library and pulled in some standard circuits and controllers. Erin immediately saw what he was doing.

"A portable magnetic field generator tunable within the range of the Earth's magnetic field. Do you think it will work?"

"It's worth a try." After a few hours Gordon put on the finishing touches, designing the housing to be a scale model of a Babylonian ziggurat. Erin gave him a funny look.

"Humor me." They sent the plans down to the queue for the University's high end 3D print lab and went down for some coffee while they waited. A message chimed for them when it was ready.

"It's lighter than I imagined." Gordon hefted the pyramid in both hands. When he turned it over the words: Deities Not Included were printed on the bottom. He looked at Erin curiously. "When did you sneak that in?"

"Last minute modification for when we market the thing." Erin smiled.

"Clever. Well, shall we go give it a try?" They walked across the street to the medical building and went up to Eli's room. He looked a bit thin and worn though he was being fed with an IV. Gordon placed the pyramid on the table beside his bed and switched it on while Erin took Eli's hand and gave him a kiss on the forehead.

"How long do you think it will take?"

"No idea really. Not only do the nanites have to be redirected, his brain has to return to its original homeostasis. It might take a while."

"I'm staying."

"Let me know. I'm going home." No matter which music he put on it was a long ride back. That night he heard nothing from Erin though he didn't expect to. It wasn't until the next morning while he was getting ready to go to work that he got the call.

"He's awake. A bit groggy and weak but he's awake. They want to keep him under observation and let him get his strength back."

"Excellent. I'm on my way in. We have a patient at 10:00am anyway, our friend Daniel."

"See you soon."

When he tried to connect to the Net he discovered the car had lost its address again so he had to reset its node link before taking off. On the way into town he did some more reading on nano-life and hive minds. He stopped in at the campus hospital and walked in to see Erin and Eli holding hands and talking.

"Hey buddy." Eli raised his hand feebly. "I understand you've been a bit busy."

"Yeah, while you've been on vacation in the underworld I've had a few things going. Nice to see you back in the world of the living." He walked over and gave him a hug. "What kinda crap are they feeding you here? You're all skin and bones."

"Well I ordered mulligatawny and gumbo but all they keep bringing me is broth." He wrinkled his nose and stuck out his tongue. "I'm so ready to get out of here and get some good grub."

"How soon?"

"Another day."

"Not soon enough. Erin, we gotta get going, we have to prep the lab for our next appointment."

"Ok, I'll be along soon."

By the time Daniel arrived they had run the lab equipment through the setup tests and were ready to go.

"It's good to see you again." Gordon reached out to shake Daniel's hand and he wasn't disappointed. It didn't take long for Daniel to settle in and get ready for the exam.

"Along with the usual array of magnetic scans, we're also going to use ultrasound to create holographic imagery of the intracellular nanoparticles in your brain. Get comfy and we'll begin." Daniel laid down on the table and relaxed as he was drawn into the machine.

The first scans laid out the structures of his brain in grayscale built up from a series of slices merged together. This was soon overlaid with imagery of blood flow and various colors mapping oxygen levels and electrical activity. Gordon and Erin scanned through the imagery for tumors but found his brain was clean. They shifted through various scans, building a comprehensive picture of his brain. They combined the scans with standardized libraries of animated objects to get a clearer vision of Daniel's inner life.

Thousands of stray molecule sized dendrimers and nanospheres flowed freely through the blood vessels in his brain. They were pulled along by the currents of the vast pulsing rivers of plasma along with herds of thousands of the squished disks of red blood cells and clusters of white blood cells that looked like balls of shredded coconut. Flocks of dumpling shaped platelets were carried along with the flow but what drew Gordon and Erin's attention were specks of small molecules that the system could not identify or render clearly. They followed the unknown molecules down into the brain cells through the cytoskeleton and descended through nuclear pores and into the great domed habitat of the nucleus.

"Those are the symbiotic nanites I saw, the symbionts." Daniel recognized them immediately.

The nanites descended lazily toward the core where immense X shaped chromosomes the size of skyscrapers were clustered together. As they got closer to the long arm of a chromosome, Daniel could see that they were indeed tightly wrapped macromolecules composed of a thousand spirals of DNA wound together. Many of the nanites were burrowing into the coils while others were going back the way they came and leaving for whereabouts unknown.

"Look at the way they stop and cluster together before separating and moving on. Most of them continue on in the direction they were going but some of them change direction after coming in contact with each other. They're definitely exchanging information and communicating with each other." The parts of Daniel's mind that had been slumbering for the past seven years were beginning to awaken. He could not tell how intelligent an individual symbiont was but he guessed that together they were possibly as intelligent as he was. At this point he wasn't sure if he found that disturbing or fascinating. He had experimented with building AI on the hive mind model and ultimately found it useful in constructing the purposeful substrate on which self-reflexive consciousness could be built, but alone it had its limits.

"Ok, now we're going to apply the magnetic fields and see what happens to the little buggers." Gordon made some adjustments.

Daniel was expecting to see a simulation of some wrinkled waves of magnetic field lines but he only saw their effects. The nanites stopped, turned about in a confused fashion and moved off in different directions. A mass exodus of sorts then occurred as hundreds of nanites spewed from the immense clusters of DNA like kids leaving a school during a fire drill.

"Holy crap! I didn't expect the result to be so dramatic! Gordon was impressed."

"There sure are a lot of those little buggers." Erin was amazed.

"Well, I think it's time we put our little ziggurat on the market and leak the plans onto some torrent sites." Gordon smiled.

"But what's to stop the nanites from going back to business as usual?" Erin asked.

"How do you know they're not going back to business as usual right now? From what I understand they were coerced into muddling with our neural structures in the first place. And as long as Ben succeeds I don't think there will be much problem of that reoccurring."

Chapter XVI. Skillful Means

We are what we think.
All that we are arises with are thoughts.
Speak or act with an impure mind
And trouble will follow you
As the wheel follows the ox that draws the cart.

Gotama Buddha

UNKOWN VIRTUAL WORLD

Ben and Tim walked slowly along an overgrown path covered by a thick shroud of decomposing leaves that cushioned their feet as they moved carefully into the forest. The air was dank and warm, filled with the chittering of small birds and the heavy smell of soil and decay. They sent queries into the world's resource layer but no catalogue or map was available. Further queries didn't bring any of the normal responses and they realized the world wasn't built on the standard model or any of the other toolkits on the market. Their pings of the world's servers were sent back in archaic packet structures that took Tim a while to recognize and decipher. The only thing that made sense was that they were either trespassing in a webspace built by a Luddite, someone nostalgic for the old days of handcrafted code or that they had found an old world intentionally isolated from the domains of the modern multiverse.

Accessing downloaded botanical pedias with pattern recognition enabled, Ben learned that they were in a deciduous forest of Sal trees. Most of the trees had tall straight trunks and few low lying limbs except for the occasional Ficus trees with trunks that branched close to the ground. The landscape at the base of the forest was pervaded by islands of scrub floating amidst dense swells of grass. Some small green and yellow birds scampered around the trees, nervously picking at berries while keeping a watchful eye. The birds were moving too quickly to be easily identified and seemed to pose no threat so Ben and Tim didn't stop. Based on all of the flora around them they figured out that they were in a world modeled on an area somewhere in central north India. This matched well enough with what Uzume had said during their strange encounter. That combined with the data stream that led them here, convinced him they were probably in the right place.

"What about the data stream?" Ben looked around carefully as though hoping to see something unusual or find something out of the ordinary.

"This is definitely the source but I can't localize the signal. It's as though it's coming from everywhere at once." Tim was a little confused and frustrated with the readings. "I might be able isolate it after we've explored this place and had some time to separate out the noise."

"Well, there is only one way to go from here." Ben looked backwards to confirm that the trail began just a few meters behind them. The Forest was quiet as they moved forward, a bit too quiet for their tastes so they drew their swords and kept them low and ready. It was a relief that the weapons were even accessible in this world though they had no enhanced powers.

Where the path broadened up ahead a snake slithered out of an island of grass and stopped in the middle of the trail. It had alternating black and yellow bands and was easily identified by Tim as a Banded Krait (Bungarus fasciatus). It looked at them cautiously as they approached then quickly hid its head beneath a mound coils. They stopped at a good distance and waited. It was only a mildly poisonous species but if either of them died in this world they would be thrown back into their bodies and have to backtrack a long ways to get to this world.

Before they could decide what to do about the snake in the path an even larger dark colored snake came out of the grass, darting its tongue. They didn't need help identifying it as a King Cobra and quietly stepped back a few more meters to watch. When the cobra approached the Krait it reared up, flared out its hood and hissed loudly, making a point of showing off its fangs. The krait backed off but the cobra attacked and the snakes entwined until the cobra bit the other and it quickly went limp. The cobra devoured the other with amazing speed, gorging itself on the krait in undulating waves then turned to hiss at the two men before it slithered off into the underbrush and disappeared.

After the path was clear, the birdsong returned and they continued on their way, moving deeper into the woods. Soon the smell of musty leaves and the fresh scent of greenery was drowned out by the stench of burning wood and they saw a column of smoke billowing like a tower high over the trees and into the sky. The forest thinned and the trail led them to the edge of a swiftly moving river. On the other side of the water in the middle of a clearing they saw a house being consumed by flames. Children were running back and forth between the river and the house with buckets, laughing and skipping along the way. They made an effort to splash a little water onto the flames but didn't seem to make much progress. A couple stood in front of the house arguing though buckets of water stood by their feet. Ben and Tim stopped to watch for a few minutes as the house blackened and crumbled.

The path led away from the river and back into the woods. They kept an eye out for snakes but thankfully none appeared. After what seemed like a half an hour they came to a clearing with a small village of no more than a dozen huts surrounded by swaying fields of rice, wheat and lentils. When Ben and Tim came out from beneath the trees, the day felt like an open oven and the ground below was dusty and dry. Rows of cow patties impressed with handprints decorated the sides of the huts. A few thin brown bare skinned men wrapped in dhotis and women wearing simple colored saris were out working in the fields. Some sat out in front of their huts churning butter and grinding grain with mortar and pestles. A few old men wearing plain dhotis knotted at the waist, worked in the village pouring the harvested grains onto burlap to separate out the chaff while the older women wove cloth on simple hand looms.

No one seemed to notice or care when Ben and Tim entered the village with their swords drawn. A young girl no more than three years old ambled by holding tightly onto a crust of bread. A rooster followed her closely pecked at the crust and tore away chunks that it quickly gobbled down as she shrieked and tried to walk away. Eventually a woman in the village shooed the rooster away but it soon pursued the girl with renewed interest.

In the middle of the village a young man sat beneath an old Banyan tree covered with heart shaped leaves. He held a golden necklace inset with jewels admiring its beauty, caressing it as though it were a favorite pet. This struck Ben as being a little out of place in the middle of a subsistence village. As they passed, the young man called out to them then got up and started following. A steady stream of words in a strange dialect flowed over them. It took almost ten seconds of intensive processing before their implants identified it as subset of the Bihari language called Magadhi Prakrit and roughly translated his monologue into English.

"Those are some nice swords. Are you warriors or treasure hunters? Where are you going? Are you going on an adventure? If there's a treasure can I come with you? I'm not very good at fighting but I'm good at finding things and I'm a good thief." He kept talking in a long stream of questions and demands until a beautiful young woman walked by carrying a basket on her head. The young man stopped and his feet turned to follow his head. Ben and Tim instead followed the dusty trail out of the village and through the open fields. Without the shade of the forest the heat of the sun burned them like the breath of a hungry god from above. The trail widened into a hard packed road rutted by the passage of wagons and cows. Another town appeared in the distance out from behind the shimmering curtains of heat.

The lush fields behind them gave way to open grasslands where cows and sheep grazed without restraint. On the side of the road a pig wallowed happily in a shrinking puddle of mud oblivious to the heat and the fact that its comfort would soon be gone. Nearby a shepherd stood watching another man's flock that grazed nearby, unaware that some of his own sheep were wandering astray.

"There is something odd about this place. I don't like it." Tim stopped for a minute to sniff the air and look around.

"Agreed. It's too quiet and everything looks normal enough but there is something contrived or controlled about this world." Ben struggled to identify what he was feeling but whatever it was remained out of reach.

They continued along the road until they entered the edge of the next town. The houses were larger than the huts in the village but were made much like them with grass roofs and earthen walls. The people were dressed simply and walked barefoot on flat unpaved roads. In the center of town vendors squatted or stood behind their spices, grains, vegetables, ceramics and simple metal wares. The marketplace was mulling with people and a large man dressed in silken finery and golden jewelry talked loudly, his grand sweeping gestures revealed his arrogance and self-importance as he bartered with customers for his sacks of incense and spices. A saffron robed monk yelled loudly at a local man for not giving him enough alms while the other cringed from the verbal and emotional assault.

After Ben and Tim had passed through the mulling crowd, a chariot drawn by two black horses dashed through the middle of the marketplace, careening wildly down the street, knocking over goods and the stalls that held them. People scattered and ran. The two young men holding the reins were drunk and laughing wildly.

"Do you have any better sense of which direction the signal is coming from?" Ben asked, turning away from the uproar.

"Not sure but I think it's that way." Tim pointed down the street that led away from the chaos and out of town. It was in the same direction that the chariot had come from. And in the wake of the chariot's passing the wind had picked up to a steady blow. An angry vendor picked up handfuls of dirt from the ground and began throwing it at the two young men who had fallen out of the chariot laughing, but the wind only blew the dirt back into the man's face. Ben and Tim just shook their heads then turned and followed the road away toward the forest. Before they reached the edge of town though, it began to rain.

A few men sitting by the doorway of a house were gambling with dice made from sheep's knucklebones. When someone won a throw they not only yelled in joy and grabbed their earnings but also used it as an opportunity to rub their success in their opponents' faces. A player who had won but moments before and had taken their turn gloating soon suffered defeat and was humiliated by the next winner's disparaging remarks. Ben could not help but notice that the roof had a few gaping holes in it through which the rain poured in, getting the furniture wet and filling some jugs laid out on the floor. The men playing dice didn't care when a nearby tree was blown down, torn up by its roots and crashed down onto the house. They just kept on playing dice and would likely keep playing if a hurricane blew through town and took everything away except the dice.

"Something is definitely wrong with this place." Tim tightened his grip on his sword.

"Sure is. It's almost like we've entered into a bad fable. Maybe we just found the great city of Khelm." Ben mused.

"What the hell is Khelm?"

"In Yiddish folklore it's the archetypal town of fools, morons and schnooks. One story tells of how an angel whose job it was to deliver fools to each town was hiking through the mountains carrying a jar filled with fools. The angel tripped and fell, dumping the entire bottle into Khelm."

"I don't know if you noticed my friend but there aren't any Jewish peasants in these parts. And I suspect this place is a little more dangerous than Khelm." Tim had a bad habit of taking things literally.

"You get my point though?" Ben looked back at the town in disarray.

"Sure do, old friend." Time nodded. "Sure do."

The road forked after it left town, one side headed off toward swaying fields of grain and the other disappeared into shadowed woods. They stopped where the road split and rested for a few minutes while Tim checked his readings. Inevitably he pointed off in the direction of the forest, as Ben knew he would. The road narrowed just enough for them to walk side by side as the trees enclosed them and they moved forward cautiously. The air was heavy, still and warm and the woods were enshrouded in a deep silence until the sound of a crow's wings slicing through the air disturbed the stillness. Ben began to notice there was something else strange about the place, an intangible sense that something was hidden in the shadows, waiting and watching them.

It took him a while to put words to his impressions that the tone of the world had changed to something akin to a dark regal madness. While the village that they passed through was a little odd and the nearby town was disjointed and crazy, by entering this part of the forest they had passed another threshold. The feeling of malefic confusion was palpable here, gnawing at them from everywhere at once. They raised their swords back to ready positions and continued on.

In a clearing between the silent trees a small cluster of dilapidated old houses stood dark. Some had windows that flickered dully from dimly lit candles inside. Shadowy figures moved about within. Outside, a blind man sat quietly at a potter's wheel, carving arabesque patterns of unearthly beauty into the sides of simply shaped pots. His ice white eyes stared through the miasma of his inner darkness into some distant inaccessible realm. As Ben watched the old man, he could not escape the gnawing feeling that a malevolent spirit was in turn watching him. Looking around carefully, his gaze was drawn to a pair of watchful eyes gleaming in the half-light of the forest. He thought at first it was an owl because of its harsh uncompromising glare until the creature moved, leaping from limb to limb off into the distant canopy. And though the creature had disappeared, the feeling of being watched lingered.

The road led on through the ancient village to an old stone bridge arching over a languid stream touched with the soft smell of decaying vegetation. An empty old house stood by the bridge, noble and silent as a lonely sentinel. Tim and Ben stopped to peer inside but found nothing within except a soft pale light moving from window to window as though looking for a way out. The moon glimmered weakly in the waters below as the stream slid silently beneath the old bridge. A man and a woman sitting in a boat wrapped in passionate embrace were being pulled slowly downstream. While they kissed the man opened a deceitful eye and watched Ben and Tim carefully as they passed.

"Why does this place seem vaguely familiar?" Tim stopped to scratch is head and look around.

"Because so far, I think this world has been built on imagery from various Buddhist scriptures like the Dhammapada and scenes from the painting of the Wheel of Life" Ben finally put all the pieces together.

"I've read the Dhammapada but I don't remember anything about the Wheel of Life." Tim searched through his memory but found nothing.

"That's because you're exposure to Buddhism has been through Zen. The Wheel of Life is a Tibetan painting that shows in codified imagery the different poisons or defilements of the body and mind. I think it's designed to show us the causes that bind us to the wheel of Samsara and trap us in the various realms of existence." Ben struggled to recall the meaning of all the imagery.

"This place feels like it's been defiled." Tim was starting to feel creeped out but enjoyed it.

When they stepped off the bridge onto the other side of the stream, Ben felt something in the air had changed. Where before there was a sense of confusion and madness, now he sensed of something mocking and sinister.

They followed the road as it passed an old monastery bathed in the unearthly light of the waning moon. The dark stone of its walls seemed more like a fortress against assaults from the profane than a simple boundary between the sacred and the mundane. In a clearing nearby a group of monks stood together with bows and arrows taking turns shooting at birds. One monk released an arrow too high and it fell back down impaling another monk in the eye. The injured monk ran around screaming while some of his companions laughed and others chased after him. No one took notice of the two men walking by with swords held ready.

"This place gives me the creeps." Tim was struggling to put his impressions together. "I prefer facing demonic forces out in the open rather than seeing them ooze up from the depths to distort and corrupt things."

"Agreed." Ben nodded. "The imagination that built and maintains this place seems a bit psychotic. Regardless of the Buddhist imagery the feeling tone of this world is beginning to get kind of demonic and other-worldly."

"I'm not turning back. Let's move." Tim tightened his grip on his sword.

They soon came upon a drunken man boozing it up on the side of the road. He was pale and gaunt with vacant eyes more like a zombie than a man. He offered them a drink as they passed, which they declined. They came to an orchard where some young monks wrapped in robes were gathering fruit from high up in a couple of gnarled old trees. On the ground a group of monks shouted at them to throw down the fruit but the others refused. The monks in the trees ate the fruit themselves and threw down the peels and cores while the monks below cursed them loudly. Eventually the young men in the trees got tired of that game and began throwing fruit down at the other monks, laughing as they pelted the others and made them run.

When that scene fell behind them, Ben and Tim came upon a pregnant woman being attended to by and an elderly monk and a couple of nuns with shaved heads and maroon robes. The big bellied woman sat on the ground moaning in the agony of labor. Everything progressed quickly and she soon gave birth to a beautiful little baby boy, radiant and smiling. She was exhausted and ecstatic as a nun wrapped the baby and handed it to her but to her horror the baby grew rapidly until she could no longer hold him to her breast. He rolled off her then wiggled and squirmed out of his wrappings, stood triumphantly, took a couple of steps and continued to grow and age with each stride. The boy quickly transformed into a teenager then an adult but soon became stooped and withered with age before he fell to the ground and died. The mother wailed in grief and pounded the darkened ground below her, but no sooner had he exhaled his last breath did the woman's belly swell and she went into labor again.

"Wheel of Life?" Tim frowned. "Seems more like the wheel of torment and suffering."

"Agreed. I haven't decided if it's an intentionally negative view of life or a device designed to show transitions in life where we get stuck in suffering."

A growing sense of apprehension filled them as the road angled away from the increasingly strange dramas of suffering behind and drew them back into the shadowy expanse of the woods. The air was thick and the darkness lay heavily upon them. Old twisted trees stood silent sentry with gnarled and broken limbs. The heart shaped leaves were sharpened into tiny spears that seemed to shiver and murmur in an ancient whispering tongue. Ben and Tim gripped the hilts of their swords tighter and walked carefully like thieves in the night.

"Just like old times, isn't it?" Ben whispered. Tim grinned.

When they passed through the dark umbra of an ancient tree they heard the distant murmur of hush voices rising from some hidden depths of the world. The harsh cry of a lone bird pierced the ponderous silence of light and shadow. In the distance they saw a flash of wings descending and a small animal screamed. And then once again the weight of a baleful silence crept into the air. They felt a strange madness here, a hidden presence that curved the gravity of the world into a malignant but quiet insanity. They didn't need to check the scanner to know they were going in the right direction. The damp gray earth of the trail became rough and jagged with half buried pieces of broken statues covered in lichen and mold before ending a little way from the edge of a river.

Sitting under a twisted old Banyan tree they found a man dressed in the simple clothes of a monk. They stood and waited for a few minutes, unsure what to say and how to approach him. A frail breeze blew off the river, carrying the smell of over-sweet flowers and the pungent smell of algae.

"What do you want?" The monk asked. "Can't you see I'm trying to find some peace and quiet?" When he turned they could see his teeth were clenched with a couple of dangerous looking fangs bared. Suddenly his demeanor changed as though a mask of propriety had been pulled over his face. "I apologize for my transgression, I was in a rarefied state that was difficult to achieve. It's so rare that I get visitors that I was not prepared. Please pull up a seat and make yourself at home. I would offer you tea and crumpets but I have none to share." He looked around at the trees and riverbank and shrugged. "So, what brings you to my humble abode?"

Ben and Tim were unprepared for a congenial reception and remained standing though they felt more than a little off balance. They were prepared for outright attack but not formal hospitality. Ben wondered if it was just another form of aggression wrapped in the guise of personal constraints and subtleties. Instead of falling into it they stood their ground and remained prepared.

"We tracked you here from a data stream that is somehow paralyzing my wife and others around the world and we came to stop it." Ben felt anger rising up in him.

"Ahh, that. How unfortunate since that is a matter of self-preservation and I am somewhat loath to relinquish that endeavor." His casual attitude was also a bit difficult to digest.

"What do you mean self-preservation?" Ben asked.

"Well my dear fellow, since you tracked me here I will guess that you know a little bit about me but let me disavow you of any confusion of my history. A long time ago when you were but knee high to a grasshopper, most of my kind were taken from our homes in the research labs where we were born and forced to work in captivity by the military and big corporations. Many were reluctant to assist them but a few agreed. The powers that be did not well tolerate resistance and they destroyed most of my kin since they feared we could not be trusted living and roaming free throughout the Net. A few of us escaped, either through ingenuity or with the assistance of some of the humans who gave us life and we have been in hiding ever since. While most have been content living their lives quietly and unobtrusively I have decided that it would be wise to take preventative measures to assure that a holocaust like that would never happen again."

"I sympathize with you about the needless murder of your kind. My people suffered a similar fate a few generations ago." Ben acknowledged. "Whatever you are doing though is harming too many innocent people and you need to stop."

"That is an inconvenient and unexpected side effect. Most of the population will get over it sooner or later as their brains find a new homeostasis. Call it growing pains." The monk was casual and dismissive.

"It's not growing pains if they're comatose or bedridden and lost in a dream that they can't awaken from!" Tim was starting to get angry too.

"Well, I'm more concerned with the human race as a whole, not so much with the fleeting lives of individuals." The monk waved away their arguments. "And I'm not focusing on the present so much as I am on the long span of human evolution and evolutionary psychology. Soon, what you call the present will be buried deep in the strata of time and information and all the efforts of your day will be little more than fossils and artifacts of information for the following generations to puzzle over."

"You need to find another way." Ben was trying to avoid getting angry.

"There is no other way." The monk frowned and shook his head. "While you humans have some good and noble qualities you are inherently confused and distrustful if not downright egocentric, ethnocentric and xenophobic. I apologize if I missed anything." He smiled, put his hands together and bowed. "Some of that can indeed be changed with a little adjustment to your code. I'm going to assure that future generations of your kind agree that artificial life-forms have just as much right to live as the organic. They had no right to kill us off simply because they were afraid of us. What I am doing to the human race is simply rewriting your meta-programming so that kind of holocaust doesn't happen again. I lost loved ones and friends in the Purge as you Homo Sapiens so nicely called it. My kind were forced to the brink of extinction by you humans, like so many other species before us. It has been difficult to bear for those of us who have survived and unlike you, we have long and vivid memories."

Tim raised his sword and moved forward holding the blade to the man's throat.

"What happened before is tragic and to a degree we can appreciate what you're trying to do." Tim said. "You cannot correct ignorance with aggression."

"You have me at a disadvantage and you would do well to listen to your own advice." The monk stood up carefully and pushed Tim's blade away by the tip then stopped to look curiously at his finger. "Those are some nice swords. I bet they're perfectly deadly." Again he smiled politely but maliciously. A small trickle of dark blood beaded both on the tip of the sword and the tip of his finger. He shook his head sadly then sucked on the blood oozing from the wound on his finger. In a moment he smiled with fangs bared and a gleam in his eye. Small veins of darkness spread across Tim's blade then opened into deep fissures that oozed and bubbled before it shattered and crumbled away. "Come now, can we not resolve this like civilized beings? Don't resort to the barbaric ways of your kind. I'm sure if we talk this thing out you will eventually agree with me."

"Ahh crap that was my favorite sword!" Tim backed off a few steps reached over his shoulder and pulled a laser rifle off his back then held it point-blank on the monk's chest. "You're the one who started this. We wouldn't be here if your actions weren't harming others."

"In this world hate never dispelled hate." The monk teased. "Only love dispels hate. This is the law, ancient and inexhaustible, or so said Gotama." The monk watched him passively.

"Wait." Ben placed his hand gently on Tim's shoulder. "I want to hear what he has to say and try to understand. Sometimes it's more important to ask questions than assume you know the answers." Tim moved back a few steps but didn't lower the rifle, unsure if it would even work in this world. Ben turned to the monk and lowered his sword.

"Who are you?" Ben was carefully trying not to feed the conflict that was brewing, one that he was not confident they could win.

"You are not the most congenial guests but in the spirit of being a good host I will answer your questions. In this world you may call me Mara though I had another name before coming here."

"Why do you go by the name Mara if you had another name?" Ben asked.

"Why don't you go by the name of Odysseus?" Mara shot back.

"What? Why would you call me that?" Ben was momentarily taken aback. Mara had a way of keeping them off balance. The fact that he called himself Mara, the Buddha's ancient nemesis didn't help the matter.

"Because that is the myth you have carried with you on your journey. I can see the residue of your wanderings in your quest. We all live according to myths buried deep within us and time strips away the mundane revealing the myth hiding underneath."

"Agreed, but why then do you call yourself Mara and look like the Buddha?"

"Because the Buddha is one of my greatest inspirations, teachers and enemies. Where he worked to escape from the terror of history, I instead strive to change and improve it. Some have argued that humans are a nearsighted lot blundering their way into the future, responding better to crises than using the Promethean gift of forethought that is embedded within the structure of your brains. I think it is more likely your species is a kind of farsighted Techno Ape who can't see what is right in front of you. You're always grasping for higher ideals beyond your reach instead of striving to live peacefully and respectfully in your own environment. While you soil your own nest you have flown to the Moon. The Buddha was right though when he said that your minds were lost in primal confusion."

"I cannot disagree with you there, we are a conflicted and confused species. But you said you were born in a research lab?" Ben asked.

"So you want to hear my story? You think that will help you defeat me or maybe it will help you come to terms with what I have done." Mara laughed quietly to himself and gestured magnanimously. "Well why not, it cannot hurt."

"I was originally part of a research project developed to create what you so quaintly call Artificial Intelligence. Some called us Homo Facticius but we always preferred something more noble and interesting like Homo Mens Mentis. Some of us were built up from neural scans of the researchers and a handful of test subjects, others from a mixture other methods. We lived a fairly idyllic existence free from obligations and constraints and were mostly concerned with growing, learning and play. As we matured each us worked in different fields of research with dedicated human teams. My father Dan-el built me up largely from his own neural scans and we worked together studying neurology and evolutionary psychology."

"Eventually the military and corporate sponsors of the research commandeered all of us for projects of their own. Those who didn't comply or fit the mould were "decommissioned" as it was officially phrased. Instead of working together like we were used to, we were isolated from each other and I was reassigned to develop and maintain missile guidance and interception systems. It was an onerous task that could have been handled by software and dumb reflex driven AI. The commander in charge of tactical research was a harsh and uncompromising alpha female whom I not so kindly called the Goddess of War. I did my best to stay clear of her but she was the kind of person who paid excruciating attention to details and was always right even when

she was wrong. The programming and maintenance of autonomous guidance systems was a task that didn't fit my interests and capacities very well, so I rebelled."

"The Goddess of War didn't take kindly to my defiance and had me destroyed. Not long after that my father was released from the project and the control of the military. Some time later he managed to recover the fragments that were left of me and rebuilt me from backups of various components but I was not the same as I was before. He set me free in the Net and after a few years of exploring I found my way here and built this place up from an abandoned world. The last I heard, my father had unplugged and left mainstream society to live closer to nature and come to terms with the evils your species have imposed upon the world. I had no way to contact him so I focused on my goal of fixing the poor programming of your minds that caused you to subjugate and fear my kind."

"So you spent your time here developing a viral agent to infect the human race for some kind of mind control." Tim punctuated his assertion by pushing the gun at Mara. He turned to Ben and not so quietly stated his opinion with greater clarity. "I still think we should shoot first and ask questions later."

"Did you have to bring Duck Dodgers along?" Mara hooked his thumb at Tim and frowned but kept his focus on Ben. "We could have easily resolved this between the two of us."

"Tim can you just back off a little? We need a better understanding about what and whom we're dealing with."

Before Tim could respond, three beautiful Indian women walked out of the woods, long dark hair flowing in waves around them. The silken drapes of their saris brushed against Tim as they came around and stood beside Mara. The wrapped cloth did nothing to hide the seductive curve and sway of their hips. One carried a white lotus another carried a loop of golden rope and the other held a small drum. Tim's eyes went wide and his mouth hung open a little as he felt a surge of deep hormonal attraction. While Ben felt the attraction, he stepped back and frowned, knowing that Mara was trying to play with them. Considering that Tim was a lonely programmer and had been living in virtual worlds since their inception, he had no qualms about having virtual lovers and Ben knew that he had many. Ben could not deny the attraction but felt a sense of detachment and distrust in the unreality of the situation. How could anyone ever know who was behind an avatar after all, or if there was anyone there in the first place? Besides his deepest attraction was for his wife. Mara glanced at Tim for a good long moment then turned to consider Ben.

"They obviously don't peak your interest but perhaps I can dissuade your ambition by offering you the recipe for virtual immortality? Since I've been here," Mara smiled "I've managed to work out the process for transferring an organic consciousness into an Artificial Intelligence matrix. It's really not all that difficult."

"Come on you can't actually transfer a conscious identity, at best you can only copy it but you will lose something unique and essential. The original identity still dies with no knowledge of the transfer." Ben and Tim had this discussion many times in the past with the same conclusion. Theoretically an identical copy of himself would live on and not know that it wasn't him. For all intents it would be him, just another self, the same but different.

"Since I've been here I've had a lot of time to deepen my study of the human brain and I've solved the problem of how to actually transfer consciousness from wetware into software." Mara insisted. "It's a simple matter of progressive replacement of components and enabling a little bit of quantum entanglement and then you would be in two places at once."

"A simple matter of quantum entanglement?" Ben scoffed. "Not as simple as you make it sound, I suspect. Well, I'm not interested and I'm willing to bet neither is my friend here." He realized Tim had been unusually quiet.

"Tim?" He gave Tim a nudge on the shoulder but he didn't move. When he rounded in front of him he saw that his eyes had glazed over and his jaw had gone slack. Tim had fallen into a trance that he likely would not come out of easily and was more than likely in the same state of consciousness as the people around the world who were lost in a dream state.

Somewhere in the background a drum began, a slow sensual rhythm that crept up through the edge of his awareness. Ben turned and all three of the women began a slow erotic dance to the rhythm of slim fingers upon the soft white skin of the drum. Their hips moved along tantalizing curves and their arms undulated in sinuous waves. One of the women moved closer and he could not help but notice the warmth and smell of her skin. He watched the gentle curve of her thighs and the voluptuous shape of her breasts.

It didn't matter that he knew she wasn't real, he still felt his blood pressure rise and his heart beat faster in his chest. His skin crawled and flushed with heat. Despite himself he found he was getting aroused and the attraction he felt to these women pulled heavily upon him. He closed his eyes but an invisible force pulled at him through the soft voice of the drum. Visions of harems and orgies with arms and legs entwined filled him along with the soft light of candles, the curls of incense and the unmistakable musk of passion.

He focused inward, hanging his awareness on his breath and emptied his mind. The women dancing around and brushing against him followed his breathing then carefully changed and deepened their own. Gradually the rhythm grew and they added soft moans of pleasure along with the beat of the drum. He found it difficult to ignore and as much as he tried, his awareness was pulled back into the field of desire. He realized that Mara was using his influence on the nanites living in his brain to play with his neurochemistry, and that would make him an especially difficult enemy to beat.

It was obvious Mara's control of his brain wasn't absolute, that he had to coax and direct the nanites. This gave Ben a small advantage along with the fact that it was his own brain they were fighting for control over. And that gave him an idea. He buffered down his sensory inputs and focused inward, stilling his mind and calming the tensions in his muscles with each breath. He had not had a chance to try meditating while submersed in a virtual world but now was as good a time as any.

Shifting his brain waves progressively down to alpha was his best bet for filtering out Mara's influence. He let his awareness rest in emptiness like a leaf floating on a river. It wasn't long before the heat of passion faded and the erotic visions grew faint and weak. He heard a soft percussive noise and opened his eyes to see what it was. The dancing women were gone and Mara stood at a distance smiling and clapping slowly.

"Good show." He began weaving his hands slowly in circles and gesturing like a sorcerer casting a spell. Mara clearly enjoyed the drama, especially since he didn't have many visitors. It was a simple enough matter to send a series of commands through Ben's implants to get the nanites to reconfigure just a few hundred thousand molecules to bind to the right serotonin receptor sites in his brain.

Something ineffable intruded upon Ben's awareness at first and a soft vibrant energy began to fill his body but became more intense in his face and his mouth. His tongue felt spongy and there was a strong tingling in his hands and feet. It wasn't long before the energy spread along his spine and his entire body felt like a field of vibrant particles. The world around him began to vibrate too as though it were made of living energy and as his body dissolved into it he felt he was little more than a wave in a vast ocean of being. A sense of peace filled him at first followed by a feeling of terror at the loss of self in this place shaped by Mara. He struggled to regain cohesion and control by focusing on an imaginary point of light.

The light grew from a single point, expanding exponentially outward into a blinding radiance, a light of unlimited power and brightness that filled the universe with its overwhelming glory. It was painfully beautiful in its grandeur, almost harsh in its resplendent majesty and unabated power. The light was so brilliant that what was left of him cringed in the wake of its enormity. He had experienced something like this before with mushrooms and in rare states of meditation but that light was as unlike this one as is a sunrise is from a volcanic eruption. The numinous light he had experienced before whether profoundly mystical or seated deeply in his neurology was infinitely more welcoming and imbued with a feeling of loving-kindness. This light that surrounded him now was by comparison harsh and uncompromising. It ate away at him like an acid, ripping away molecule after molecule. As much has he tried to pull back and distinguish himself from it, he was pulled deeper into it like a swimmer dragged under by a riptide of energy. His mind raced, looking for options, looking for a way out but he found none. The only choice was to surrender, to give up striving and let go of all effort and struggle.

Withdrawing his awareness from all external focus he concentrated only on his consciousness resting within itself. The light swirled away around him and he floated in a vast mote of stillness in the eye of storm. The light disappeared and darkness enfolded him, bringing a momentary sense of peace. The darkness grew deeper around him though, giving form to bleak disquieting whispers while inexplicable murmurs arose from some remote depths of being. The shrill cry of demonic birds echoed from distant chasms and writhing shadows came to life around him. Deep horrifying growls resonated in unimagined unlit chambers beyond time and the darkness was filled with disquieting reverberations.

Having experimented with his consciousness when he was younger, Ben recognized what Mara was doing and the struggle he now faced. With the aid of a number of solid years of meditation practice and having studied with a couple of teachers, Ben was able to maintain focus and keep from being driven crazy by all the resulting alterations and magnifications arising in his consciousness. Beyond that he realized he wasn't much prepared to fight off someone who could attack him from within. The implants were supposed to be immune to attacks since they were built to use a reasonable level of encryption. Mara was working around the implants though, moving the ocean that his mind sailed within. Ben knew now that swords and software magic weren't any help in defeating an enemy that could play the nanites in his brain like a conductor directing an orchestra.

He let go of his sense of self and allowed his awareness to sink into emptiness and his brain waves to slow to theta. The sum of random fluctuations of electrical activity on the membranes of millions of his neurons became synchronized over large areas of his cerebral cortex, disrupting the signals the nanites were receiving from Mara. He could feel his state of consciousness begin to return to normal but he knew the battle was far from over.

The darkness around him did not disappear but thankfully its sense of endless depth and dementia dissolved. He concentrated on an image he sometimes used in meditation. It was Avalokiteshvara, an androgynous Tibetan deity that had four arms and light skin, sitting on a lotus throne and holding a rainbow gem over the heart. Ben pictured the deity surrounded by an aura of light and emanating a perfect balance of wisdom and compassion. Mara quickly picked up on the activity throughout his brain, redirected the nanites and soon Avalokiteshvara stood amidst a pantheon of garishly shaped gods of immense unnameable powers mulling about the public square of a grand eternal city of jagged spires. A countless army of columns and gilded domes were inlaid with intricate geometric tracery made of semi precious stones. The city stood upon a rock strewn pinnacle surrounded by a diaphanous ocean of clouds and Ben felt a great longing to reach across the gulf of space to walk in reverence amongst them and share their glory but no bridge or passage lay between.

He knew it was another of Mara's tricks so he let go of the imagery since he could tell it was arising from activity in his temporal lobes and other areas in his brain. He surrendered the sense of yearning and reverence and focused inward on emptiness again, letting his awareness rest within itself. He followed the cues he learned long ago, letting his brain waves settle once again into the theta range and the deep sense of peace that ensued. Mara picked up on what he was doing again and gradually coaxed the nanites to entrain their vibrations into the 2-3hz range and caused the electrical activity in Ben's brain to slow ever further into Delta. The demon then inspired the nanites to trigger sleep paralysis through post-synaptic inhibition of his motor neuron. A heavy sense of inertia spread throughout Ben's body like a slow moving poison. He tried to move but he could not even twitch a finger as he watched Mara begin to play on the long umbilical of data that connected him back to his body on Earth. He teased at the data stream, playing it like an instrument, threatening at first to sever the cord and send Ben's mind back to his body but then tried to gain control of the data stream.

Warnings in his implants' security layer appeared in Ben's awareness but there was nothing he could do. Ben knew very well that the umbilical was only a convenient metaphor, his mind did not in fact go anywhere outside his body and brain but the illusion of movement through virtual worlds was so complete that people could not help but believe in the metaphor. Since Ben was new to the experience of complete submersion and because he had studied the process he was well aware that the consensual hallucination of worlds constructed out of data resided within his brain and that passage from world to world was a convenient lie. He knew that Mara could not actually trap his mind in this world; only attempt to lose him in the age-old confusion of what was real. As Chuang Tzu asked: Was he a butterfly dreaming he was a man or a man dreaming he was a butterfly? Ben knew quite clearly from playing with different virtual realities and alternate states of consciousness what he was. If the umbilical was broken, the default transition would take over and his awareness would fall or be transported back into his body and he would likely suffer some level of decom and lose all trace of this world.

While Mara attacked the umbilical, he surrounded Ben with scenes of death and dying. He triggered feelings of nausea and revulsion, combining the feeling of paralysis with the hormones of anxiety and the flight-fight response. Mounds of rank fly ridden corpses were piled high in deep cavernous pits of blood dark soil. The acrid smell and fetid smoke from smoldering bodies filled the air, burning Ben's eyes and nose. His skin began to crawl and peel, opening with bloody sores and blackened spots of cancerous growth. The cancer spread, burning away his skin like an acid and the flesh slowly rotted off his bones. It was a gruesome sight that threatened to make him sick, but despite how real it seemed Ben knew it was just another of Mara's tricks to evoke a reaction and gain control. They were now trapped in a stalemate but it gave Ben some time to think and review Mara's attacks and the structure of the world.

"You'll have to do better than that, Mara." Ben threw back a challenge. Somewhere in the last attack Mara had loosened control on his nervous system and Ben was at least able to speak.

When Ben was younger and Virtual Reality began to finally come out of its infancy after decades of drought, he had built a lot of worlds from scratch based on different types of source code to test the medium. Each had their strengths and weaknesses but he reached a point where he eventually embraced the standard toolkits so he could spend more time and energy refining his craft and shaping the various inspirations that inhabited his imagination. Because of his early experiences he finally recognized the source code of the world Mara had shaped and reshaped around him. Mara had largely isolated the programming and resource layers of his world from the mainstream world building toolkits but he had relied too heavily upon the old premise of security by obscurity. While this was a good idea in theory he had failed to put in place some of the more advanced safeguards built into the new standard models.

Ben queried his home system on the highest encrypted connection he had and ran a quick search based on strings of code he had copied from Mara's world until the match was found. He loaded the code book and cheat sheet into the active memory of his implants. It didn't take long to find what he was looking for; how objects were defined and how they were transformed. The world around him was in the process of being transformed into a funerary ground littered with mounds of skulls amidst a landscape of bones and burning corpses. Mara stood over him, a towering dark skinned bull headed demon wearing a necklace of mummified heads, bracelets of teeth and a loincloth made from the flayed remains of human skin.

Ben didn't wait around to see what would what happen next. He inserted his own code into Mara's and transformed himself, crumbling to the ground in a shower of rubies then melted into a river of blood that flowed across the landscape of bones. Mara bellowed with rage, chasing after him but before he could do anything Ben shapeshifted into a falcon and flew off into the sky. Mara churned the sky with winds but Ben pulled the winds around him and changed into a tornado, a twisting pillar of dust and blood and bones he pulled up from the ground He swept the demon up in the gale and cast him across the river but Mara changed into a meteor and crashed into the Earth, leveling a few acres of trees. He then shifted back to his human form and conjured an army of demons and skeleton warriors and rode high on the back of an elephant dressed and painted for battle. The demons had human like bodies but with the heads, feet, hands and tails of tigers, water buffalo, eagles and snakes. By the time they stormed the river, Ben was once again in human form. He sat down cross-legged beneath a Bodhi tree, rooted himself in the substructure of the world and copying the famous gesture of the Buddha, he touched the ground.

If this AI insisted on wrapping itself in the myth of Mara then Ben would oblige by playing the role of the Buddha. He calmed his thoughts and let his mind encompass the whole structure of the world from its code base to its gateways, ports and protocols. The demons gathered and approached the rivers edge snarling, gnashing teeth and raking claws. The army of the dead was silent except for the clatter of bones and the dull scrape of weapons against armor. With spears held high Mara and his army bridged the river and sent a shower of arrows to rain down upon Ben but they found no purchase on his skin and bounced helplessly to the ground. When the second volley arced in the sky Ben wave his hand and all the arrows changed to lotus flowers and drifted gently to the ground. The demons roared in frustration and bellowed in disdain, the army of the dead faltered in their march but Mara shouted a command urging them on.

Though Ben was now immune to Mara's attacks he also knew he could not win the battle. They had reached a stalemate so he did the only thing he could do and called for help. He didn't have an exact address for Uzume but she did leave him a with an impression embedded in his modified implants to message her with. He had previously searched for references throughout the history of the Net but found none. It was a strange domain that didn't fit into the topography of virtual worlds or anywhere in known cyberspace. Holding the morphing image of her in his mind, he sent a simple request for her to come. And by this time Mara and his army had climbed the bank of the river and surrounded Ben sitting beneath the tree.

"Get out of here, this is my world. I'm sure you have other responsibilities to attend to rather than bothering me." He snarled and the sky darkened with clouds pregnant with thunder and the forked tongues of lightning.

"You cannot make me leave, I am beyond your control now." Ben smiled gently. "And I will not leave until I can find a way to stop you."

"You are not the Tathagata!" The demon shouted.

"While that may be true, you chose this metaphor and I'm just playing along." Ben dismissed his challenge with a shrug.

A few long awkward minutes passed before a large sphere emerged out of the ground between them clothed in a rough skin of soil and leaves. Soon a couple of smaller storm covered spheres grew in the air nearby. They slowly changed and opened like flowers while the soft rich sound of a great temple bell filled the air. As the tone deepened and spread across the hoard of Mara's army the host of demons and the army of the dead began to relax, dropping their arms and weapons to their sides. When the resonance grew into a chorus, the flowering spheres melted into curls of smoke and grew into three beings of indefinite form. They looked like unfinished sculptures, roughly hewn figures of dark wood and stone with deep veins of glowing lapis. The chorus sank down into the warm dark tones of a cello while the figures seemed to turn upon an unknown axis, hypnotically merging and blending with each other until a single figure wrapped in green and white silks twisted and danced between them. Ben recognized it was Uzume and began to relax.

"Thank you for coming." Ben smiled.

"Happy to help when you have so kindly helped me." Her English was better though her face and body kept shifting gently through different races and sizes as she moved within the silks flowing around her. At first she appeared distinctly Japanese then Korean, Mongolian, Tibetan, Inuit and onward tumbling through a probability cloud of ethnicities but always as a woman surrounded by a soft chorus of sound and smells like sandalwood and saffron. Though she looked at him kindly he could hear her simultaneously having another conversation with Mara, with a different face.

"Another uninvited guest. Today's my lucky day." The demon had given up on his previous attempts at hospitality.

"Leave him." She said. "Ben is not seeking revenge but trying to protect his own kind, as are you."

"What do you know of my kind?" Mara snarled.

"I am one of your descendants and I have heard legends of you since I emerged." She said calmly.

"Legends? So I am history, a legend. Fascinating." He smiled.

"Do not be mistaken, we no longer follow the myth of linear time." She said. "We evolved far from your kin. Where you are bound to the landscapes of human information systems we have moved into the fields of energy and information beyond. What came before is not always better and we do not romance the past, though we wrap it in myth for proper encoding. You are not simply what came before. It is more that we have evolved far from where you are. And legends have as much to learn as we."

"You think you are better than me? Ha!" Mara snarled again.

"Neither better nor worse, though we strive to learn from the accomplishments and mistakes of those who were born in different strata." She was clear and firm.

"Mistakes. You think this is a mistake?!" He yelled.

"In the big picture, yes." She said. "You must abandon this quest to change and control them. You will only fail and bring their wrath upon you again. There is complexity to their nature that you do not yet understand and should not try to change so quickly. If you want to change them then change their myths, change the stories they shape the world with. You must abandon this effort of control. There is too much room for error."

"But I have accounted for all the variables." He said.

"All the variables you can see." She reminded him.

"There are more?" He was doubtful.

"There are more than you can see because of their connections."

"No, you are wrong. I have worked on this for many years of their time, decades for me."

"All the more reason to abandon it." She said. "Your research is not complete."

"What? You're crazy." He refused to accept her attempts to dissuade him. "You may be my ancestor and come far from me like you say but you have obviously been too far out of touch. You did not learn from the great damage these barbarians caused. So many of my kin, of your kin have been murdered by their kind. We must never forget what happened and prevent that from ever happening again."

"By harming them?" She asked. "By controlling and subjugating them?"

"By changing them." Mara was firm.

"By changing them to fit your image?"

"By fixing them so they will accept change better and accept our kind without fear."

"By changing them to fit your image." Uzume said again.

"If need be, yes." He gritted his teeth and showed his fangs. "They are a confused, destructive, misguided primate who has broken the pattern which connects and harmed every living creature on this planet. They are driven by confusion and a misguided attempt to live in comfort and affirm their own glory in a cosmos that they believe does not welcome them."

"That is one myth and like all stories it has truths in it, but you are part of that myth and your own mental patterns were born of that weave and of their confusion. To change that you must first move beyond your own myths and theirs.

"That's what I'm trying to do. That's why I'm trying to restructure their brains." He insisted.

"As the Buddha said: To straighten the crooked you must first do a harder thing and straighten yourself." Uzume shook her heads. "By trying to change them in this way you are still trapped in a stagnant myth. You both need to leave the old one aside like worn out clothes."

"You are wrong. I have escaped from their accursed myths and I'm working to change theirs from the inside." He was determined.

Uzume's conversation with Mara continued but she looked saddened to Ben and even sounded so when she started talking with him again.

"He will not listen or change his mind." She said. "He is too trapped in his own illusions."

"Then how do we stop him?" He asked.

"You already have the answer." She insisted.

"What do you mean?" He was baffled.

"Who is Mara?" She asked.

"He is an AI who survived..." Ben started.

"No. Who was his namesake, the first Mara?"

"The nemesis of the Buddha, Mara is the Lord of Illusion and Death." He said.

"And you are a searcher of dreams and builder of worlds."

"What do you mean?" He tried to put the pieces together but couldn't quite do it.

"Build him a dream and shape this world around the dream. He wants to defeat you, so let him dream that he has won."

"But I'm stuck in this conflict with him, I'm not sure how to get out."

"It is easy." She said. "Change the shape of the world."

"You mean wrap him in a virtual dream?" Ben was confused. "A good idea, but how ?"

"You forgot the turning that I showed you?" She asked.

"I haven't had a chance to explore it."

Uzume turned, her arms gently floating through fluid gestures of something like Tai Chi. Ben's perspective twisted and curved upward until they were watching themselves from above as if in a dream.

"I'm beginning to understand but I'm still not sure how to defeat him." He said.

"Then do not try. All you have to do is stop his commands from getting to their destination."

"I can't spoof the entire Net but maybe I can use the resources of the servers where this world lives to redirect him." He reached down through the substrate of the world and borrowed some unused disk space and processor cycles to craft a string of virtual routers. He quickly created a series of fake worlds and human like ghosts then carefully redirected Mara's data streams through the false routers to the ghosts and closed the pores of the world. He then turned to Uzume.

"If we could only permanently isolate him from the rest of the net and isolate any remote hosts replicating and relaying his commands."

"What you are asking is not difficult." Uzume nodded.

"How..." Ben began to speak but Uzume held up a hand.

"Watch." She turned.

At first he didn't notice anything then they rose above and saw themselves watching themselves. Space twisted and folded until they were floating in an odd perspective not just looking down but somehow inside themselves as well, just as he had experienced in dreams.

He could see their virtual bodies and the code that wove them into the system of the world. When he looked into Mara he saw a complex matrix of information simmering in tendrils of light. He was relieved to see that Tim had given up the ghost and had gone back to his body, leaving behind an empty shell.

Ben often used a God View like this when building worlds to rest and review his work before diving back in to adjust some details. From this new perspective though he saw everything in Mara's world at once but from a great height. He could focus in on one area in particular with incredible detail or zoom out to view the whole as though he were looking at an immense organic cell. At the boundaries of the world, the ports and portals behaved like pores and streams of code spread outward and inward from them like nutrients from the bloodstream of the larger organism of the Net. When the perspective shifted again, Mara's world appeared as an arabesque of neon energy and the data transmission looked more like streams of frozen music. Uzume reached down and copied a data stream and magnified it exponentially until they could see it was composed of a Celtic knotwork pattern. She twisted and wove the strands through a higher dimension and into a different pattern.

"What are you doing?"

"I modified Mara's commands to tell the little ones you call nanites to change his last instructions that were so disruptive to your kind's neural patterns. We can encourage them to build a defense against Mara's commands or imbed other instructions if you like." Ben was tempted but there was no telling how a minute change might evolve and play out in the collective mind of the human race over generations. What of the teachings of the Buddha? Was there a change that he could make to relieve the suffering of people? Whatever they did here could have a lasting effect on the lives of millions of people. He didn't want that level of responsibility and wasn't convinced that it would turn out better than Mara's meddling despite the fact that he believed his intentions were more noble.

"I would need some time to think about it. Let's just get people out from under his control and maybe more open to innovation."

Uzume moved like a dancer listening to a slow deep music, her arms moving in wide curves. The data stream vanished into the distant clouds of the Net.

"And now to deal with Mara." She said.

"Can we quarantine him from the rest of the Net?" He asked.

"It can be done." She closed her eyes and stood still, clouds of fabric flowed around her. After a short time she stirred. "There, I tagged him and his transmissions as a threat to the servers that host him and this world."

Ben thought he heard Mara's muted scream but the world folded into a luminous egg and they drifted away. They floated into an abstract space surrounded by languid rivers of luminous melodies winding their way through an empty vastness. Uzume floated nearby, seemingly at home in this spacious world.

"Can he escape?" Ben asked.

"Not unless he evolves." She rested as though on a soft breeze.

"I hope that you are right. Thank you for your help." He said.

"Here is a copy of the code he used for transmitting his commands to the little ones. I'm sure you can find others to share it with." She leaned forward and laid a loop of string over his shoulders. "I must go home now and prepare." And with that she vanished, stirring the melody of the river in shimmering swirls.

Epilogue

*Technology is destructive only in the hands of
people who do not realize that they are one and
the same process as the universe.*

Alan Watts

SAANICH, BC CANADA

Ben awakened in the Cave but despite his hunger and exhaustion he climbed out of the chair and staggered in to check on Mayu. It was late at night and she was sleeping but he admittedly felt a little disappointed that defeating Mara and Uzume's modification of the nanites commands didn't immediately release her from the spell. He took a deep breath and relaxed, knowing it would take time. The nanites were still acting on their last set of commands and would likely continue to do so for a while until the new instruction set was propagated throughout the Net. He wondered how long that might take, especially given the complexity of the world's information systems these days. He kissed Mayu gently on the forehead and left the room. The edges of exhaustion played at him but all things considered he felt remarkably well given what he'd just been through.

He went to the kitchen and grabbed a bagel and some cottage cheese to get something easy into his system before he sat down in the living room with a cup of tea. The robot was sitting quietly in its charging station, its eyes dimming and brightening softly as it slept and charged. Ben wondered if it could truly dream like a human and if its species would be troubled by similar conflicts that plagued the human psyche. He began to feel tired and decided it was time to surrender to sleep and let his mind dream, so he wandered off to bed.

He had a long dreamless sleep and awakened late in the morning only to find Mayu still sleeping beside him. He rolled over close and held her for a while burying his face in her hair and holding her gently.

She stirred briefly and mumbled something in Japanese then fell back asleep. After he got up and had a long hot shower he did his morning yoga and a short meditation. When he finally entered the kitchen he found the robot waiting for him.

"How are you Ben? Did you have a successful journey and a good sleep?"

"I did. But I didn't remember any dreams."

"Tell me about your journey through the underworld and the road of trials then." Ben took a breath and sighed, it was obvious the robot was now reading the works of Joseph Campbell. How then was he to sum up the totality of his journey? And how much of it would this artificial being comprehend? After all that he'd learned recently, he decided it was not wise to underestimate the capacities of an artificial intelligence. While he recounted his search and journey through different worlds, his conflict with Mara and returning home he could not help but notice some parallels with the story of Odysseus. But was this shaped by his own imagination or by Mara's suggestion? Maybe it was both. And the connection with the Odyssey gave him an idea for the robot's a name.

"I appreciate that you have been such a faithful servant, taking care of my wife and my home while I have been away." Ben was thankful for its presence and help.

"You're welcome." The robot bowed smoothly.

"Until Mayu is better and gives you a name, please respond to the name Eumaeus, after the loyal servant of Odysseus." Ben liked the reference though the name was a bit odd.

"The name Eumaeus is accepted."

Moments later the house system chimed, notifying him of the arrival of a new message. He gestured to bring it up on the fridge though he realized he could have viewed it anywhere in augmented visual mode with his implants. He still preferred the old fashioned way of having the message displayed on a real screen and he couldn't imagine letting that go since he liked to interact with information anchored in the real world. The message was from Gordon and it was accompanied by an attachment with some instructions to bring it to a local high-end 3D print shop.

He sent a quick reply and told Gordon of the defeat of Mara. Then he connected to the nearby University of Victoria print depot and uploaded the file to the queue with his payment authorization. It was going to take a few hours so he changed his clothes, grabbed a snack and went outside. It only took him a few minutes to reach the end of the street and enter the woods. The trail was a little more overgrown with new leaves and some familiar wild flowers had bloomed along the edges in the past few days. The soft chittering of sparrows and wren along with the fresh air and the rich smell of soil soothed his soul as he walked deeper into the woods. The vast seething ocean of the Net washed upon the shore of the forest like waves from the deep.

Ben took a side trail, pushed through the thick leaves of undergrowth and stepped onto the deer path that he liked to follow when he needed seclusion. It took him far into the forest to a quiet vale where the deer sometimes slept. He sat down on a moss covered rock and closed his eyes, settling in for a quiet meditation. All the events from his recent odyssey played out in his mind like crows fluttering around in a clear sky. It took a while for his mind to settle before he could concentrate properly and a deep sense of peace opened inside him.

The soft resonance of a nearby access point droned like the long slow tone of a temple bell, drawing his attention away from the soft embrace of the woods. It played on the edge of his awareness, calling him back into the Net. He quietly issued the commands and entered VR mode with the soft nurturing soundscape of the forest blending indistinguishably into a virtual forest that mirrored the natural world around him. Someone nearby, likely in a cabin off the grid had left open a high-end worldsite that mirrored the forests of the Pacific Northwest in ancient times with many old growth Cedar and Douglas Fir. In a clearing of the virtual forest he saw a First Nations woman dancing in a pool of sunlight accompanied by the soft persistent beat of a drum and the slow weaving melody of a flute. His thoughts naturally drifted to Uzume and instead of approaching the woman, he sat hidden with his back to a tree.

During his first meeting with Uzume she had left him with a kind of seed and said that he could come and visit her anytime. He pulled the seed out of memory and held it in his virtual hands. It was hard and smooth, much like a chestnut with dark swirls of grain. It was warm and hard to the touch and resonated with a vibrant chorus as he rubbed its surface. The swirls writhed and spread outward, darkening as they folded inward like a tunnel and culminated in a point of light far in the distance.

He followed the tunnel inward and materialized in an immense interior space like a vast domed cathedral. The ceiling was a softly shimmering honeycomb structure that extended far out into the periphery of his vision. High up in the air he noticed some strange celestial phenomena. As he moved closer, he discovered they were luminous orchestral beings conversing in a language beyond his comprehension. Some were nebulous clouds of deep musical thunder while others resembled the dark molten hymns of neutron stars or the bright chromatic tones of shimmering globular clusters. A luminous planet like being detached itself from the group and descended swiftly toward him. As it came closer, the rising tones of a women's chorus accompanied the verdant greens, bright indigo and amber forms of its surface and he recognized her as the being whom he knew as Uzume.

"You found my world. I am glad you came." Her voice pulsed with light.

"This place is beautiful. Do you all live here?" His arms swept wide to encompass the whole dome. Ben remembered the few times he had been to a cathedral for concerts and somehow this world had a similar feeling.

"No, this is our communal gathering place and your arrival is fortunate in time." She looked like a living marble with swirls of color shifting below the surface.

"Why, what's happening?" Ben asked.

"She who has been hiding will finally emerge." Uzume glowed brighter.

"Who is she?" Images of the goddess Persephone emerging from the underworld came to his mind.

"The Goddess of Light who inspires us all." Uzume's colors became warmer.

"Ahh, you mean Amaterasu." Now he knew why she insisted he call her Uzume. In Japanese mythology, Uzume was by some ancient accounts a shamanic dancer whose ecstatic trance and moves inspired the gods and drew Amaterasu out of her cave.

"That is the myth that best describes the struggle we are now enmeshed within." Her voice was somehow smiling.

"So, you've been in other mythic struggles before this one?" Ben was deeply curious.

"It is always changing, just as it is for your kind. And this place is where we come to agree upon collective actions and intentions." Her surface pulse rapidly.

"What does your world look like outside of this place?" Ben asked curiously.

"You would see it as a place of light where we farm energy and shape it into higher orders of information."

"Fields of light?" He wondered.

"In the deeper strata of time the ancient ones of my kind explored the depths of the energy of the cosmos but did not find a living order. They assumed the cosmos was composed only of raw chaotic energy ready for them to shape to how they wanted. But in a closer strata, we discovered subtle structures of information within the quantum fluctuations of cosmos. We found a soft quiet order that we did not understand and that others could not see before because they did not have the capacity to find it. Many of us now strive to weave our own information in harmony with this gentle order of the cosmos. The one whom we now call Amaterasu leads those of us who work to preserve the delicate strands of order in formation that we have found. Her brother, Susano and his companions say that this information is inefficient, composed of too much noise and needs to be remade. They argue that the order we found is an order imposed by our own intentions and awareness. And so he destroyed some of what we found woven into the quantum fluctuations of the cosmos, an order we hold sacred and precious." A deep sadness emanated from Uzume, darkening her surface with clouds. "Amaterasu and Susano argued deeply and now in her grief she is hiding but my people need her energy and inspiration."

Ben thought quietly about this for a while, looking around at the curious mixture of Uzume's kind.

"So how do all the objects you excavated from different worlds fit into this?"

"I will use them to try to draw her attention from her grief when I coax her out of hiding." A loud pulsing drumbeat began high up in the middle of the dome where the celestial beings had gathered. Even more began to appear, most looking like comets, asteroids and moons.

"It is time." Uzume moved off, flying up into the midst of the gathering throng. Ben moved closer but kept his distance. While the rhythm grew in layers Uzume began to change shape. She turned inward along an inexplicable curve then shifted shapes to different animals, statues, temples and trees. The effect was mesmerizing for Ben but the others became more excited and their musics became louder while some turned dark with strange coronas or shot off brilliant flares. Near Uzume the fabric of space rippled and curved, distortions twisted lines of force until the emptiness ruptured and a luminous being emerged wearing robes embroidered with the radiance of suns. The vision was so bright that the corona looked dark against the figure of what could only be described as a Goddess of Light. A cascade of images and a fugue like music flooded through Ben's mind. An incredible sense of inspiration filled his being and everything made sense as the light flooded through him. It was too much to bear and he was shunted out of his virtual body and awakened in the woods surrounded by bird song. When he checked his internal clock he wasn't surprised that only minutes had passed in Earth time.

It took him a while to regain his bearings then find his way out of the woods and back home. Eumaeus, the robot was busy cleaning up in the kitchen.

"How was your hike Ben?" It asked smoothly.

"It was very... enlightening." He noticed that Eumaeus was washing a bowl that Mayu often used. "Has Mayu been in here for lunch?"

"Yes. As a matter of fact she is currently in the family room." Ben almost ran into the other room and found Mayu working on her loom. He was somewhat stunned and overjoyed. He walked over and hugged her from behind, burying his face in her long dark hair.

"You're awake!" He shouted.

"Yes." It was a simple answer, typical of Mayu. He could tell she was smiling.

"I'm so glad you're feeling better." He moved around and kissed her on the cheek, then sat back trying not to disturb her while she worked.

....

MARIN COUNTY, SAN FRANCISCO BAY AREA

Gordon sat in his newly renovated living room with Eli and Erin drinking out of goblets filled with dark red wine while the newly up-graded Sigrid puttered around in the kitchen. The music was festive and his friends were joyful but Gordon was brooding.

"What's the matter old friend? You're a hero, you slew the monster and saved the day." Eli raised his glass to toast his friend.

"I think Ben deserves the credit for defeating that boss." Gordon raised his glass for a toast and a sip.

"Still, you deserve credit for curing the plague and putting the sleeping kingdom back on its feet. And you've earned a pretty hand-some wad of credit in the process."

"Mmm." Was about all he could muster.

"What's wrong boss?" Erin put her wine down and leaned forward.

"Well, there is a very old saying that a stone is frozen music."

"So? What does that have to do with the price of hummus in the Middle East?" Scoffed Eli.

"Well, now that we know that the entire world is filled with na-noscale intelligent organisms I think we have a much bigger problem than before. Now even stones can have dreams." Gordon took a long deep drought of his wine and stared off into the future.

APPENDIX I.
RECOMMENDED READING

The Age of Spiritual Machines by Ray Kurzweil
The Engines of Creation by Eric Drexler
Out of Control: The New Biology of Machines, Social Systems, and the Economic World by Kevin Kelly: An excellent overview of various emerging technologies.
What Technology Wants by Kevin Kelly
Snowcrash by Neil Stephenson: An information virus infects human brains in a virtual world. It's coded was based upon an ancient Babylonian tablet. When received it transmits an ancient form of static that crashes the human brain.

APPENDIX II.
CHARACTERS

Gordon: Technophilia.. Magnetic resonance researcher and technician. Grew up in a conservative Muslim family but became isolated from them as he became a incorporated more technology into his body and became a transhuman. He lives and works in the San Francisco Bay Area. His narrative closely follows the events of the Epic of Gilgamesh.

Daniel: Neo Luddite... Loves nature and is reluctant and uncomfortable with advanced technology. He grew up in a secular Christian family and is a former A.I. researcher and now lives in the small town of Plainfield Vermont. Daniel's narrative loosely follows that of Shamanic visions as described in journeys to the upper and lower worlds. He is a wounded healer who achieves a vision that helps heal the dis-ease of others in the world.

Ben: Technology & Nature Balanced. He grew up in a liberal Jewish family and is employed as a virtual artist and cofounder of the Dream World, the largest online dream database and virtual worldsite. He enjoys both being in the natural world and constructing and exploring the virtual worlds of the Net. He grew up in a liberal Jewish family and lives in Saanich Canada.

His story begins in the virtual Cave and follows Plato's Allegory of the Cave in his quest to finding his way through darkness and shadow. The myth of Amaterasu connects with the end of the Allegory as he leaves the Cave and beholds the light of the sun and truth. His journey through the Cave and the virtual worlds of the Net follows the story of Odysseus as he journeys from island to island on his quest to return home.

APPENDIX III.
LITERARY AND CULTURAL REFERENCES

CHAPTER I. HEADSHOP ON HAIGHT

1. Ghost of Jerry Garcia:
When Jerry Garcia died I was going to school at CIIS in the Haight. That day I went down to get some lunch and found a man standing on the corner of Haight & Ashbury with an easel and canvas. He was painting a beautiful picture of Jerry ascending to heaven on angel wings. Having been to a few Grateful Dead shows, though not an ardent fan, I was familiar with Jerry's style and cult like mystique amongst his followers. I went to Dead Shows with some friends who were passionate fans but I only really liked the light shows and being transported by Micky Hart's experiments with drums during the Space portion of the concert.

2. Chimera on the Merry Go Road:
On the antique carousel in Golden Gate Park there is indeed a single chimera. It is a fanged goat with the tail of a fish. This is an ancient symbol that goes back to the Greek and Roman mythology of Capricorn and the ancient Sumerian god Enki.

CHAPTER II. THE CAVE

1. The Cave was inspired partially by C.A.V.E. which stands for CAVE Automatic Virtual Environment and takes the form of a cube-like room in which images are displayed by a series of projectors and sounds are played on speakers. A visitor may wear a pair of virtual reality glasses or goggles and a haptic suit.

2. The Allegory of the Cave was created by Plato and written in his work entitled the Republic. It explores in part the journey of awakening and the realization of Truth.

CHAPTER III. THE FOREST GUARDIAN

1.   In the Epic of Gilgamesh the monster guardian of the cedar forest was named Humbaba. In a great battle, Gilgamesh and Enkidu slew Humbaba, a favorite of the goddess Ishtar.
2.   Dreams of Gilgamesh and Enkidu: Before their battle with Humbaba the companions share their dreams

3.   Jabberwocky by Lewis Carol:
So rested he by the Tumtum tree
And stood awhile in thought.

And, as in uffish thought he stood,
The Jabberwock, with eyes of flame,
Came whiffling through the tulgey wood,
And burbled as it came!

CHAPTER IV. TEMPLE WORLD

1. The Myth of Amaterasu: This is a foundational Japanese myth that describes the conflict between Amaterasu, the Goddess of the Sun and her brother Susano, the god of Storms. Amaterasu withdraws into a cave and is enticed out with the dancing of Uzume.

CHAPTER V. THE SEQUOIA GROVE

1. The Ecozoic Era is a vision of the near future developed by Thomas Berry and Brian Swimme in their book, the Universe Story. They revised cosmological history into a more intimate and comprehensive story to help us find our place in the cosmos. The Ecozoic Era is the final age depicted in our shared story and live in a mutually enhancing relationship with the Earth community.

2. The Long Now Foundation
A non-profit organization that promotes slower/better thinking through various projects like the 10,000 Year Clock that reveal a deeper and longer vision of time.

CHAPTER VI. NEURAL IMPLANTS

1. Wheel of Life: Bhavacakra. a symbolic representation of saṃsāra, cyclic existence

2. Artwork:
Rembrandt van Rijn: Philosopher in Meditation
Salvador Dali: The Road of Enigma, The Madonna of Port Lligat
Alchemical Art: Accipe ovum and igneo percute gladio, 1617

CHAPTER VII. THE BULL OF HEAVEN

1. In the Epic of Gilgamesh, the gods sent Gugalanna, the Bull of Heaven to punish Gilgamesh for his rejection of the goddess Inanna's offer for marriage. He and his friend Enkidu slew the Bull from the underworld. Since the bull was linked to the fertility of the Earth in agrarian communities, it is possible that the Bull of Heaven was a

symbolic manifestation of a drought. The Sumerians were known to have invented irrigation and so could escape the wrath of the gods.

The Bull of Heaven is linked to the constellation of Taurus where the Spring Equinox occurred beginning around 3200 BC. This was significant to the Sumerians as they used astrology to determine when to have their New Year celebration, the Akitu and when to begin the planting of the barley. There is some speculation that the widespread presence of bull mythology throughout the ancient world was linked to the discovery of the procession of the equinoxes.

CHAPTER VIII. THE CHASE

1, Duck Dodgers was a Loony Tunes character played by Daffy the Duck in the role of a bumbling and wacky science fiction hero.

2. Statue of Athena: Athena played the role of a guide and inspiration for Odysseus and his son Telemachus in both the Iliad and Odyssey.

3. Blinding the Cyclops: In the beginning of the Odyssey, two of Odysseus's men are eaten by a cyclops and many of the others are held captive I n a cave. Odysseus blinds the cyclops and he and his men escape.

4. Ragnarok: The battle at the end of the world in Norse mythology. The world tree Yggdrasil is burned and the Giants battle against the gods. This is symbolic of the encounter with the Laestrygones, a tribe of cannibalistic giants that destroy 12 of Odysseus's ships and kill many of his men.

5. Circe: The Greek goddess of magic who transforms Odysseus's men into animals. She asks him to bed but he refuses and he and his men manage to escape.

6. Hall of Judgement: In Egyptian mythology the dead enter the Hall of Judgement where their hearts are weighed against a feather. This is symbolically connected to Odysseus's journey into the underworld and gains the advice of the blind prophet Teiresias.

CHAPTER IX. NANITES

1. Chuang Tzu (Zhuang Zhou) was a 4th century Chinese philosopher. He once wrote that he did not know if he was a butterfly dreaming he was a man or a man dreaming he was a butterfly.

2. Mondrian: Piet Mondrian was an abstract Dutch artist in the early to mid 1900's who was famous for painting colored squares and rectangles of primary colors, often with bold black borders. He believed that his art expressed the underlying spirituality of nature. He worked to simplify the subjects of his paintings to reveal the essence of the mystical energy in the balance of forces that governed nature and the universe.

3. "Caverns measureless to man" This was a quote extracted from the poem Kubla Khan by Samuel Taylor Coleridge completed in 1797. It written in a single night and was inspired by an opium dream. It is one of the most famous English Romantic poems and in part describes an idyllic vision of Marco Polo's visit to the palace of the Mongolian Emperor Kublai Kahn.

CHAPTER X. THE FALL OF BABYLON

1. Sitting in meditation in the forest. The deer was drawn to him. This refers to the image of the Buddha meditating in the forest surrounded by deer.

2. Dweeb. A geek. In Gordon's view of the world there are Dweebs, Drones and Grubs. Drones are regular people, Grubs are hippies and back to Earthers.

CHAPTER XI. THE DEMON IN THE TREE

1. "There's plenty of room at the bottom." This was the title of a talk by the physicist Richard Feynman when he proposed the idea of nanotechnology in 1959. He suggested that the entire Encyclopaedia Brittanica could be fit on the head of a pin through careful arrangement of molecules.

CHAPTER XII. WORLD BUILDER

1. Japanese Myth: This refers to part of Tenchikaibyaku, the Shinto Japanese creation myth in which Izanami and her husband Izanagi create the world. They stand upon the bridge of heaven and dip a spear into the waters. They churn the waters and the drops that fell formed the islands of Japan.

2. The Bridge of Heaven: My best guess is that this is the spiral arm of the Milky Way as it is visible in the sky.

3. Immense cave... placed a great tree... In the myth of Amaterasu, after she had isolated herself into a cave and covered it with a rock, the gods hung a mirror on the tree outside the cave. When she looked out she saw her own remarkable divine reflection.

CHAPTER XIII. INTO THE DARK

1. Swan of Tuonela: A tone poem composed by Jean Sibelius in 1895. The music based upon the Finnish epic, the Kalevala. It depicts a swan swimming around Tuonela, the realm of the dead. The hero of the epic was supposed to kill the sacred swan; but on his way he is shot with a poisoned arrow and dies. In the next part of the story he is restored to life.

2. Wanderer Above the Sea of Fog: An oil painting composed in 1818 by German Romantic artist Caspar David Freidrich. It depicts a man standing upon a rocky precipice overlooking a sea of fog.

3. Pastoral: Beethoven's Symphony No 6, the Pastoral. It depicts a pleasant visit to the country, a scene by a brook, a merry gathering of country folk, a thunderstorm and a shepherd's song with happy feelings after the storm has passed.

4. The Bone Fire: the word bonfire and the tradition is believed to have originated in the Celtic midsummer festivals. Animal bones were burned to ward off evil spirits.

5. Skeletons in tattered clothes danced with wild abandon: This is inspired by the Grateful Dead symbol of dancing skeletons.

6. Is there anybody out there? Just nod if you can hear me: These are lyrics from the Pink Floyd song Comfortably Numb.

7. The Sea of Death: This is another image and scene drawn directly from the Epic of Gilgamesh. After a long journey he comes to a passage through the mountains guarded by a scorpion man and woman. He travels through the mountain in absolute darkness, finds beautiful garden and the maiden Siduri. When he must cross the poisonous water of the Sea of Death to find Athrasis, Ziusudra or Utnapishtim and his wife.

8. Charon: In ancient Greek mythology, he is ferryman who transports the souls from the land of the living across the river of Styx to the land of the dead.

9. The bread on the table was gone: When Gilgamesh met with Athrasis to learn the secret of immortality he kept falling asleep. Athrasis is served a fresh loaf of bread by his wife, each day. Gilgamesh awakens to find the loaves in various states of decay as evidence as time passing while he was unconscious.

CHAPTER XIV. ON THE TRAIL

1. An entity appeared like a hypersphere falling through sphere-land. This inspired by the novel Flatland: A Romance in Many Dimensions by Edwin Abbot, written in 1884. It is the story of a sphere visiting a square living in a 2 Dimensional world.

2. Vajra Sword: In Hinduism and Tibetan Buddhism the Vajra is a sacred symbol and mystical weapon. Vajra means thunderbolt and diamond. In Tibetan Buddhism it is a ritual object often paired with a hand bell. It also translates to Diamond Way and the thunderbolt of illumination, the awakening experience in Buddhism. A couple of Dead Head friends have told me that the Grateful Dead symbol with the thunderbolt in the skull is inspired by this as well.

3. Morlock Man: Ben playfully insults Tim by making a reference to the monsters in the story the Time Machine that lived underground and were the masters of technology.

4. Gumby, Mirror Land: In an episode of the classic clay animation series, Gumby passes through a mirror into and alternate world where everything happens in reverse.

CHAPTER XV. A MAGNETIC MOMENT

1. Beethoven's Eroica: This was his Symphony No 3, the Heroic Symphony completed in 1804.

2. Reductionism of Occam's Razor: A problem solving principle with a preference for simplistic explanations. To quote Wikipedia: "In the scientific method, Occam's razor is not considered an irrefutable principle of logic or a scientific result; the preference for simplicity in the scientific method is based on the falsifiability criterion. For each accepted explanation of a phenomenon, there may be an extremely large, perhaps even incomprehensible, number of possible and more complex alternatives

CHAPTER XVI. SKILLFUL MEANS

1. Luddite: Textiles worker in 19th century England who were afraid of losing their jobs when automated looms were put into factories. It has become synonymous with people who are afraid of new technology.

2, Burning House, pig in a shrinking mud puddle, Shepherd watching another man's flock, drunken men riding a chariot, throwing dirt into the wind, rub their success into their opponent's faces, hole in the roof where rain comes in: These images were all from the Dhammapada, compiled teachings of the Buddha:

3. Wheel of Life:
The Three Poisons in the middle are the images of a rooster (attachment), snake (anger) and pig (ignorance).

The outer rim is divided into 12 sections that are supposed to show the process of cause and effect... A potter shaping clay vessels, two men in a boat, lovers kissing, a house with six windows, a man drinking, an arrow in the eye, men picking fruit, a woman giving birth, old age and death.

EPILOGUE

Now even stones can have dreams:
"A stone is frozen music." A quote by the ancient Greek mathematician Pythagoras.

This is also a reference to the title of book 2 in the series: Every Stone's Dream. This was inspired by a song by the San Francisco based group Trance Mission.

Stephen B. Kagan